The Roux In The Gumbo

Kim Robinson

Kim's Publishing

The Roux In The Gumbo

Publisher's Note:

This novel is a work of fiction. Any references to historical events, to
real people, living or dead; or real locales are intended only to give the
incidents either are the product of the author's imagination or are used
fictitiously, and their resemblance, if any, to real-life counterparts is
entirely coincidental.

Library of Congress number on file with Kim's Publishing

The Roux in the Gumbo Revised Edition

Acknowledgments

As I will in every book that I write, I give praise to God for getting me where I am today. I want to thank my husband Colin who has helped me every step of the way, I love you.

To my children Davonne, Colin Jr., and Colina, thank you for your encouragement. Mommy is going to do something fun with you for being so patient on those days when I couldn't get off the computer, and for all the days you spent with me at book signings.

To my grandmother, Helen, my aunt Genevieve Smith, their mother and my great-grandmother, Annie Thompson. Sadie Rodgers, Melvin Paul Broussard, Melvin Paul Broussard Jr, Curley Broussard, Willie Bruce, Poopie, Jeanane, Clarence, Pat, Terry. I hope you are looking down from Heaven and know that through this book you live on. I will love you forever.

A lot of people in my family helped me write this book by giving me their memories, and I want to send my thanks and love to my parents, Clyde and Anna Lee Harold, my aunts, JoAnn Broussard, Francis Muhammed, Claudette Vinegar, Phyllis Broussard, Mary Broussard, Yvonne Broussard, Joyce McZeal, Evelyn Shears, Barbara Robinson, Lorena Haywood, to my uncles Johnathan Broussard, Curly Broussard and Butch Broussard.

To my cousin Stewart Smith who took the time to find all the photos and send them, I want to say thanks. To my cousins Tracy, Kenya, La Keisha, Johnathan Jr. Aiesha, Asia, Hakim, Munir, Dana, Michelle, Poncho, and Christopher, Larry, Virginia, you guys get your stories together because we are going to write a book, I love you.

To my home girls; Sheila Barber, Wanda Moreland Tucker, Michelle Oliver, Zenia Clinton Robinson, Deborah Greene, La Juana Evens, Deborah Calloway, thank you for believing in me, even when I didn't believe in myself. "Ain't no stopping us now!"

To Neshee Publication, Aalim and Heather, I am truly blessed to have been lead to you. Thank you for taking me into your family.

To Emma Rodgers, and the staff of Black Images thank you for helping me and so many other writers.

To Delores Thornton, Lauretta Pierce, Diane Tugman, Heather Covington, Belinda Williams, Nicole Stevenson and Denise Campbell, Sheila Goss, Vanessa Johnson, Yolanda Johnson, Vincent Alexander. Thank you for having my back, I am so glad to have your lead to follow.

To Karen Quinones thank you for taking the time to explain the publishing business to me.

To Whiskey Creek Press and my Creek authors family, Neshee, Jadore, Mardi Gras, thank you for giving me my start.

To my web mistress Diana Hatch, thank you for all your help and support, I could not have done any of this without you. To my typesetter Misherald Brown, thank you and little J. for giving you the time to get the work done so fast.

From The Author

Can you believe that it has been 12 years since I held the first print copy of The Roux in the Gumbo in my hands? That book is tattered and worn, but a love for writing was born with it. I still use that book for signings, though the pages are falling out and the cover has since been changed.

Just like that book I have gone through changes, inside and out and my writing reflects this through growth and improvement that has come about with each class, webinar, instructional book and conference.

I keep learning things about this business every day. Trust and believe the publishing industry is as crooked as the letter S. Aspiring authors there are a lot of people lying in wait to take advantage of your desperation to get your story out in the world, but don't let it discourage you. Make sure you google and check out every person you work with.

Since my first book was published I have went through some physical maladies, but the thing that helped me to keep it moving was my determination to keep writing, it was an escape that worked better than any pain pill. Now Cancer free, both knees and a shoulder replacement and seven books later, I am ready to get back out in the world and start fresh. Watch out world, here I come, feeling much better with a new energy and gratefulness that I pour into my work.

While putting this trilogy together I have gone back over the book and repaired grammar and spelling mistakes while keeping the integrity and base story. I hope that you enjoy this as much as I have.

I would like to ask that you take a moment and write a review and share it with your friends. Writers need their Amazon numbers to stay current. I worked hard on my literature and your feedback is what keeps a writer doing what they do. We need your opinions, whether they be good, bad or indifferent. I get an amazing and wonderful feeling every time someone takes a moment out of their day to let me know what they think of my work.

Dedication

Watching the shell that remains of my maternal grandmother, devoid of her vibrant life, her encouraging smiles, and constant conversation was the final factor in my decision to vote with the rest of the family to let her expire. We could not allow her to continue to endure so much pain.

Throughout her entire life, this woman took good care of any and everyone who came into her world. It just does not seem fair. Then again, how often was fair a factor for black people?

Anyone who had ever been in the company of her spirit would know that she would not want to exist this way– her body twisted from multiple strokes, limbs failing, and the cancer eating away at her spine. This was more than any soul should have to bear. To starve her to death seemed so cruel, yet it was the only legal way to let her pass on. The fate of someone who had fed half of Los Angeles was to starve to death.

Helen, whom everyone called 'Mother,' would feed anyone who was hungry. She always said, "Anything I give, God will make sure I get back tenfold."

You had to know her to understand her way of thinking. Maybe this book will help to clarify and glorify a woman who is certainly an angel in heaven.

When she died, she left seven children, twenty-four grandchildren, and thirty-eight great-grandchildren.

Mother was the kind of woman that no matter what you did she is "gonna" still love you unconditionally. Don't get it twisted now, she would be the first to tell you when you did wrong, but still be there for you.

Anyone could knock on her door or come into the café, and say they were hungry and she would feed them. If you needed clothes, she would take you to her second-hand store and dress you. Many people took advantage of this, but she knew exactly what was going on. More often than not, when these people got on their feet, they came back to repay her. Some said they could never do enough for her. Her good deeds were often the catalyst in helping them get their lives together.

Mother always said, "Folks is folks. There are good white folks and good black folks. There are bad white folks and bad black folks. She also said, "Every person's life is like a pot of gumbo, you get out what you put in."

Gumbo is a popular Louisiana dish, a kind of soup. There must be a million variations on how to make it. Every person who makes it thinks theirs is better than the next. I have seen people arguing over what is the best way to make this dish. Just like life, everyone has some input on what would make the next person's life better. Some people want more sausage, more shrimp, or no shrimp. Some want crab or oysters. Some prefer more spice, more file' (feelay).

One thing they all have in common is a Roux (Roo). Roux is the gravy base and the foundation of this dish. It gives the soup its flavor and is what makes you get that second bowl. Everyone has a Roux in their life. Someone who influenced every step they took, and gave their life direction. Mother was my Roux.

In order to see into this incredible woman, you have to know what came before and what came after. That is where we are going in this book. Let's go, it is going to be an adventure.

Laissez les Bon Temps Rouler
(Let the Good Times Roll)

Author's Notes

To see photos of the people in the back of the virtual book or go to my website, www.Kim-Robinson.com, click on the book cover and page down or go to the back of the print book.

Since this book spans over two centuries, there is a family tree in the back to help you keep up

They Live On

Life does not start at conception or birth
A soul takes millenniums to create
To raise and nourish future generations of worth
Ancestors who bore fruit, come back to relate
Leaving shared beliefs and astral dreams

Memories and professions passed on with bites of recipes
Cuisine perfected through time with spices of personalities
herbs of love, marinades of meetings
baste in other's life experiences

A sculptor preserves a person with clay
A photographer immortalizes a face, a physique
A producer creates a movie to tell a history
An artist paints a likeness of a profile or day

To get to tomorrow, you have to have yesterday
Their stories should be told. It is what they deserve
To be passed on to children to come
I write to preserve

~Kim Robinson

My Family's Gumbo

3 lbs. snow crab, cleaned and washed

15 chicken wings, cleaned and washed

1 lb. chicken gizzards, chopped fine

4 lbs. diced smoked sausage (Hillshire Farms) Fry lightly to remove some of the grease

3 lbs. large shrimp, peeled and deveined

4 packs dried shrimp

2 lbs. baby shrimp

4 stalks of cleaned and diced celery

3 diced onions

3 packs of onion soup mix

2 cans of okra: drain off liquid and fry in ¼ cup of oil to remove the slime.

Gumbo file' (ground sassafras leaves)

Seasoning salt

Black pepper

Celery salt

Prepared rice

Roux:

½ cup of vegetable oil

½ cup of butter

1 cup of flour

I know they didn't have Onion Soup Mix or blenders and Cuisinart's back in the day, but I am sharing my current day changes.

Gumbo:

Fill a large stockpot half way with water and set on high to boil. You can divide ingredients into 2 or 3 smaller pots. I prefer this method, because it takes a while to get the water to boil. It will also decrease the chance of your gumbo sticking to the bottom. There is nothing worse than a burnt pot of gumbo. "Chile just thinking about it makes me want to cry."

Gumbo is something that every time it's made it just gets better as you add or take away ingredients to tailor to your taste. Much like a fine suit of clothes. Other variations have bell pepper, tomato puree, oysters, crawfish, rabbit, turkey or chicken, parsley, green onion and garlic. I could fill this book up with various ways to prepare this dish. Do not be afraid to experiment.

I put my gizzards, onion and celery in the blender before adding to the boiling water so that I get the flavor without biting into a tough gizzard. Add gizzards, onion, celery, onion soup mix, dried shrimp, sausage and chicken.

When it reaches a rapid boil, reduce flame to low and cook for an additional 20 minutes while you make the roux.

Roux

If you prefer a thicker soup, add more flour. Heat the oil and butter over medium heat. Sprinkle flour over grease while constantly stirring, so as not to scorch, based on your preference. I prefer a nut brown or caramel color. Some people like a darker roux. You can taste as you go along.

Add Roux and stir, use the soup from the gumbo pot to deglaze the pan. Add chicken, crab legs, black pepper, seasoning, and celery salt. I pre-fry my okra to get the slime out. Be very careful with celery salt, it can overpower the other flavors. Add 1 teaspoon to entire pot. You can always go back and add more. Boil for 35 to 40 minutes. Add shrimp and crab, boil 5 minutes more. Remove from heat add 1 teaspoon of gumbo file to each pot. Serve in a bowl over rice.

Sprinkle file' to taste. Do not be afraid to get your fingers dirty. Also, do not forget to suck the gravy out of the crab legs before you open them up.

You have to let the gumbo cool down all the way before you refrigerate.

It can be frozen for up to three months. I prefer in Tupperware containers or Ziploc freezer bags. Enjoy and drop me a line and let me know how you like it.

kim@kim-robinson.com

Life Is What You Make It

To be a woman around times of slavery
You are subject to acts that are unsavory
In order to keep your head up through the depravity
You command from your soul a certain kind of bravery

The only true freedom that you have, no one can enslave
With your brain you fight back
Even if outwardly, you behave
For the people who keep you back and bound in chains
You pray to God that one day they will know this pain
They can put chains on your arms, your legs,
and even your behind,
But the thing that can't be restrained is your mind.

Keep the curtains drawn on the windows of your soul,
Your eyes…
Don't let them see the strength that is inside, your pride
Say your prayers every day; hold on to your faith
Just in case the afterlife is the place
The place where you get your taste
Of the good life, our oppressors don't appreciate.

But with some hustle and creativity
You might not have to wait
And the days and nights in this life don't have to go to waste.

Life is not how you take it,

Don't spend all your time looking for answers
Your life is what you make it.

Gizelle

Gizelle welcomed the feel of the cool sheets against her skin. She crawled exhausted into her bed, naked as always during the humid summer. As she slept, her subconscious took her back to a night twenty years ago in 1850. She was twelve years old and alone in the middle of the night. Scared, tired, hungry, and sick, she sat crying and shivering under a huge magnolia tree in driving rain, deep in the bayou near Lake Charles, Louisiana.

Gizelle decided to sit and wait. Surely, one of the water moccasins or some deadly spider would put her out of her misery. No matter what, she was not going back to the plantation.

Before Gizelle was old enough to be weaned, she had been wrenched from her mother's breast and sold to the Sunrise Plantation. They should have called it the Graveyard because so many slaves were buried there. They worked clearing the bayous so the boats could navigate through the waters to bring in materials to build plantation homes and slave quarters. They also brought in seed and supplies to cultivate the fields of cotton, rice, and sugar cane; anything that was agriculturally profitable.

The overseers did not allow slaves who labored in the fetid water to get out as they watched others pulled under by the alligators. If the poisonous snakes and spiders did not kill them, the elements would. They worked regardless of rain or snow. Those who fell ill were left on the bank to die. The owners could always buy more slaves.

During the epidemics, cholera and yellow fever laid claim to many. Hundreds expired from colds, croup, or the many diseases that thrived in the swampy water. The soles of their feet split open from the fungus brought on by standing in dirty water for too long. They bound their feet with bandages but without proper treatment, the cuts developed gangrene. The limbs were amputated. Cripples sat in pirogues to transfer the debris from the water to the bank. A slave was lucky to make it through a year working at Sunrise.

Gizelle's dark skin dictated that by the age of four she was sent to the fields to pick cotton. When she was nine years old, the overseer gave her a gift. He raped her. He had been doing so for three years now. He had very strange and unnatural desires, and she could not take it anymore. She would prefer death to the tortured existence she was living.

Each time lightning brightened the sky, Gizelle prayed for God to end her life. Finally, the storm passed. She gathered Spanish moss from the trees and made a pallet. She closed her eyes, hoping they would never again open.

"*Cher, Cher,* Wake up chile! What are you doing here? Get up *Cher* you are soaking wet. Come with me. Open your eyes," the voice said.

Gizelle heard the words but did not want to open her eyes. She did not want to be alive. Maybe God was a woman, or maybe he was busy and had sent an angel for her. She peeked out with one eye. Nope it was not God; God did not have long white hair that hung down to his waist. She opened the other eye and looked into eyes that looked like a cat, colored a greenish-gray. Her face was soft with what seemed to be concern. No one had ever looked at Gizelle with such kindness.

"Can you stand, *Cher?* Are you hurt?" The woman touched Gizelle's forehead and found it burning with fever. "You poor chile, you come with Tallulah; I will make you better."

Gizelle rose shakily to her feet and leaned against the strange woman. Tallulah was the tallest woman she had ever seen. When Gizelle got dizzy and could not walk, Tallulah carried her.

Tallulah took her to a cabin built three feet above the ground alongside a creek, allowing the water to flow under rather than through the house when the water was high. It was a cozy habitat.

Three large rooms were more than adequate for Tallulah. One, a large inviting kitchen kept warm by the stove where she prepared her food. Another was the bedroom, which boasted a four-poster bed with night tables and an armoire that covered an entire wall. The custom furniture would have done any mansion proud. The last room had a massive desk on one wall. The other three walls were bookshelves, overflowing with books and mementos of her life. The collection of Indian and French artifacts spoke volumes about Tallulah's heritage.

Gizelle dreamt that someone removed her wet clothes and placed her in a large metal basin filled with lavender scented water that had been warmed in a teakettle that sat on the top of a big pot-bellied stove. Her hair was gently washed and braided. She was spooned hot soup; the tastiest she had ever eaten, nothing like the slop at Sunrise. The woman held a cup for her so she could sip delicious honey-sweetened herb tea. It soothed and warmed her from the inside out.

When she was out of the tub, Gizelle's body was rubbed down with oils that made her skin feel smooth and soft like a baby. The towel was soft, like freshly ginned and cleaned cotton. She wondered if she was dreaming, or maybe this was heaven. Wherever she was, this was where she wanted to be.

Gizelle awoke in the comfort of a soft feather mattress. *This must be how the people in the big house slept,* she thought. She was afraid that if she moved, her surroundings would disappear and she would find herself back on the floor of her cabin. Tallulah warmed the sheets by filling a bottle with hot water and rolling it between them. The quilt smelled as if it were filled with fragrant flowers. She drifted back to sleep.

Tallulah—1850

As Tallulah bathed the child, she noticed scars, welts, and burns. Tortured slaves were a familiar sight for her. She spent her days making rounds to plantations in the area. Some plantation owners believed in caring for the blacks that worked for them, not that they considered them human, but just as horses or dogs could get sick, so could slaves. They did not mind the small retainer. It was much less than the cost to care for a sick slave or replace a dead one.

Tallulah worked wonders on slaves and animals. It seemed she always knew which herb would revive her patient. Many physicians who refused to work on blacks came to her for advice on perplexing cases. Some white people found her much more effective than the college-educated doctors; before long, they joined her list of exclusive clients.

The fullness of Gizelle's breasts, and the life-giving milk that leaked from her swollen nipples, along with the slight roundness of her stomach alerted Tallulah. She would wait for Gizelle to get better to ask if she wanted to keep the baby. If not, she would prepare a brew from the black cohosh plant. If taken early in pregnancy, it causes the necessary bleeding to bring down the period and abort the fetus. She had prepared this for many women with great success. Tallulah lay down next to Gizelle and went to sleep.

Tallulah was French and Indian; the result of an affair her mother, Jennifer, had with a tall Muskogean (Black and Indian) warrior named Sachwaw. She was nearly five feet, eleven inches tall. She had bronze skin and a slim figure that even at her age of fifty, was statuesque.

Tallulah came into the world amidst great tragedy. Jennifer's husband, Jacques Boneaux, a French Diplomat with blonde hair and blue eyes, could not deal with the horror of his wife's betrayal.

Jacques—1800

Jacques rushed home after receiving word from one of his slaves that Jennifer had borne the child. Upon entering the foyer of his massive plantation home, he saw the doctor coming down the stairs. "Congratulations Jacques," he said as they shook hands. Jacques offered him a flask of bourbon.

"Let's celebrate, Doc."

Doc took the flask, closed and returned it without taking a sip. "Your wife and daughter are resting, both healthy and fine." He put on his coat and hat.

Jacques could not help feeling something was amiss. Doc's eyes never met his. He seemed nervous and in a hurry to leave, much as a man with something to hide.

Jacques had never known him to refuse a drink. Yet, he had begged off, saying that he had to get home to his wife as he hurried out the door. Jacques had spent many a night in brothels with Doc and he had never seen him in a rush to get home. Actually, it was just the opposite, and who could blame him? Jacques had met the good doctor's wife and she was far from attractive. Pictures in their home professed to the great beauty she once was. When she got pregnant with their only son, she had put on quite a bit of weight and after the birth, she continued to blow up like a balloon, which distorted the once pristine features of her face.

No, he thought, Doc just said they were fine. Then he remembered he had a baby. He took the stairs two at a time.

Jacques stood at the bedside watching Jennifer in her slumber. He could not help but smile at the blissful serenity of her sleeping, angelic face. They had been married exactly one year ago during this very month, December of 1800. Their fathers had been childhood friends in France and had come to America to make their fortunes in slaves and cotton. From the day Jennifer was born, their parents spoke of their marriage.

Growing up, Jacques and Jennifer rarely saw each other, as he was away at boarding schools. When they were together on holidays and gatherings, he was so enchanted with her that he did not quite know how to act. She was a lady, born and bred.

Jacques remembered deflowering Jennifer on their wedding night. For a moment, he felt guilty and even considered not consummating their marriage. When he entered the room and saw her slim figure, so blonde and beautiful, her creamy skin accentuated by the glow of the candlelight, he had to have all five feet six of her. Jacques felt just as eager as he had when he was twelve and his father had arranged his first encounter with a slave girl named Riva.

Jacques had fantasized about being with Jennifer for so long that he lost all self-control. He showed no consideration for her feelings. His father's instructions about the delicate task of handling a virginal bride left him. He laid her down on the bed and thrust himself into her. As he entered her warm moist flower, before he could pull out, he spent himself. My God! he thought. This had never happened before. He was grateful she was a virgin and knew nothing of the way sex should be. Even a whore on Bourbon Street would have laughed herself silly over his performance. He was ashamed and hated himself for being such an inconsiderate buffoon.

Jennifer

Jacques mistook Jennifer's tears as an indication of pain. He held her close, all the while telling her, "It will be easier and much better next time, *Cherie.* I rushed so as not to hurt you," he lied.

My God, Jennifer thought, as she lay there crying, just as she and her mother had rehearsed. Had she blinked she would have missed the entire act. She could not believe what had just happened or, to put it more bluntly, what had not happened.

Had Jacques only known her tears were not of pain but disappointment; what he thought was the blood of a virgin was actually her monthly period. It had been so easy tricking him since he had not bothered with foreplay, or any preparations for her benefit. He had simply pushed her down, entered, and it was over.

Jennifer had not been a virgin since the age of twelve when her body had begun to change. Her father, Marcelle could no longer be satisfied with fondling her, something he had been doing since she was the tender age of five.

Jennifer was under the impression that all fathers played with their daughters in this manner. Until one day, she found the courage to broach the subject with her mother, Elizabeth.

Elizabeth – 1815

Elizabeth questioned her fourteen-year old daughter, Jennifer, at great length. "Never speak of this to anyone but me."

She listened to every detail, before explaining to her precious child, "What your father is doing is a heinous, terrible sin. I want to make it abundantly clear to you that it is definitely no fault of yours, and you must do what you can to prevent it from happening again."

Elizabeth gave Jennifer several excuses to use when her father approached her in the future. She warned her, "Do not let your father know that you have spoken to me. I promise you that in the near future, I will make everything all right."

Elizabeth held Jennifer for a long time as she confessed how dirty she felt. Marcelle had told her, "The only way it is a sin is if you tell anyone. If you do, God will never be able to forgive you, and you will burn in hell."

Elizabeth took her distraught daughter to bed and tucked her in. She sat with her until she fell asleep. Blinded by tears of rage, she felt her way along the wall. When she finally made it to her bedroom, she crumpled in a heap on the floor next to her chamber pot and threw up. Marcelle would pay. Elizabeth swore on everything she held dear that she would see him punished.

For Marcelle and Elizabeth, marriage had been a necessity when they found themselves expecting a child. It was bound to happen one day and they were happy about it. She was seventeen and Marcelle Le

Croix was twenty. He went directly to both their parents and told them the predicament, knowing what the outcome would be. This was what everyone had always predicted for them.

Marcelle and Elizabeth had summered and played in the surf together on a stretch of private beach in the South of France. It was only natural for them to fall in love. They had been playing doctor since

Marcelle was five, but when he was thirteen years old, they became intrigued with sex after hiding in the closet and watching his parents through the French doors of the closet. There was plenty of opportunity for them to experiment because their parents were often abroad, leaving them to be raised by servants.

When the time came for Marcelle and Elizabeth to go to boarding school, they chose schools close to each other. They spent all their spare time together. He paid a townsman handsomely to let them use his small flat for privacy.

After the marriage, things seemed to get even better. Marcelle was patient and loving during sex. He had traveled with his father to Japan when he was fourteen. By the time he returned, he knew everything about making a woman achieve orgasm after orgasm before finally taking his own release. He enjoyed the preliminaries more than actual intercourse. He would massage and lick every inch of her body, awakening every nerve in her being. Elizabeth, in turn, took instruction quite well.

Elizabeth thought she knew Marcelle. She loved watching him

in the evenings while he sat telling Jennifer stories until they both fell asleep. He spent countless hours teaching her to ride the horse he had given her on her eighth birthday. Package upon package arrived at their door whenever he was away on business. Her love and desire for him had never once waned until this day–not until this hour. How could he have violated their wedding vows by doing something so egregious and Machiavellian to Jennifer? She felt a hatred for him that she never imagined possible. She had to calm down, think of what to do. She prayed to the Lord for strength.

Elizabeth began to complain to Marcelle. "You never take me anywhere." She bade her time. Two weeks later Marcelle invited her to accompany him to New Orleans.

While Marcelle was occupied conducting his business and purchasing new slaves, Elizabeth sought out a *voodooiene.* One of the housemaids had told her to go to Congo Square and ask for Marie. She had no trouble finding her. She explained her predicament.

"What would you like to see done to him?" Marie asked. Elizabeth did not hesitate, "I want him to suffer and then I want him to die!"

"You come back tomorrow, I will have something ready that will help you, *Mademoiselle.*"

When Elizabeth returned Marie gave her a pouch, "Add one teaspoon from this pouch to his food at each meal. Stir it in well. It will not take long and you can be sure he will suffer."

Elizabeth asked, "What is it?"

The *voodooiene* put her fingers to her lips, rose and left the room, indicating that their business was finished. She did not tell Elizabeth that the pouch contained finely ground glass and a touch of dried and powdered White Oleander.

Elizabeth could not bring herself to do the deed for two weeks. Each time she started to prepare Marcelle's meal some tender memory would pop into her head and stop her. She put it off telling herself that she would wait until tomorrow. Despite everything, Elizabeth still loved him, but she loved her daughter more.

"*Maman,* I cannot stop the alarming feelings. My mind tries to fight it but my body cannot. I try to avoid father's attentions, but he does not hear me when I say no."

Elizabeth knew that she must rescue her tormented, confused child. The first few days, every time she added the fine powder to Marcelle's food, she cried. Soon her tears were not borne of remorse, but anger. Each time Jennifer came to her in tears telling of another time that she was unable to keep her father's roaming hands and mouth off her body before he violated her, it got a little bit easier.

Elizabeth cried when she looked upon her daughter's sad face and noticed the sparkle was gone from her eyes. Jennifer was withdrawn and sullen. She never laughed anymore. Now that she knew what her father did to her was wrong, she swore she could not be around her friends. In her mind's eye everyone could see her sin. She would not go to school or church. For a while Elizabeth let her stay home.

After a month of Jennifer's depression, Elizabeth called her to the kitchen to witness as she prepared Marcelle's dinner and explained what she was doing. As miraculous as it may have seemed in the days that followed, the weaker Marcelle grew, the stronger and happier Jennifer grew.

Elizabeth never turned Marcelle down when he came to her bed and she hated herself for not being able to control her body from the multiple orgasms any more than Jennifer could. She wondered why she still succumbed to his attentions even though she hated him so. Afterwards, when he fell asleep, she would leave the room and cry.

Marcelle complained about his stomach. He threw up after each meal. After a month he was throwing up blood. The pain got so severe that he could no longer put off seeing a doctor. The doctor could not figure out the problem. He had blood in his stool and urine. He could not keep solid food down. His diet consisted of cush-cush (cornmeal mixed with water and fried, then placed in a bowl with milk and sweetened with honey) or mashed potatoes or plain rice. So much for the spicy cuisine he preferred.

Elizabeth was the perfect, loving, concerned, stoic wife. She showed just the right amount of distress as the neighbors and friends filed in daily to visit poor Marcelle, bringing remedies they swore would help.

Everyone loved Marcelle. He had been a successful businessman and was known to be quite generous with anyone in financial distress. Marcelle, with his best friend and business partner, Francois Moreau, had done well since they had invested in the business fifteen years ago. They married in a double ceremony and honeymooned abroad on their move to the United States. They had made their fortunes within months, not that they needed it mind you; they were both of wealthy families, it was an adventure, and a profitable one.

Marcelle's parents came and brought doctors from Europe, but to no avail. Family, friends and acquaintances traveled from across the water to see Marcelle before his inevitable funeral.

Lizette

Elizabeth, being the understanding wife that she was, sent invitations to women who she knew Marcelle had slept with over the years. She invited his mulatto mistress, Lizette, and the two bastard children she had by Marcelle. Elizabeth had known about them for years. There were no secrets among the coloreds and she was so kind to her servants that she was privy to any gossip about the Master's affairs. She always gave them coins for their confidences.

When Lizette arrived, she was visibly nervous because she did not know what to expect from Marcelle's wife.

Elizabeth was glad to meet her after all this time. She had often wondered what she looked like. "You can take the children upstairs to see their father and afterwards I will mind the little darlings while you have some time alone with Marcelle. The doctor said he doesn't have much longer so please, take your time saying your good-byes," Elizabeth said.

Lizette's apprehension dissipated as she looked into this woman's eyes. There was no deceit and the touch of her hands was as comforting as her mother's had been.

When the children came out, Elizabeth came from her seat in the hallway with Jennifer. Her heart bled for the tearful children; she sat and consoled them. She introduced Jennifer to Lizette's daughter, Jeanine, twelve years old and the boy, Marcus, eight. Marcus was a bronze duplicate of Marcelle when he was a young boy. Jennifer and Jeanine took an immediate liking to each other. They went upstairs to Jennifer's room with Marcus in tow.

After a few hours, Lizette came downstairs. Elizabeth saw the tears in her eyes. She went to her and put her arms around her and let her cry on her shoulder. "Come, Lizette, please join me for a bit of libation, I am sure you can use it as much as I," Elizabeth said. She poured them both a generous glass of sherry.

Two bottles later, Elizabeth and Lizette knew everything of each other's lives and the history of their relationships with Marcelle. They laughed raucously as they compared notes about his sexual prowess. Neither harbored any animosity for the other. They understood their roles in his life and felt lucky to have had someone as good as Marcelle. Elizabeth forgot for a minute that she was the reason he was dying.

Jennifer came downstairs. It appeared she was pulling Jeanine along against her will. The poor child was begging her, "Please don't tell, I don't want to go to hell."

"It will be all right, trust me," Jennifer reassured her. She whispered in Elizabeth's ear, *"Maman,* Jeanine also."

Elizabeth understood immediately. This young child had also been a victim of Marcelle's perversities.

Elizabeth looked at the poor girl who stood before her. Tears streamed down her face. She had the same eyes as Jennifer and at this moment they brimmed with tears of fear. Elizabeth could not ignore the child's pain. She pulled her to her bosom and held her tightly, "Do not cry; everything will be fine. I promise you will not go to hell for telling and you have done nothing wrong. It is his sin, not yours," Elizabeth whispered.

Lizette was puzzled, "I demand to know what is going on," she slurred.

"Jennifer take Jeanine and Marcus upstairs and provide them with something to sleep in." She turned to Lizette. "Be patient. Please accept my invitation to stay here tonight. It is much too late for you to travel back to the city and we have much to talk about."

Lizette agreed without protest; she liked this woman and instinctively knew that she meant them no harm.

Jennifer pulled Jeanine toward her and put her arm around her. "Come little sister, I will take care of you."

Lizette expected to hear Elizabeth reprimand the child for calling a Negro her sister. When she dared to look at her from beneath her long lashes, she was relieved to see Elizabeth was smiling.

"We must swear to let them spend time together. Jennifer is lucky to have a sister and a brother. I always longed for siblings when I was a child. Unfortunately, for some reason God never blessed my mother with another child. Come let us retire to the great room where the cushions are more comfortable and the brandy is stronger," Elizabeth said, and proceeded to explain the nature of Marcelle's misdeeds.

Lizette's nostrils flared in rage and tears fell from her beautiful eyes, "I had my suspicions, a bad feeling that I stupidly refused to acknowledge. I have been saving money for years and was going to send Jeanine and Marcus away to good schools where they could acquire an education that would take them far away from any life shadowed with servitude or compromise. I even keep them out of the sun, hoping that they will both stay light enough to be able to pass as white if necessary. I never dreamed that it was already too late to protect my baby."

Lizette lowered her head and cried. She was lying to herself –
she had known. She had been jealous of the attention that Marcelle paid
to Jeanine. He had taken her out for long carriage rides and shopping
trips. He never invited her or Marcus to accompany them. The gifts
he gave Jeanine were not appropriate. A father did not give expensive
jewelry and frilly undergarments to a child so young. She kept quiet for
fear that if nothing was going on, she did not want to put the idea in his
head. If it was happening, what could she do about it? She wished she
could kill him.

Lizette had explained to Elizabeth earlier in the evening that she
herself was only eleven years old when Marcelle solicited her aunt, the
proprietor of one of the more prominent brothels in town. He had seen
Lizette coming from her small bedroom on the third floor one morning.
Clients did not go up there.

Lizette's aunt had been her guardian since her mother had died
of cholera. She had only planned to wait one more year before auction-
ing off Lizette's virginity to the highest bidder. After that, she would
preview her at one of the balls. It was a Louisiana custom called *pleas
sage or Placage*. Prosperous men entered into sponsorship of young
girls of mixed race. There was a ball held every year. The girls' guardian's chaperoned them.

When a man chose a girl, the guardian negotiated a contract for
finances and trust. This way should something happen to the man, or if
he tired of the arrangement, the girl and any children that resulted from
the relationship would not be left with nothing.

This arrangement included education for the children. A generous protector would grant them their freedom, some at birth, but usually
they held out until the eighteenth birthday to ensure the fidelity of his
mistress.

Many sponsors did not honor these commitments. A good lawyer in any other era could have made them keep their promise, but in times of slavery they were dependent upon the good graces of the man. Many watched their children be sold on the auction block.

Lizette's aunt knew a good deal when she saw one. It could do nothing but help her business to have Marcelle La Croix as her niece's protector. The association would afford her many benefits. If she ever needed a favor, he would not turn her down; not to mention the monies she would receive before he took possession of Lizette. She negotiated a handsome arrangement for Lizette, and an even more handsome one for herself.

Lizette knew that her life was destined for the same direction as her mother's. She dreamt of running away, but had nowhere to go. Lizette often heard the girls talk about Marcelle. He was a favorite. He only saw young girls…the younger the better. Every brothel in town knew that if they acquired a virgin to contact him immediately. He was always the highest bidder at the virgin auctions.

Lizette could have done worse for herself. Marcelle was generous with money; she had a fine home with servants and he was kind and considerate. He turned her into a woman who craved him and soon was addicted to the pleasure he gave so expertly. He taught her how to please him from the moment he woke in the afternoon, until he left her late at night to sleep in his own rooms or return home.`

Marcelle's seed gave Lizette the children she adored more than life. She had fallen in love with him and settled into her station. She focused her energies on making a better future for her children. She wanted Jeanine to grow up, find a free man, and marry for love. She never wanted her daughter to know what it was like to be at the mercy of someone else's whims. She had seen women prosperous one day, and destitute the next, it happened as easily as the wind blew should the protector fall on financial hard times, or tire of his mistress for whatever reason or on a whim at the end of the day they were his property.

What Marcelle had done to their daughters was worse than any slave auction or ball. To be forced to become sexually active before her time was wrong, but with her own father, despicable. He should burn in hell. If she had not been concerned about their futures, she would have told him so.

Elizabeth swore to Lizette, "If Marcelle has not put his affairs in order and given you and your children freedom before he dies, I myself will see that it is done."

The two women sat on the couch and finished a decanter of brandy. They fell asleep holding each other, just as sisters would.

When Lizette left the next day, it was with emancipation papers for herself and her children, along with a large bank draft that would keep them in luxury throughout their natural lives. All signed by Marcelle's own hand.

That afternoon, the doctor told Elizabeth that Marcelle would not make it through the night. She sat quietly by his bed; he slept fitfully. He woke coughing blood. She sat on the edge of the bed and looked into his eyes. "I have loved you ever since I can remember Marcelle. You have been such a wonderful husband."

He squeezed her hand in gratitude and looked up at her with eyes that said he loved her and was sorry for leaving her like this. He could no longer speak; the tissue in his esophagus had torn from the constant vomiting.

Elizabeth stood, "I am glad that you are dying. You are a vile, insufferable beast and the world will be much better off without your kind. The doctors never had a clue that I was poisoning you. When I served you supper, I was serving you your death."

Marcelle's eyes widened and through the pain he asked, "Why?" Blood rose and dripped over his lips. He attempted to sit up, but the sudden movement left him strangling on the blood that was rapidly rising in his throat.

She could see the question in his eyes, "Any man who sleeps with his own daughters should be made to suffer for eternity. Death is more than you deserve."

Marcelle never imagined that Elizabeth knew. He closed his eyes in shame and they never opened again.

Jacques

As Jacques looked down at his beautiful wife and mother of his child, he could not help but realize how much he loved her. He picked up the small bundle wrapped in his exhausted wife's arms and gingerly pulled back the hand-crocheted blanket. His heart stopped. The child that he assumed was his, clearly was not. Thick black hair and olive skin told the true fraternal story.

He grabbed Jennifer by the hair and pulled her out of bed. "You will tell me who the father of this bastard child is!" Jacques screamed.

Before Jennifer was fully awake, Jacques was dragging her out to the barn. He strung her up, and beat her as if she were a slave. She had no choice but to confess the details of her secret assignations with the Indian.

She realized he could very well kill her at this moment. She had nothing to lose, "Had you been more considerate as a husband and lover, I would not have found it necessary to look elsewhere for satisfaction. You are an idiot Jacques. You were no comparison to my father who had been bedding me since I was twelve. I missed the feelings that you never once took the time to give me. I found them with someone else while you were on your many whoring trips with your mistresses. I wonder if they are as disappointed with your skills as I have been this past year. The moment you cut me down from here, I am taking my beautiful daughter and going to my lover," Jennifer spat in his face.

The overseer had reported to Jacques that Jennifer had been spending a lot of time with the local Indians. He had assumed it was something she had been doing for amusement. He had not given it a second thought; he should have.

Jennifer told Jacques, "I never loved you the way I love Sachwaw."

These words were more than he could bear. He had no control over the rage that consumed him, or the arm that held the whip. When he finally regained his composure it was too late. Jennifer was dead. Jacques cracked his whip at the slaves who ran forward to cut her down. "I forbid anyone to cut her down." He left her wide-eyed body tied to the post for all to see.

Elizabeth ran past Jacques into the barn. She was taken aback by what she saw. She could not believe what he had done to her beautiful child, "My God, you monster! What have you done to my baby girl?" she screamed.

No matter what Jennifer had done, she did not deserve this fate. Elizabeth knew about her daughter's frequent clandestine meetings. She did not blame her one bit for her actions. Jacques had several children by slave women, the result of the many nights that he left Jennifer's bed to go to the slave quarters. He had never given Jennifer any attention. He did not know the first thing about being a husband. He spent months at a time away from home under the guise of business. When he returned to town, he stayed with his mistresses for days before coming home to his lonely wife.

Elizabeth and Jennifer had known about Jacques and his two mistresses before they were married. One a Mulatto, the other a Quadroon, he had fathered seven children between them. They had every comfort that the white wives had and more, a fair trade for not being able to have his name. They lived in fine town homes located in the center of town. Their clothes were of the finest quality; they never missed an opera or play and often traveled with him, while Jennifer stayed at the plantation house in the country, cut off from the world.

Elizabeth cried for her daughter's soul.

The next morning Jacques was waiting in the area where the overseer had seen Jennifer with the Indian. It was not long before he heard a whistle and saw a dark, muscular figure. He raised his gun and shot the form as it got out of a small pirogue. The tall Indian fell at the water's edge.

Jacques approached with caution and when he looked upon the fallen man, he was delighted to see that he was still alive. He had only clipped him in the shoulder. He did not want the savage to die without knowing why. He cursed the man and even though he knew he probably could not understand a word of the French he was speaking, he knew that the man knew who he was. "You filthy savage, you will not live to defile and rape another white woman," Jacques said.

Jacques shot him again in the stomach. He wanted him to suffer a slow, painful death. He walked back to where he had been hiding and picked up the bundle he had left there. He opened the blanket the child was swaddled in and placed her next to the Indian. "The both of you will be eaten by alligators; it is what you deserve."

It was not until Jacques returned and saw the slaves standing and looking into the open barn that the finality of his actions made him sit down on the ground and cry with remorse. He spoke aloud, "How could Jennifer betray me? I worshipped her in every way. She was my fine porcelain doll, her beautiful features, and hair as soft and shiny as corn silk. She was to be worshipped, not touched. I gave her everything I possibly could. Did she not have the finest wardrobe? The best house? The best slaves? Why had she done this?"

When Jacques had bedded her, she had lain like a perfect, southern-bred lady. She never moaned or showed any enjoyment; not like his mistresses or the slave wenches. This was as it should have been for a southern woman. It was common knowledge that women of breeding did not enjoy sex. It was something they did only to reproduce.

The things Jennifer had said when questioned, Jacques could not believe his ears. He thought that he was sparing her the unpleasantness of sex. To listen to her describe the passion that she felt for this Indian was unendurable. The savage was not even human. No more than an animal, yet she had enjoyed being with him and described sexual acts that he had never experienced. Could she have been telling the truth about her father?

There was obviously something wrong with Jennifer and he had fixed it. There was no way to change it now. He was not worried about legal action. No one would blame him, least of all the law in Louisiana. He felt justified in what he had done.

Sachwaw

Sachwaw had passed out and woke to a searing heat in his stomach. But there was something else, something that needed urgent attention. There was a baby lying next to him crying.

Sachwaw rolled over onto his side, and saw Jennifer's beautiful eyes looking at him from a tiny face with olive skin. The situation became clear; this was his child, his and Jennifer's.

Sachwaw felt a surge of strength. He would not die this way. He had a child to look after and a woman to rescue. He struggled to his feet and took the blanket from beneath the child. He tore it in two and tied one strip tightly around the wound in his stomach. The first shot had gone straight through his shoulder and the bleeding had stopped. He picked up the child and with much effort tied her to his back with the remaining strip of cloth.

It took Sachwaw a few minutes to manage to climb back into his pirogue. He tried to lift the paddle but the effort was too much for him. He thanked God that the current of the water was in his favor. When finally he got close to his village, he rolled out of the small craft and crawled to the edge of the village.

A squaw passing by the water heard the baby crying and placed her gourd on the ground and went to investigate. When she saw Sachwaw, she screamed out. Many villagers ran to help. Sachwaw's mother, Weena, immediately started giving orders.

The medicine man instructed four men to carry Sachwaw carefully to his tent. Weena took the child. She looked upon her granddaughter's face. Many times, Weena had seen Sachwaw with the blonde woman. She had begged him to stop seeing Jennifer and spent many nights praying about it. She knew this relationship was destined for disaster.

For three nights Sachwaw was delirious with fever. He called out for Jennifer the entire time. He dreamt of the day he met Jennifer. He had been fishing when he saw her stumble to the ground after tripping over a fallen tree limb. He ran to her aide. As he turned to walk back, her hand on his arm stopped him. She found him intriguing. They fished that afternoon. Sachwaw taught her how to bait her hook and she was eager to throw her line into the water. When she caught a fish she was as excited as a child. After catching five fish, Sachwaw made a small fire. He taught Jennifer how to scale and gut the fish in preparation for cooking. She watched with interest as he skewered the fish on sticks and stuffed them with herbs that he had searched out. As the fish cooked he taught her words from his tribal language and she in turn taught him English. He enjoyed basking in her beauty. He ate two fish himself and watched with much amusement as she devoured the other three.

As Jennifer returned to the plantation she thought only of meeting him the next day. She had been lonely for male attention and Sachwaw was every inch a man. She had never felt this comfortable with Jacques. Sachwaw aroused those feelings that her father had first stirred in her and more. She did not feel she was doing anything wrong and when she found she was with child she assumed it to be Jacques.

Jennifer knew the truth when she suckled the beautiful baby to her breast for the first time. She did not expect Jacques to return for a few days and by then she and her daughter, whom she had named Tallulah, would be gone. She would take her mother, find Sachwaw and they would disappear. She discussed her plans with her mother. Elizabeth's only comment was, "Do what makes you happy my child; if you love him go to him and I will be there for you. We have more than enough money to sustain us for ten lifetimes." She fell asleep making plans for their escape, but it was not to be.

One week later when Sachwaw recovered enough to walk, he was on his way to find Jennifer. Every day the medicine man had to stop him from getting up. He had seen her spirit several times, but thought he was hallucinating; regardless, he knew that she needed him. He arrived at the plantation in the early morning and waited.

Sachwaw saw Jacques driven away in a carriage. He waited for hours, never seeing one sign of Jennifer. He made his way to the barn and entered through the back door. He would wait here for a chance to get into the house. He smelled something that made his stomach turn. He entered the dark barn and stood still while his eyes adjusted. He looked for a way to get up to the loft so that he could study the second floor and find the best way to enter the house undetected. He saw someone leaning against a post. As his eyes grew accustomed to the dark, he realized he was looking at Jennifer's beautiful hair. Open welts covered her bare back and her hands were tied around the post. He called to her. Why did she not move or answer? What were all these flies doing in here?

Sachwaw looked into her lifeless eyes. Maggots crawled over her blood-encrusted back. He wanted to scream out. He could not stop the bile that rose into his throat. He ran to a corner and threw up. This had been Jennifer's fate because she had loved him. Had he any notion that the child was his he would have never let her remain here. What kind of evil spirit could possess a man to do something as terrible as this to someone so kind and beautiful? Sachwaw knew the answer, the white man's greed and desire to own and control everything.

Sachwaw cut Jennifer down and waited for the cover of night to bury her remains. He now knew that he had not been hallucinating; it was her spirit that he had seen. He found a blanket and shovel, wrapped and carried her to the place where they had met. He returned to the barn and cried in silence as he waited for Jacques return. The shock of losing Jennifer coupled with his weakened state; it was no wonder he soon fell asleep.

Sachwaw woke to the sound of the carriage returning. Jacques lurched into the house and back out again. He had not had one sober day since his wife died. He went to the slave cabins and after a few minutes returned with a very young girl.

Sachwaw waited for an hour and went into the house through the back door, silently making his way through the kitchen and up the stairs. He found the bedroom where he had seen the candlelight from outside. He entered the room. Jacques was asleep, lying face down on the bed. The girl was sitting up in the bed, tears flowing from her eyes. She could not have been more than twelve years old. There was a piece of bloody cloth between her legs. Her eyes widened when she saw Sachwaw move from the shadows. He put his fingers to his lips, warning her to be silent.

In one fluid motion Sachwaw sat on Jacques' back and grabbed a handful of his hair, pulled his head back and cut his throat. Then he left as quietly as he had come.

The young slave girl, Effie, got up. She smiled to herself as she made her way back to the slave quarters. She was happy about what had happened to the master. She had always liked Mistress Jennifer; what he had done to her was cruel.

Effie knew what Jacques had done with her was a sin. Jacques had grabbed her arm and pulled her from her bed and she was on her way to the big house before she knew what was happening.

Effie's mother, Riva, rose from her bed in a panic. She knew better than to try to stop the master. She jumped from her bed, begging him not to take her little girl. "But Master she's your own daughter. Don't do this. I'll go with you instead. She still be too young," Riva pleaded.

"Go back to bed, Riva. She's the same age you were the first time I bedded you, and what difference does it make if she's my daughter? You were my father's offspring, which makes you my sister. That just means any children she has will fetch a higher price. I made a tidy sum off the four that you birthed for me. You say one more word and I will sell you."

When Jacques got Effie to the bedroom, he made her drink a snifter of the strong horrid tasting brown liquid, then pulled her dress up, lay on top of her and took her. After three painful minutes it was over. He was snoring before she could roll him off. It took her forever to get out from under him. She had wished him dead and gotten her wish. Ha! Ha!

Effie had always thought that one day her father would free her. That dream had been shattered right along with her hymen. She picked up a bag that he had placed on the night stand when he had come in. She twirled the bag that contained two hundred dollars in gold coins around her finger, and despite the pain between her legs, she smiled and hummed her way back to the cabin to tell her mother what had happened. They ran away the next morning.

Elizabeth

Elizabeth saw the Indian come into the house. After the child left Jacques' room she entered. She knelt beside him and lifted his eyelid back. Yes, thank the Lord he was dead. She turned and went to bed.

After the funeral, Jacques' brother John hired a new overseer for his own plantation and moved into his brother's house. He was a gambling, unsuccessful businessman who had run through his inheritance like a racehorse.

He never was a mind to pay attention to the running of the plantation that his father left him. He discovered too late that the overseer was robbing him blind. He had never had much love for his brother who was the one father had favored. This was a Godsend to him—not to mention a new vein of cash.

When Elizabeth asked, John was only too eager to build her a cabin at the back of the property and deed over one hundred and fifty acres of land. Having her around was more unnerving than his brother and sister-in-law's ghosts that roamed the house every night. He knew his brother would turn over in his grave, but he never thought he would come out of it. He had always heard that people who die bad do not stay dead. Every night, he saw the two of them in their chambers. He decided to have a new wing built onto the house and sent for a Voodooist and a Priest to try and exorcise the restless spirits.

Jacques' attorney contacted John regarding Jacques' mistresses and their children. He told the solicitor to bring them all to the plantation. He had envied his brother and the often fantasized about the two beautiful women. He was confident that the women would go along with his arrangements rather than end up sold and, or separated from their children. He was right.

John installed the two women in the house with him and sold one of the houses in town. He was a bachelor and had always preferred colored women. He allowed them to bring their own servants to cook and clean. Their children were installed in the old wing with nannies. When the new wing was built, he had an extra-large bed made. Each of his concubines had their own quarters flanking the master bedroom. Physically, they were quite entertaining. Jacques had trained them well and he now knew why it was necessary for them to live next door to one another, they enjoyed each other as much as he enjoyed watching them.

There was only one problem in John's new life - what to do with Elizabeth? She was the only damper on an otherwise perfect arrangement. She walked around in black gowns and sat in her daughter's room talking to her day after day. John offered to buy her a house in town, but that was not what she wanted. He could not wait until her cabin was finished. He stopped construction on his new wing so the workers could concentrate on finishing her cabin. He assigned slaves to work her acres. Whatever she decided to grow would ensure a yearly income. What did he care if she wanted to live like a pauper in a cabin instead of in a house with servants? Now he could get back to the business of enjoying his new house and its inhabitants.

Elizabeth took all of her daughter's jewelry, her pick of the furniture and moved into her small cabin. She had plenty of money of her own from her inheritance, not to mention Marcelle's estate.

She could have moved into town, but there was something comforting about the Bayou. She was used to the sounds of the crickets and cicadas. The reptilian inhabitants seemed to accept her as if she were one of them. When she took her pirogue out, it seemed as though she and the animals had a special connection.

Elizabeth had an alligator that lived under her porch and several snakes stayed in her yard. They saw no reason to go anywhere since "Hoot," the huge owl with a massive wingspan, perched on the porch day and night, fed them well. He would swoop down on a mouse, rabbit, possum or some other unsuspecting animal, feast upon the unfortunate victim and share the remains with the resident alligators and snakes.

Wooden bowls nailed to tree trunks and branches served as feeders, keeping the trees around Elizabeth's house filled with an infinite variety of birds. Their feathers of blues, yellows and reds brightened the trees; their sweet chirpings were the Bayou's music. The Bayou had its own fragrance, a perfume resulting from the mixture of amaryllis, magnolia, peonies, and jasmine melding together in soothing aromatherapy.

Elizabeth's garden was lush with tomatoes, bell peppers, onions, and herbs. Wild berries were thick by the creek; everything grew rapidly under her green thumb. The cabin had three large rooms. Elizabeth cooked over a wood-burning pot-bellied stove. The Bayou afforded an abundance of shrimp, crawfish, and catfish. She liked life just the way it was—simple.

All these things, mixed with the twinkling of the fireflies in the early evening and her daughter's spirit, tied her to this place.

It had been a year since Jennifer's murder. Elizabeth decided that today she would go and tell the Indian what had happened to Jennifer and the child. She felt he should know. Jennifer had often spoke of her visits with the handsome Indian and Elizabeth knew that she was smitten with him from the way her eyes sparkled.

Elizabeth often saw Indians hunting around the property. She followed one to the village, and asked for Sachwaw. A little boy ran into a tent and when he reappeared Sachwaw hesitantly followed.

Sachwaw had seen Elizabeth a few times and wanted to talk to her, but was afraid the woman would be harboring anger. After all, her daughter had died because of him. He often left game on her steps when he went hunting.

Elizabeth offered him a small bundle. Sachwaw looked inside and discovered a picture of Jennifer and the knife that he had used to cut Jacques' throat. He had dropped it next to the bed. When he looked up at Elizabeth, the smile on her face explained that she was in alliance with him.

A small child toddled up to Sachwaw and wrapped her arms around his legs. Sachwaw bent down and picked up the child and handed her to Elizabeth, "Tallulah."

Elizabeth's breath caught in her chest and she started to cry. The child had Jennifer's eyes. This was her grandchild. She had assumed that Jacques had killed the child and buried her in the shallow grave that she stumbled upon one day. She often went there and placed flowers for Jennifer and the unnamed child. God had given her back a piece of her daughter. She sat on the ground, holding the child close as she cried.

Elizabeth and Sachwaw talked for a long time. It was not the child's grave she had found, but Jennifer's alone. She was relieved to know her daughter had a decent burial by someone who loved her.

Elizabeth met Weena, Sachwaw's mother, and some of the other women in the village. They instantly liked one another. She stayed the night and learned about the Muskogean communal ways. She ate with them in a circle and slept in a hut with Tallulah, marveling at how much the child reminded her of Jennifer at the age of one.

After dinner, Elizabeth and the villagers danced by the fire. She had not danced so much since she was a young girl. They smoked dried leaves from a long pipe. She was giddy from the sweet, acrid smoke. She had never laughed so much in her life. She liked it so much, they made a gift of the pipe and gave her a pouch full of the herbs.

Sachwaw said Jennifer had told him 'Tallulah' was what she planned to name the child if it was a girl. Tallulah was the name of Elizabeth's grandmother. She had often spoken of her to Jennifer.

The child was smart and affectionate. She sat in Elizabeth's lap constantly and when she moved about never let go of her hand. She knew that this lady was an important part of her life.

The next evening, when Elizabeth prepared to go back to her cabin, Sachwaw put Tallulah on his shoulders and walked with her. By the time they arrived at the cabin, Tallulah had fallen asleep. He placed her in the bed.

Elizabeth poured herself and Sachwaw a glass of brandy and lit her pipe. They sat and talked late into the night. She told Sachwaw all about Jennifer's youth and he told her all about his. Eventually, the bottle was empty. Elizabeth talked and talked until she heard a thud. Sachwaw's head had hit the table. She laughed as she got a blanket and covered him. She climbed in the bed with Tallulah.

The next morning, Elizabeth rolled over and bumped into something warm. Tallulah was smiling at her. She tickled the child and giggled with her as she used to do with Jennifer when she was a baby. She rose to prepare breakfast. Sachwaw was gone.

Sachwaw visited daily bringing food for Elizabeth and Tallulah. He and Tallulah spent almost every day together. Elizabeth spent a lot of time at the village and sometimes Weena would visit and stay for a few days. Tallulah grew up very happy. She knew how to hunt, fish, fight, and learned Indian cures from the medicine man.

Elizabeth took Tallulah into town and had her dresses made. Tallulah preferred her dresses that Weena made of deerskins. Within minutes the frilly dresses were covered with dirt. Finally, Elizabeth grew tired of fighting the losing battle and gave up, letting Tallulah wear what she wanted. Was it not for her long beautiful hair, no one would have known she was a girl.

Tallulah

Tallulah started school when she was five years old. She often got into fights with the other children who teased her about her height and Indian heritage. It did not happen too often because she always won. She was a bright child and excelled at school.

Tallulah's childhood went by quickly. She was happy and lucky to live in a world filled with so many people who loved her. She knew everything there was to know about the fields and often worked alongside the hands. She loved the feel of the dirt between her fingers and toes. She could hunt and fish with the best of the boys. She hated wearing shoes, and as soon as she walked out of the schoolhouse, would take them off and sling them over her shoulders.

When Tallulah was sixteen, Elizabeth passed in her sleep and was buried in tribal tradition next to Jennifer. Sachwaw consented to Tallulah's marriage to Shaw. They grew up together and had been in love since childhood. They married on her seventeenth birthday and lived together in the cabin. Their only regret was Tallulah never got pregnant. Shaw was a great hunter and treated her as if she were something precious. They laughed a lot and were very affectionate.

Elizabeth had been seeing the town doctor for years. She met the doctor when he came to buy herbs from the medicine man. She was quite fond of him and she and Tallulah accompanied him on his rounds and started learning about medicine. By the time she was fifteen years old, she was so good that if he were busy, he would send word for her to go and tend his clients. When he died, she took over his rounds. She did this for over sixty years.

Shaw's death was a mystery, but clearly a racist act. His body was burned and hung from a tree. Tallulah was forty-five years old when he died and she knew she would never love another man. The same year brought the death of Sachwaw.

Most of the tribe had moved or died; there were very few left. She had plenty of clients to keep her busy. As far as family, she was alone. She was grateful that she had received enough love to last her a lifetime.

Gizelle

When Gizelle woke, she felt much better. Tallulah felt the child's forehead and smiled at the cool touch. She rose to prepare a breakfast of fried ham, eggs and fruit. She brought in a tray and gave Gizelle a shirt that had belonged to Shaw.

Over breakfast, she asked Gizelle questions, but the child would not speak. She was afraid. At least she was feeling better. A sick person could have never eaten so quickly, or with such relish.

Tallulah reassured Gizelle, "I will not send you back to wherever you have come from, and you are welcome to stay with me as long as you want. Do you know that you are pregnant? Do you want to keep the child? It's not too late if you don't want it; you are barely more than a child yourself."

Gizelle started crying. Tallulah walked around the bed and held her.

Gizelle spoke, "I don't want to have this child; it's that evil overseer's." Once she began talking, it seemed she could not stop. She told Tallulah all about her life on the plantation.

Tallulah prepared the black cohosh tea and gave her two cups. They took a walk along the creek to check the traps that were full of crawfish and crabs while Tallulah told Gizelle of her own life.

They returned to the cabin and Tallulah put chili peppers, mustard seed, bay leaves, dill, coriander seed, and allspice cloves in the boiling water before adding the crawfish. Gizelle found it even better than the soup.

Tallulah laughed at the way Gizelle ate. It was as if the child had never eaten before, but then she told her that the food they gave slaves was terrible. It was no wonder the child enjoyed her cooking so much. She gave her two more glasses of black cohosh tea before they went to bed.

The next morning Gizelle woke to pelvic cramps. Tallulah gave her a good helping of brandy in chamomile and mint tea and told her to go back to sleep. She filled a bottle with hot water, wrapped it in a cloth and placed it on the child's stomach. By noon she was bleeding. Gizelle lay in bed for four days.

Gizelle asked about the books that Tallulah read aloud to her. "How do you do that?" She lay next to her in the bed so she could look inside the book at the words.

She was surprised when the child started to recognize and point out simple three and four letter words and told her, "There is no reason why you cannot read and write. Of course, you would have to keep it a secret, and not let anyone see you doing it. It's against the law for slaves to be educated. If you promise to keep it a secret, I will teach you."

Tallulah reached into a chest and pulled out her old school books. Gizelle studied the books for hours. When she was up and around, she sat next to the creek or on the porch for hours studying and using a stick to copy the letters into the ground. When she encountered words that she could not make out, she made a little mark next to them with a piece of charcoal. When Tallulah returned she would ask her about them. Gizelle learned fast, and felt very proud when Tallulah praised and told her what a smart child she was. Within three months, she was reading and writing fluently.

Gizelle would jump around with glee when Tallulah brought books home that she bought and borrowed from her clients. She knew that magic feeling of being swept way on the words of a novel leaving the present behind. She had experienced it herself and encouraged Gizelle to see the words in her mind. Gizelle never found a book that she enjoyed more than the Bible.

Before Doc died he gave her all his college and medical books. Soon Gizelle was understanding them too and applying the knowledge to her medical rounds. Gizelle became Tallulah's assistant, just as she had been to old Doc many years ago. No one ever came looking for Gizelle, but Tallulah still told people Gizelle was her slave.

Gizelle was soon competent enough to make rounds on her own. She was well known for healing by the time she was sixteen. She had a gift of predicting things about the person or animal they had seen. Each prophecy and vision came true. She would tell Tallulah that someone was about to have her baby and low and behold, before the day was over, she was sent for and the child was born.

Gizelle had warnings for people and Tallulah would pass them on. They would laugh when she told them, but soon after, they would return and let her know that she had spoken the truth.

Soon people began to ask questions about loved ones or their futures. Gizelle could close her eyes, and within a few minutes, have an answer. Sometimes she would lie and say that she did not see anything.

She did not see any reason to scare people or share bad news. Her visions could not be changed. The warnings she would share. Anything else, she kept to herself.

There was one thing she told each and every one of them, and that was to pray. Tallulah had taught her religion and she believed in God. God had sent Tallulah to Gizelle. If anyone could change things, it was God.

Tallulah made it known to all that she had given Gizelle her freedom. She had legal papers drawn up so Gizelle would never have a problem and could move freely about the countryside. The men who hunted down runaways for a reward knew Tallulah, or of her reputation and importance in the community, and never bothered Gizelle. It was not long after she received her emancipation papers that slavery was abolished. But, she still had to have her papers with her at all times. Reconstruction era came with its own set of problems.

Gizelle began tending all the rounds. Tallulah was too tired as of late, and had total confidence in her apprentice. They had lived together like mother and daughter for almost twenty years. At eighty-two years old Tallulah passed peacefully in her sleep.

Gizelle was thirty-six years old and alone for the second time in her life. She had friends and clients, but Tallulah had been her family. She missed her. She laid her to rest in the place Tallulah had shown her, right next to her mother and grandmother. Gizelle had a huge crypt erected and had her body interred. She put all three of their names on the crypt.

Gizelle visited Tallulah every day. She spoke to her often, knowing she was still with her. She always felt and saw spirits. There was a saying that people who die bad do not stay dead. There was another one: if a spirit had someone that they were not sure would be all right without them, they would stay behind to look after them. The latter was the case with Tallulah.

Tallulah had often told Gizelle that she would like to see her married with children.

"I never want to see a man that way again. I have seen all the man I ever want to in that old overseer. No thank you, Ma'am."

Tallulah tried to explain the difference between the overseer and a loving husband, but Gizelle would have none of it. Men approached her in town; men of means, attractive men, but she was not interested. Truth be told; she was afraid.

Gizelle had seen other people in love and envied the tenderness and affection in their eyes and actions…the way their hands folded into each other's, the touch of their lips, the security. She would not know how to begin, she was afraid of how it would end, until one morning….

Gizelle had birthed a child; when she knew that a baby was coming she stayed in town. Just as she had dreamt the night before, the expectant mother's water broke. The child had come seven hours later, loud and healthy.

Gizelle was on her way home when a young boy ran up to her and grabbed her arm. "Please ma'am come quick, my sister is in trouble. We live up the street. Something is wrong. The baby don't want to come."

Gizelle examined the girl. The baby was breech, trying to come out feet first, one leg wedged into the unconscious girl's pelvis. She had passed out from the pain. The girl's mother pleaded, "Please, can you save them?"

Gizelle washed her hands in the basin and poured oil over her hands up to her elbows. She knelt before the child, took the babies thigh in one hand and pushed the baby back into the womb. With one hand on top of the girl's stomach, she maneuvered the baby's body around until she could feel the head in the correct position.

Next, she poured cold water on the girl's face to revive her. "I need you woke because we have to get the baby out quickly." To the mother she said, "Get behind her and lift her up to help force the baby down and out." It was over in two minutes. The child's hearty cries made everyone in the room laugh with relief.

As Gizelle prepared to leave, the mother told her, "I have birthed many a child and never in my life have I seen one try to come into the world ass-first like that. I am grateful for your help; my name is Rebi and this is my daughter, Celeste. Over in the corner is my oldest boy, Grayson, but everyone calls him Grayman on account of his gray hair. The small one who sought you out is Mason, my youngest."

When Grayson stood, their eyes met. He was six feet, two inches tall and had caramel skin. His smile was mesmerizing. Gizelle could not speak, the words stuck in her throat. His intense look awoke something in her that she had never felt before and she did not know how to handle it. She moved past him and picked up her bag. She mumbled something about another client and ran out the door.

Grayman

Gizelle did not stop running until she was around the corner. Out of breath, she sat down on a bench to wait for her heart to slow. "What is wrong with me?" she said aloud to herself.

She almost jumped out of her skin when a voice behind her said, "That's what I would like to know. Why are you running? I hope not from me."

Grayman was right behind her. He took her hand and placed a pouch of coins, "You forgot your money. I am sure this will be enough." He sat down next to her. The touch of his fingers on hers was like magic; calming, yet exciting. He turned her hand over and studied her palms as if he were reading a book.

"What do you think you are doing?" she asked.

"I am reading your future through your palm little one."

She had heard of this and card reading but never put much stock in it. She laughed nervously.

His brow furrowed, "You doubt me?"

Gizelle did not know what to say. How could she doubt anything coming from this man? How could she believe anything coming from him without knowing him? Why did she want to? Why did he make her feel this way? She wanted to get up and run away, yet she wanted to take his arm and put it around her and never move.

Grayman started telling her about her past—slavery, Tallulah, the aborted baby. He told her things that no one could know. Gizelle was shocked and embarrassed at the realization that if he knew all this, he also knew about the old overseer. If she had entertained any romantic thoughts, she could forget them now.

Gizelle stood and gathered her things and tried to hurry away.

Grayman stopped her with his hand on her arm, "Don't be afraid. It is a gift that I have; you have it also." He was right, but the only thing about her gift was she could never see her own future.

"I can help you develop your gift. No, I will help you because I have seen myself in your palm. I am your future and the things in your past are just that; in your past, Cher. You are a strong woman to have survived all the things you have had to endure."

Gizelle raised her eyes to meet his. Warm, brown pools invoked that unfamiliar feeling again. She mumbled something about being tired and going home to rest.

"Yes, I can see that in your eyes," he said. "You go home and rest, Cher. Tonight, I'll come to you and we will have dinner together. I have heard much about you and have a business proposition I would like to discuss. There is much we can teach one another."

"I am not interested," she hurried away. Gizelle had lied. She was definitely interested. But in what? The man? The palm-reader? Or both? She knew full well that she was interested in him—everything about him.

On her way home, Gizelle stopped by the grave. Tallulah and Jennifer were waiting for her. The spirit of Tallulah told her, "I know of the man you have met. He is indeed your future, there is good there, but if you are not careful, evil will touch you." Gizelle listened as Tallulah told her about the study of Voodoo, the worshipping of snakes and gods from another country. "Voodoo is a religion that is based in Christianity and can help give people hope and put their lives on God's path. He is well educated in this religion. He could use it for good, but he also knows the dark side. He must realize that hoodoo is of the devil and should not be used at all. Gizelle, be careful that his life's lessons and consequences do not fall upon you. For the most part he is a good man. Now, Cher, I can go on to rest because I know that you will not be alone."

That was the last time Gizelle saw Tallulah's spirit. She often felt her presence but never saw her again.

Gizelle arrived home and started to prepare something to eat, but the long day caught up with her. She fell into bed and a deep sleep. She was exhausted from the events of the day.

Grayman returned to his mother. Rebi laughed at the smile on his face.

"I paid Gizelle," he said.

"Yes, but why are you smiling like the cat who ate the canary?"

"I like her Mama, and I am a little more than curious about her."

Rebi

Rebi had heard about Gizelle's reputation as a healer. With her skills and her son's knowledge of Gris-Gris, the two of them could easily make their fortunes together. Rebi was always looking for ways to line her family's pockets.

She made a special charm and lit a white candle for love to ensure her son's destiny. She felt that this woman would be good for her first-born.

Rebi was the daughter of a Voodooist from Haiti who had been kidnapped and enslaved. He never stopped practicing the religion that had been bred into his family for generations, and it did not stop at Rebi. She taught her children. She had traveled the South like a gypsy with her father, husband and children, practicing voodoo and selling charms.

Rebi had done well for herself and her family, and even better when her husband, Lucien, died at the hands of a jealous man who caught him in bed with his wife. He was supposed to be delivering a charm, but ended up being seduced by the woman. It was not the first time he had slept with one of Rebi's clients, but it would be the last.

Rebi did not grieve the loss of her wayward husband. He had never done anything but exploit her and squander her earnings. Her savings grew rapidly after his death. She no longer had his gambling debts emptying her purse every week. Many times she was forced to pay debts that he had incurred with people who were not to be played with and threatened to kill him.

Rebi had saved her money and was looking to buy a house, settle down, and in a few years, retire. Her children were her life and she meant to see them happy. She had done a good job raising them. They all made their own money and could have gone off on their own, but chose to remain with her.

Celeste was good at doing hair. She had several affluent clients who would not let anyone else touch a hair on their head. She made daily rounds to their homes to see to their coiffures. Celeste's husband, George, worked on boats and was often out to sea. He had been gone for three months this time and would be proud to see his son when he returned.

Grayman drove a carriage for one of the most affluent French men in town. Born with a caul over his face, he could see things … important things. Just by touching people or something that belonged to them, he could see their past, their secrets and their futures. He was a great help to Rebi.

Little Mason, her nine-year-old son, shined shoes from his little box next to her booth in the marketplace where she sold charms and herbs. Rich, white women bought them as amusing gifts for their friends. Their attitudes changed after seeing their friend's hopes and desires fulfilled. Celeste and baby George were faring well. They had been lucky. For a moment, she doubted that the gods would let her daughter survive the birth. She realized that without the competent young woman who had performed nothing short of a miracle, her daughter and grandchild would have died. Rebi smiled as she bathed and prayed over her first grandchild.

Dinner Is Served

Gizelle slept the entire day. Her dreams were of the man she had met that morning. She pulled the covers up around her and rolled over, bumping into something; someone. It was him. Grayman was here in her bedroom, sitting on her bed smiling.

She rubbed her eyes, trying to remove the confusion. Certainly she must be dreaming, but she was not. He was actually here. She pulled the covers up around her nudity.

Grayman lifted a tray off the bedside table. She could smell the shrimp, rice and red beans. Her mouth watered. Gizelle reached for the tray and then realized this man had come into her home without her invitation. If memory served her right, she had told him she was not interested. She rose up to tell him to leave, anger formed in her eyes like storm clouds. "Get out and never come here without my invitation, which will not be forthcoming in this lifetime."

Grayman laughed, rose and walked to the door of the bedroom. "I and your dinner will be waiting for you in the other room," he said.

Gizelle jumped up and followed him, "What makes you think

you can just come into my home?" She looked around. He had prepared the meal on her stove. There was a bottle of brandy and flowers on the table, which was set with her china dishes and crystal glasses. White candles burned throughout the room.

Grayman sat at the table and smiled strangely.

This angered her further. "What are you grinning about?" Gizelle screamed.

He rose from the table and approached her. He handed her a glass of brandy, which she drank in one swallow. His smooth fingers suggestively traced their way down her spine, "I had come to discuss business, but now looking at you this way, I am beginning to have other thoughts."

Gizelle looked down and realized she was naked. She screamed, turned and ran into the bedroom. She was so embarrassed. She could hear his side-splitting laughter through the door. Suddenly she could not ignore the humor of the predicament. She had to laugh herself.

They were still laughing when Gizelle joined him at the table in a deerskin that had belonged to Tallulah. She enjoyed the meal. He was a good cook, which was one art she loved but never found much time to do.

Grayman told her, "I cook almost every day for my family. Someday I will have a restaurant so I can cook all the time."

Gizelle found this interesting and realized she wanted to know more about Grayman. No, not more, everything! The brandy gave her the courage to tell him so.

"I grew up in New Orleans and was in my early teens when my family was emancipated from slavery thanks to my mother's skill. She cured the master's only son. The doctors were at a loss when the child got yellow fever. He came very close to dying when Maman approached the master to help save his son. The deal was if she succeeded he would grant her freedom in return. The master did not think this woman could do anything to make a difference.

Maman had learned of a mixture of herbs from a famous Voodooiene that helped many survive the cursed disease. The woman had shared the recipe for the tea with her, making her promise to use her knowledge to help others.

The master was so grateful for his son's recovery that he gave Maman two hundred dollars in gold coins and honored his promise. He freed not only her, but also her father and children. He purchased her husband from the neighboring plantation and freed him also.

Gizelle was curious about palm reading and asked him about it. She listened eagerly as Grayman explained what each line stood for. He showed her his charms and explained what was in each one and what the desired outcome should be. He also explained to her the visions and knowledge that could be read in cards.

"My knowledge and this pocket watch are all I have left of my father."

She held it and read the name written on the inside.

"It had been his master's watch."

She noticed that the watch was broken, the hands forever frozen at half past eight. Clearly this did not matter to him, she could tell by the way he carefully put it back into his breast pocket.

They talked for hours. The brandy, along with his ardent attention, was making her feel giddy and light-headed. She cleared the table during an awkward silence.

Gizelle found herself wondering how Grayman's lips would feel on hers; his hands on her body made her remember the desire in his eyes. She blushed. She had never felt desire before and it must have shown.

As she moved past him to clear the table, he pulled her down onto his lap and kissed her. His tongue probed deep inside her mouth.

She found herself giving in to his lips upon hers. His tongue on her neck made a warmth spread through her body and an unfamiliar moistness gathered between her legs.

Gizelle tried to stand after he released her. Her legs were so weak that she could not rise. She leaned back into the comfortable strength of his arms, where he held her for a long time in silence. This must be how it felt to be a child in the safety of a loving parent's arms. She wanted nothing more than to sit here forever. He rocked her gently, all the while humming a soothing tune in her ear.

Grayman had known from the moment he touched her hand that he was going to be in her life. In one instant he had seen the hurt and pain of her past, she had suffered. He felt her desire for him but instinctively knew this was not the time. He wanted her body, but he wanted her trust and friendship even more. He felt something very special, something much more important than the swelling of his manhood.

He noticed her even breathing. Sleep had overtaken her. He lifted and carried her to the bedroom. She stirred in his arms as he lay next to her, but did not wake. They slept through the night, a sweet, comfortable, satisfying sleep, her back against his chest.

The aroma of ham and fresh baked biscuits aroused Grayman. He opened his eyes. Gizelle's big, light brown eyes studied him. He took a swallow of the lemon-mint tea that she offered. This was how he wanted to wake up every day.

They fed each other from the plate, giggling like children. By the time they finished eating, both were entertaining other thoughts. Grayman slowly pulled down the shoulder of Gizelle's dress. As the breath from his lips blew across her breast, the small nodule hardened and so did he. He spent long excruciating minutes going from one breast to the other as if he were a hungry infant who could not get his fill. He loved her smell; her hair was still moist from the perfumed soap that she used in her bath. Her skin was soft and smooth as silk. He unclasped her skirt. She stood, letting it fall from her waist. She started to climb under the covers, but Grayman stood stopping her so he could familiarize himself with her body. He stood next to her, running his fingertips over every inch, marveling at her ample hips and the perfection of her petite frame. The blemishes on her body were like beautiful badges of honor telling her history.

With every stroke of Grayman's fingertips and each gentle kiss, her breathing became more laborious. She reached up and unbuttoned his shirt. His muscles rippled with every movement. She loosened the button that held his underpants together, they dropped around his ankles, leaving his large penis waving like a flag, hard and erect. She had seen plenty of male forms, but not in this manner. She had not had sex since the overseer twenty some years ago.

Grayman sat her on the end of the bed and placed his hand on her chest. He pushed her torso down and placed one leg over each shoulder. His tongue and lips found the small, hard bundle of nerve endings between her legs. She had never experienced the series of explosions that wracked her body. Finally, she grabbed his head to stop him because she was having difficulty breathing.

With one hand, Grayman pulled Gizelle's body into the center of the bed. He kissed her deeply, at the same time entering her moist flower. The waves washed over her body more intensely now. She could only scream and hold on to his wide shoulders as she attempted to ride out the painful pleasure she felt time after time.

Once, twice, three times his body shuddered and she felt warm semen bathe her insides before he collapsed on top of her. They both mercifully drifted into sleep with him still inside. Her legs and arms wrapped around his waist and neck. Both of their bodies shook involuntarily from little after quakes of orgasm.

It was early evening when Gizelle awakened. The sun was going down. She rolled over, hoping to arouse Grayman again. He was gone. She felt panic. Why did he leave? This could not be happening. Was that it? Would she ever see him again? Was she just something he had amused himself with? She fell back on the bed and cried into her pillow. Then slept.

When she woke, she decided to eat something before pouring herself a drink. She would have gone straight to the brandy, but knew without food first, she would regret it.

When Gizelle walked into the front room she found the pocket watch resting in the center of the table with a flower next to it.

Marry Me

When Grayman left Gizelle's cabin it was with a bounce in his stride. He felt good about his decision to ask her to be his wife. He headed home and discussed it with his mother. Rebi was delighted.

Rebi rose and went to her bedroom. She came back and gave him a beautiful antique ring set with one perfect half carat diamond on a lacy band. The ring had been her wedding ring. She had stopped wearing it when Lucien died.

With tears in her eyes Rebi said "I thought I was going to have to wait and give this to Mason for his bride, but there is a God, Hallelujah. My boy is getting married!"

Mason and Celeste heard her and came into the room, not believing their ears. Grayman had never even dated a woman more than three times. When they saw the look on his face as he intently studied the ring, they knew he was serious.

The whole family went to a church service on Sunday. This time it was a different church–Gizelle's. Grayman had done some investigating to find out where she worshipped.

Gizelle tingled all over when he sat down next to her. She was relieved to see him. He looked so handsome she could barely concentrate on the preacher's sermon. He noticed and suggested they go outside.

They sat on a bench. "I have missed you, Cher."

She confessed that she had not been able to think of anything but him.

His family joined them after church. They all looked like they were harboring a secret and kept grinning at her. Celeste asked her question after question and told her she wanted to do her hair. Rebi quizzed her about her cooking skills. She was a little overwhelmed at all the attention.

Grayman smiled and said "Relax and get used to it. You will understand later."

Gizelle rode home with them. Grayman promised his mother they would be back in time for dinner. They rode out to the country and he pulled a blanket and picnic basket from the backseat. They walked by a creek and found a nice spot under a tree where they enjoyed fruit, cheese and wine while they talked for hours. Grayman seemed a bit nervous. Finally, he could not wait any longer. He took the ring from his pocket, got down on one knee and proposed.

Gizelle put her hands to her face. She could not speak.

"I cannot tell, Cherie. Is this good or bad news for me?" He pulled her hands from her face.

She was crying and smiling. Finally she nodded.

"Is this a yes? Does this mean that you will be my wife?"

She nodded again. He stood and let out a yell. He pulled her up from the blanket, kissed her and swung her around dancing as if there was a band playing. She laughed because she could also hear the music.

"I will be the best husband there ever was."

They made long slow love that afternoon.

When they arrived at his house, everyone was standing at the door waiting.

"Yes, she has agreed," Grayman said.

They all started whooping and hollering and dancing in the front room.

Celeste's husband, George walked in just in time for the celebration. His boat had returned that afternoon. He met his beautiful son. He could not have been more proud. He would not put the sleeping child down. Even as he sat and ate the feast that Rebi and Celeste had prepared, he kept baby George in the crook of his arm. The roast chicken, sweet potatoes, salad, cakes and pies never tasted so delicious.

George was happy to be back. He had to think of a way to make a living without going back to sea. The last trip had been quite unsettling for him. Bad weather had almost sunk the cargo ship, 'The Anna.' George was sure that he was about to join his father in his watery grave. Often he saw his father's spirit while at sea. They struggled to bring down the sails while trying to stay upright against the strong winds.

His father's spirit spoke, "Make this your last voyage. Your son has been born. I do not want that child to grow up without a father as you were forced to do."

George's father, and everyone else on the supply ship returning from Haiti, had gone down in the eye of a terrible storm.

George was thirteen years old and for a year afterward he would sit on the docks every day waiting for his father to come home. When he was sixteen and working on the ships, he had to acknowledge his father's death. Early one morning while on deck, his father's spirit visited him. He took his father's warning seriously and asked Grayman if he knew of any work.

Grayman told him, "I am buying more carriages to hire out. You can work for me."

Rebi talked about looking for land on which to build a big house. She hoped they would all consider living together. Grayman said that he thought it was time he had his own home.

Gizelle thought of a better idea and asked Grayman if she could speak to him in private. When they sat back down at the table, he asked Gizelle to tell them what she proposed. She explained to them that Tallulah had left her one hundred and fifty acres of land and that a 300 acre parcel of the neighboring property would be up for auction the next week. If they wanted, they could build their homes there. That way they could all be close. It was the answer to George's prayers. He had been saving for years and said, "Count me in." He had a family now, and with some land, he could farm. Celeste could not have been happier.

"So it is settled, I will have all my children living close to me. What more could I want? Except some more grandbabies." They all turned and looked at Gizelle who lowered her head and giggled.

"I will get right on it, Maman," Grayman said as he and Gizelle rose to leave. Grayman took a carpetbag with his belongings from his room. He would be living with his fiancé.

Rebi and Celeste got started on wedding plans. Rebi told Gizelle to leave all the arrangements to her.

Gizelle and Grayman jumped the broom two months later in the field by her house. It was a beautiful ceremony under a tree that had been tied with hundreds of ribbons, making the bayou look like something from a child's fantasy book. There were twenty tables covered with pretty fabrics and food their friends brought.

Everyone had their instruments. The congas, banjos, washboards and steel guitars were in full Zydeco swing until early the next morning. Rum and Tafia poured freely. It was a happy time. Every one of Gizelle's clients came, including the white folks who had come to love her over the years, all bearing gifts. Grayman's boss attended and gifted him a bag of two hundred gold coins.

Gizelle's Wedding Present

Grayman gave Gizelle her gift after the last guest departed. He told her that she was pregnant. It was strange that as many babies as she had brought into the world, her husband could tell her about her own pregnancy before she was aware of it. He even told her that it was going to be two boys - identical twins. His father had been a twin.

They made leisurely love that night, none of the urgency that they usually felt, but no less passionate. Afterward, they slept with his head on her stomach.

In the months to follow, Grayman helped organize and oversee the building of two cabins—one for Rebi and Mason; the other for Celeste and George, who now had another baby on the way.

He bought Gizelle her own automobile and taught her to drive. They hired men to work in the fields and started growing produce. Grayman rented an empty storefront in the town square so they could open a real business. Soon their store was one of the most frequented in the city, by all races.

George had worked on almost every ship that came into port. He went to the docks daily to purchase fabrics, spices and anything else he thought would sell in the store. He was allowed first pick since the captains respected and remembered what a good ship hand he had been. They were happy to see him settle down with a rapidly growing family.

Rebi assisted Gizelle on her rounds. Soon she would be too big and planned to spend the last month of her pregnancy and the first few months with her baby boys at home.

Grayman's carriage service was rapidly growing. He now had five carriages and three automobiles. He made time to spend with Gizelle, but was a nervous wreck. If she moaned or showed any discomfort, he would call his mother. Finally Rebi stayed at their cabin.

When Rebi was busy, Annie, a girl who Gizelle was teaching medicine and mid-wifing, moved in with Rebi. Grayman ordered three more rooms added on to the cabin. His boys needed their space. They were also building a grand house where they could all stay whenever they were a mind to.

Celeste's hair business was growing. She apprenticed three young girls to take over the clients. Celeste had a few exclusive clients who paid handsomely for her in-home services, and had one girl that she was training to replace her in this area since she was expecting another child. She took over a shop next to the store and opened a salon.

When Gizelle's boys finally came, they were healthy and strong. The delivery was easy. They named them Jimmy and Jerry. They were Grayman's pride and joy. He spent every extra moment with them. Gizelle sometimes joked that he would breastfeed if he could.

Jimmy and Jerry were good boys and they grew tall. They were smart and quick to learn everything from farming to building. They loved driving the full wagons from the fields. They took an interest in going on rounds with Gizelle learning medicine. They had learned about reading palms and cards from Grayman. Both were sighted and knew to be careful and not share their visions with anyone but the family.

Bad Medicine

There was only one thing that Gizelle did not like about her life; Grayman's practicing of Hoodoo. People came to him for charms for love, money, health, these she had no problems with; these were Voodoo, which was for good and based in religion. A line of salt around your property would help to ward off evil. She always made sure it surrounded all their homes.

It was the dark side; 'the Hoodoo' that she did not approve of. The charms and rituals designed to bring harm. He and Rebi sold them all. If you wanted someone dead, they would fashion a wax coffin, place a few strands of the unfortunate person's hair inside with some other ingredients and bury it in a graveyard. Soon the person would die. If you wanted someone sick, you could place a charm under their doorstep or bed - Gris gris bags made up of things like powdered lizard eggs, jackass hairs and feathers brought about different events. Hoodoo invoked fear in her. No one should be able to play God.

There was also the threat of the other voodooist looking to eliminate competition. Who knew which person would turn the black art against Grayman? 'What goes around comes around.' Several women were hurt by Grayman's marriage; jealousy could be very dangerous.

Grayman was washing Gizelle's car when he found a pouch tied under the seat. She often went into town making medical rounds. Anyone could have put it there. When Grayman examined the contents, he recognized it was to cause illness. He checked the car that he drove and found an identical bag tied under the front seat. He meant to find out who put it there. This was bad medicine.

Grayman discreetly followed her on her rounds for two weeks. He arranged for someone else to take over driving his exclusive client. He paid his drivers a portion of the weekly fares and rented out the other five coaches.

Grayman was able to make these purchases with money from their last crop of cotton and rice. George had become a full time farmer overseeing the four hundred acres of crops they cultivated.

At the end of the second week, Grayman watched a boy he did not recognize tie a bag under Gizelle's car seat. He knew the child was doing someone else's bidding. He had slept with a woman a few times and when he stopped seeing her, she swore that she would make him sorry. Lucia had sent him several messages.

He ignored her. He now knew what, "Hell hath no fury like a woman scorned," meant.

Grayman waited for a while and the boy came out of the small house in the center of Main Street. He went to her door and knocked. When she cracked open the door, he slammed into it with all his force, sending her sprawling to the floor. He stood over her and threw her gris-gris bags into her face and grabbed her by her collar and pulled her to him.

His face was inches from hers. She could see the spit spraying from his mouth as he spoke in anger, "If you ever try to hurt me or anyone in my family again, there is no magic that will help you because

I will kill you. I will strangle the breath from your body with my bare hands if I even think you are trying to do me harm," Grayman said. He dropped her and turned to walk out.

Lucia screamed, "Stop, please. I need to talk to you. I am sorry, but I love you. It's not fair that she should have you and I have nothing."

Her words stopped him and when he turned around, she was standing with her blouse in her hands. She unbuttoned her skirt and let it fall to the floor. His anger had excited her.

Lucia was nothing like Gizelle. She was tall and voluptuous. He remembered the nights he spent with his head buried between her full, ample breasts. She held one in each hand as she tried to entice him. He found himself taking a step toward her, then thought of his wife and sons and stopped cold. He shook his head as if to clear it. "I cannot do this, Lucia, I love my wife and she has given me two beautiful sons. I am sorry but I never felt about you the way I feel about her."

He approached Lucia; taking the blouse from her hand, he draped it around her shoulders "You are so beautiful, and you deserve someone who can love you as much as I do my wife. You should never want a man who you have to trick into loving you. Don't be bitter, Cheri, it does not become you." He wiped the tears from her eyes.

Grayman walked over to the bar and poured them each a glass of rum. "Come, sit with me and we will talk this out if you like. I think we would make better allies than enemies. What do you think?"

"I am so sorry, Gray. I am a desperate woman and have never had a lover as ardent as you. I understand your marriage and respect your feelings. You are a good man. You could have retaliated with stronger medicine than mine, yet you didn't. You even sit here now and offer me your friendship after what I have done. I am so ashamed and, yes, if it is not too late, I will gladly accept what you offer. You never have to worry about me betraying you again."

"Lucia, we are having a birthday party for the twins next week. They will be seven years old. I want you to come. I feel that loneliness is your only crime. Let me show you that having good, true friends is much more important than having a lover. I, myself, will undertake the task of finding a man good enough to be your husband, your lover and, most important, your friend."

She hugged him as he left her. She felt good about her new alliance with her former lover, and decided at that moment to rethink her actions. If he could be that forgiving, that gracious and understanding, then she vowed to strive to follow in his footsteps. There had to be something better than the empty, meaningless life that she led. She wanted a real, true love, not men whom she could not stomach for more than one night. Since her protector had died, she had been on an endless search for another to take care of her. She decided to start taking care of herself.

Grayman could not get home fast enough. He told Gizelle the entire story. He swore that he would no longer practice any Hoodoo that would bring harm to anyone. He now understood how detrimental it could be to people's lives and he wanted no part of it. Gizelle's prayers had been answered. The only dark shadow in her life was removed.

When Gizelle met Lucia at the party, she felt sorry for her and decided to help Grayman find her a companion. She could not be mad at her in spite of what she had tried to do. She understood loneliness. She had been lonely and did not even know it until she had met Grayman and become a part of his family. The funny thing was they did not have to look hard. Grayman's boss came to the party. He was enchanted by Lucia. His wife had died a few years before and he too had endured an endless string of bed partners for whom he had no feelings. They left the party together and after that were always in one another's company. The last time Gizelle saw Lucia was to birth her son. A few months later the small family moved to Paris.

Jimmy And Jerry

The party was not only to celebrate the children's birthday, but a way of letting all the school-age children know that their parents were proud of them for being so brave. They had been through a lot of adversity trying to go to school. Marie's two oldest; little George and Chasity, and the field hand's children dealt with a lot of racial tension.

The parents of the black and Indian children who attended the school had to accompany them because some days white men stood outside to scare them off. When this did not work they burned the schoolhouse down. It was rebuilt only to be burned down once more. They were not discouraged, they rebuilt again.

One day while the children were at school, Jimmy went to the coat closet to sneak a piece of pound cake that Gizelle had packed in his lunch. The back door of the school opened and a bottle with a flaming rag in the top came flying inside. The liquid spread the fire rapidly.

Jimmy tried to stomp it out but the liquid splattered on his pants and he caught fire. Screaming he ran out the back door. He saw a man riding off with a white sack over his head.

Jerry heard Jimmy's screams and tried to go out the back, but the fire was too menacing. He ran back through the front, yelling, "fire," so everyone could move out. When he was running toward the sound of his brother's screams his leg started to ache something terrible. Often times one of the twins would get hurt and the other would feel it. One of them would be home, the other out in the field or at the creek and the one at home would go to Gizelle or one of the adults, and say that Jimmy is hurt, or Jerry fell in the water. They were always right.

Jerry saw Jimmy running around in circles and tackled him down to the ground. He held him tight and rolled in the dirt until the flames went out. The schoolteacher knelt down next to them to check Jimmy's leg. She saw that the fabric fibers had fused to his skin. She tore off her headdress and wrapped it.

The children followed the teacher as she carefully picked Jimmy up and took him to a cart used for hayrides in the back of school. They lifted him onto the cart; each child grabbed a space on the handle, since they did not have a horse they would pull him home.

The school was enveloped in flames, smoke rising in black, billowing clouds. George and the other workers were in the fields when they first smelled, and then saw the smoke. They loaded up in three automobiles and drove as fast as they could. The roof of the school was caving in when they pulled up. Fear clutched their hearts, making it hard to breathe. George had to be tackled to the ground, lest he run into the flames to find his children.

One of the workers saw a dust cloud in the field. They loaded up and headed for it. George said a prayer as they approached the children. Little George ran to meet his father. He told him everyone had gotten out in time.

"Thank you Jesus," they all exclaimed.

George saw Jerry holding Jimmy up on the cart. His stomach

turned when he saw Jimmy's leg. He gingerly picked up the child despite the screams of agony and ran to his automobile.

Jimmy said, "Uncle George, I just wanted a piece of cake."

George held the child close so that he could not see the tears of rage rolling down his face.

Gizelle and the other women heard the horns blaring from the kitchen where they were preparing lunch. As they walked out they were assaulted by the smell of smoke coming from the school.

Gizelle tried hard to fight back the tears as she applied a poultice made of crushed garlic, aloe vera and lavender oil to Jimmy's leg. She made chamomile tea with a healthy dollop of brandy to help him sleep. She sat in the bed holding and rocking her boy.

Jimmy kept saying, "I just wanted a piece of cake." Finally, he fell asleep.

Jerry held his mother while she broke down in tears. She blamed herself for Jimmy's injuries. She had dreamt of something happening to the school and the children and ignored it. She would never dismiss her dreams again.

How would the children get their much-needed education so that one day they could do something to change this world? She would pray on it and hope that God heard her and would send an answer soon.

Stand Up

One of the field hands had gone back to the school. He wrote in the dirt in large letters:

THE CHILDREN ARE AT GRAYMAN'S THEY ARE ALL ALIVE

This way, when the other parents saw the burning cinders of the school, they would not feel the fear he had.

Grayman arrived followed by the parents who worked in the city, followed by the sheriff. Word had spread like wildfire and almost the entire black population assembled in the front of the house. They were all too familiar with the Ku Klux Klan's dirty deeds and were determined to do something about it. They had been to the school and were relieved to know that the children were not in the ashes. They headed for Grayman's house and waited until the sheriff left to talk. They all agreed to wait and see what the law would do this time. It was not long before they realized the law would do nothing to help them.

Two nights later, the church went up in flames and a cross was burned in front. The Reverend was hanging from a tree. He had been castrated and mutilated after being forced to witness the rape of his wife and daughter by the hooded men.

The colored towns' people knew they had to take matters into their own hands. Their conviction to be free and not have their rights denied gave them courage. Many would rather die than continue to live with fear and degradation.

The Klan was starting to lose power. Several events had put them in a bad light. Their leaders had been seen for what they were - thieves and land-hoarders. Many of their families had lost their fortunes, built on the backs of slaves during the civil war. They all cherished dreams of the South rising again. By hook or by crook they meant to see blacks back in slavery where they felt they belonged.

Several government and state officials were up on charges. One of their leaders, the Grand Wizard, was indicted for second-degree mur-der. When the others distanced themselves, he turned over signed con-tracts and financial records connected with several bad deeds and orders for murder. The membership declined from over six million to three hundred thousand. People were starting to attack the Klan all over the country, and they were desperate to stay in power.

Grayman and several parents and towns' people contacted an organization called NAACP, National Association for the Advancement of Colored People. They sent money to help rebuild the schools, and lawyers with information about the organization to teach them what their civil rights were. Blacks, Indians and some sympathetic whites all got together to rebuild the school and church.

There was a man who went by the name of Jedd. He had been a member of the Klan and when he decided to get out was threatened. His thirteen-year old daughter and wife had been harassed and were always in fear, but they stood behind his decision.

Jedd had a friend that was still a member and when drunk

bragged about the Klan's plans. The Klan was going to burn down the school again the next night. He told Grayman. Jedd was one of the men who had helped rebuild the school and church and looked at blacks as people with rights. Telephones started ringing all over the county.

That night, over sixty men - black, white and Indian were armed and hidden in the branches of the trees that surrounded the school. When the Ku Klux Klan rode up with their torches burning, they were doused from above with gasoline, setting both men and horses on fire. Men ran out of the school and dragged the Klansmen off their horses.

The sheriff and several of his deputies were un-hooded, along with store owners whose clients were majority black, two lawyers and the gas station owner. The thirty Klan members received the same treatment that the Reverend had gotten.

The vigilantes had dug a huge hole in the middle of the planting field. They threw them all in and covered the hole. The next crop of cotton that was planted over the hole was one of the best yields they ever had. The boles of cotton were huge; three times the size of the rest of the field. Guess it was something in the fertilizer.

Buddy Leaves

Buddy and his wife, Martha, lay on the bed in the small shack they lived in with her Aunt Loretta. Martha had just told him she was pregnant. He looked at the calluses on her palms, then into her dark-chocolate face and beautiful doe-shaped eyes and made a decision.

"I'm leaving, Martha. I don't want to see our kids raised this way. I'm not ever going to watch our children break their backs and cut their fingers in any field. Our children are going to have an education. I'm going to be more than a sharecropper. I'm going to find work. I'll be back for you. I'm gonna put you in a house where you don't have to work. I'm gonna take you out of these rags and dress you up fine," Buddy swore.

Martha was sure that he would never come back. She decided she was not going to be like her friends, forced to do degrading things to support themselves when their men found out they were pregnant and left.

Martha went to her Aunt Loretta, "How can he leave me when I told him I was 'bout to have his baby?"

Her aunt walked around the back of the rocking chair and put her arms around the distraught girl, "Honey, that boy done been smitten with you for a long time. I heard what he said to you and that ought to be making you love him just as much as he do you and this baby," Loretta said as she caressed the small mound that was beginning to show under Martha's shift. "There's a new day coming for black folks and he just wants y'all to be a part of it. Don't never discount a man for trying to make his dreams come true; we gonna pray and he'll be back just like he said, 'fore that baby is born."

Since Martha was good with a needle and thread, she started making quilts and doing alterations for people. She saved every dime she could get her hands on.

Buddy had been her first love since she was nine years old, working in the fields picking cotton. She could not imagine being with another man. Her aunt had faith in God and she also knew people. If she believed he would be back, he would be back.

When the men heard that Buddy had left, Martha received several visitors. They knew she was pregnant, but it did not matter. A lot of men had been jealous of Buddy for having a woman so devoted to him. Two of them proposed and offered to be father to her child.

"I thank you for your offer, but Buddy is my husband. He'll be back for us." She told them this even on the days when it was difficult for her to believe it.

One day Martha opened the door and her heart soared.

"I'm looking for Martha, I left her here about eight months ago, would you happen to know where I can find her?" Buddy said with a big grin on his face.

Martha could not speak. She started crying. He pulled her into his arms and held her for a long time. Some of the neighbors had seen him walking down the street in his porter's uniform and were all outside watching.

"Pack a bag honey, you are going with me to California. I told you I would be back in time. I already have us a place to stay and everything, but we don't have a lot of time. The train leaves in two hours," Buddy said.

Martha had dreamt about this day. She had to pinch herself to make sure she was not dreaming. While she packed, he told her all about his new job on the railroad and his travels since leaving Louisiana. California was the place where he wanted to raise their children.

She did not have but one bag. In it she had a jar that held the two hundred dollars she had saved, a few dresses and a picture of her parents who had passed a long time ago and some baby clothes.

Martha said goodbye to her Aunt Loretta, "You take good care of my niece, you hear me?" Loretta hugged Buddy goodbye.

"Yes Ma'am and when we get good and settled, I'm gonna come back for you" Buddy promised her.

The neighbors wished them well as they made their way toward a new life.

Train Ride

Martha was on the train heading for California. She had never dreamed of living anywhere but Louisiana. "Hallelujah," she kept saying.

Buddy had teased her unmercifully about her figure. "Please don't make me laugh no more, Buddy. You gone make the baby come, my stomach is already hurting."

"Alright, I'll leave you alone for now, but you better get used to it, cause for the next ten years that's how you gonna be looking," Buddy said.

Buddy checked on Martha every now and then when he could get away from his duties. The last few times he had come she had been sleeping so he made sure that her blanket was covering her and placed an extra pillow at her feet.

Buddy walked into the car with dinner for Martha when one of the passengers slipped and fell. Buddy put the tray on a vacant seat and rushed to help the man up. As Buddy helped the man to his feet, he noticed that his coat was wet. Then he noticed the water on the floor.

"I'm so sorry sir, I wonder where this water came from. If you'll give me your jacket, I'll be glad to…" Buddy's voice trailed off as he noticed that the water was pooled under Martha's seat.

"Martha, Martha wake up," Buddy said as he went into the seat where she was laying over on her side sleeping. He pulled the blanket from her. She sat up half asleep; wondering what he was so excited about. She felt the moisture on the back of her dress. It was time.

"Buddy, my water done broke," Martha said.

Buddy stood there as if in a trance. The man that he had been helping realized what was happening and patted him on the shoulder. Buddy stood there frozen. The man slapped him into action, "Wake up man. This woman is about to have a baby."

"Baby, do you know what to do?" Buddy asked.

"Not really, but it couldn't be that hard. So many other people have done it," Martha said.

There was an older woman on the train by the name of Rebi. She took over, barking orders in a no nonsense tone that had everyone jumping to do her bidding, "What is your name, Cher?" Rebi asked.

"Martha, ma'am. Are you a midwife?" she asked.

"The very one you need to give praise to God for sending me to help you bring this child into the world. I need you to turn and put your feet up on the seat right next to your backside so that I can see where we are," Rebi said.

"Young man, are you the daddy?" Rebi asked, never even glancing over her shoulder. She used her hands on the outside of Martha's stomach to find the position of the baby.

"Yes, Ma'am," he said. "I really do 'preciate your help, and I want you to know that I can pay you," Buddy said.

"Right now, I need you to get lots of clean towels and some warm water. Get moving! This child is coming now," Rebi said.

Buddy was back within seconds. The men left the car. Three women came to offer help. Two of them were white. One got behind her and lifted her up every time the pains came. One leaned over the seat in front of her and held her hand. The other stood by with a sharp sterile knife to cut the cord.

Buddy kept walking into the car to see how things were going, even though he had been told to stay out. Every time he popped his head in the car, Martha took the opportunity to scream out her anger over him leaving her. "You didn't even bother to come and see me! I hate you! I love you. Get out of here. Buddy, where are you? You should be having this baby and then you'll know how much it hurts!" With that last bout of yelling Buddy decided to get back to work. Two hours later the child was pulled out of Martha's womb just as the train pulled into Los Angeles.

Buddy was amazed with his son. They named him Train. Martha rode in the cab with her mouth hanging wide open. This town was really something. She asked questions that Buddy patiently answered. She loved the apartment that he had rented and furnished.

Two years later, they bought a house and true to his word, he sent for Martha's Aunt Loretta. The day that Loretta met Buddy at the train station, her suitcase held a bible and three quilts. In her purse an envelope held two hundred dollars, a gift from her friends.

Martha and Buddy were working on their third child. He had been right when he had told her to get used to being pregnant because that was how she would be for the next ten years. No sooner did one child arrive than another was conceived.

Annie's Family Is Gone

Annie Thomas was born in Lake Charles, Louisiana in 1904. No one ever really had a clear picture of her parentage. The only thing known was that they were sharecroppers. "They died young, indentured by debt," was all she would ever say.

Annie had one brother, Buddy, who left when he was seventeen years old. He was her mother's first born. He was light-skinned with wavy hair and beautiful features. She had not seen him since she was seven years old.

Buddy worked in the fields with Annie's father. Annie's father never treated him as his own son. Annie's mother had been raped by an overseer when she was twelve years old. Nine months later, Buddy was born. Annie was born ten years later fathered by the man she had jumped the broom with.

During Reconstruction era, most of the slaves became hired hands who were paid a salary. Most of them knew no other way of life so they accepted terms that sometimes made them more of a slave than they had ever been.

Plantation owners put up stores where the employees could buy food, clothes and supplies to plant and harvest in the yards of the shacks they rented while they continued to work. "It's okay if you don't have the money to pay. You just put your 'X' on this here piece of paper and I'll extend you all the credit you need," the owners would say. The total usually was more than they could ever hope to pay off with their meager earnings. The storeowners were eager to credit their pay towards the ever-growing bill. After a few years they were back in slavery, trying to work off the debt.

Some owners would offer to sell their hands a small piece of property. Several generations of ancestors would have to work their natural lives away before owning the land free and clear. Of course, the owners left out these minor details.

Some of the newly freed people did not want to stay in the same place and have to deal with the masters who had kept them in bondage for so many miserable years. They left the plantation to make their own way in life. Many found illegal ways of making a living.

Who could blame Annie for leaving after growing up picking cotton and watching her parents die with only a shack to show for it. Annie understood why her brother left and, when her parents both got sick and died, she walked away wanting nothing to do with the land that the owner said she was responsible for. She was eleven years old. She had no idea of where to find Buddy or even if he wanted to be found.

Annie, Are You Pregnant?

Annie spent the early part of her life in Lake Charles and in the surrounding towns of New Iberia, Lafayette and Broussard. She worked hard and did many things to make enough money to support herself and later her three children.

Annie was fourteen years old when she got pregnant. Chocolate brown skin with budding breasts, narrow hips and jet-black wavy hair fell just below her shoulders.

Her first love was Willie Simpson III, the son of a plantation owner. They called him Willie the III. Annie cleaned upstairs. In three years, Willie the III had grown attached to her. They talked, played games and had picnics by the lake. His attitude changed when her pregnancy became obvious. They never really discussed it; she had told him she was having his baby as he panted over her during sex. He said, "That's nice." Annie assumed he would do the right thing.

Their afternoons remained hot and steamy until Annie's stomach got big. Then Willie the III started ignoring her. He spent more time with his friends talking about college. Annie assumed he would be attending a local college. She had no idea that most graduates went away to college to get away from their parents.

Annie listened to Willie the III and his friends talk about their future vocations as she cleaned the room. To these young white men, she was invisible. She was just another 'house-cleaning-black,' who did not have eyes or ears and knew they had better not repeat anything.

Willie the III did not bother to make excuses when questioned about never being around. He said he did not have time, with graduation coming and preparations for college.

She asked, "What about the baby?"

He said, "Don't worry about it, everything will be fine."

One day Annie was cleaning a lamp in the hallway and the light shining through her clothes showed the roundness of her stomach... Maureen, Willie the III's mother, who had been watching her asked, "Annie, are you pregnant?"

Annie told her "Yes Ma'am."

"Is the father one of the men in the field? Do I know him? Are you going to be wed?"

Annie answered "No, yes, and I hope so."

Maureen looked at her, puzzled.

Annie said, "Ma'am you asked me three questions. No, he is not a field hand. Yes, you know him very well, and I do hope to be married soon."

"Well, who is the father?" Maureen asked.

Annie proudly told her "Your son Willie the III."

Maureen's jaw dropped. They were fond of Annie, but not that fond. After all, she was colored. Maureen started crying and screaming, then fainted. Her husband heard the commotion and came running in.

He told Annie to fetch the smelling salts and when she returned, Annie asked, "Is Ma'am okay?"

"She will be just fine. This is one of her many spells; it will pass. Annie you can go on home since your day is finished. I will see to her," Willie Jr. said.

Annie left.

Maureen did not like sex and Willie Jr., being the pervert that he was, took advantage of her spells. He viewed it as an opportunity to have his wife's body, which was otherwise off limits. She always denied him, unless she had imbibed too much sherry or was unconscious. If he was quick, he could finish before she came around. He was not in the least bit concerned about what had caused the spell, he just knew that he had to hurry.

She regained consciousness just as he was letting out a loud groan and his semen bathed her insides.

"You are a disgusting pig. Why do you always take advantage of my weakened state? You sir, are no gentlemen and your son is following in your footsteps," Maureen said.

"Woman, what are you talking about?" Willie Jr. said as he buttoned his pants.

"Your son has gotten Annie pregnant, and I want to know what you are going to do about it. The stupid child has the preposterous idea that he is going to marry her?"

He turned so she could not see the smile on his face. Well, apparently she was right. He was a chip off the old block. Well, they say that the apple never falls far from the tree. His first child had been born when he was fifteen and he had added ten more mulattos to the list over the years. Yep, that's my boy. "Maureen, don't worry. This is not a problem. We will give the girl some money and this will all go away.

Don't fret yourself over this. These things happen all the time."

The next day when she showed up for work, Annie received a cold greeting from the head housekeeper "Your services are no longer needed." He shoved an envelope into her hand and attempted to close the door.

Annie stuck her foot in the door and opened the envelope, and looked at the money. She raised her voice "Is this all that their grand-child is worth?" She threw the envelope past him onto the floor. "Can I please talk to Willie the III?"

Maureen came downstairs, "Annie, my son has left for school far, far away. You are never to come to this house again. I hope this will be the last I hear of this unpleasant situation," She instructed the butler to close the door, which he slammed in Annie's face.

Annie walked to the end of the street, sat on a bench and cried. She knew once her lover learned of what his parents had done, he would come. He would never abandon her.

For a month Annie sat in her rented room waiting for Willie the III. She held onto hope. What was taking him so long?

Willie The III

Willie the III loved Annie as much as a white boy could a colored. He enjoyed her company, especially in bed and they had taught each other everything.

Unfortunately, Willie the III had a fiancée, Caroline; they were expected to be wed at the end of the summer. This was an arrangement their parents made when they were children.

He would have preferred to marry Annie, but his mother would not have the family name soiled and it was against the law. That afternoon when he walked into the house, his mother was sitting on the couch crying and his father was trying to tell her that it was not the end of the world.

"What's not the end of the world?" Willie the III asked as he entered the room.

"Don't you dare act as if you don't know what this is about; why didn't you come to us when she first got pregnant? We possibly could have helped the girl. She has the preposterous idea that you are going to marry her. Who put that into her head I'd like to know?" Maureen

106

screamed at him.

"Maureen go on to your room and let me talk to the boy," Willie Jr. said taking her by the arm and leading her to the staircase.

"I want to know why…"Maureen's voice trailed off.

"I will handle this woman, now be quiet and go upstairs," Willie Jr. said.

Willie Jr. walked back into the room and closed the two big doors. He poured two glasses from a decanter of brandy and handed one to Willie the III "We are going to raise our glasses high to my boy, a chip off the old block. I was beginning to wonder if your seed was any good boy," Willie Jr. said, patting him on the back. "I'm proud of you son. Don't you worry about a thing, I'll take care of this."

"What's gonna happen to Annie, pa?" Willie the III asked.

"Well your momma doesn't want her working here no more and all that talk about you marrying her is just plain foolishness. Once upon a time we could have taken the baby and got a good price for a high yellow child, but now that slavery is over, these niggers get the darndest ideas in their fool heads. We will give her some money and send her on her way. I wouldn't worry about it," Willie Jr. said.

"But Pa, it ain't right we should send her off like that even if she is colored. She is having my child. Shouldn't we let her keep on working for the child's sake?"

Willie the III did not want to be without Annie. He had planned to have her work in the house after he married Caroline. He could have her there as a live-in maid. That way while his wife was sleeping, he could sneak down and be with her. He had been with white girls before and it was not the same satisfaction for him. Why did she have to go and tell his mother about the baby?

"You damn fool. That child probably ain't even yours and, if it is yours, it ain't yours. Boy, did you forget that you are gonna be marrying

Caroline in a few months? What do you think she would say about this? You will forget all about Annie and that child or you will be out of here on your ear without a dime. I don't mind you pestering no nigger, but anything else is out of the question. Keep things simple for all involved, you will not see her again. I never want to see the little bastard. Do you understand boy? You are gonna marry Caroline, and me and her daddy are going into business together to make sure your future is secured. I don't want to hear another word about it," Willie Jr. said.

Willie the III realized there was nothing he could do for Annie. He would never go against his father's wishes. He had to think about his life and Caroline's. Besides, coloreds had babies all the time.

Willie Simpson The III Is Married

One day Annie was cleaning windows for a woman she did odd jobs for. Now the best way to get a window clean, the kind of clean with no streaks or smudges, where you don't even know that it's a window you are looking through is to use equal parts vinegar and warm water with newspaper. Nothing else works as well or as fast.

Annie was about to crumple up a sheet of newspaper when she spied the smiling face of Willie the III standing in a tuxedo, eating a piece of cake with a beautiful, blonde girl. She took the paper to her employer and asked, "Can you read this to me please, Mrs. Martin?" Annie could not read.

"Oh yes, this is the announcement for the wedding of young Willie to his high school sweetie," Mrs. Martin said.

Mrs. Martin proceeded to share the details of the beautiful wedding in detail, "Anyone who is anybody in Lake Charles society was in attendance. It was one of the biggest events of the season. Maureen outdid herself this time. They spent a fortune. Maureen and I went to school together you know," When she turned around she noticed Annie seemed distressed.

Annie did not want to cry, but she could not stop the flow of tears. Suddenly the room started to spin. She woke on a couch with Mrs. Martin holding a cold towel to her forehead and smelling salts under her nose.

"What's wrong with you child? Why are you crying so?" Mrs. Martin asked.

Suddenly, it was all too much for Annie; the words flowed from her mouth like water.

Mrs. Martin listened, stroking Annie's brow, all the while shaking her head, "Tsk, Tsk, you poor thing. I heard rumors but I never pay any mind to old hen's gossip. It never dawned on me that it was you that they were talking about. How could Maureen be so cold as to throw you out without a job, and that Willie? Why, you are only a child. He took advantage of you. Well you just stop crying now. I'm going to help you with this mess."

When Annie returned to her room that afternoon, the reality of being alone hit her. She knew Willie was not coming. No one was coming. No person in this whole world was going to be there for her and this child. She was scared; no, not scared, terrified.

That day Annie's heart turned to ice. It would be a long time before she would ever trust another man. She was a survivor, what else could she do? Annie had no family and was feeling very alone. She was young, pregnant and had no man. She had some friends, but not the kind you could depend on to do anything but say, "I told you so" or "You need to learn to stay in your place" or something that would add to her distress.

Gizelle Meets Annie

The following day when Annie showed up for work, Mrs. Martin introduced her to Gizelle. "She is going to examine you to make sure the baby is okay. You should have seen a doctor when you first realized you were pregnant."

Mrs. Martin gave Annie an envelope and when she opened it there was two hundred dollars. Mrs. Martin had spoken to Maureen on Annie's behalf. Maureen would do anything to keep the scandal quiet. She assured her that she would compensate the child monetarily for the sake of the baby and silence. Regular payments would come through Mrs. Martin.

While Gizelle was examining Annie, the child asked, "Can you get rid of the baby? I don't want it."

"It is not possible; the Be'be is already too big." She felt Annie's stomach and told her, "You are at least six months along. You need to get your mind ready for this blessing that God has seen fit to give you. No more talk about not wanting the Be'be. The child will be touched by it. Whatever the father has done is done. You have to pick up your spirits so that this baby girl will feel welcome and loved in her life," Gizelle said.

Annie started to cry and told her the whole story. She also cried because she realized that Gizelle had said, 'baby girl.' She had prayed for a boy. She did not want to bring a girl child into this heartless world. She hoped her girl would never go through the things she had.

Gizelle explained to her, "There are other, more important directions that you should be channeling your energies into. Later, after the child is born and only then if you still want me to, I will help you serve a little justice to the family who has used you like so much toilet paper and thrown you away. All you need to do is trust in God's will. He will make sure that these people get their own cross to bear, because there is such a thing as karma and those old sayings be so true, 'What goes around comes around,' and 'You reap what you sow.' Think about your daughter who has not done anything to anyone and deserves and needs love since she is not going to have a father, Annie. You will have to prepare to be both mother and father."

When Gizelle left Mrs. Martin's house, she took Annie with her. They stopped at the boarding house to gather her few possessions. Rebi heard the automobile approaching and walked out onto the porch. Gizelle told her Annie's story as she slept in the car.

Rebi decided Annie should stay with her since most times Mason slept in town at the store. They woke her up. She got out of the car and took in her surroundings before following Rebi into the house. Rebi reminded her of her own mother.

Annie was so much like Gizelle when she was her age; alone, pregnant and scared. Gizelle believed God wanted her to help Annie, just like Tallulah had helped her.

For the remainder of Annie's pregnancy, Gizelle taught her everything she needed to know about taking care of a baby. She took her along to assist with some baby birthing. Once Gizelle sat back and told Annie to take over. She was surprised when it came as second nature to her. When she held the baby in her arms to hand to the mother, she was overwhelmed with the beauty of what she had just done. She started crying. Everyone understood. Gizelle had birthed dozens of children and it still managed to bring tears to her eyes every time.

Annie loved living with Rebi. She felt she was part of a real family. Her parents had been in the fields night and day and by the time they came home, could do nothing but fall into bed and sleep. This family always had lunch together, usually outside under the big oak tree in front of Rebi's house unless it rained. They went to church every Sunday. Every now and then Annie would go but she did not have much belief in God. Sunday dinners were an elaborate event.

One night there were two babies coming. Gizelle told Annie that she would have to go and deliver one of them. When Annie returned, she was proud of herself. She handed Gizelle the money, but she shook her head, "The money is yours. You did the work, so you have earned it, Cher."

That is when Annie started going with Gizelle on all her rounds so that she could help with the midwifing and doctoring. Gizelle taught her things like healing and herbs. Bay leaf for stomach ails, sarsaparilla roots for fever, poultices and always a prayer.

Annie helped birth Gizelle's twins. She moved in with her for a few weeks. She loved the boys. They were the first babies that she had ever spent time around. She was amazed by something they did every day.

Three months passed quickly. She and Gizelle walked every day because it would make her delivery easier. One day Gizelle suddenly stopped and closed her eyes.

Annie was used to this; she was having one of her visions.

"You will be a Mama before the sun rises," Gizelle said.

Annie woke up drenched and the sheets were soaking wet; it was her time. She went to Rebi's room and knocked on the door. Rebi went down to the front porch and rang the dinner bell. It was loud enough for Gizelle to hear. She saw a lantern shining at the other houses that sat four acres away and knew they were on the way. She looked in the other direction and saw the light on at Celeste's house. Everyone was there within minutes.

Annie knew it was silly, but suddenly she was afraid. As the pains came she did the oddest thing, she began laughing uncontrollably. With every spasm that shot through her pelvis she could not stop laughing. Everyone in the house laughed along with her. The child came into the world five hours later with a loud cry.

She was healthy and normal. She had all of her fingers and toes and a crown of curly black hair. One could not help but marvel at the contrast in color; it was as night is today. The baby was the color of rice. Annie looked down on her daughter and said, "Hello Lil' girl, I'm your momma, and your name is Helen."

The next week, Mrs. Martin came bearing gifts. She blew into the room like a summer breeze and sat in a rocking chair with Helen while Annie opened box after box of clothes, toys and shoes.

Mrs. Martin was splitting her sides with laughter as she explained to Annie that Maureen had given her some hush money. Her first impulse was to turn it down but she decided to take it and make a trip to New Orleans. There she had the time of her life buying presents for Helen. There were enough clothes to last until Helen's third birthday. She also had an envelope for Annie with two hundred dollars inside.

Annie spent hours holding Helen the first few days. She swore to herself that she was going to protect her daughter from the evils of the world. The only thing troubling her was the fact that Helen looked so much like her father. Annie had a constant reminder of his betrayal.

A few weeks later Annie was ready to get back to work. Gizelle found her a job. She would be cleaning house for the town Judge and his wife.

Rebi kept Helen, Gizelle's twins and Celeste's four children during the working days. Grayman dropped Annie off in the mornings and she rode back with Celeste at noon, who had to suckle two months old twins, Kate and Kathy. There were also three other infants whose parents worked in the fields. Grayman, Mason and the fieldworkers came to lunch every day. The nursing mothers would sit around the parlor gossiping about the events of the day as the babies fed. Then they would join the others for lunch, take a nap and head back to work.

By the time Helen was two, she would join Annie at work. The baby loved helping her momma. She would go from table to table with her little dust rag. Annie would sprinkle the lemon oil on for her and she would rub until she could see herself. Then she would call Annie and say "See, shiny, Mommy."

Even at home, Helen was not happy unless she could snap and shell peas, shuck corn, shell shrimp, crack pecans, roll chicken in flour, or corn meal the fish. Her favorite task was to mix up eggs. She was so bright and smart. Annie knew she spoiled her, but she was her baby girl.

Annie loved changing Helen in dresses with matching bonnets and hand-made shoes. She would send her outside to play, knowing she would get dirty within the hour.

Rebi would say, "Leave that child alone. I see you changing her clothes every two minutes."

Helen did not like it either. When she saw Annie coming with fresh clothes and a brush to comb her hair, she would run away screaming.

People in town assumed Annie was the nanny to this little white girl. She never told them any different. When she was four, Helen would ask to play with the little white girls who lived down the street from the Judge. Annie got pleasure seeing her daughter playing with the girls. Their mom's treated Helen like any other white girl. They did not ask and she was not telling.

Annie was walking down the street with Helen one day when an automobile slowed down next to them. Maureen was inside. She did not stop, but circled the block three times staring at what she knew had to be her granddaughter. Annie's envelopes came more frequently.

Mrs. Martin told Annie that Willie's wife had miscarried twice, and the last time, the doctor said she would not be able to have any children.

Helen would talk all the way into town. She pointed her pudgy little finger and asked, "What's that?" Helen named the things she remembered on the way home, "Tree, bird, cow, horsey." Motherhood is wonderful, Annie thought.

When they pulled up at the Judge's house, Annie pointed her finger and said, "Man."

There was a man standing out front. It was Willie the III. Annie said the name aloud. Grayman looked at the man. He knew the story. Annie and Helen got out of the car.

Grayman asked, "You need me to get rid of him?"

"No, we'll be just fine," Annie said. She was angry with herself because her heart still fluttered at the sight of him.

"Hello, Annie. How are you?" Willie the III asked.

"What do you want?" Annie said harshly.

"I was hoping that we could talk?" he said as he bent down to examine Helen.

"We ain't got nothing to talk about," Annie said.

"Oh come on, Annie, don't be that way. I know that things must have been rough on you, but, we were young and my parents made me leave. My mom told me she was trying to do right by you, sending money and all. I got a solution to all our problems that could make up for all this."

Annie turned on him with rage in her eyes, "And what's that Willie? What do you plan to do, turn back the hands of time and marry me and make things right? Cause that's the only thing that could fix things for me and that's just impossible, now ain't it?" Annie questioned and poked him in the chest.

"Uh, that's not quite what I had in mind. You know I can't marry you," Willie the III said.

"Oh, Why not? You married somebody didn't you? Then I go and find out I wasn't nothing to you and she had been your sweetheart longer than me. You ain't nothing but a weasel. I will thank you to leave me alone," Annie said.

Annie opened the latch on the gate and turned around to pick up Helen and found that he had scooped her up, "She looks just like me, doesn't she? Hello little girl, I'm your daddy."

Helen looked at the man and then at her mother and started to cry and reach for her. She did not know this man, she did not like him because he made her mommy angry.

"You got no right to be telling her that, Willie. There's a big difference between making a baby and being a father," Annie said.

"Listen to me, Annie. I can take better care of her than you can. With her looking white and all, she could come and live with me and be raised privileged. We would even pay you to have another child, and if it is a boy and looks white, we could take that one off your hands too. That way you would not be trying to raise the children alone. They would have a mother and a father. You could visit them, or even come and live in as a maid; it would be like old times. I am her father you know, I have a right to her."

Annie could not believe her ears. He was proposing to take her baby girl. "You low down snake. You should know better than to think I would let you and that barren bitch you married take my child."

She took Helen and walked through the gate. He followed her "Annie, you know that I can take her from you. You need to think about this," Willie the III pleaded.

With those words, Annie halted in her tracks staring at him for a few seconds before opening the front door and picking up an umbrella. She turned on Willie and started beating him upside the head with it, "You son of a bitch, don't you know I will kill you dead before I let you take my daughter from me?" She screamed.

She was in mid-swing when Grayman came running up and grabbed her from behind. Something in this gut had told him to stay close, and it was a good thing because if he had not been there, she would have caved this boy's head in.

The Judge had heard the entire conversation. He knew all about Mr. Willie Simpson the III. Gizelle had told him about Annie's problem before they hired her. He had been friends with the Simpson's for over four decades. It took both men to restrain Annie. The boy had taken a good whack on the head and lay on the ground.

Grayman told him, "You had better get up and get while the getting is good."

The Judge told Willie the III, "Take a walk with me around the corner, son. I want to have a word with you." The neighbors were watching and had heard the whole thing.

"So, you think you can just walk up after four years and take Annie's child? You got her pregnant at the age of fourteen, then walked off and abandoned her. No sir. Not in my county, and I am the Judge. I happen to be quite fond of Annie and Helen. If you think I would sit back and let this happen you are sadly mistaken. Do I make myself clear, son?" the Judge waited for an answer.

"Yes sir, but could you please ask her to think it over? It's the best thing for the child," Willie the III said.

"And why is that, because your wife can't have children? If your wife could bear children would we be having this conversation? You need to realize that she is a mother; has been since day that child's life was conceived. She's a woman, as you obviously know, not a cow or a slave. Women do not just sell their children like a side of beef, and frankly I see it as a lack in your character for you to be willing to add insult to injury by asking her to do such a thing. I trust that this will be your last time contacting Annie?"

"Yes sir, but please, just ask her to think about it."

"No, I will not. She heard you and if, which I doubt very seriously she ever would, if she decides to consider your offer, she will get in touch with you. I am going home and have my breakfast now. You have a good day."

When the Judge walked back into the kitchen, Helen was crying and Annie was stomping around cursing up a blue streak. His breakfast was on the table. He picked Helen up and sat her on his lap.

"Don't worry about it. Unless you contact him, he knows to leave you and Helen alone."

Annie's Club—1921

Celeste had two boys and two girls. Rebi kept them while Celeste worked keeping the affluent white women's hair beautiful. She no longer went to their homes; they came to her shop in town unless it was a special occasion.

Little Mason was no longer little. He was single and happy. He was the father of two boys; Tanner and Jake. He tended the store. Mason was handsome; girls and women were always vying for his attention. His sons were products of affairs with girls whose families were not happy about it. When the girls started to show, they stayed with Rebi until their children were born. After that, the women went on with their lives, no one the wiser. Mason doted over his boys.

Rebi had a young man living with her. Her favorite saying was, "I don't want nuthin' old but some money." She had met Gerard at a party. He came home with her that night and never left. He had proposed several times but she kept turning him down. She liked things just the way they were. They often traveled on business and returned with gifts for everyone. The children loved him because he was like a child himself. He played in the yard with them every chance he got.

Gerard lavished affection on Rebi. She deserved it and wished she had met him when she was younger. After six months, Rebi found herself forty-four years old and pregnant. He could not have been happier. He had never settled down long enough with any one woman to have a family. He walked around proud as a peacock, telling anyone that would listen, "I'm gonna be a daddy."

Gerard was a moonshiner. He taught Rebi to make gin and beer. They built stills on the backwoods of the property. Since prohibition started in January 1920, they were raking in money hand over fist.

Nights that Annie was not helping Gizelle; she went with Rebi and Gerard. Many a night they were out back distilling, bottling, and boxing up the White Lightning. Annie's favorite part was the deliveries. Rebi took her to the speakeasies, hoping to find the child a husband. It was not natural for a woman to be without a man. Rebi knew Annie's pain, and felt like a good man would fix everything.

Annie was growing fond of the Louisiana nightlife. She loved the illegal clubs, the liquor and the excitement—not to mention the gambling. Most nights, a fight broke out over a woman or a man or someone caught cheating. She loved the constant action.

Rebi had to drag her away from the circle around the arguments and fights. "Girl, one day you gone stick that little nose of yours into one of those circles and get it shot or cut off," Rebi said.

The Judge and his wife never saw cause to criticize Annie's work. She was meticulous and had lasted longer than any maid they had employed before. She started at daybreak and was done by noon.

Annie worked other jobs also. During festivals and busy seasons she worked at two hotels in the evening cleaning rooms. During her breaks, she would go into the kitchen where she watched and learned as they prepared all the fancy meals that the patrons liked.

She learned about seasonings and herbs from Gizelle and Rebi. Annie was a good cook and enjoyed it almost as much as she enjoyed watching people eat her cooking. Annie knew what herbs to feed a person to ward off illness and bring about or abort pregnancy or to improve energy. She even knew how to feed a man to improve his performance in bed. Garlic and onion warded off colds.

Annie felt that one of the best things that you could do for a person was to feed them. Gizelle always said, "Food is meant to nourish the soul," and, "Don't ever cook when you are angry. Only cook when you are in good spirits and have pure, pleasant thoughts; those feelings will be passed on with every bite, otherwise you can make a person sick or kill them."

When the Judge's wife died, Annie became his cook. The Judge heard from his wife the day she died that the way she had hooked him was by putting her menstrual blood in his food. It was said that this would make a man love you forever. He never had figured out what made him want to be with this woman so bad; she was not even very attractive. Now he knew. After this revelation, he was funny about his eatin's and would not eat anything prepared by anyone but Annie.

Annie's cooking accounted for the Judge's obesity. The first year after his wife passed, the Judge put on twenty pounds and twenty more every year after that. She must have known a thousand different variations to prepare the Gumbo's and Jambalaya's, shrimp, crawfish, and crab that she would pick up fresh on the way to work each morning.

Many people owed the Judge favors. Some of them could only pay with goods from their gardens and farms. These installments kept his kitchen stores brimming with fresh cuts of pork and beef that Annie turned into pure heaven as only she could. Nearly every morning when she approached the steps to the Judge's house, there were fresh vegetables on the front steps.

The Judge often told Annie that her desserts were going to be the death of him, but that did not stop him from polishing off half of a pecan pie, chocolate cake, bowel of custard or dozens of fruited beignets before going to bed. Not once had Annie returned in the morning and been able to find a crumb left of the other half. He would have finished it off during the night; he claimed that the rich desserts would call to him in his sleep. Her pralines he could not live without; she would wrap them in wax paper and he would put a dozen in his briefcase every morning.

When the Judge traveled, Annie prepared his meals so he could carry them with him. If he was to be gone more than a few days, he made arrangements wherever he stayed for her to be able to cook for him and she was paid double to accompany him. If he was going out to dinner, he would eat before he left and drink his way through the meal. It was like that until the day the old Judge died.

One day on her way home, Annie noticed a 'For Sale' sign in front of a lot that had two houses on Main Street. Since Rebi now had Gerard, she felt it was time for her to get her own place. She had several envelopes from the Simpsons and Rebi never would allow her to pay room and board, nor would she take any money for looking after Helen. Gizelle would not take any of the doctoring money, and she now took care of all the business in town.

Since he was such an experienced businessman she asked Grayman to inquire about the property. Two days later she owned it, free and clear, paid in full.

The whole family went with Annie to her new house to get the keys. Mr. Macklin, the Realtor, was waiting. Annie approached with Helen on her heels. Mr. Macklin opened the door and then he noticed her. He stood entranced for a few seconds; not long, but long enough for Rebi to notice.

He knelt down in front of Helen and pulled a piece of taffy from his pocket, "Who is this pretty little girl?"

Helen stepped behind Annie and peeked around her skirt.

"This is my daughter, Helen."

He would never have imagined this child had colored blood in her veins, but that is not what captured Mr. Macklin's attention. The child looked exactly like his daughter at that age before her death over two years ago.

"Well, enjoy your new home. Here are your keys. Paperwork is all in order. You know where to find me should the need arise," Mr. Macklin said.

The family went inside. Mr. Macklin drove to the end of the street and parked. He sat watching Helen laugh, run play with the other children in the fenced-in yard for over an hour. He was disappointed when everyone came out of the house and drove away. He followed them.

Mr. Macklin knew in his heart that Helen was his daughter come back to him.

Within two weeks painting and repairs were done, the house was furnished and Annie moved into her house and gave a big housewarming party. She was excited about owning her own home and was living alone for the first time in her life.

One night Annie was sitting in Mary's Speakeasy. She watched Mary perform Billy Holiday's "God Bless the Child." The lyrics began to take on a personal meaning:

Them that's got shall get,

Them that's not shall lose

So the Bible says

And it still is news

Mama may have

Papa may have

But God bless the child

That's got his own

Right then Annie decided that since she liked the nightlife so much, why not be a proprietor instead of a customer? She started to put the plan together in her mind. She knew how to make the liquor. She had spent enough early mornings with Rebi and Gerard distilling and bottling. It would be easier to get it from Gerard though. She was a great cook. It could be a restaurant and a club. She would hire men to handle the gambling tables. She was going to do it!

The next day Annie discussed her plans with the family and they agreed that it was a great idea. Everyone wanted to invest. Grayman offered to cook on days when he was not too busy. Gerard said he always wanted to be a bartender and Celeste would waitress a few days a week. Mason would oversee the gambling tables.

Annie and Celeste went with Mrs. Martin to New Orleans to buy furniture. She knew all the best stores, and the best speakeasies. Annie talked to the owners who gladly gave her good, sound business advice.

Annie talked to the Judge and he promised to keep the law off her tail as long as she kept cooking for him. Every illegal establishment in town paid him in some fashion to keep their doors open. It was going to happen no matter what the law said, so they took the money and turned a blind eye.

Grayman sent in carpenters to expand the kitchen, front room and add a large room in the back for gambling. They built a bar and booths with tables for people to eat and drink. He hired a bartender and three men for the gambling tables. A local lumberman named Tree, who was six feet five inches tall, would be there in case of trouble. Within a month Annie's was open for business. People drank, gambled and partied all night.

Mason would bring supplies from the store for the menu, which varied each night. Annie rose at five o'clock in the morning, and was at the Judge's by six. She would finish cooking and cleaning by one o'clock in the afternoon. If there were any clients who needed healing or mid-wifing, they knew to call or send for her at the Judge's house. She visited with Helen at Rebi's for a few hours. After that, she went home and slept until seven o'clock in the evening, then got up and started cooking. She opened her doors at seven o'clock and closed at five o'clock in the morning.

From two to five in the morning, Tree took over so Annie could sleep. If there was some high stakes gambling going on, she would let Tree keep the place open after she left for the Judge's.

Annie used the other house to rent rooms out to the local prostitutes and gleaned a portion of their nightly take. The money was growing in leaps and bounds.

Annie turned out to be a tough, hard-core hustler. She had a lot of heart. If a person did not know, it did not take them long to realize they did not want to be on her bad side. Life had made Annie a mean-hearted woman with no tolerance for any foolishness or disrespect. By the time she was nineteen, she had matured. Annie was five feet five inches, small but full of fire, black as tar, and breathtakingly beautiful. Her long, silky hair flowed down to the middle of her back. Her figure could stop a train, not to mention a man's heart.

After Gerard and Rebi stopped making liquor, Annie started distilling the White Lightning and brewing the beer herself. Her liquor was so good; two shots could knock a person on their ass. Even after prohibition, people preferred Annie's over government-approved liquor.

The house took a percentage of all the gambling winnings. They played cards and shot craps. Annie ran a tight ship and made sure there were no slip-ups or cheating. The night's take was usually accurate, but if it was not, the difference came out of the employee's salary.

Annie had no patience with people playing games with her and was easily riled. When you are dealing with people who drink and gamble, you have to be tough, or they will run over you.

One morning, about four o'clock, as things were winding down, there was a knock on the door. It was the police. They had come to take Annie to jail. Earlier, she had caught a man switching the dice. If you take a pair of dice and file the edge just right it will change the balance and every time you roll, they will come up seven or eleven. He palmed the other dice and switched them randomly so as not to cause suspicion. The gambler dropped one of the sheisty dice. When the bouncer went to put him out, he demanded to see 'The Black Bitch' that owned the establishment.

Annie heard him threaten to hurt her if she did not give him his money. He was surprised when Annie pulled her straight razor from between her breasts and in one fluid motion cut him across the face. It would have been his throat, but he moved just in time. The next slice was his shoulder, and before she could swing her razor the third time, he was screaming like a woman and running out the door.

Annie told the bouncer to go let the Judge know she would not be around in the morning to fix his breakfast because she was in jail. The Judge's irritation was not due to the crime she committed but that he had to get out of bed at half past four in the morning to go to his office and arrange to drop the charges. The Judge often frequented Annie's establishment. He had a fondness for working girls since his wife died, and the prettiest ones worked at Annie's.

Annie was out of jail in time to check her books and make sure the Judge's breakfast was on the table by seven o'clock that morning. She never stayed in jail more than an hour. She gave them plenty of cause and opportunity to pick her up. But, no matter what she did, it wasn't bad enough for the Judge to miss a meal.

Toodaloo

There is a story that is famous and still rings like a church house bell in Lake Charles to this day. The event actually changed a woman's name, among other things.

Annie did not take truck with anyone messing with a man that was hers. Mary was a singer and a liquor customer of Gerard's who owned a club. Tall, voluptuous, brown-skinned with long legs who had a very strong attraction to other people's men. She would sleep with them, inform their wives or girlfriends, and then lose interest.

As bad luck would have it, Mary was interested in Annie's man, Oscar. Oscar had lasted longer than most, because Annie was not planning to give her heart to anyone ever again. She had been hurt badly and one month was usually the length of her relationships, but somehow Oscar had been around for three.

Mary was determined to seduce this man. She had been trying for two months, but he kept playing hard to get. Why should Annie have all that man to herself? So, when Oscar came walking in the door with Annie, she set her cap. Mary wiggled her big hips extra hard while she was performing, and kept making eye contact with Oscar. She loved to sing Billy Holiday songs and was performing "Them Their Eyes."

Oscar definitely noticed her. He thought, Oh sucky, sucky, now she is really putting it on.

Mary would slide up to the table and bend over so Oscar could see down her bosom, and when she wrapped up the song she fell into his lap, kissing him.

Oscar just laughed at this floozy. He knew she was using her feminine wiles to get his attention, but he did not pay her any mind. He was in love with Annie; not to mention he knew what Annie carried between her breasts.

Mary did not get Oscar's attention that night, but she did get Annie's. Annie warned her, "This is my man and you need to find someone else to set your sights on."

Mary walked away and Annie went to the restroom. When she returned she stopped cold. "Well, I'll just be goddamned," she said to herself as she watched Mary sitting next to Oscar. The slut was actually drinking her drink. Annie stood and watched from the other side of the room. Every time Mary put her hand on Oscar's thigh it got closer to his groin. Oscar was shaking his head. He kept removing her roaming hands, putting them back on the table.

Mary was not discouraged. Finally, Oscar, tired of the game, rose and went to speak to one of the band members. Annie approached the table. She stood listening to the conversation between Mary and Lucy, a woman seated at the next table. "Girl you better give up on that one. He don't want you. He got his nose wide open for Annie," Lucy said.

"Chile don't you know. With a little work, I'm going to have him in my bed. He'll be saying, "Annie who?"" Mary said.

Lucy was waving her napkin trying to signal her to shut up because Annie was right behind her listening to every word.

Annie tapped Mary on the shoulder "With all these men in this room you can't find anything better to do than run after mine like a bitch in heat? I done warned you once and you didn't pay me no mind. I'm gonna leave now and take my man with me because you don't know that fat meat's greasy."

"Well go on and leave, but why don't you leave Oscar here. He'll be in good hands. You think you can come in my club and tell me what not to do? I can do anything I want, including whip your ass if you don't get out of my face."

What did Mary go and say that for? Annie socked her in the face so hard that her feet left the ground as she flew up into the air. Lucy picked up her glass just in time before Mary landed on the table and broke it.

Lucy looked down between her legs into Mary's face and warned, "Chile, if I was you I would stay right there. Do yourself a favor and don't get up."

Mary shook her head to clear it and picked up a table leg and charged at Annie. Annie had reached into her bra and had her straight razor out and ready for business. Mary was big, but Annie was quick. She sliced Mary several times before she even realized she was cut. Grayman and Rebi had taught her how to use a straight razor and Mason had taught her to box, and most important, how to duck. She evaded each of Mary's swings.

Mary looked down, saw the blood on her clothes, and fainted. An ambulance was called. They cleaned the wounds before taking her to the hospital.

Thanks to Gizelle's tutelage, Annie knew just where to cut a person, be it to kill or to hurt. There were no arteries or veins damaged, but she had twelve cuts; one in the vaginal area.

In those days, they referred to a woman's vagina as her Toodaloo. From that day forward Mary was known as Mary Toodaloo. Annie was not arrested since the police now knew that it was a waste of time.

Mary was not aware that Annie worked for the Judge; she tried to have her shut down using a cop she had been dating off and on. He tried to set up a raid on Annie's place, but when the other policemen realized who the target was, they all backed out and warned him that the Judge would not be pleased. He put the brakes on the raid and told Mary he could not help her. She dropped him after that.

Mary thought of revenge every time she looked in a mirror and saw the scars that Annie's razor had left on her jaw and chin. Her clitoris had been left without foreskin and she avoided anyone touching or looking at her there because of the embarrassing questions that followed.

Mary decided to take another route. She sent to New Orleans for a Voodooist. The Voodooist turned out to be an old friend of Grayman's. He went to Annie's to put the pouch of medicine under her porch, and couldn't resist going inside when he smelled ham hocks and red beans, which was one of his favorite meals. It couldn't hurt to have a bite to eat.

When he saw Annie, he remembered her from Grayman's. Just that Sunday he had enjoyed the hospitality of his good friend's home. Realizing this was the club that Gray had told him about, he made tracks to the kitchen. As he ate his ham hocks, greens and cornbread he told Grayman why he had come to town.

They both headed back to Mary's. Grayman told her, "If anything happens to Annie, if she should choke on a chicken bone or meet with an untimely accident, you are in trouble. I am also part owner of the speakeasy and know that you tried to have us raided. If anything bad happens, you Mary, will be the victim of very bad medicine."

Mary knew of Voodooist reputations, having grown up with an Acadian Mother raised in the Bayou. She knew that terrible things could happen.

Grayman stood up over her and grabbed her face. Looking in her eyes, he pulled out the pins that held her hair up and released her. There were several strands of hair in the pins. He then showed her a small black wax coffin. Her heart beat wildly, her chest heaving. Her eyes could not contain the terror that she was feeling as Grayman took her hand and with his knife trimmed some shavings from her fingernails and dropped the pieces with the hair into the coffin and used a candle to melt it closed.

Mary knew that all they had to do was bury the coffin in the graveyard, say a few words and she would be dead. She decided the best thing to do was leave town and set-up shop somewhere else. Mary was gone before morning.

On another occasion there was a white man who had come to the house, purchased his White Lightning and left. It was the night before Juneteenth and a lot of people were traveling to their relatives or preparing to receive them. Business being so slow, they had closed early.

The man waited across the street until he felt everyone was gone. A few minutes after he saw Tree leave, he came back banging on the door with an empty bottle.

Annie opened the door, he was ranting and raging that the liquor had not been any good. Funny thing was he was demanding another bottle. Annie told him, "Wait here."

When she came back into the room the man had come inside. Why didn't I close and lock that damn door?

He thought because he was white he could intimidate Annie, "After all, selling bootlegged liquor is against the law."

She was tired from a long day. She had worked at the Judge's and birthed three babies. She wanted to rise early to get out to Rebi's and help cook for the big Bar-B-Q and Fish Fry the family had planned.

She just did not feel like dealing with this situation, so she gave him the bottle she had gotten out of the kitchen, "Here, take this and go."

He turned as if to go out the door. Just as Annie was about to close it, he slammed his weight against the door and sent her sprawling across the floor, hitting her head on the edge of a table.

Things went black for a few seconds. Annie struggled to sit up, blood trickling out of her hair and down her face.

He stood over her, unbuckling his pants "I'm going to teach your uppity-black-ass how to treat a white man. You want to keep your doors open, you make sure you take good care of me. I want my liquor and my pussy free or the Ku Klux Klan will be burning a cross on your yard along with this place and you in it, you understand me nigger bitch?" He put his bottle down on the floor as he unsteadily tried to step out of his pants that were tangled around his shoes. Then he fell.

Annie saw her chance. She jumped up, grabbed the bottle and brought it down over his head. She smiled as she watched the blood pouring out of a wound. She placed her foot on his Adam's apple, opened the bottle and applied pressure to his throat. When he opened his mouth, she poured in half of the bottle of liquor; he was gagging and swallowing. She poured the remainder over his body.

"So you one of them KKK men who go around hanging folks and burning down schools with children inside, huh?" She walked away from him and while he scrambled to pull his pants up she picked up a candle that was burning inside a wine bottle, held it behind her back and walked out the front door. She stepped to the side of the porch. When he came running out after her, he started cursing because he did not see her. He decided to leave. As he walked down the steps he heard her say, "Yoo hoo, Mr. KKK, over here." As he turned toward the sound, she brought the candle around as he approached her and the liquor soaked clothes caught fire. He went running down the street in a screaming blaze.

They came and arrested Annie and as usual, the Judge had her out in time to fix his breakfast.

The Judge hated what the Ku Klux Klan stood for. He charged the man with breaking into her house and trying to rape her. What Annie had done, he labeled as self-defense. After a long hospital stay the perpetrator was released to jail. When his brothers came to bail him out, he was denied bail and the brothers were held and only released after a stern warning from the Judge about mistreating coloreds in his district.

Larry And Horace

One night a regular named Larry introduced Annie to an old friend of his, Horace. She knew Larry was a collector for an Italian restaurant owner who was mob connected. She wanted to know what Horace did. Even more important, what was he willing to do for her? She was instantly attracted to his dark chocolate skin, pearly white teeth and enchanting smile.

Horace was five feet, ten inches tall and his attire? Well, "sharp as a tack," comes to mind. He had on expensive shoes and two diamond rings with stones as big as peas.

Throughout the entire night, every time Annie glanced in Horace's direction, which was quite often, he was watching her. Whenever she brought them another drink he tipped her well. By the end of the night his tips added up to fifty dollars. He was a man after her own heart.

After putting his drink down, she commented on how beautiful the ring on his pinky was. She lifted his hand to get a closer look. Actually, she was trying to see if his hands were as soft as they looked; they were.

As she turned to walk away he stopped her with a hand on her arm. He downed his drink in one swallow, stood up and took her hand and put the ring on her left hand, third finger, "With this ring I thee wed," then picked up his hat and walked out the door.

Annie stood glued to the floor with a silly grin on her face. Horace definitely knew how to make an impression. All day, every day, all she thought about was Horace. She had no choice, every time she looked at the bright, two-carat diamond it made her think of him; as she prepared the Judge's food it sparkled at her, while she bottled up the White Lightning it shined at her, while she fed Helen it twinkled at her. Her heart that had been broken by Willie the III, started to beat for Horace.

Larry came in alone every night for two weeks, to Annie's great disappointment. He knew that she wanted to ask him about his childhood friend because he knew the effect Horace had on women. In Greenville, Texas, they had grown up on a cotton farm. He had been watching his friend 'Love em' and 'Leave em' for more than twenty years. They dreamt of having a life without cotton and white folks, and had both been successful when Horace met a numbers runner, they had been working for him for fifteen years.

Wilma, Larry's wife, ran numbers in Louisiana. Larry had trailed her back home from Texas. They had been together for the last five years, married for two. They had a two-year-old son, Larry Jr. and just found out they had another child on the way.

Larry came into the club with Wilma about three o'clock in the morning. Annie could not take it anymore and picked up a bottle and three glasses from behind the bar and sat down at their table. Blunt and to the point, she blurted out, "Okay Larry, I want the skinny on your friend."

Larry and Wilma started laughing. Wilma reached in her bra,

which doubled as her bank, and pulled out a roll of bills, peeled off two twenties and handed them to Larry.

She slapped Annie on her hand, "Girl you done cost me forty bucks. We had a bet on how long you could hold out. Looks like Horace done worked his magic again."

"I wondered how long it would take you to fold," Larry chided.

Wilma often saw Horace when she made runs to Texas where he lived, and warned Annie, "Chile don't let your heart get set on that one. I have yet to see him with the same woman twice."

Larry picked up his glass "You know how it is Annie, he's kind of like you."

They all laughed. By the time the bottle was empty she had heard Horace's life story. Larry's parents took Horace in at the age of nine when his parents, who were sharecroppers were hung.

A white man broke into their cabin and raped Horace's pregnant mother. He was returning from the pond where he had been fishing, when he saw the man enter the cabin. Hearing his momma's voice raised, he looked through the window and saw her wrestling with the man who was trying to kiss her. He dropped his line of fish and ran into the cotton field to find his father.

Horace's father burst through the door and pulled the man off his wife. The overseer had seen the man go running out of the field and followed knowing what his friend had been up to. When the overseer and three other white men arrived at the cabin, Horace's father was beating the hell out of the rapist. The overseer yelled "Nigger get your filthy hands off that white man."

They beat his father bloody. His mother realized they were killing her husband and picked up a knife from the table and stabbed the overseer in the chest. They knocked her unconscious and dragged them from the cabin and prepared for a hanging.

Horace's dad saw him and waved him away, lest he be hanged too. Horace hid under the porch with his hands clasped over his mouth trying not to cry out.

After they took turns raping her the child was beaten from her stomach before they strung her up. The seven-month fetus dangled by the umbilical cord. She watched in horror as they beat the dangling child with a stick; her fingers feebly reaching for the small bundle as the life left her body.

His father gurgled while trying to hold on to his own life as his feet searched for ground that was not there. Finally with a sickening crunch, his neck snapped.

One of the men laid his pistol down on the porch. They were sitting and drinking liquor from a jug and slapping each other on the back while bragging about what a good job they had done on the niggers.

"Well, I guess we better take poor Wilbur's body home. I sure ain't looking forward to telling his wife," one of the men said.

"Might as well get it over with," the others rose and they headed inside to recover the overseer's body.

Horace grabbed the pistol that was left on the porch and the shotgun left leaning against the tree and waited behind the tree.

The men struggled with the overweight body. As they went down the steps Horace leveled the shotgun and pulled the trigger spraying them with buck shot. He often hunted with his father and was an accurate shot. The men went down before they knew what was happening.

Two died immediately and the other two were hurt badly but still conscious. When the shotgun was empty, he used the pistol. Horace picked up a stick and beat their brains out.

Horace was sitting under his parents' bodies, crying when lights coming down the road pierced the dark. The overseer's wife had come looking for her husband. She went to the crying boy, "What happened here?"

"I don't know. I came back from fishing and found them like this. I tried to get my parents down, but I ain't big enough. I tried to wake up the men on the porch to help me, but they won't move."

The woman pulled the young child to his feet and led him to her automobile. They drove to the plantation owner's house. He sent for the sheriff and the undertaker who could not make head nor tails of the massacre.

Horace was taken to the neighboring plantation, where Larry and his parents lived. A group of men went and cut his parents down. A few days later they were buried in the colored cemetery.

Horace joined the army when he was eighteen and after a year, was honorably discharged. He was shot in the leg by what they call, 'friendly fire.' If you watch close you can see he still has a slight limp. He gets a monthly disability check from the government for the rest of his life.

He had gotten married before going into the army. Broke his heart when he found out she had been stepping out him while he was away, he went back to playing the field vowing to never marry again.

Now that Annie had all the information, she just needed Horace to show up.

A week later, Annie was preparing plates of fried chicken, cabbage, cornbread and macaroni and cheese for the customers. She felt arms around her waist, "So, how is my wife?"

It did not matter that Annie did not know this man, it did not matter that she had only seen Horace once before, She was so excited she could have wet herself, she turned and threw her arms around his neck and their lips found one another's and stayed there.

Every customer in the house stood in the door of the kitchen clapping. Everyone knew the story and were laying bets on whether he would ever come back.

Annie told Lucy to take over the food. Tree would handle everything else. Horace was taking her out to do the town.

They went dancing at a swanky establishment that one of his boss, Luigi's associates owned. The place was, 'Whites only,' but somehow this did not apply to Horace. They partied until early morning then went out to breakfast. Over breakfast they talked about Helen.

They went back to Annie's and made love through the morning. Feelings rose in her that she had not experienced since Willie the III. They slept in each other's arms, secure in the knowledge that they belonged to one another—body, mind and soul.

In the late afternoon, he woke her up and told her that she needed to get dressed.

She looked at him puzzled, "Where are we going?"

"We decided last night that you are my woman, correct?" Horace pulled her out of the bed.

"Yes. We going to get your clothes from Texas?"

"No, it's time for some new clothes, we will go to the tailor together. You and I are going to have outfits made that let everyone know we are together. It's time I meet my daughter, and from now on she needs to be with her mother, you understand? Ain't nobody else supposed to be raising our child but us," He lifted her chin, so that she could see the sincerity in his eyes, "I know that a man takes the calf with the cow. Now, get moving woman. Our little family is going to the State Fair."

Four year old Helen sat on Annie's lap and eyed the man who sat next to her mother, she had never seen her mother with a man. This made her curious.

Horace looked back at the pretty child.

Rebi called Gizelle, and she called Celeste and so on. Even the hired hands with their wives and children showed up to see Horace. For Annie to bring a man here, he had to be something special.

Annie was packing Helen's things as she explained that she would be back for visits, but she and Horace were going to take care of her daughter now. You could see the pride in her eyes.

Grayman, Mason and George grilled Horace. Grayman told him, "I consider Annie and Helen my own children..."

Mason interrupted, "They are my nieces."

George piped up, "And mine."

Grayman continued, "We hope you plan to do right by them. You being so fancy with them Texas ways, we want to make sure you not playing with her heart; she been hurt before you know. You the first one she's ever brought around the family and Helen."

Horace did his best to assure them, "Alright, I understand and I'm glad to know that ya'll care about and love them, which is just what I want to do. Ya'll ain't got nothing to worry about, I plan to take good care of them as long as Annie lets me."

Horace felt like he was on trial. Even the kids wanted to know if he going to be nice to Helen.

Annie was getting Helen dressed when she remembered they had Horace in the living room...

When she entered the room they told her that she needed to leave, they were not finished getting to know Horace yet.

Annie let it go on for another half hour before coming to his rescue, "I'm sorry everybody, but we have a day planned. Horace is taking me and Helen to the State Fair."

Grayman stood up, slapped Horace on the shoulder and said, "That's a good idea young man." He looked at the others, "What ya'll waiting on, go and get ready. We going to the Fair."

Horace was amused at their protectiveness, but he understood and respected that family comes first.

Grayman, George, Gerard, Mason, Horace, Rebi, Gizelle, Annie, Helen, Little George, Jimmy, Jerry, Kate, Kathy, Tanner, Jake and all the field workers and their families loaded up in their cars and were off.

They had an amazing time. Horace and Annie were like little kids. He played every game there was and won. They had so many prizes, dolls and stuffed animals that they had to give some away because there was not enough room in the cars to carry them all back.

Horace was good to them. He treated Helen as if she were his own child. When he was in town he took Helen to Rebi's during the day when Annie worked at the Judge's. He added structure to Annie's life. Her focus was now on family and she was the happiest she had ever been.

He oversaw the speakeasy with Annie at night, ran numbers during the day. Horace and Larry were partners in more than a few lucrative ventures.

Horace had taken one look at his first wife, and immediately knew that he loved her. Now, ten years later he had the same feeling about Annie. He had not planned to get serious with anyone ever again, but when he saw Annie that night going about running her business, so confident and sure of herself, he could not help but be charged by the electricity between them.

Horace had his own idea of what a wife and mother should be. Annie was nineteen and wild. He felt the reason why things would work out better for them this time around was because Annie was just Annie.

Leslie, his first wife had pretended to be something that she was not. He had married her and she was a virgin. Then he was drafted. By the time Horace came home, she had slept with everyone in town. He blamed himself for leaving her alone so soon after the wedding. He was willing to try to work things out. That's why it hurt so much when she asked for a divorce.

Annie on the other hand, would be everything to the person that held her heart. They had a lot of issues in common; both had lost their families at an early age, both were adopted by people who genuinely loved them, both had been heartbroken over their first love, both had experienced several unsatisfying relationships and most important, commitment meant loyalty above all else.

They were at Gizelle's for dinner one Sunday. Annie and Horace were wrestling when Gizelle walked over and grabbed Horace by the arm, "Stop all that rough housing, don't you know a pregnant woman can't be doing all that craziness?"

Both of them stopped and looked at her as if she had lost her mind.

"Oh my goodness, you didn't know did you?" Gizelle asked.

Annie realized that she had been sick the last few mornings. She thought she had drank too much the night before. Gizelle was never wrong.

Horace started whooping and hollering. Everyone came over to see what was going on. Horace was so happy; this would be his first child. He doted over Annie. He would not let her stay in the club late, at ten o'clock she was sent to bed like a child. He said that a pregnant woman had no business in a speakeasy.

Annie did not argue; she liked the way he took charge.

Horace rarely came in the door without some little toy or trinket for the baby. He constantly showered Annie and Helen with gifts of clothes, furs and jewelry. He was great at running the club. The books increased in profit as more people started coming after he hired a band. He decided more security was in order. He hired a crew of builders to remodel the house. The new second floor was the club, complete with a bandstand for the entertainment he planned to book. A marble bar ran along one wall. A doorman was installed to let people in, or not.

The kitchen was expanded complete with new restaurant appliances. The first floor had built in booths lining the walls. He hired waiters and cooks. Annie and Grayman oversaw the preparation of the menu .He built more rooms onto the other house and hired more girls.

Every Sunday they went to church. Annie did not set much stock in religion since God had not answered her prayers when it came to Willie the III. Horace insisted that she go. Her views started changing, along with her life and her figure. She was in love, a real love that was reciprocated.

Sunday afternoons were spent at Rebi's. Larry came with his growing family, along with the people who worked the fields and Grayman's employees. The men languished down by the creek, fishing, drinking and playing stick ball with the boys.

The women prepared the elaborate Sunday meal. The menu always varied from one Sunday to the next. Tables covered with chicken and deep-fried turkeys, fish, shrimp, fried blue crabs, crab cakes, okra, salads and coleslaw, crawfish, hams, dirty rice, macaroni, red beans and rice and numerous other dishes.

Annie, Helen and Horace always stayed over until Monday, because by the time they finished eating, drinking and dancing, no one wanted to leave and there was plenty of room.

Helen loved it in the country with all the other small kids. Sometimes she would stay through the week. She loved school. When she moved into town with Annie full-time, Horace drove her out every morning to go with the other children, and Grayman would bring her home in the evening.

During the summer she would go with Annie to the Judge's and play with the white children in the neighborhood. She never felt the difference in their races, until one day she went to one of her friends' parties. Jenny was having her sixth birthday party and Helen had been there while her mother was setting up the preparations the day before. Jenny had not invited Helen who just assumed she was supposed to go. She was so excited and Annie had no idea that Helen was not invited. Jenny's family knew that Helen was colored, but the girls played so well together they did not see any reason to stop them.

Helen walked into the party in her pretty dress with her hair all done up in curls, and her patent leather shoes. She did not know any of the other girls, who were all from Jenny's school. Annie dropped her off. When they got inside in front of the others, a girl who had arrived at the same time as Helen said, "Your nanny dresses really nice."

Helen told her, "That's not my nanny, that's my mommy."

All the little girls looked at Jenny, "Your mother lets you play with niggers?"

Jenny pulled Helen to the side and told her she should wait in the kitchen. Helen heard what the girls were saying about her. She walked out the back door.

When she arrived down the street at the Judge's, she was crying. She told him what had happened. He explained to her that people who felt that way were just ignorant and she should not pay them any mind. He told her, "You are just as good as any of them in the eyes of God and that is the important thing."

The Judge called Annie and she came and picked up Helen. She was so upset about her baby girl being hurt that she went down to Jenny's and walked in when the mother opened the door.

"Is something wrong Annie?" the mother asked. Annie gave her a look that said it all.

"How can you let a five-year-old child just walk out the door alone? If you did not want her here, you should have said so when I dropped her off," Annie said.

"I had no idea she had left, and of course Helen is always welcome here."

Annie felt she was lying through her teeth and told her, "That's not how your daughter and her friends feel." She walked to the table where Jenny was opening her gifts. Jenny was holding the China doll that Helen had given her. "Isn't this the most beautiful doll you have ever seen?" Jenny was saying to her friends.

"Let me see that?" Annie said. Jenny handed it to her.

Annie turned around and walked out the door.

The mother followed her out the door and down the walk trying to apologize for any misunderstanding.

"Oh I don't think there's been no misunderstanding, we understand each other just fine," Annie said.

From that day on, Annie took one of the other kids with her to play with Helen.

Jenny came down the street one day, "Can I play?"

Helen looked at her and said, "Go away Jenny, you are not my friend anymore."

This time it was Jenny who went home crying.

Annie's water broke on a Sunday afternoon. Celeste sent Kathy to the backfield where the men were playing ball to fetch Horace. Annie and Gizelle were in the bedroom and they started preparing for the birth. Annie knew just what to do and was calm. She had birthed many babies since Gizelle had taught her to midwife. She could have done it herself, but it was nice having Gizelle there with her and she told her so.

"Gizelle, do you realize that you are the closest thing I got in this world to a mama, and this is my second baby that you have bought into this world? I just want to thank you," she said.

When Gizelle turned and looked at the girl with a tear in her eye, she told her, "You have been like a daughter to me and I am thankful to God that he put us together." She went to the head of the bed, pulled Annie in to her arms and hugged her. "Now we better cut out all this mush and get that baby out of there."

Horace came bursting through the door like a hurricane. He had run the entire way.

Grayman came in a few seconds later laughing his head off, "I told this boy to wait so I could unhitch the horse from the wagon but he just took off running. You know I don't rightly think that the horse could have gotten him here any faster. Come on boy, this is women's business. Let's go out back." He lifted a jug over his shoulder and headed out the door. When he noticed that Horace was not following, he walked back and pulled him by the arm.

"I want to stay," Horace said.

Annie beckoned him, "Honey, it be bad luck for the father to be in the same room while a baby is coming in the world. Don't worry, me and the baby going to be just fine," she whispered.

Still, he hesitated.

Gizelle took him by the arm and led him out of the room, "You go on now, this won't take long at all. The baby's head is already peeking out," she said as she closed the door.

Grayman and George laughed as they watched Horace pacing back and forth like a nervous boy. They knew how he felt, but it was starting to get on their nerves. Finally, he could not take it anymore. George stuck his leg out and Horace tripped over it sprawling onto the grass. George leapt up and sat on him, "Boy I got to do something to stop your pacing, you wearing my shoes out." They all laughed. Horace grabbed him and they started wrestling across the yard. George had him pinned when Celeste came to the door and announced, "It's a girl and they are just fine."

Even though George was six feet, two inches tall and just as wide, Horace threw him off like he was a little boy. He jumped up and ran into the house. He was moving so fast that he slipped on some water next to the bed, fell and bumped his head on the side of the bed, knocking himself out.

After they checked to make sure Horace was breathing, they picked him up and put him on the other bed. Everybody laughed till their sides ached.

Horace came to an hour later and even though his head was throbbing from the big knot, he jumped straight up out of the bed and walked over to where Annie was sleeping with the baby on her chest.

Gingerly, Horace picked up the child. She was so tiny, he was afraid he would break her. Carrying the baby, he slowly walked to the chair and undid the blanket she was swaddled in. He marveled at her perfection: little miniature fingers and feet, a cap full of jet-black curly hair and skin the color of dark chocolate. They named the baby Genevieve, after his mother. She was later known as 'Gena.'

Horace sat in that chair with the baby for hours. Helen came in the room; she was five years old now. He lifted her up in his lap and showed her the new tiny infant who was her sister.

"Now that you have a new baby are you still going to be my Daddy too?" Helen asked.

"I'm always going to be your Daddy unless you fire me; are you going to fire me, baby girl?" Horace asked.

"Never, ever," Helen said and the three of them fell asleep, the baby in the crook of his arm and Helen with her head on his chest.

Annie awoke and was alarmed for a moment because the baby was not on her chest. She rose to get out of the bed, then saw Horace in the chair with the babies. She lay back down and went to sleep.

They stayed until Friday. All Horace wanted to do when he was not running back into town to check on the club and his numbers business was sit and hold the baby. The only time he would relinquish the child was when Annie had to feed her; he even changed her diapers. When someone else did hold her, he hovered over them so nervously hopping from one foot to the other that they would sense his anxiety and give Gena back.

When they got back home, Annie was surprised when she walked into her house. The additions to the back of the house had been finished the week before. She walked towards the bedroom and Horace said, "If you're looking for the bedroom you are going the wrong way, I moved it." He led her to the back of the house. She stood breathlessly taking in the beautiful room; it was huge. It had an even bigger nursery right next to it complete with the finest furniture you could buy. Satin curtains hung in a soft peach color to match the quilting on the headboard.

The nursery was yellow and white with a beautiful canopy bed for Helen and a crib for Genevieve. Annie looked around, her mouth hanging open in disbelief. "How did you get all this done?"

"I hired a woman from New Orleans to decorate on that last run I made with Larry and Wilma. We picked out all the furniture while we were there. I had to lay out plenty of extra cash for them to deliver it Sunday while we were at church. The curtains and everything else Wilma and Larry did as a gift for the baby. They take their God-parenting roles serious. What do you think Baby, you like it?" Horace asked.

She walked to him and pushed him down on the rocking chair and sat on his lap, "I love it…and you." They sat for a while and watched Helen jumping up and down on the bed as Genevieve slept in her new crib.

Annie felt life was good. She realized she had a lot to be thankful for, but she also had a foreboding feeling. Gizelle told her that she saw something in her future. She was going to have to pray for strength.

She tried to dismiss the warning, but deep down she knew she could not take it if anything were to happen to Horace.

What good was worrying going to do? For now, she just had to be grateful for each day.

Wilma

Larry and Wilma were happy together. They were married, had a son and were expecting. Wilma was now a full-time mother and home-maker. Larry took over her business. She was tired of running numbers and luxuriated in the joys of domesticity.

When Wilma was a teen, her mother had a live-in lover. He raped her and when she told her mother, she was called a whore and thrown out. Not knowing how to take care of herself at fourteen, she ended up on the street turning tricks in order to eat and pay room rent.

She had been on the street for four days when she met Oren. He was forty-four years old. When he offered her a place to stay, she jumped at his offer. She did not love him, but was grateful for the sanc-tuary he provided. He took her out with him sometimes, though she preferred that he did not. He was very jealous and every time they went out, he accused her of flirting with someone.

Wilma did not know men existed who did not find it necessary to beat on their women. Growing up watching an unending parade of men beat her mother, she really did not know any better. For Wilma, Oren's jealous rages and beatings were normal. She endured black eyes, broken jaws and ribs. One of his beatings resulted in a miscarriage. The next day he was always repentant. He would buy her presents in the form of an apology and promise it would never happen again. Of course it did. One night, Oren was drunk and arguing with a client he had cheated by changing his number. The man hit Oren. Oren shot him. He was sentenced to five years in jail.

Wilma took over his numbers territory. She knew all his customers and the route. Word quickly spread that Wilma was fair and her business ran well for three years.

Wilma met Larry on a run to Texas, and invited him back to Louisiana. He showed up for a visit a few months later and stayed. She loved Larry with all her heart. He was good to her. He worked for the same organization that she did, so when he moved, it did not disturb anyone's books. Larry sold heroin ran numbers and spoiled Wilma rotten. He loved to give her diamonds and furs and made her feel as if she were something precious to be loved and cherished. Not once had he ever laid a hand on her and he was a wonderful lover, and later a great father.

When Oren was released from jail, the first thing he did was talk to the Italian, Luigi, about getting his job back.

"Your job is no longer available, and in case you were wondering neither is Wilma," Luigi said. Luigi took great pleasure in telling him about Wilma and Larry. He had never liked Oren anyway; he was a dishonest crook, and stupid. He had never made half as much money as Wilma running numbers and Larry was a bigger money maker than Wilma. Hiring Oren did not add up to good business sense.

Oren had done nothing but think of Wilma the entire time he was in jail. He knew she was not the waiting type, but he never dreamed she would be married, and she had a kid.

He hung out at some of the clubs knowing that he would run into Wilma eventually. She was not as glad to see him as he would have liked.

"What, no hug and kiss for an old friend?" Oren said.

Wilma stood and hugged him, "Of course, I'm glad to see you Oren, pull up a chair, I'll buy you a taste."

Wilma called Annie over and introduced her to Oren. She was there to meet Larry and hoped he would hurry up; she felt uncomfortable being alone around Oren.

"So Wilma, what have you been up to?" Oren asked as he eyed the ring on her finger.

"Well I'm married, and have a beautiful son."

"That's good, Baby. When do I meet the man who has been keeping my woman on ice while I have been locked down?" Oren asked.

"What do you mean keeping me on ice?" Wilma huffed.

"I mean I'm home now, you and I can take up where we left off," Oren said.

"Uh, huh, that's not going to happen, Oren. I'm happy, and I love my husband. I'm glad to see you and all, but I'm not looking to leave Larry. Do you understand?"

"Oh I understand. You know, if you're worried about the boy Wilma don't. I would love to have a son. I would treat him just as if he was my own. I know a woman like you can't just sit around and wait for five years. I'm not angry. I still love you Wilma, and I know you still love me, I can see it in your eyes," Oren said.

At that moment, Larry walked up and overheard the last of the conversation. He looked the old man in the eye and said, "Yeah baby, answer the man's question. Do you still love him?"

Oren looked at the man who had taken his job and his woman.

He decided to play it cool. He stood up and offered his hand. "Hey man, I'm Oren, I'm sure Wilma must have told you about me."

Larry shook his hand and said, "Yes, she has. He turned back to Wilma, "Answer the man's question honey, I'm in suspense. Do you still love him?"

Wilma stood up and wrapped her arms around her husband. "Honey, you know who I love. And with that said, I have to go home to our baby boy. Oren, it was nice seeing you again," she gave him a pat on the shoulder, "I'm glad you're out. If you need a loan or anything, just tell my husband and he'll take care of you." She kissed Oren again and left.

"Let's have a drink," Larry sat down. They talked about prison. "Man, wasn't a night that passed I didn't think about Wilma. I like to wore my right hand out. Worked every time, if you know what I mean?"

By this time Horace had joined them because Annie told him what was going on, he knew this could go either way. He saw the storm clouds forming on Larry's face.

"Excuse me, I have to go to the head," Larry said.

"Let me give you a word of advice buddy, lay off the talk about Wilma. That's not cool; they are married and she is the mother of his son."

When Larry returned Horace stood up, "Man I'm beat, I'm going to bed. I'll see you tomorrow; nice to meet you, Oren. Remember my advice, it can only do you some good."

"I apologize Larry, maybe I've had too much to drink. I hope I didn't get on your bad side. Hey, the bottle is empty, how bout I get us another," Oren raised his hand to get Annie's attention.

"Man you just need some TLC, you been away too long. We need to take your mind off that five finger mambo you been doing for the last five years. Hold on a tic."

Larry returned with Lizzie and a fresh bottle. He picked up his hat, "Man all this talk about Wilma makes me want to get home and do some dancing myself, if you know what I mean? You enjoy the rest of your evening, Oren, I'm leaving you in good hands, Lizzie is the biggest money maker we got in the joint, don't worry about the tab, it's on me," Larry shook Oren's hand and left.

"Lizzie, huh? Tell me what you gonna do for me and this five year cherry," Oren moved closer to the busty brunette.

She stood and picked up the bottle, "Follow me, Big Daddy, I'm not much for talking. I'm a show you type of woman."

Oren followed her to the house next door. He had to admit, this was much better than his fantasies. He got right down to business. After the first time, he poured himself a full glass and gulped it down, "Who the hell does he think he is? He's probably at home screwing my woman right now. He even gave her a child. I could have done that. You know, I was her first real man. That's why I know I'm going to get her back," Oren said.

"Well in the meantime, let's see if you can do a little better than the last. You were like oatmeal, done in three minutes. Come on, Big Daddy, show me what you can do," Lizzie said trying to change the subject because she could see he was irritated.

He climbed back in the saddle and stayed there until she complained, "You are wearing me out, honey, hold on a tic, I'm going to have to call in some help." Lizzie went down the hall. Soon another woman walked in. Alice was even prettier than Lizzie in a full-figured sort of way.

When Oren woke up at noon, there was yet another woman lying next to him asleep. He must have really been drunk because this one was not attractive at all. He pulled the covers back and was stunned to find that this was a man wearing a woman's gown. He dressed in a hurry and left. He did not want to know what happened.

Oren went to a restaurant and as he ate breakfast, formulated a plan. He stole a car and staked out Luigi's. He tailed Larry for two days. The second night he followed him into Annie's.

Larry made room for him when he approached the table, "How you doing, man? How is life treating you? I heard you had a good time the other night, they said you sampled everything on the menu."

"Yeah, I think I got a little greedy, what do I owe you?" Oren asked.

"Nothing. I told you it was on the house, and I do mean on the house. Horace wouldn't take the money, so actually you should be thanking him."

I'll make sure I do that," Oren picked up the glass Larry had poured him.

Larry picked up his fork as he saw Annie coming towards him with his order of smothered pork chops, scalloped potatoes and green beans, "Thank you Annie, I been thinking about your cooking all day, I love my Wilma, but lord help her, she can't cook worth a damn."

"You know we always got you covered here," she looked at Oren, "What can I get you."

"I'm alright."

When she walked away Oren turned to Larry, "I need to talk you seriously about Wilma,"

Larry stopped chewing and slammed his fork down and pushed his plate of food away, "What about my wife, Oren?"

"I still love Wilma and I know she still loves me. I need my old territory back too. The way I see it, you got my woman and my job. I'm back now and I want them both returned. I know that the only reason Wilma doesn't want to leave you is because of the boy, and I just want you to rest assured that I will make him a good father; raise him just as if he were my own. You can't fault a woman for taking care of her child, but we both have to face the fact that she's still my woman."

Larry stood up over Oren and raised his voice, "I put a ring on that woman's hand, not through her nose. She is free to go wherever she wants. Did you ever think that the reason why she might not want to be with you could have something to do with all the beatings you gave her? You ever think about that? See, I have never laid a finger on her. If she wanted to be with you, she ain't scared of me, she would say so. Oh and as far as my son goes, I don't need another man to be a father to my children. Yes, Wilma is pregnant again, going on four months now. That woman can walk away, but Larry Jr. and the one she is carrying will stay with me. Why would I let you anywhere near them? Yeah Oren, I know all about the child that you beat out of Wilma. Now, you done pissed me off and ruined my appetite." He picked up his hat and left.

Horace came over to the table where Oren sat eating the food that Larry had left, "Man you are barking up the wrong tree," Horace warned.

Oren ignored him. He knew where Larry was going. He had given him a chance, but the fool just did not get it. Now he had to take a different approach.

Oren drove to Luigi's where he and Larry stood outside laughing and talking. He parked and walked down the block, easing up behind them he raised his gun and shot them both. Oren grabbed Larry's bag that held the money and betting slips and sprinted down the street where he had left the car.

A waiter heard the shots and came out to investigate. Seeing the two men lying on the ground, he ran back inside to call an ambulance. Within minutes, they arrived and were able to stop Larry's bleeding from his chest. Luigi was already dead from the wound to his heart.

A guest at the restaurant called over to Annie's and told Horace what had happened. Horace and Annie went to pick up Wilma on the way to the hospital.

They took Lizzie with them so she could watch Larry Jr. and she talked all the way to Wilma's, "I'll bet it was that Oren fellow from the other night. When he got drunk all he talked about was getting Larry out of the way so he could get Wilma back. I thought he was just drunk and talking shit. I told Larry that he had it in for him. Larry said he was harmless and would soon get over losing Wilma. I tried to lay it on him good since he just got out of jail and all. I figured if Wilma had been with him, maybe he was a good guy. I been without a real man in my life for so long, but all he wanted to talk about was Wilma this, and Wilma that. He called every one of us Wilma while he was doing it."

Word spread like fire. Larry was in surgery for over four hours. Finally the doctor came out, "All we can do now is wait and pray. We were able to remove the bullet from his lung, but it's up to him now."

Luigi's relatives and associates were in town within hours, looking for answers. They came to the hospital to talk to Larry, but that was not possible because he was unconscious. They told Horace to call them as soon as he came around.

Horace, Annie and Wilma stayed at Larry's bedside for two days. Finally, he opened his eyes. Wilma rushed to his side. He beckoned Horace over. When he leaned down Larry said one word, "Oren," before passing out again.

It seemed that Luigi who was a Mob Boss had been under investigation for quite some time. The FBI stood outside the door waiting to talk to their only witness.

Horace knew that the Italians liked to take care of things their own way.

Wilma heard what Larry said. She picked up her purse and coat.

"Hold it girl, where you think you going?" Horace said.

"I'm going to find that fool," Wilma said.

"No you're not. What you gonna do is sit here with your husband and let me take care of this. We don't need those Italians thinking Luigi died because of you. Think about Larry and Larry Jr. and…" he tapped her stomach. "How Larry and I ended up with wives that think they are Ma Barker or Bonnie Parker, I'll never know. Ya'll need to realize that you have men; men that can take care of this sort of thing."

Horace and Annie picked up Larry Jr. He was going to the club to check the books for the last two nights before he took the kids and Annie out to Rebi's for a few days.

Tree stood outside looking distressed, "Boss, some white men inside wanting to talk to you. I told them we closed, but they say they don't care, say they is gone wait 'till you come."

Horace went around through the back door and woke the girl's and Lucy. "Lucy you get the girls out through the back door and to the side street, Tree will be waiting for ya'll. Hurry up!"

"Tree, I need you to drive them out to Rebi's," Horace said.

"I don't know Boss, I got a bad feeling about these guys. I should stay here with you, just in case?"

"Tree, you can come back, but right now I want you to take my woman and kids out of here so that I know they are safe."

When they arrived at Rebi's, Grayman was just leaving for work, "What's going on?" After he heard the words, "Horace," and "White men," Grayman went inside and made a phone call. He rang the dinner bell and the worker's came in from the field. It was not long before they were on the road. Three more cars joined their caravan en-route. More men were waiting outside the club when they pulled up.

Grayman stood in the doorway listening to Horace explain, "I want to know just as bad as you who shot my friend and my boss."

The gun in the middle of the table and the blood on Horace's shirt indicated that the Italians did not believe him.

"I'm tired of playing around. Why don't we just beat it out of him, you know how these people can be," one of them said.

At that moment Grayman cleared his throat. He and twenty men stood there, making it clear that Horace was not alone. Ten more men came in through the back way.

"Make damn sure you use it," He handed Horace a phone number and left.

Grayman had heard about the shootings. Driving people around, you get wind of everything. That is why he knew exactly where Oren was. He had been hiding out at a hotel in town the last two days. The hotel waiters reported every move he made.

Horace dropped Tree at home, and went to spend some time with his girls before climbing into bed with Annie. He made love to her. It was the kind of love that a man makes when he knows that he is about to do something so dangerous that it may make this time, his last time.

Annie knew he was going to seek revenge. She spoke to Gizelle and was assured there had been no more visions. She told her that the vision she had told her about was close, but not now.

Annie fell asleep holding her man in her arms and woke alone.

Rebi told her that Horace had taken all the kids fishing, and had left her a message, "Be ready to fry up a whole mess of fish, we ain't coming back without 'em."

They stayed at Rebi's for four days.

Horace ran the club and came back every morning to take the Judge the food Annie prepared for him. The Judge and The Mayor had received visitors; the FBI, and the Italians. The Italians felt that the handsome payoffs they had been getting for years warranted their involvement.

The Judge had an idea. He shared his thoughts and breakfast

with Horace, "The person who did this is obviously hoping that Larry will die since he is the only witness. We are going to put word in the papers that Larry did die. This way, the guilty party will think it is okay to surface. You and our out-of-town visitors can take it from there."

The next morning, an article was in the paper:

Larry Adams; the victim of a shooting on Main Street died last night after fighting for his life for four days. He left behind a wife who is expecting, and two year old son.

Larry was much better. Released that same morning, he slept peacefully at the club with Tree at his side. Wilma was at home playing the grieving widow.

Ozzie, the neighbor who lived across the street, sat in his window watching Wilma's front door. If anyone came to the door he was to call Horace. In case he missed the arrival, she would signal him by closing her front room curtains.

Wilma had only been home for two hours when there came a knock at her front door. She looked out the window, low and behold, Oren stood there with candy and a bouquet of flowers. She closed the curtains and opened the door.

It took all her self-control not to shoot him right between the eyes. She was grateful when Horace arrived ten minutes later. She had endured enough of listening to Oren lie about how sorry he was for her troubles.

"You know it goes without saying that if there is anything I can do to help, all you have to do is say the word. I know it is too soon for you to be thinking about anything. I just want you to know that I am here for you in your hour of need," Oren said.

"Thank you, Oren, you don't know how much that means to me."

Horace told Wilma, "I came to take you to make the arrangements for the funeral."

Wilma began to cry. Horace poured her a drink, "I am sure going to miss my buddy."

"You know, I only met him twice, but I could see he was a real stand-up guy. I really hate that the little fellow has been left without a daddy. Wilma, maybe I could stand in for Larry every now and then. I could teach the boy to play ball, take him out for ice cream or something?" Oren said with a pitiful look on his face.

This was just too much for Wilma. She looked down into her glass afraid of what she would do if she looked up.

Horace sensed that if they stayed any longer, she would blow the whole thing. "Wilma, I guess we better get going so we can meet the undertaker," Horace said.

Wilma burst into hysterical tears. She missed her calling; she should have been an actress.

"Horace, let me go with you. It's too much for Wilma right now," Oren patted her back in a comforting yet suggestive way that made her skin crawl.

"That's a good idea. We would appreciate that Oren," Horace said.

"Anything I can do to help Wilma, all you got to do is say it and it's as good as done," Oren said.

On the ride over, Horace told Oren all about how far back he and Larry went. When they arrived, they went into the back room where the Italians were posing as funeral directors.

Tree walked back to the office of the funeral parlor where Horace appeared to be filling out some papers. Tree held his hat in his hand. "I just saw him, he looks like he's sleeping," Tree said.

One of the Italian men said, "Yes, I am quite proud of the job I was able to do." He picked up the papers that Horace had pretended to sign. "These all appear to be in order. Shall we go and view the body?"

Horace went into the viewing room ahead of the others. Larry was lying in a coffin with his arms folded across his chest. He had actually fallen asleep. Horace kicked the coffin to wake him up before Oren heard the snoring. Larry stuck his tongue out at Horace and made a funny face.

Horace could hardly stop himself from laughing. "Ya'll did a right fine job on Larry." He took a step back. "What do you think Oren?"

Oren approached the coffin and looked down, "I have to agree with you," When he turned for one last look, Larry's eyes popped open. He reached up and grabbed Oren by his tie. "Why did you kill me?" Larry said in a raspy voice.

Oren could not believe his eyes, "Oh Shit! Oh Shit! Oh Shit! They said people who die bad don't stay dead, I never believed it before. I'm sorry! I'm sorry!" Oren screamed.

Larry sat up in the coffin.

Oren's bodily functions let go and he pissed and shat himself. He was backing away from the coffin scared out of his wits, "You got to understand, I loved her, she was all I thought about for five long years. I just wanted her and my territory back, you can understand that can't you?" He squatted in a corner of the room. There was a sharp pain in his chest and his arm went numb as he tried to reach for his gun.

Everybody started laughing and Oren realized this was a set-up.

Wilma walked into the room and kicked him in the face. His nose started to bleed. "You son-of-a-bitch, you tried to kill the only man I ever loved. What makes you think you could take me from the only person who ever treated me right?"

Finally, Larry said, "Somebody stop her, I just bought her them damn shoes and she gone get blood all over 'em."

It took Horace and one of the white men to pull her off. Then she thought about how he used to beat her, and of the child he had made her miscarry. She broke free. She took her pistol from her handbag and shot him before hitting him upside the head with it.

Oren could not move, his chest was hurting something terrible. He was struggling in an effort to stand up, then he passed out. He woke on a metal table used to drain the blood from corpses before they pump them full of embalming fluid.

One of the Italian's said, "Hey he's woke."

The other man was holding a big needle connected to a long tube. They were planning to pump him full of the fluid while he was still alive. Oren clutched at the excruciating pain in his chest.

The man approached and looked into Oren's unseeing eyes. He realized Oren was dead. "Damn this nigger done died. Shit, I never get to have any fun."

Soon Larry was up and around, doing just fine. The Judge was happy, everything was back to normal. The Italians left town and Luigi's brother Antonio took over the restaurant. The FBI left when they found Oren with bullet wounds in his arm and shoulder, carrying the gun that killed Luigi. The coroner said he died of a heart attack. It was business as usual for everyone except Luigi and Oren.

A Lonely Man

Mr. Macklin had become a regular dinner customer. Annie did not mind because she always had the food ready early. Each day he would come a little bit earlier. One day he came while Annie was giving Helen and Gena their dinner. After that, he showed up at the same time every day.

"Being a bachelor and all, this is the only way I can get a good healthy meal." This was the only way he could think of to spend time with Helen. One day Annie asked him about his family. He told her that they had gotten sick and died. She left it at that.

Several times, Mr. Macklin went to Rebi's on Sunday afternoons under the guise of presenting an offer on their property. He said some people were interested in the land for development. Of course they declined, but invited him to stay and eat. He would always sit in the yard and talk with the kids, especially Helen.

He always seemed to be riding by when the kids were walking home from school. He would stop at the store and buy soda pops or penny candy and sit for a couple of hours and tell them stories or read books.

Rebi noticed that he always held Helen on his lap. She had a bad feeling about that man; nothing she could put a finger on but a bad feeling just the same. She shared this feeling with Annie.

"He's probably just lonely, not having any family and all," Annie tried to assuage Rebi's doubts and hoped to God she was doing the right thing.

One Sunday after church, he pulled up while they were eating dinner. He pulled some trunks out of his car and when the men saw him struggling they went to help him.

"Annie, my house has gotten too big for me. I was packing up to move and thought that maybe Helen could use the things that used to belong to my daughter. Most of them are still brand new. It would be a shame for them to go to waste," Mr. Macklin said.

Annie told him "Well I sure do appreciate you thinking of my Helen, Thank you Mr. Macklin. Why don't you come have supper with us?"

He gladly accepted her invitation and pulled up a chair right next to Helen. He had been watching her grow from the time she was two years old and every year he was more and more convinced that this girl was his daughter come back to him. After dinner, he pulled the trunks over and showed her all the beautiful things he had for her. He pulled out dress after dress all with matching shoes and hats. There were several beautiful China dolls.

Helen felt like it was Christmas. A lot of the clothes still had the tags on them. He asked the girls to try them on. They would run in the house and come back out in a different outfit and model around. After everyone told them how pretty they looked, they would run back in and change. They did this for over an hour and still had not tried on everything.

Mr. Macklin was pleased as pie to sit and watch the fashion show. This was his little girl, he knew it - he just knew it. He had bought himself a camera and took pictures of everyone, but he took a lot more of Helen.

After that he and his camera came every Sunday. His new home office was wallpapered with pictures of Helen. There was a movie theatre in town and Mr. Macklin often took the kids to the picture show and bought them all the popcorn, candy, and pops they could eat. He always sat right next to Helen.

Every year on her birthday he would ask Annie to let him take her shopping. He took her to the best stores in town to buy her whatever she wanted.

Annie told him that he spent too much on her and asked why, since he never took any of the other children shopping.

Mr. Macklin showed her a picture of his daughter. She looked exactly like Helen. He told her that Helen reminded him of his daughter and it helped to ease the pain. Her birthday had been two days before Helen's.

Annie felt sorry for the man and figured his attention was not hurting anyone.

Franklin

Grayman's taxi business had been prosperous for over twenty years. He received offers from people to buy his business, but turned them all down, even the ones that came with threats. He had just received another such offer from Mr. Franklin.

If Mr. Franklin could acquire Grayman's business, he would have a monopoly on the whole town. He was not happy that Grayman turned him down even after he increased the offer.

Franklin was a member of the Klan, what few were left in these parts. He had Grayman's drivers robbed and had hired a group of men to harass the drivers and their clients.

Franklin called a meeting at his house to come up with a plan of action to get rid of this coon once and for all. When the meeting was over and the men left, Franklin was excited about their plans. So excited that he could not wait to get upstairs to his hot young wife Suzie.

When she met Franklin Suzie was sixteen, blonde and pretty. Her father, James needed to pick up his pay from Franklin's Taxi Company, so that they could buy her some new clothes.

Franklin saw Suzi and James when they walked into the garage. He went to the dispatcher and got an assignment and told James that he really needed him to work that day.

James could not turn down the opportunity to make extra money.

Franklin told him to get right over to the address on the slip of paper.

"Do I have time to drop my daughter at home?"

"Have her wait in my office for a bit while I finish up a couple of things and I'll take her myself," Franklin volunteered.

Suzie sat in the office listening to the radio while Franklin finished up some paper work. The radio was loud, but not loud enough to cover the rumbling of her stomach.

"For such a little thing your stomach is making some big noises." Franklin chuckled.

Suzie blushed with embarrassment. She had not taken time to eat because her father had promised ice cream and shopping.

"All that noise is making me hungry now. What say we go and get a bite to eat before I drop you off?" Franklin asked.

"Sure, what are we going to eat?" Suzy said.

"What would you like?"

"Don't rightly know what there is out this way; I ain't had food from in town before 'cept ice cream."

"You mean to tell me you have never had a meal in a real restaurant before young lady?"

"No sir."

Franklin looked at her for a long moment. He had a thing for young girls, and she was a petite little thing, just the way he liked them. "Is there something special that you had planned today?"

"No sir, well not now since Poppa has to work. He was going to buy me some dresses on account I have grown out of what I have."

"Well then I would like to personally treat you to the finest restaurant here in town if that's all right with you. Of course we can go shopping first, but I would consider it an honor." Franklin said.

She looked down at her dress, which was actually so small she had to wear a sweater over it. She had to walk on the backs of her sneakers because they were too little.

"If you are worried about your father, how could he possibly mind? Anyway if he does have something to say, I will simply fire him. I had planned to anyway."

He saw the alarm on her face and laughed, "Hey, I was just joking, James is one of my most dependable men. How about I radio him and get his permission. He should be arriving to the call I sent him on."

Franklin went to the dispatcher's desk, "James, this little darling of yours seems to be hungry. You have any objections to me taking her for a bite to eat?"

"No, if she's a mind to go, I don't have no objections. I forgot I was supposed to take her to get ice cream, so she ain't had nuthin' to eat this morning, but I got to warn you, she can put away some food," James warned.

James wife, Catherine, was a wonderful homemaker and mother - until she vanished a few years ago. Before that James was a happy man. He drove taxis in the evenings, and during the day took care of the farm he had inherited.

Catherine was good at quilting, and her work brought in a good piece of money. She sold her quilts and clothes on the side of the road and at fairs, along with her pickling, preserves, vegetables, honey and dairy products the farm provided. They were not rich, but they more than got by.

In the evenings James and Catherine sat with Suzie for hours as she taught them to read. They had never gotten any book learning and made sure their daughter took full advantage of the opportunity the integrated school provided.

Every night when James came in, Catherine would sing to him. She had the prettiest voice in the church choir. He always said that if he could just have one of her songs every night, he would work his fingers to the bone and be glad to do it, for he knew he was married to the prettiest woman in town, inside and out.

Suzie was about twelve years old when she came home from school and couldn't find her mom. There was dough for bread on the sink covered with a wet towel. A chicken was roasting in the oven. Quilt pieces lay on the table in the pattern she had planned to sew them together. She never did come back.

After a month, James set out to find Catherine. He left Suzie with cousins in the next county, promising her that he would be back. Finally, after six months of searching to no avail, he hired a private investigator and brought Suzie back home.

Suzie tried to do everything the way her mother had as best she could. She had dreams of her momma coming back home. Some nights she would wake up and smell her essence as if she were sitting right next to her.

James lost his smile and aged rapidly in Catherine's absence. He no longer farmed. The only income was from driving double shifts. He lost so much weight that he did not look like himself anymore. Suzie begged him to eat. Sometimes he called her, 'Catherine,' when he got good and drunk. He had known in his heart that his wife had not walked away from them, and visions of her in distress haunted him. He could not rest until he knew where she was.

On the rare occasions when James was sober, all he talked about was finding his wife - then one day he stopped talking about her at all.

The investigator showed up one day with a report, complete with photos, from a down river, town sheriff. James intuition had been right. Catherine's body had surfaced on the Mississippi River Bank two years ago. They did not get many unidentified bodies around those parts. The coroner said she had been beaten to death before being thrown in. From the scratches on her body it seemed that the current had taken her quite a ways on the river bottom. When no one claimed her, she was buried.

James never could bring himself to tell Suzie about her mother. But, at least he could stop looking now.

James gave Suzie a couple of dollars every week, the rest he drank. She bought sugar and flour so that she could make biscuits and bread. They still had one cow that she milked every morning. The chickens afforded her eggs and meat. Sometimes she made ice cream using the fresh berries that grew by the creek.

At fourteen, Suzie altered her mother's clothes to fit her, letting them out across the bust. Seeing her in her mother's dresses seemed to disturb her poppa so much that she tried to get dressed after he left in the mornings. By the next year, she had outgrown them and told him so.

James brought home ill-fitting clothes that were used and tattered. He noticed how bad they looked as she held them up. He took them from her and threw them into the fireplace. He promised she could get some store bought clothes the next day.

Fine Dining

"Well it's settled, you and I are going to have ourselves a fine day. I ain't had a pretty face sitting across from me at a dinner table since my wife died. You make sure you have a good time, and know that you are taking pity on a lonely, old man's soul," Franklin held his elbow out to her. Suzie giggled as she put her arm through his.

Suzie had never been in a department store. She stood with her mouth agape.

"I would like to outfit this young lady in your finest," Franklin said.

The sales woman walked around Suzie, assessing her size, "Will we be needing everything, Sir?"

"Everything, I think five outfits should get us started," Franklin said.

She smiled at the thought of the commission she was going to make, "I'll be right back."

She returned with an armful of garments and a woman who measured Suzie's feet, moments later she took, "Would you be so kind as to follow me to the dressing room, Ma'am?"

Suzie looked behind herself to see who the woman was talking to and realized it was her, she giggled, "My name is Suzie. Nobody has ever called me, 'Ma'am,' before."

Suzie did not recognize herself in the finery. Even the silky underwear felt good against her skin.

She walked out to show Franklin and he clapped his hands together, "Beautiful, tell me, do you like it, my dear?"

"Oh yes," Suzie gushed. She tried on four more outfits and kept the last one on.

Franklin spoke with the saleswoman before guiding Suzie out of the store and down the street where she stood dumbfounded in the entrance of the elegant eating establishment. The tables were set with several silver forks and she did not know anything about which one to use for what.

Franklin told her, "Do what I do." He explained the forks, plates and crystal glasses.

The food was so pretty she was not sure she should eat it or continue to stare at it. It was delicious. When the waiter came by with the dessert cart she seemed to have trouble deciding.

"We will take one of each," Franklin told the man pushing the cart. They took one bite of each decadent treat passing the small plates back and forth.

"Suzie, I am a lonely man. Have you ever thought about getting married?"

"I never gave it much thought."

"Would you consider it with me? I know that I am old, and far from attractive, but I would make up for this by doing everything in my power to keep you happy. You could purchase any home that suited you, complete with servants. We can travel anywhere you want. Paris perhaps, or maybe a cruise. Rest assured I have more than enough money to keep you amused."

Suzie's fork was in mid-air, "I don't believe my ears Mr. Franklin, why are you making fun of me?"

"I'm sorry, I should not have spoken. I should have known that someone as young and beautiful as you would never want to be with someone like me," Franklin signaled the waiter and pulled a flask from his pocket and took a large swallow.

"Are you being serious?"

"So I haven't insulted you?" Franklin was hopeful when it came clear that she seemed to be mulling his proposal over in her mind.

"Let me get this straight - you are saying that I can live like this every single day, go places I have only seen in magazines, wear these kind of clothes and all I have to do is marry you?"

"Yes, that is exactly what I am saying," Franklin reached across the table and took her hand in his.

"Why me? I mean you have only laid eyes on me this very day. I thought you had to be in love to marry someone. What's the catch?"

"Being with you today makes me feel young. I have not had this much fun in a long time and I cannot think of any other way to make it permanent, can you?"

Suzie did not realize that any amount of money that she could possibly spend would be a savings in comparison to what Franklin spent in whorehouses. For all the funds he spent, he could not even take them out in public. Franklin had many friends and business associates who married younger girls. He was not a fool. He knew that she would never love him, but neither had his first wife.

Franklin had barged in on his wife and her lover in a hotel in New Orleans. He had hired a man to follow her because he knew something was going on, and she spent too much money to disrespect him this way. She was supporting a younger man with his money. Several of his associates had seen them in public. He would not tolerate being a laughing stock. He murdered her with his own hands and framed her young gigolo for the crime. He was now rotting away in a work camp.

As long as Franklin could have Suzie's young body all to himself, he did not mind spending the money.

"OK," Suzie said.

That was six years ago. Franklin disgusted Suzie. Sex with Franklin was revolting. Franklin had gained a lot more weight over the last two years, and sweat like a pig all the time, even in cold weather. He had to take extra shirts with him everywhere he went and changed several times a day. He stank of cigars and liquor.

Franklin had strange taste. He liked Suzie to dress up in costumes and spank him with a whip called a cat-of-nine tails. He would write out little scripts for role-playing.

Suzie had all the money she could spend and a group of girlfriends that she lunched and shopped with. They were married to old men also. They taught her ways to stay busy and unavailable. They all had lovers. Suzie was afraid. Franklin had told her if he ever caught her with another man it would be bad for not only her, but her father too.

Suzie traveled with Franklin. He wanted her at his side for the operas, balls and parties. They had to keep up appearances for business. Most people mistook her for his daughter, but he gleaned great pleasure from letting everyone know that she was his wife. She hated the rude remarks he made to his friends about her in bed, "Well if I die, it will probably be in bed trying to satisfy Suzie. She can't get enough of me," Then he would let go with that stupid, raucous irritating laugh of his. She was bored to tears suffering through his business dinners and parties that she hosted for his associates and their wives. She had taken cooking and etiquette lessons.

Suzie did not understand the big problem they all had with the colored people. Why not hire them and let them work? Many a time, she had to listen to Franklin's complaints about some poor colored man named Gray something. He had it in for him, simply because he did not want to sell his business. Suzie listened, letting the information go in one ear and out the other, except for one time, she was appalled at what she heard, Franklin planned to have the man maimed to scare him into selling his business.

They lay in bed, "Oh Franklin, why can't you just leave the poor man alone? He doesn't have half the carriages and cars that you do, you said so yourself, how much more money do you need?"

"I don't expect you to be able to understand these kinds of things my dear, but if we let these people get too much, they will want it all. We cannot lose control of our country to a bunch of niggers."

Suzie puled the blanket over herself and turned over to go to sleep. Of course, Franklin had other ideas. She wondered how much longer he would live. Her friends joked about the day they would be free, meaning the day when their old fart husbands would drop dead and they could have what they really wanted, the money.

Grayman Gets Hurt

Grayman was leaving his Taxi office and walking across the street to his car when a truck came speeding toward him. The lights of the car came on just before it ran him down.

He woke to someone slapping him in the face.

"Yeah he's still alive," said the man who had gotten out of the truck. The man arranged Grayman's legs straight out in front of him, before returning to the cab of his truck.

Grayman turned his head and saw the car coming for him again. He screamed out as the tires ran over his legs. He lay moaning from the pain when he heard the car shift into reverse and run over his legs again. The car stopped; he could hear the men laughing. Grayman mercifully passed out before they ran over his legs again and drove away.

Calvin, was looking out of his upstairs window when he saw the truck hit Grayman whom he knew well. He ran the office for the cab service the last twenty years. He grabbed his shotgun and yelled for his wife to call Mason and the medics. By the time he got down to the street, the truck was turning the corner.

Grayman was alive, but unconscious. Calvin ran inside the garage and yelled, "Get some blankets and towels, somebody done ran Gray down."

They could already hear the ambulance siren. Mason arrived in time to climb in the back of the ambulance.

Gizelle had begged her husband to sell. She warned him about her visions, but when it came to the business he had spent so many years building, he would have none of it. He would start talking about his constitutional rights.

Gizelle sat in the hospital waiting room thinking of what she could have done to stop this from happening. She realized that one of the reasons that she loved him was because he was so brave and stuck to his principles.

Everyone came to the hospital. Calvin told Horace and Larry what he had seen. Gizelle told them that Franklin had been the man who had been pestering Grayman to sell. They could not be sure, but they had a good idea that Franklin had to be behind this.

Grayman would never walk again. His legs had been shattered so badly, all they could do was amputate. They kept him asleep with morphine.

Gizelle and Rebi used every form of hoodoo and voodoo they could think of. Poultices, candles and prayer. They stayed at the hospital for a week. Even the children would not leave.

Finally, Grayman was strong enough for them to focus on the second leg, they hoped they could save it. The doctors said that Grayman had a good chance of regaining the use of the second leg and with a prosthetic he may even be able to move around. He did not wake up for two days.

Two weeks later an attorney came around to the hospital with an offer for Grayman's business. He pulled himself up and looked the lawyer square in the eye and shouted, "Get the hell out of here."

"Don't you know what could happen to you the next time if you don't sell now? Don't be a fool man."

Gizelle and Mason were coming down the hall when they heard the raised voices. He grabbed the man by the collar and they both started beating him. The man wrenched free and ran down the hall.

Horace and Larry were having a drink in a club while discussing f some business. They overheard some drunks bragging about what they had done to a nigger.

"The stupid fool still wouldn't sell. Well now we get to have some real fun with him."

"And his wife that brother of his too."

"Yeah, Franklin pays a pretty penny, don't forget that. I'm planning to buy that car that I had my eye on. Can you believe that nigger had the nerve to beat Sam up right there in the hospital." the white man said.

Horace went to the phone and called Mason. He and Larry stood outside waiting. Five cars pulled up. Mason went back in the club with Horace who pointed them out. They waited outside until the villains came out of the bar. They watched them get into their cars and followed. No one ever saw the two men again.

Horace went to Franklin's door. When he opened it, Horace asked, "May I speak with Franklin?"

"I'm Franklin, what can I do for you?" he asked.

"I have a message for you from Grayman who is like a father to me, it's about the business."

"I knew he would finally come around. How much does he want for it?" Franklin asked as he stepped out onto the porch. He was not going to invite this nigger inside of his house.

"This much," Horace said and put the pistol to Franklin's temple and pulled the trigger.

The fat body hit the ground and he shot him again in the chest.

As Horace turned to close the gate, he looked up and saw a white woman standing in the upstairs window. It must have been Franklin's wife. He could have gone back and shot her, but he did not believe in killing innocents.

The next day, Gizelle asked Annie to take a walk with her, "You remember I told you that Horace was going to have to leave? Well it's time." She told her that she should let him take Gena. She was going to need this time with her father because soon he would not be able to see her again.

Horace spent the night with Annie. The next day they went to the hospital and he leaned down and spoke in Grayman's ear, "I took care of that debt you owed."

Grayman was grateful, but sad. He knew that the boy was going to have to leave soon.

As Annie served the Judge his breakfast he said, "Sit down for a minute Annie, I need to talk to you."

She poured herself a cup of coffee and sat

"Say a certain person had information about a person who had possibly committed a murder. A justified murder, but a murder all the same. Say this person knew that someone had been hurt badly, and a member of the person's family had sought revenge and gotten it. Someone saw this person and it would only be a matter of time before the authorities would know who it was that they were looking for. They will be expecting me to issue a warrant for that person's arrest in the very near future. Now, it would be against the law for me to let that man's wife know that. Say the guilty party were to leave the state and be out of my jurisdiction. It would be hard for them to identify and charge him with the murder. Trial would be impossible if they could not find him.

Divulging this kind of information would be against the law and I could never do that. Do you understand what I am saying, Annie?"

"I do, and I'm sure that whoever that person is would be very grateful to you."

She left and rushed to the club. She told Horace what the Judge said.

Larry was with him, "I already talked to my cousin in Texas and he said he would welcome some help down there on his farm. He's got girls Gena's age and a big house."

Horace looked at Annie, "I guess it's settled then; I'll leave day after tomorrow."

Now Suzie could collect on Franklin'8s insurance policy and sell the company and live the rest of her days in style. Hallelujah! She no longer had to deal with Franklin sweating over her. If there had been a way, she would have killed him herself.

The sheriff questioned her, but Suzie definitely would not be a witness to someone who had done her such a good turn. She told them that she had been asleep. She also told them all about her husband's plans to kill Grayman. Franklin had made a lot of money, but his greed was so strong that he wanted to take a man's life to get more. He deserved to die.

If Suzie could find the handsome man, she could think of a lot of ways to thank him. Witnessing the murder had turned her on so much that after she watched him walk away she had gone to and played with herself until she had the most satisfying orgasm she had ever experienced. Since then he had been the subject of her fantasies.

Suzie decided to find him. She had a friend named Sally who frequented the black nightclubs. She said that there was nothing like a black man, every time her husband went out of town, she would go and find herself one.

Suzie had always been curious, and now she wanted to find out for herself. Even though she was supposed to be in mourning, no one that she knew would be frequenting any black establishments. Suzie called her friend Sally and went to bed to rest up for later that night.

Suzie and Sally headed for Annie's club. She was in the place for a two minutes when she noticed a painting behind the bar. It was him. When the waitress came to their table she asked, "Who's the man in the picture? Is he here?"

"Wait a tick, I'll check," the waitress went to find Annie.

Annie appeared a few seconds later and sat down across from the giggling women, "I'm Annie, what can I do for you Ma'am?"

"I'm looking for the man in that picture. Can you put me in touch with him?" Suzie asked.

"What business you got with my husband?" Annie said.

"Oh I see, well is there some place we can talk in private?" Her disappointment was evident

Annie led Suzie to a back room.

Suzie put her drink on the table, "It's about a legal matter. You see, my husband is Franklin… I mean was. He owned the other cab company in town. Now, I don't know all the details, but I think he did something bad to that man; what's his name? Gray something or other. I overheard Franklin making arrangements to have him killed. Now he has paid for that with his life. The way I see it, he got what he deserved. Don't get me wrong, I would like to thank the person who has made me a very rich widow." Suzie explained.

Annie told her, "I'm sorry for your loss, but I still don't know why you want to see my Horace."

"You see … Annie is it? Don't be sorry, I'm not. I was standing in the window and saw what happened—all of what happened."

"The Sheriff said that you told them that you had not seen anything. Why would you lie if you saw someone kill your husband?"

Suzie took Annie's hand in her own, "Because I am finally free of him, the only remembrance is all his millions. Now I can have all his money without having to be bothered with him. So you see, your husband, Horace is it? Well he has done me a big favor. I would like to warn him that one of my neighbors did see him, and maybe do something more for him, financially that is, to show my gratitude."

"Thank you for your concern, but I think you must have Horace confused with someone else. Anyhow, he had some family fall sick and went to see them. I don't know when he will be back, but like I said, I'm sure that Horace wouldn't be involved in anything like that. I'm sorry you have wasted your time, but you stay and enjoy yourself. Everything is on the house," Annie rose and walked out of the room.

Annie did not know what Suzie's game was, but she was not playing and neither was Horace. She did not know if the woman was trying to help the Sheriff catch Horace, or if she just really wanted to help. If you asked her she had a thing for him. Some women got all hot and bothered behind that kind of thing. Whatever it was, she could forget it. Horace was leaving and he was leaving now. She went to the bedroom where he was sleeping with Helen and Gena to tell him about Suzie.

Horace had planned to leave in the morning; he wanted to spend as much time with them as possible. He was going to Texas and lay low until things cooled off. He had liked helping his parents in the fields when he was a kid. Where he was going was not far from where he had grown up. The first thing Horace planned to do was stop and talk to his parents. He never went to their graves, their spirit was at the tree where they died. He wanted them to meet their granddaughter. He was grateful that Annie insisted he take Gena.

Horace had said that he would rather go to jail than go on the run and leave them. At least that way, they could visit him.

Annie would not hear of it, "Men die in jail, or turn into women," not that she thought that could happen to him. She felt that if he just disappeared for a while things would cool off and he could come back.

Gena would be fine with her daddy. They made love. She promised to send word when everything had cooled down. She knew that they would be watching her and the club.

Helen did not understand why Gena was going somewhere with Horace and she could not go. This had never happened before. She watched her mother pack Gena's clothes. She cried when her mother told her that they had to go away for a while so that Horace could stay safe. She did not want anything bad to happen to him, but she was going to miss them something terrible.

Suzie And Tree

After Horace and Gena left, Annie went to check the books before turning in. She was puzzled to see Suzie draped over Tree of all people. The woman was drunk off her ass.

Tree was blushing and loving it. Suzie was the first white woman to show interest in him.

Annie warned Tree, "Watch yourself, now." She knew that he was well aware of the problems they had with the law and could be trusted not to put them in a cross.

That night Suzie she had her first taste of chocolate, and she loved it. You see, Tree was big everywhere and he was an ardent lover who went for hours, until she screamed out for mercy.

Annie was cleaning the club when she found an envelope that was addressed, 'To Annie, From Gratitude," with two hundred dollars nestled inside.

Suzie had never known a man as gentle as Tree. He made her feel special in every way. They had long conversations and spent a lot of time laughing. She had never known any black people before, but after getting to know Tree, his family and friends, she decided they were much nicer than most of the whites she knew.

Suzie asked Tree to accompany her to see Grayman. She had been calling the hospital daily to see how he was faring and knew he was going home that day. She took care of her business in the accounting office before locating and introducing herself to Grayman and his wife.

Gizelle had heard about Suzie. She decided that the child was sincere as they talked over a cup of tea in the cafeteria. When she returned to the room, Grayman was in a wheelchair ready to be released. "Where do I go to take care of the bill?"

"Oh I thought you knew… your bill has been paid in full by the lady who was here this afternoon." The nurse pushed Grayman out the door.

After their first night together, Suzie insisted that Tree stay with her. The lawyer assured her that she had enough money to live in style for her lifetime and any great grandchildren she might have.

She spoiled Tree rotten, buying cars and clothes and they were always flying off to some faraway place for vacation.

This did not sit too well with a lot of the white men in the area. They bought some land close to Gizelle and built a beautiful house. She and Suzie had become fast friends, she was soon considered one of the family.

Tree still worked at the club on the rare occasions when they were in town, not because he needed to, but because he wanted to. He did not need any money, Suzie made sure that he had his account at that the bank. She gave him the Taxi Company and he partnered with Grayman to take over all the territory.

It seemed like Annie started having problems as soon as Horace left. She spent a lot of time fending off men trying to step into Horace's shoes. She made it clear that she was faithfully waiting for her husband's return, no matter how long it took.

Annie had to re-establish the fact that she was the owner of the club and just because her man had handled all the problems for her when he was there, it was not like she could not take care of things herself.

Tree was at the club one night, he loved Suzie but he also missed the nightlife. She was at home, probably throwing up. It seemed that lately all she did was eat and throw up, He held her long hair back and washed her face with a towel and prepared peppermint tea to settle her stomach which was getting bigger by the day. He could not wait for the baby to be born.

Annie was running a card game, when in her most controlled voice she told a man, "I don't allow no cheating in my house, I know what you are doing and if you don't stop, you are going to be sorry."

"You crazy bitch, I ain't cheating. You done gone and insulted me."

You could say just about anything to Annie, but unless you were looking for big trouble, you did not call her, 'A Bitch.'

Lucy saw the storm brewing and went to get some help. The man pulled out a gun and set it on the table. Annie had been sitting there with a large browning sporting knife in her lap.

Tree came through the door with Larry. Annie held up her hand and said, "Uh huh, I don't need any help, I will handle this myself."

The man was ranting and raving and swinging the gun around.

Annie told him, "Put the two cards that you palmed back on the table and I'll let you leave."

"What you mean you gone let me leave? In case you're blind or something, I'm the one holding the gun here."

There was a pot of two hundred dollars on the table. He reached for it. Before he knew what happened, Annie threw the knife which landed in his chest.

The surprise on his face was so comical that everyone had to laugh.

Tree and Larry moved to take the dead man out.

"Don't touch him, go call the police and then ya'll get on out of here."

The police came and took her away at quarter to five. She was back home by half-past five because the corpse still had the gun in his hand. It was called self-defense and once again the Judge had his breakfast on time.

Horace Takes Gena To Texas

Horace and Gena drove and sang songs and played a game called 'I Spy,' as they drove for six hours to Texas. They stopped and ate sandwiches that Annie had packed under the tree.

"This is where I come when I want to see my mother and father," Horace explained to his four year old.

"Why do you come here?"

"Because this is the last place I saw them alive," Horace explained how they died.

Gena watched him talk to them as if they were there. Then she saw them. Three people; her grandparents and the baby. They smiled as if to say they were pleased to meet her. Horace saw them too. She joined in as they talked for hours.

"We are going to have to leave now if we are going to make it to Claude Jr.'s before dark," Horace rose and started packing up. Claude Jr. and his family lived two hours away.

When Horace and Gena arrived at their destination they were right on time for dinner. Claude and his family were just sitting down for dinner of fried chicken, potato salad and corn.

Claude Jr. and Horace caught up on what had been happening in their lives. It had been twenty years since they had played stickball in the fields together.

During the Civil War, Claude Senior had been captured while trying to defect to the Yankees. The patrollers who combed the roads for runaway slaves returned him with an 'R,' branded on his chest for run-ner. He received fifty lashes and had never felt such excruciating pain. He prayed for God to send Moses down to take him.

Plantation owners were scared to death because the Yankees were whipping the confederate army into a steady stream of coffins. They were desperate for recruits. When they called for volunteers the first time, most of the plantations were left with an overseer, usually older men, and young boys.

So many slaves had run off to fight with the Yankees that what-ever Southerners were left, no matter what age, they had to be pressed into service. They promised slaves their freedom if they would fight for the cause.

"We'll take care of you after the war," Claude's master bribed. "We are fighting this war for your sake. Who else is going to feed and clothe you? There are plenty of free niggers up North starving to death 'cause they have no way to feed and house themselves. Ain't we always fed and clothed ya'll? Even when you people are too old to work in the fields, don't we let you live out your days in peace right here? You think them Northerners going to take care of ya'll like we do? No sirree."

The master put it in writing; not that Claude could read, but his wife, Laurie could. She was taught to read by a maid she befriended while traveling North with her mistress. She told him that the note said, master will deed over a plot of land and free you, long as you fight for the Confederate army.

Claude's wife, Laurie had given him four children; three boys that were sold as soon as they could walk, and a girl, Clara, who now carried his baby.

The master knew that he would tire of Laurie one day. After giving birth a few times, wenches were no longer attractive to him. Mind you, they held up better than most white women, but when they started to sag, it was time to replace them. Clara was twelve years old when he told Laurie, "Go fetch Clara." Had she known what he had in mind, she would have taken her child and ran away. She was forced to sit with her daughter's head in her lap as he took her virginity.

After that night, Laurie slept next to the kitchen, where she worked helping the cook. She was bitter because she felt that sleeping with his own daughter would surely damn both of their souls to hell. She had hoped the reason he had not sold Clara was to free her.

Laurie watched Clara come down the stairs crying and held her while she complained about the master's doings. She explained to her, "Honey, you have no choice, but you have to hold your head up and know that one day it will be over."

Laurie and Claude had been sweet on each other for almost eighteen years since the day the master had brought him to the plantation. They knew it was dangerous for them to be together as long as she was the master's bed wench. She started eating more, hoping that if she got fat the master would no longer want her.

Claude worked in the fields during the day. At night, he was used for breeding. He had fathered over thirty children. The master gave him a gold coin for each child, but he would have given back every coin if he could have kept just one of his sons. He watched his children sold away with a heavy heart.

Claude and Laurie had come up with a plan. Laurie did not want him sleeping with any other wenches. He would pull out and spill his seed on the floor so as not to get the other women pregnant. He did not have to sex her friends who knew about the plan.

When Laurie and Claude were put together for breeding, she got pregnant quickly. She went to the master and asked to marry with Claude. The master gave his consent. He had just bought two more studs because Claude's seed was no longer as potent, except with Laurie.

Claude was the only one who had come home alive from the war. The master died in his very first battle. He knew he would not get what the master had promised, because Texas slaves could not be legal landowners. He made a deal with a wounded Yankee, Harry Grant.

Claude was bringing the master's body home when he ran across a Yankee soldier in a field with his leg wounded. Claude did not have anything against this man, so he changed the man's uniform for his old potato sack clothes, this way, some person who had lost all their slaves and family to the war would not try to kill the soldier. He could have sworn he saw the dead master trying to sit up when he helped the Yankee into the wagon.

The way Claude saw it, these people were doing what they had to, just as he had been forced to work for the Confederate army carrying water, digging ditches or any other drudgery they could think of that did not require blacks to bear arms, lest they turn on the white folks that fought to keep them enslaved.

When Claude had tried to go over to the Yankee's where he knew the coloreds had guns. He thought if they gave him a gun he could kill the master himself. To his dismay, they told him that he would be of more use as a spy. Every night, he crept off and met a colored man a few miles from camp to give him news. His help enabled the Yankees to ambush the Confederate soldiers; it had been a quick defeat.

Claude stopped at his cabin. Laurie helped him get the soldier inside. He took the master's body up to his parents. The father was old and senile, and the mother was grief-stricken and at a loss. She did not know what she would do now. Her only boy was dead. Who was going to run the place? There was no one to get the harvest in since so many of the slaves had run off, and the overseer had not returned from the war. The white men she hired, robbed them blind. The smokehouse had been broken into twice, the thieves absconded with all the winter meat and provisions.

The parents stood at the graveside as their boy was lowered into the ground. The father had a moment of sanity and turned and looked at his wife, "Things are just not worth living for—no slaves, no son, the South has lost." He hugged her and went and sat on a fallen log under a tree. She sat alongside him and leaned back, telling him, "The Lord will provide."

She heard his snore and realized her husband was sleeping; not a bad idea. She closed her eyes. When she woke it was coming up on dusk. She shook her husband to wake him and he keeled over, dead. She cried for a while, then struggled to her feet to go back to the house to get some help with her husband. Before she knew what she had done, it was too late. Her hearing was not what it used to be. She had not heard the rattlesnake's warning and did not realize she was bitten until she saw the snake sliding away. The poison quickly took effect. The last white owner of the plantation fell to the ground.

For a month, Harry was knocked out most times by the teas and liquor that Laurie fed him to quiet his screams, lest some white field hand discover him. The slaves who knew he was there, knew that this man had almost lost his life fighting for their freedom. They were eager to help the man get better.

When finally Harry was coherent enough, he with the slaves for hours, teaching them to read, write and cipher. With Laurie's herbs and poultices and six months of rest, Harry's health was restored. He was grateful to these people who had saved his life. He knew, that even though Claude had what he thought was a legal document, the courts would never allow the promise. Slavery was not over by a long shot, and it would take years to clear up all the red tape the South had come up with. He vowed to remember the kindness of these people and help them.

No one knew what was going to happen to the plantation. Soon, Northern soldiers came spreading word that they were free. Claude led them to Harry who penned a letter to his family who assumed him dead.

Harry's father was a Congressman, and as soon as he received the letter, he and his wife set out to go get their boy. Harry told them what these people had done for him. Claude and the other four slaves who held the worthless pieces of paper asked if he could help them get their land that was promised.

The Congressman knew these people, though free, had no place to go. He checked with the bank and found there was no legal owner left to the land. No more family existed; the papers the slaves had were as useless as Confederate money. He pulled some strings and spread some money around and ended up with the deed to the property. He called the slaves to the big house and told them that he was the owner now. They should pick the plots of land that they wanted and it would be theirs.

Claude chose forty acres on a hilltop; he was given one hundred and forty acres. The rest of the land was divided among the other newly emancipated slaves. Now they felt free.

Harry and his parents moved into the remodeled and refurbished big house. There were over one thousand acres of corn, cotton and sweet potatoes. The slaves would work the fields and after harvest receive a portion of the profits.

They had their own lands that they could take care of in the evenings and on their two days off. There were no overseers. They were not necessary. These people were working on their own property for their own lives, and if anyone asked, they told people they were share croppers who worked for Mr. Harry Grant. This way, they would have no problems with the vigilante groups who were going around terrorizing colored folks who were trying to start a new, free life.

Harry and his parents lived some months in Texas and the rest of the year up North. They were not concerned with the running of the plantation. When they came down South they found that the coloreds had always been fair with the crops. Their monies were always waiting for them.

Harry put their share back into the property. They discussed what was needed around the place to make life easier for everyone. They bought livestock and built a cotton gin. New houses and barns were erected.

Claude and Laurie were happy. Their second child since emancipation was on the way.

Harry married his childhood sweetheart and brought his wife down in the spring. When it came time to go back North, she decided she loved it here and wanted to stay. She was pregnant, and Harry was so elated over the upcoming child that he granted her every wish.

Harry got up early every morning and worked side-by-side with everyone else. He ran around showing them mail-order catalogues for fancy equipment that he swore would make the work easier and the plantation run smoother.

They hired the newly freed to work the land and help around the growing community, which included a church, store and schoolhouse. They had no problems with the Ku Klux Klan because as far as they knew, the plantation belonged to a white man. There was no prejudice on this land, white and black children went to school and played together without problems.

Horace and Gena blended right into farm life. He was reminded of how much he had enjoyed working side-by-side with his father. He and Claude Jr. both spoke of how nice it would be to have a son to carry on for them. They both only had girls: Horace had Gena and Helen, and Claude Jr. had Sherri Ann, Margaret, and Ann Marie.

Gena told Annie over the phone that this place was like being at Rebi's. She missed her mother, sister and everyone else back home, but it was not because she was lonely, from early morning till supper she had dozens of children to play with. She liked school and spent lots of time with her father, who she adored.

Horace had talked to Larry a few times and was told that Annie did not seem happy. She was drinking way too much, and gambled away a lot of the nights take. Grayman's leg was infected and they may have to amputate it. He would be in a wheelchair for the rest of his life. Gizelle and Mason's boys were drafted into the army. George and Celeste were doing well and the farm was making plenty of money. Rebi and her brood were all doing fine.

Prohibition had been over for some time, but Annie still had the club running. Of course, it was not like it used to be. Most of the money came from the gambling and girls. She missed her man and everything irritated her. She had gotten used to Horace handling the problems and suddenly she had to deal with everything herself again.

Horace decided that he was going to bring Annie and Helen to Texas. Larry could handle the club or they could close it. He did not care; he was missing his family too much. He called and told her and she agreed that nothing was more important than being together. She started making arrangements immediately.

Claude Jr. and Horace went into town to sell a load of cotton. The broker that they had been dealing with for years had died and his son was now the proprietor. When they declined his less than honest, short offer, the man called Claude Jr. an, "Uppity nigger who needed to be taught a lesson."

Claude Jr. had never had to face this kind of prejudice before. Horace had, and told him, "Let's go."

Claude Jr. was angry, and called the man a thief as Horace pulled him back to the truck. They had stayed came in town for a while buying gifts and having some drinks. Horace explained that all they had to do was let Harry's son, Jordan bring the load back so they could get a fair price.

Claude Jr. and Horace headed home with their cotton before it got dark. They were almost home, drunk and singing at the top of their lungs when they happened upon a broken down truck blocking the road. They got out to see if they could help and found themselves surrounded by the broker and some of his friends who came out of the tree line.

The broker said, "Since Claude Jr. called me a thief, I have decided to accept this here load of cotton as your way of apologizing for back talking me."

The other men jumped onto the truck and started throwing bales into the road. Claude Jr. ran to stop them and the fighting began. When four of the men attacked Horace, he pulled out his gun. When the dust cleared, two of the white men were dead.

The sheriff and his deputies appeared out of nowhere. He looked at the dead men, then to Horace with the gun in his hand. He arrested them both even though there were only two colored men against ten whites.

Horace and Claude Jr. were beaten before they were taken away. A neighboring farmer had seen the whole thing and called Claude's wife and told her what happened. She called Annie. Annie and Gizelle came the very next day. They went to the jail and tried to see Horace, but were told he could not have any visitors for some reason that did not seem fair. Annie called and The Judge sent a lawyer. They stayed at Claude Jr.'s, trying to see them every day, but were denied.

The lawyer was told that Horace and Claude Jr. had been transferred to the next county, for their own safety. They went there the next day, but were told they had been sent somewhere else. When they arrived at the next county they were told that they had been sent back to the original jail to stand trial. This went on for over two weeks.

The lawyer was being harassed and threatened for attempting to represent niggers who had killed white men, but he bravely stood his ground. When the day came for the trial, Horace and Claude Jr. had still not been seen. Right before time for the trial, they were told that they both had a fatal accident at the work camp and had already been buried.

"We didn't know how to reach the next of kin, so being Christian men and all, we went on and put them in the ground...disease and all, you know."

Annie and Gizelle took Gena and headed back to Louisiana. Two years later, the lawyer who had continued to investigate their case, found out that they were beaten to death. They had never made it to any prison.

Helen—1930

Lake Charles was changing. Railroad tracks were now on Main Street. A row of storefronts sprang up across from Annie's. There was a shoeshine parlor, a small grocery store, beauty shop, barbershop, ice cream parlor and tailor's.

Helen sat on their front porch watching the comings and goings. She had gone to school for a little while and really enjoyed it, soaking her lessons up like a sponge.

With time, Annie had changed. She drank until she passed out every night. She argued and fought all the time. She told Helen, "You look too much like that damn no-good daddy of yours." She beat Helen for any little imagined thing. Helen understood that her mother was sad and heartbroken over Horace's fate; so was she.

Helen had to help with the business at night. Annie had taught her everything about the business and she ran things with efficiency. The customers thought she was so cute. Some thought they could take advantage of her because she was young.

Annie had also taught Helen how to cheat at cards and dice. This way she could recognize if they tried something crooked, then it was only fair that she turn it back around on them. Most of the customers knew better than to pull anything in Annie's place.

Every night, Helen got out of bed to run the club when Annie was not capable. She was either too drunk or had started gambling. It was up to Helen to stop her. Some nights, that just was not possible and Annie would lose far more than they had made. The next day, Helen was punished.

Lack of rest had Helen falling asleep in school. It was so embarrassing to her that she just stopped going. Annie did not think that book learning was important for girls anyway. Many mornings Helen woke up to find strange men in bed with her mother. She did not like these men, and obviously neither did Annie, because as soon as she woke she put them out. Annie got depressed after these nights because she would be angry with herself. She was not even able to remember how she ended up in them. She did it as a distraction, something to numb the painful loss of Horace.

Annie started working more with the Voodoo and Hoodoo. Gizelle had told her to leave the dark side alone, but Annie was intrigued by it. She had learned from Grayman before he stopped practicing it. She also learned some other things from a friend of his who came in town a lot. He always spent the night at the club because he would be in no condition to drive out to Gizelle's or back to New Orleans after a night of working girls and liquor. Annie would coax him into teaching her more.

Annie was bitter. Her new saying was, "Confusion is my heart's desire, peace I do despise." She never went to church anymore; she said, "God don't do nothing for me but take everything away, I'll stay out of his house and he can stay out of mine." Things went on this way for years. Then one day she met a man named Bob on her way home from work.

Bob was a preacher. One day as he was overseeing the building of his new church, he decided to speak to this woman who he had seen walking by every day. Annie was carrying two bags and they looked heavy. He waited until she got to where he was standing and plucked the bags from her arms, before she could protest he asked, "Which way are we going?"

Annie looked up at the man and said, "This way."

Bob made small talk, and unlike the other men in her life, did not make a pass or even ask to see her again. He was attractive enough, but after he told her he was a preacher, she dismissed any carnal thoughts.

Every day for two weeks Bob waited for her. Then one morning, when she came out to go to work he was waiting in front of the house in his car. For three months he dropped her off and picked her up when she was finished. He had come for dinner a couple of times and the girls seemed to like him.

Bob's church opened. He asked her every week to attend, but she always declined. He talked her into letting the girls go.

Finally, one day Bob said, "I guess the only way to get you into my church is going to be at our wedding," and he presented her with a ring.

When she did not say anything, Bob took her hand, "Annie I'm asking you to marry me, to be my wife. I'm waiting for an answer."

"Bob, you are a preacher and I am a sinner; now how is that going to work out?" She looked closer at the shiny diamond.

"If God can forgive sins and not judge, so shall I."

They were married six weeks later. Annie had to close down the club, which was not making much money anymore and she stopped selling liquor. He also did not like the Voodoo, said it was demonic, but she still did it every chance she got. She started going to church and soon found herself listening to his preaching. He was good at delivering God's word. Their lives had a semblance of order again and Helen went back to school. Bob would take the girls and pick them up after. After service, they all caravanned out to Rebi's on Sundays.

Sometimes church life got to be a bit much for Annie, these times she would go out to the clubs. He would be sitting on the porch waiting for her when she returned. He would preach at her until she apologized and tell him it would not happen again, and it didn't happen until the next time, which seemed to be about every three weeks.

Annie got pregnant. Bob was ecstatic; he did not have any children. He became her shadow. She could not move or go anywhere without him. She was starting to feel as though she was suffocating. She could not have any fun or go anywhere. He did not like spicy food and wanted to oversee her cooking and what she ate. When she was not working, she had to be at home, or in church with him.

Annie had the baby. It was a boy and they named him Robert–Bob for short. He was a healthy baby and gave them all a lot of joy. Helen and Gena took care of him when they came home from school. During the day when Annie was at work, he stayed with Bob.

Annie really tried to get into Bob's life, but it was not the same as when she was with Horace. She could not love him the same way. No matter how hard she tried it just was not happening. She was tired of his constant Bible-thumping and criticizing. It seemed like he corrected every little thing she did; it was nerve-wracking. And the worst thing of all was, he was no good in bed. He was so quick that if she blinked she would have missed the entire thing.

After having come to know real lovemaking, it was hard to deal with a man who was not concerned with satisfying her needs. It left Annie feeling unsatisfied and frustrated. Whenever she made suggestions about what he could do to make her feel good, he would say, "Those things are not of God." Then he would get his Bible out and start reading to her about her role as a wife and mother.

Annie tried for as long as she could, but he remained insensitive to her needs. He did not like to go out to Rebi's on Sundays and it showed. He did everything he could to distance her from everyone he didn't think appropriate, God fearing people. He said she needed to make new friends. She tried, but had nothing in common with his stuck=up parishioners. Most of them thought it was a disgrace for a preacher to have taken up with her. They all knew of her reputation and the den of iniquity that she called a club.

More than a few women in the church would have loved to take up with the preacher, and they did not keep it a secret. When Annie was seen going into a hotel room with the chef at a hotel where she was his assistant by a maid – Gladys, a church member who had been abandoned by her husband years ago, and did not waste any time letting Bob and everyone else know. She had always dreamed of being a preacher's wife.

When Bob confronted Annie, she told him the truth. She had known the chef for years and he satisfied her physically, something that Bob did not do. He went and got his Bible and started reading to her about the evils of the flesh. He said it would take him and the Lord to save her sinning soul. He made her quit working at the hotel. He even told her that he would try some of the things that she had suggested. Things got a little better, but not much.

Annie told Bob that she missed her family and was going to start taking the girls to Gizelle's after the first service. He told her that he did not think those people were the kind of company she should be keeping, but if she felt she had to go he would join her there after the last service. He knew that these people, though they attended his church sometimes, were not god fearing.

The next Sunday they rode out and Bob sat through the whole meal quoting the Bible. No one could talk about anything without him preaching. Finally everyone got so uncomfortable that they just stopped talking. When it was time for him to head back for evening service he told Annie, "You and the girls get ready to leave."

"I'm not going, we will be home later."

When Bob arrived, Annie and the kids still were not home. He called to find out what was going on. Gerard told him that the kids were there, but Annie had left with Rebi. He went and picked up the children and got them ready for bed.

At two o'clock in the morning, one of his members called and told him that his wife was in a club gambling, drinking and dancing. When she came home it was five o'clock in the morning.

Bob was waiting in the front room. He tried to talk to her but then realized that she had passed out. He picked her up, took off her clothes and put her in the bed. He prayed over her for the salvation of her tarnished soul.

The next day Annie was feeling terrible, she did not wake up until noon. But she had herself a time the night before and it was worth it. She had not danced like that in the last two years. She realized that she missed the lifestyle and the church life was not for her.

Bob walked into the bathroom when he heard her throwing up. He placed a cold towel on the back of her neck. She could not deal with the look in his eyes. She knew that he was a good man, and that she had once again disappointed him. She was not cut out to be what he needed. She knew that by now some of his members who were in the club right along with her had called and told him about her carryings on. She lay back in the bed and waited for the lecture, but it did not come.

Bob knew that she was still feeling bad; now would not be the time to talk. If he broke out his bible she would likely hit him over the head with it. He brought her a bowl of soup and some crackers on a tray and left to take care of some church business.

He sat and thought about what to do. He knew that she had not grown up with the Lord in her life. He also knew that she had suffered a lot of trials, and sought out the fast life as a way of easing her pain. He tried to tell her that God could take all the pain away if she would give herself over.

In Annie's eyes she had disappointed Bob so many times that he should realize by now that she may never be ready.

Bob picked up the girls from the school and when they went into the house she was fixing dinner. They sat at the table and he blessed the food. Through the meal, they listened to the girls talk about their day. After dinner she cleaned up and prepared the kids for bed. They played a game together until time for the girls to be tucked in. They listened to their prayers and he read them a bible story.

Bob went into the bedroom, sat down on the bed next to Annie and took her hand. "Wife of mine, what are you going to do? What do you want to do?"

"I want to be a good wife, but the things that you expect do not include the things that I like to do. I went out last night, and I admit I went a little wild because I hadn't done it in so long, but I had a good time. I know you don't approve of my family, but those are the people who were there for me when I had no one else in the world. I know it ain't right for a preacher's wife to be out alone, but you never want to go anywhere. You don't dance; when I had the club plenty of preachers came, and just 'cause you only drink red wine, you still drinking, so what's the difference, liquor is liquor. Also, I think that music is music and the music in your choir just does not move me to get up and cut a rug, something I have always enjoyed doing. Everything that you consider a sin, I call fun. "Robert, why did you marry me? You knew all about me from those women in your church. What did you think? If you could save my dark soul, it would show everybody what a great preacher you are? Bob, I do love you in my own way, but I don't think I can be the kind of wife that you need and I don't want to hurt you. I know that church is the most important thing in your life. Now, I done tried for going on three years, but it's not working for me. Bob, you gonna have to let me go, but I want to thank you for trying." She hugged him and kissed him on the cheek.

Robert insisted they try for another year. He even went with her to clubs once a week, but could not deal with her when she got drunk, and he was not comfortable in these places because it made him rethink his church members who were carrying on something terrible. They figured they would go to church and say some Hail Mary's and all would be forgiven so they could go out and raise more hell the next week.

Finally, they divorced.

Bob took up with Gladys. He still took the kids to and from school every day. He gave Annie money for the kids every week and in the long run they found that they were better as friends. Annie even came to church sometimes.

Annie opened her club on the weekends.

Helen And Mr. Macklin

Helen had to take care of Gena every day. She dressed her for school, fixed breakfast, and walked her to school. Then she would go home and clean up the club, the house, and start dinner. She always tried to make everything nice for Annie by the time she got home from work, because if things were not just right, she would get beat.

Gena loved Helen, but also resented her. She would do things to get her in trouble. She knew that if she did not do her chores, Helen would do it because if it was not done she would be blamed.

Helen could spend time arguing with Gena, but it was easier to do the work and get it over with. When Annie found out, to the girls surprise, Gena got beat this time. Helen was warned not to do her work for her. "She has to be responsible and work just like everyone else."

Helen did not get in trouble for doing Gena's chores, but she did get in trouble for not making Gena do it. She felt as if she could not win for losing.

Gena teased Helen about looking so white. She told her that momma loved her more because she had loved her daddy. She also teased her because she did not know who her father was, and said he did not want to know her, seeing's how he never came to see her.

Helen enjoyed Mr. Macklin's visits. Sometimes she pretended he was her father. When Mr. Macklin showed Helen a picture of his little girl, she realized the reason he took such a shine to her was that she looked like his dead daughter.

Helen loved to see Mr. Macklin coming up the walk, always bringing her gifts; a doll, jacks or a comic book. On her birthdays and holidays he took her shopping for pretty dresses and shoes.

Before Mr. Macklin left, rain or shine he would take her across the tracks for ice cream. Not the cone kind that you got from the corner store, but the real kind from the ice cream parlor, with whipped cream and cherries on top. She would sit in the little white cast-iron chair and try to make her ice cream last forever.

Mr. Macklin could sit and talk to Helen for hours. Not once did he take his eyes from her face. He always commented on how much he wished that she were his little girl, and if his daughter were still alive, he knew they would be the best of friends.

She never had a problem going into the ice cream parlor with Mr. Macklin, even though blacks were not allowed. The man who owned the store knew that she was black because he bought liquor from Annie, but overlooked it because Macklin was his landlord.

On Helen's thirteenth birthday, Mr. Macklin came by in a shiny, brand new Buick. He told her he had bought it that morning because he knew it was her first teen birthday. He said that every little girl was supposed to ride in a new car on her first teen birthday.

Mr. Macklin took her shopping as always. He said that he had to show a house on the other side of town. When they stopped in front of a really pretty two-story home on the white side of town, Mr. Macklin opened the door for Helen.

A white couple waited on the porch. He introduced Helen as his daughter. This really made her feel special. Helen followed along behind them as Mr. Macklin pointed out all the features that the house had to offer to the young couple. When they entered one of the smaller rooms upstairs, her breath caught, the room was so beautiful. You could tell that the little girl who lived here had everything any girl could ever want.

Mr. Macklin told Helen that she could wait here while he went downstairs with the young couple and talked business. He handed her a book, "Here, look through this; I won't be long."

Helen could read the book even though she had been forced to stop going to school. Helen loved to read and devoured everything she could get her hands on. The book was filled with fairy tales; the very same kind of stories that Helen would daydream and create in her mind to escape her own life.

As Helen peeked around the room at all the toys and things, she could not help but wish that this were her house. There was a dollhouse made exactly like the house that they were in, same color and every-thing, with little furniture and people. The closets in the dollhouse had clothes that were just like the clothes that hung in the closet that Helen peeked into.

She went back to the window seat and lost herself inside the magical fantasy world that unfolded in her mind.

By the time Mr. Macklin returned, Helen was on the last story.

"Read to me," he said picking her up onto his lap. She folded right into him and was so comfortable that she wished she could make the story last forever. She imagined that this must be what it would have been like to have a dad. She thought of the times with Horace. She really missed him. Bob had been nice enough, but he was nothing like Horace. All he ever did was read the Bible and make them sit in church all day.

She liked church, but at such a young age, to be expected to sit through three services was a bit much.

Helen envied her friends who had a live in father. She didn't know what her father looked like, his memory was a blur. She remembered the day he was arguing with her mother about taking her away, but not his face. Children should at least know what their daddies looked like.

Mr. Macklin ran his hand through Helen's hair. This did not bother her, until he started massaging her shoulders. Then he was rubbing her waist and it tickled. She tried to continue reading but his touch was growing bolder. His fingers went to her thigh and she started to squirm. When his hands were just before the crotch of her panties she stopped reading and asked him, "Please stop; my momma always told me that this is not right. I'm a good girl."

"Now Alice you know your daddy loves you and I would never do anything to hurt you."

She jumped off his lap, "Mr. Macklin, my name ain't Alice. I'm Helen, remember? Are you all right, Mr.Macklin? You don't look to be your regular self." She was scared now. "I think I need to be getting home now, 'cause momma is taking me to Gizelle's for my birthday party." Her party was the next day, but she could not think of another reason why she would need to leave right then.

"Come here to daddy, Alice. You didn't finish your story. I want to know what happens next." She picked up the book and sat next to him and started reading.

Suddenly, Mr. Macklin picked Helen up and carried her to the bed.

"What are you doing? Stop!" she yelled.

His breathing had gone raspy and he kept rubbing the front of his pants. When she got up enough nerve to look him in the face, what she saw terrified her. She knew what was going to happen, "Please stop," she pleaded repeatedly. She froze as he snatched her underwear off and pushed her dress up over her small, undeveloped hips. She did not know what to do. He did not see the tears rolling down her face, or the pain as he forced her small, frail body down on the bed. He did not hear her cries and pleading as he tore her tiny vagina. He slammed away at her, huffing and puffing, until finally he let out a cry and collapsed on top of her aching and torn body.

Helen continued to stare at the ceiling. When the pain had gotten to be more than she could bear, she had a way of disconnecting her mind from her body. It was the same thing she did when Annie beat her. She lifted her soul out of her pain-wracked body and floated around the ceiling until it was over.

Mr. Macklin looked down at the crying child. At that moment he wanted to kill himself for what he had done to this innocent girl. He started to cry. They sat that way for about a half hour with Helen staring at the ceiling, silent tears running out of her eyes and into her hair. He rocked back and forth, crying like a child, begging her forgiveness.

Finally, Mr. Macklin rose. He got a towel and tried to clean the blood off the insides of Helen's thighs. She sat up and put her underwear back on. He talked to her as if nothing had happened.

Mr. Macklin went about the business of cleaning a spot of blood off the bedspread. When he finished, he put the towel that he used into a paper bag. He helped Helen up and arranged her clothes. He got a brush and repaired her hair, "You have the most beautiful hair. I could just sit and comb it all day. That's what I used to do with my little girl you know, and this is the prettiest dress."

Mr. Macklin was back to being himself, the man she knew. She wanted to ask him if what he just did to her was something he used to do with his little girl too, but she didn't. He took her hand and they walked downstairs.

"Go and wait in the car."

Helen walked out the door and down the path but instead of going to the car she continued down the street.

Mr. Macklin's car pulled up and he got out and led her to the car, "Helen, I'm really sorry about what happened in there and I hope you can forgive me."

Mr. Macklin stopped before reaching Helen's house. He turned to her and took her hand, placing something in it, "Helen, please do not say anything to anyone, because the only person who would get in trouble is you."

He went on talking but she did not hear what he was saying. She got out of the car. She did not look in her hand as she walked down the block to her house. She never remembered this block being so long. By the time she reached her front door her crotch was hurting something terrible. It felt like she was on fire down there. She was grateful that no one was home. She stood by the door crying after she closed and locked it. She walked in her room and undressed to take a bath. She looked in her hand and saw a roll of money. It was what he had stuffed in her hand when she was getting out of his car. She did not want anything from that dirty old man. She threw the money as far as she could; it bounced off the wall and rolled under the bed.

Helen lay in the claw-footed bathtub and cried. She did not know how long she had been there when Gena came in and woke her up.

Gena saw the water was pink, "Ooh look at the water. Did you cut yourself?" Gena asked.

Helen did not say anything.

"Momma! Momma! Helen is hurt. Come quick." Gena cried.

Annie came into the bathroom and looked at the water and assumed Helen had started her period, "When did it start?"

She thought about telling her, but remembered what Mr. Macklin said about her getting in trouble, "Earlier today."

Annie had told her about periods, and decided to go along with her assumption.

Annie took her wet hair down and washed it for her. She looked at her fingers and told her to get out of the tub because she was beginning to shrivel up like a prune.

Helen got up and dried off. She noticed that the blood was still coming.

Annie walked in with a box of sanitary napkins and a belt to hold it on. She showed her how to use it. She led her into the bedroom and told her to lie down. She rubbed her down with some oil and gave her a cup of hot tea made with ginger, cramp bark, chamomile, and strawberry leaf. Then she placed a bottle filled with hot water and wrapped it in a towel against her pelvis. Helen liked the times when Annie was nice like this. It made up for all the other times.

Helen was glad her mom didn't know the truth. For some reason, she felt like it was her fault. She knew that if she told her mother she would probably kill Mr. Macklin. She remembered what happened to Horace when he went to jail, and she did not want to lose her mother too.

She remembered a time when Annie had gone to jail for attempting to kill a man. It was about two o'clock in the morning. Annie was drunk and gambling. Helen had to run things. She was dealing cards when one of the white customers started making remarks about wanting to go to bed with her, "Look mister, I'm just here to deal you these cards. Now, you wanting something more, I suggest you go next door."

The other man at the table told him, "Unless you looking to get cut, you better leave Annie's little girl alone."

"You telling me that this is that black woman that owns the place daughter?" He looked at Helen and said, "You're colored…I thought you was white. Somebody need to hang a sign on you. That don't bother me none, I wants you just the same. How much is it gone cost me? Hey, you still got your cherry? I'll pay extra for that." He pulled on her arm.

"I done told you I don't do that," Helen said as she tried to free herself.

"You think you too good or something?" The man's raised voice got Annie's attention.

The other man got up from the table as he saw Annie approaching. The whole place went quiet. Helen was wrestling with the drunken man by now. He never saw it coming. He turned toward Annie when he heard her voice, "Turn her loose right now."

He laughed, "I got an idea. How about we have some real fun with mother and daughter at the same time, what do you say momma?"

"I say, we ain't for sale, you need to go next door for that. Now I'm not gone tell you again to turn her loose."

"What's your problem? I said I would pay. Y'all too good for money or something?"

That was it. Annie pulled out her straight razor and sliced the hand that was holding Helen.

When he let go and spun around to attack Annie, let's just say that the only action that man's penis saw that night was the sharp edge of Annie's razor. It was rumored that she cut it off.

He went screaming out the door.

Sure enough, the sheriff came and took her away, but she was back by morning. If Annie would do that to a man just for trying to mess with her, Helen hated to think what she would do to Mr. Macklin if she knew. No, she did not think that telling Annie would be a good idea.

Gena came into the room. She had tears in her eyes and whispered in Annie's ear, "Is she gone die momma?"

Annie laughed and said, "No your sister is not going to die." She explained to Gena about women and their monthly periods. Gena was relieved. They sat playing cards while Annie went to the kitchen.

"Whatever you want, I'll fix. What do you want to eat?" Annie hugged her.

Helen loved this day. She was getting all of Annie's attention, "Gumbo."

"Well then gumbo it is," As she walked out of the room, she kissed her on the cheek and Helen saw a tear in her eye.

"What's wrong, Momma? Why you crying?" Helen asked.

"Oh, I'm just silly. I'm crying because my little girl is turning into a woman. Damn I must be getting old, you think?"

"Naw, Momma, you ain't gone never get old," both of the girls said.

When Annie left the room Gena said, "I was so scared you was dying, I'm sure glad you're not. Do it hurt a lot?"

"It feel like when somebody punch you real hard in the stomach but worse."

"Helen, I'm sorry for all those times I was mean to you. It was because I was jealous, you looking white, and being so pretty and all. That stuff about your daddy, I know he came and tried to take you away from momma, she told me. I was mad that even though you don't know him that well, at least your daddy didn't go and die," she climbed up in the bed and hugged her big sister.

"Your daddy was the only daddy I ever had. Bob was okay, but Horace was fun. I really miss him."

They both fell asleep and when they woke up they ate Gumbo. Rebi and Gizelle were clucking over Helen and her new womanhood.

That day when Annie had given Helen the sanitary napkins, she really did start menstruating. Helen was relieved because she was afraid that she might have been pregnant. The way Annie explained it, when a man put his penis inside of you he fertilized an egg that was waiting inside of your womb, as the egg grew it turned into a little baby who lived in a space that was padded with menstrual blood. If you had not had sex after twenty-one days, the body says, 'we don't need this blood in here,' and pushes it out.

Gena tried to be nice for a while, it did not last long though. Rebi and Gizelle had stayed over that night. The next day they went to church and after, rode out to Rebi's. Helen had the best birthday party, and got mostly money for gifts. Annie had made the best cake. They played games.

The only thing that spoiled her day was when she stood up after cutting her cake, Jerry started yelling, "Helen is bleeding." She was so embarrassed. Annie explained to her that she had to change the pad more often or it would get full of blood and spill over, soiling her clothes.

"Momma, I want to go home now."

"All right, baby."

Helen

It was almost three years later when Helen was moving her bed and saw a wad of bills. She picked it up and counted it. With every note, the memories of that afternoon came rushing back at her.

Wouldn't you just know it? There was two hundred dollars in twenties. What was it about white folks and two hundred dollars? Was that the set rate for violating a black person and smashing their pride and dreams? Annie had told her about the money that her father's parents had given her when they found out she was pregnant and the envelopes that he had come every month after, and were still coming.

Helen pushed the memory from her mind and hid the money in the cigar box under the loose board where she saved her tips. She never told anyone about that afternoon and Mr. Macklin never came back.

She was seventeen years old and worked at the hospital for people who could not take care of themselves. Some had mental problems, were retarded or just old. One of the patients was Mrs. Macklin. One of the nurses told her that the reason why Mrs. Macklin was there was because she had gone crazy when she walked in on her husband pestering their seven-year old daughter. She picked up a heavy candlestick and when she swung at her husband's head, at the very instant of impact, he must have sensed something, because he moved. When he tried to grab for her, she lost her balance and the candlestick came down on top of their daughter's head, splitting her skull in two. The child died.

Mr. Macklin ran out of the house. When he returned two whole days later, he found his wife in the same room holding her bloody, dead child in her arms.

All the anger that Helen had been harboring drained away. The death of his daughter and his wife's sanity was the high price he had paid for his terrible sins.

Every week, Mr. Macklin would attempt to visit his wife, but the only greeting he ever got when he stepped into her room were her screams as she relived that terrible afternoon. She saw him walking down the hall a few times. He did not know who she was and she did not see any reason to remind this stooped and broken old man. He was living a hell on earth.

Court 'in

Annie ran off any of boys who came by trying to court her daughter. It was not a problem though; Mr. Macklin was still fresh in Helen's memory.

Helen had blossomed out and was beautiful by the time she turned seventeen. She had a lean, curvy figure, which combined with her long silky hair, had the neighborhood boys flocking around her like bees to honey. She paid them no mind though.

She worked at the hospital from seven in the morning and headed home in time to walk Gena and Bob home from school. The local boys knew of Annie's reputation with a razor. She never had to run any one of them off more than once…

That is, until Melvin came along.

Helen had gone across to the store to get some fixin's for dinner and as she passed by the barbershop, as usual, there was a lot of whistling and cat-calling.

Melvin Paul Broussard, who lived in the neighboring town of Broussard, where he worked in his family's pool hall and shine parlor, was visiting a friend. They had been sitting around shooting the breeze when he looked up to see what was attracting so much attention. He was stumped. Melvin had to catch this one. She was a heart-stopper. He could tell that she had a beautiful figure under the plain cotton shift she wore.

Melvin was no slouch himself. Even the most snotty, choosiest girls in the county considered him a good catch. Melvin was known as Stepper, because of the dapper clothes he wore. He and his brothers were never caught out without their tailored suits; wide-brimmed hats, spats and they all carried walking canes.

Melvin's oldest brother's name was Joe but he was called Dapp, next came Sadie and she was something else too; Curley, who was known as Playboy; and the baby brother Warren who was known as Valentino. Sadie had raised Melvin and Warren after their parents died in an automobile accident. They all lived up to their monikers; the Broussard boys were breaking hearts left and right.

The Broussard's were not rich, but well off for black folk's standards at that time. Their parents had left property and a shoeshine parlor, which was where Melvin and Warren worked. Joe and Curley played in a blues band. They were older and already on their own at the time of the accident.

"Who is that?" Melvin stood up and walked to the door for a better look.

"She ain't for you, Stepper. She got a momma who makes sure don't nobody mess with Helen. Believe you me, you don't want to tangle with Annie and her straight razor. I wouldn't advise no man to go sniffing around that door unless he wants his nose cut off," the old barber said.

"Well, I ain't just any man," Melvin picked up his hat and cane and followed Helen. He liked the fact that no one else had been able to court her; this made him all the more determined.

"Hey, Hey pretty lady. Let me help you carry that bag. It looks heavy and I wouldn't want you to strain your beautiful self."

Helen turned to the stranger, ready to tell him no thank you, and that she would appreciate it if he would leave her alone. The words caught in her throat when she looked at him with his fine clothes, pleated pants and jacket made out of some of the finest linen she had ever seen. His black hair was naturally silky and wavy; his mustache penciled in. Oh boy, he was something to see. His skin the color of dark coffee; he was handsome all right. She could not say anything. She stood there and blushed. When she came to her senses she was so flustered and embarrassed that she turned and walked hurriedly across the tracks.

This did not deter Melvin one bit. He fell into step beside her, hooked his cane over his arm and took the bag from her, "My name is Melvin Paul Broussard. What's yours?"

She did not stop walking, nor did she look him in the eye but she did whisper her name, which he already knew and had made up a little poem:

"Helen, Helen, Sweet as a summer watermelon."

Helen looked at him and giggled. She worried a stone with the toe of her shoe as she listened to him talk. It did not matter that she was not saying anything. He didn't seem to notice. He talked on and on about himself and what he did for a living and where he lived. He generously sprinkled in compliments about her face, hair and complexion. Oh, he was a silver-tongued devil!

"I don't think it's a good idea for you to walk me home because my mother will get upset."

Melvin looked her in the eye, "Your momma is probably just scared of losing her baby girl."

"Whatever the reason, I don't want to make her mad and neither do you."

"I don't know about that. I think I need to meet her and see for myself. Is this where you live?" Melvin asked. By this time, they were approaching the fence in front of her house.

Annie stood just inside the door. She had seen the whole thing as she had been watching Helen out the window from the time she had come out of the grocery store. Annie opened the door. "Helen, get inside with those groceries and get started on dinner." She looked Melvin up and down.

Helen went inside without as much as a backwards glance.

Annie came out onto the porch, "I don't want to see you sniffing around my daughter anymore; I know what you are with all your fancy clothes and cane. If you think you're going to add my child to your stable of whores, you can just forget it."

"Hold on now Ma'am, I ain't no pimp. My mother was a woman. I work hard for my money and the next time you see me I will be about proving it. My name is Melvin Paul Broussard. You have a good day now." He put his hat back on his head and swung his cane as he walked away whistling.

Annie smiled to herself. She liked the fact that this one had a little backbone, unlike the others who would run away with their tails tucked between their legs. She knew that she would be seeing this one again. She went inside.

She knew the way that Helen pretended to be extra busy prepping the sausage, corn and okra that she was expecting her to fuss, "That one was a real good-looker wasn't he?"

Helen dropped the corn that she was shucking and turned and looked at her mother with her mouth hanging open.

Annie walked into the other room laughing.

Helen

Maybe, just maybe, Helen thought as she listened to her mother's laugh. She turned back to the sink, giggling. Her mother had been telling her about men lately. Helen realized she was preparing her for courting. Maybe the time had come when she would let her start seeing boys.

The very next day there came a knock on the door. It was early Sunday morning. Helen opened the door and was shocked to see Melvin standing there with a bouquet of flowers.

"You better go before my mother sees you," Helen whispered.

He touched her on the side of her face, "Don't worry, it's your mother who I come to see."

Helen knew she must have been hearing wrong. Could he possibly be here to court her mother? She was crushed. Annie came up behind her and Helen ran to her room to die.

Melvin held the flowers and box of candy out to Annie, then gave her several sheets of paper.

"Come on before you let all the heat in." She walked back to the kitchen and sat down at the breakfast table.

Melvin sat down at the place that was set and picked up a fork and helped himself to the ham, eggs and toast she had just cooked.

She put her glasses on and looked at the papers. She could not read very well but good enough to know that the papers were deeds to property. The papers had his and his sibling's names on them as owners.

When Annie looked up he was eating. She laughed and said, "Humph, I like your nerve. I don't remember inviting you to eat breakfast."

Melvin winked and said, "This is good, can your daughter cook like this?"

"Yes, she can," Annie said laughingly.

Annie had done some investigating of her own about Mr. Melvin Paul Broussard and had learned all about his family. "I don't guess you got any papers about the gambling and after hours joint that the pool hall is a front for, do you?"

He raised an eyebrow and looked at her, "Now you being in the same business and all, would know that putting something like that on paper wouldn't be too smart."

So he had done his homework too. She liked this boy; *he had backbone.*

"I am a businessman and I am here to court your daughter, with your permission. As a matter-of fact, I would consider it an honor if you would allow me to escort you and your family to church."

When Annie walked into Helen's room, she was lying on the bed crying. "What in the world is wrong wit' you, Chile? Get up and dry your eyes; make yourself look presentable. You got a young man come a courtin' and you in here crying…unless of course you want me to send him away? He say he wants to escort us to church. You better get moving if you want some breakfast before he be done ate all I done cooked."

She burst out laughing at the smile that lit up her daughter's face.

Helen could not believe her ears. She jumped up and hugged Annie, "Momma what do I wear? What did he say? You like him Momma? Ain't he handsome?" Helen asked all in the same breath.

"Slow down, Chile. You don't never let a man know that you like him too much. You have got to always keep your wits about you or else they will be taking you for granted. That's the mistake I made with your father, and I do not expect you to make the same one's I did. Now get that new white suit down. That way, when you two walk in church together you can give those old bible-beaters something to talk about. Hurry up child."

Helen hugged her again and said, "Thank you, momma."

Annie went to wake up Gena and get herself dressed and ready to go to church. She called Rebi, Celeste and Gizelle and told them, "Get yourselves to the ten o'clock service at church. Chile, I got something you got to see. Helen got a boy come to court her."

Gena walked into the kitchen and sat down. Melvin walked back in the room after washing his hands in the bathroom and Gena's eyes opened wide, "Who Is You?" she asked.

"I'm Melvin; I come to see Helen. Who are you?" He pinched her cheek as he sat down.

She giggled, "I'm Gena, but momma just gone run you off like she do all the rest."

Gena was shocked when Annie came out dressed in her church clothes and asked Melvin, "Ain't that girl finished dressing yet?"

"Yes Ma'am. She done ate and everything; she just went to go and get her Bible," Melvin said.

"What you sitting there with your mouth hanging open for, Gena?" Annie asked.

"I just don't believe that you gone and let Helen start courtin' is all."

"Why not? She's seventeen now. I raised her right."

The whole family walked into church. The sight of Annie being there was enough to turn some heads, but Helen with a boy was enough to get the whole place buzzing. They went out to Rebi's after church. Melvin fit right in with the men.

Annie told Melvin he could keep company with Helen at the house, only when she was at home. Melvin came by every Saturday, Sunday and Wednesday afternoon. They would sit and talk and sometimes Melvin was able to sneak a kiss. On Sundays they would go to church then out to Rebi's. Some days Annie did not go, but Gena and Bob were always with them as chaperones.

Helen loved holding hands with him. Although he shined shoes practically every day, his hands and nails were always clean and manicured.

A couple of times, Annie chaperoned them to a Fais do-do. They went on Sunday hayrides, which are big picnics with tons of food, music and dancing. Helen was in love for the first time. Annie consented to them going out on a date alone after six months.

Melvin

The date that both of them had been looking forward to for so long, did not turn out the way that either of them had planned. Melvin was taking her to meet his sister. They had stopped by the pool hall first, and she had two glasses of wine.

The weather was nice and they had a leisurely walk. When they got there she was admiring the house, but something was amiss; his sister was not home.

Melvin gathered Helen into his arms and started kissing her ardently. It was really nice to be in his arms and the feather-soft feel of his lips turned more insistent as his tongue probed her mouth. His hands felt really good as they slowly massaged her shoulders and then the small of her back.

Somewhere in the middle of all this passion, Helen realized that Melvin's hands were touching her bare back. Suddenly, she was acutely aware that he had unzipped her dress, and an alarm went off inside her head.

He gripped her tighter when she tried to pull away. She asked him to stop as she pushed on his shoulders. He did not seem to hear her.

Helen realized that he desired more than just petting, "I'm not ready for this."

Melvin got angry, "I been courting you for six months now. Don't you think it's time for you to show me whether or not you really care for me? If I have to go one more night dreaming and fantasizing about you, I am going to die."

Melvin tried sweet-talking Helen and when that didn't work, he said, "You are just a little girl. If you are going to act this way after all this time then I just won't be around anymore."

She still insisted that she could not do this yet. "I do love you, Melvin. As far as I know, I ain't never courted anyone else, but I know this is not right. What if I get pregnant? We aren't married, and my momma would kill me."

Two years ago her friend Marie's mom had discovered that she was pregnant and had kicked her out of the house. Marie, with no one else to turn had gone to the boy who had gotten her pregnant. Though he had been with her more than five years, and knew she had not been with anyone else, he called her a stupid bitch for letting this happen, and told her that he wanted nothing more to do with her. Annie helped Marie. She took her to Rebi who took her in, gave her a place to stay and helped her find a job. Helen was scared and knew that what Marie had faced would be nothing compared to Annie's anger.

After his attempts to assuage Helen's fears with words and touches didn't work, Melvin got really angry. It was as if he turned into a monster or something. He forced her down onto the bed and tied her hands to the bedpost with one of his silk ties.

Helen cried, tears sliding down her pretty face, and she accepted with resolve the fact that this experience was not going to be any different than the one other terrible time that she had endured sex, "When a man loves you, isn't he supposed to be tender, and want to wait until you are married?"

Melvin did not hear her pleas. At this moment he did not care, he wanted her. For the last two months Melvin had no desire for the other girls he had been with. They were always throwing themselves at him, and he used them just like the tissue that he used to wipe himself off. After he slept with them, he was no longer interested in being around them. He had no desire to talk with them or even look at them after he had released his seed; he just wanted to be rid of them. The feelings and desire he had for Helen were different, and he knew that she was a virgin, unlike most of the others' he had been with.

Melvin looked down into Helen's eyes as he started to undress and something in his stomach knotted up and the strength drained from his loins. He realized that he loved this woman. Not the one-night-stand kind of love he had for the many women who had thrown their favors at him the same way a person threw beads off of a Mardi Gras float... the kind of love that would not let his first time with her be like this.

Melvin untied Helen, dried her tears and sat there and held her in his arms until she was calm. He apologized over and over again. From the mental exhaustion of the evening, combined with the alcohol, they fell asleep in each other's arms.

It was four o'clock in the morning when Helen woke in a panic. She was shaking when Melvin woke and realized she was moving out of his arms. He could not understand what was wrong or why she was crying. He had not done anything. She explained the source of her fear—Annie.

Melvin and Helen walked home as fast as they could. She should have been there four hours ago. He kept trying to tell her that he would explain to her mother, and would not leave until he knew that she would be all right.

When they arrived on her block, Helen begged him not to come in. Images of Annie and her straight razor were going through her mind.

Melvin would not hear of it. He held her hand as they approached the porch where Annie was standing waiting for them with a shotgun.

When Melvin opened his mouth to explain, Annie raised her hand and shotgun at the same time, "I don't really care what happened and you can just turn around, the both of you, cause we got somewhere to go."

"Where Momma?"

Annie looked Melvin in the eye and said, "You were supposed to have my daughter back here four hours ago. If you haven't spoiled her tonight, you should have, because now you are going to marry her."

To both Helen and Annie's surprise, Melvin smiled broadly and started to laugh. Melvin turned to Helen and got down on one knee and took her hand. He reached in his pocket and pulled out a small diamond ring and proposed. He had planned to do this earlier that night but he was so horny, and the way things had gone, he figured he would wait for a better time. So as far as he was concerned, this shotgun wedding worked out just fine.

Annie woke the Judge and Melvin and Helen were married with plenty of time for Annie to get the Judge's breakfast on the table.

Helen And Melvin

After their impromptu wedding and a huge breakfast, Helen and Melvin left the Judge's house.

Melvin promised Helen that they would have a real wedding just as soon as it could be arranged in a church with their families; the white dress and everything.

Helen made a joke about not being able to wear white by then.

They laughed about it on the way back to his house. Melvin figured he had better tell Sadie before she heard about the wedding from someone else. Word spread fast and far in Louisiana and if someone else told Sadie something about her brothers and she wasn't able to say she already knew, they would have hell to pay. Actually it had never happened because they were a really tight family and usually ran everything by her before taking any action.

Sadie was the brain behind the gambling, liquor and bookmaking that they did in the back of the pool hall and she took care of the two properties that were rented out.

When they walked into the house, Helen was so nervous she did not know what to do. She kept wringing her hands as if they were a wet rag. Melvin noticed and took her hand in his, "Sit down and relax. My family is going to love you just as much as I do."

Helen calmed a bit and Melvin went into one of the bedrooms and came out after a minute and went into another one. He came out with his brother following close on his heels. They were both laughing and smiling and when Warren approached her with congratulations and a great, big hug, she knew that Melvin had told the truth, at least as far as this brother was concerned. His sister, Sadie, was a horse of a different color.

When Sadie came out of her room, she did not appear to be happy about being woke out of her sleep. Helen was afraid that Melvin's news did not make it any better. When Melvin introduced Helen as his wife, Sadie's' jaw must have dropped down to her knees. She felt for the couch and lowered herself onto it. All the while, she was staring Helen in the face as if she were a gator that had crawled out of the bayou and was about to eat her.

Helen started wringing her hands again. Thankfully, Melvin sat next to her and put his hands over hers to still them. They sat this way for about two full minutes. Even Melvin started to get a bit worried.

Sadie finally said something, "Do you love him, I mean really love him?"

"Oh yes Ma'am, very much."

"Well that's a good thing because you gon' need that and then some to deal with a Broussard man."

Sadie took her hand, "How far along are you?"

Helen looked puzzled.

"You're pregnant, ain't you?"

"No Ma'am, I'm not pregnant. We ain't done anything like that yet."

Again Sadie's jaw dropped, "You ain't slept with her yet and you married her? Is that true?"

Melvin told her it was true.

Sadie started laughing. "Well I guess there ain't no doubt that he loves you. Smart girl; you know it's hard to sell a cow after you have given the milk away for free. So what are your plans?" Sadie turned to Melvin.

"We are going to stay here until we figure out where we want to live," Melvin said.

"Uh, uh! Boy you a married man now," Sadie went in the room and came back with a set of keys, "The family that was leasing the house on St. Charles Street just moved out last week." She handed the keys to Helen.

She popped Melvin upside his head and said, "Don't think you are not going to have a proper wedding. I'm gonna talk to the Reverend just as soon as services are over."

And so she did. The wedding was scheduled three weeks later.

Helen went into her stash of money that she had been accumulating over the past few years; it was over two thousand dollars. She went into Lafayette to a seamstress she had heard of with a picture of a beautiful bridal gown that she had seen in a magazine years ago and saved. She and the woman looked through samples of fabric until they found one that looked just like the picture. It was to be a beautiful gown. The lady told her she would have it done in time. Gena and her friend Marie were going to be her maids of honor and Marie's daughter would be her flower girl. She picked out all of their dresses and paid the woman to make them.

Helen and Marie went to New Orleans, where she picked out brand new furniture for the cute little two-bedroom house that was now her new home. It was her house and she could not be happier. She spent all her time sewing curtains and turning it into their little love nest.

Melvin could not believe it when he walked into the house and saw all the sparkling new furniture that had been delivered that afternoon. Someone who lived down the street called and told him that there were two big trucks sitting in front of his house. He rushed home to see what was going on. He wondered where she had gotten this kind of money from, but did not feel like he should question her when she said that this was her wedding gift to him.

Helen loved being married and feeling all grown-up. She loved having her man come home to the dinner that she had waiting for him on the table with candles she had made herself, adorned with flowers that she had picked out of the garden that the previous owners had started. She had already added some vegetables and herbs to the garden. The next thing she wanted to do was put in some fruit trees so that whenever they had children, there would be a shady spot in the yard where she could spend her afternoons with her babies.

Every night Helen and Melvin made love. Helen had finally found   out what all the commotion was about. When she experienced her first orgasm, she thought she was dying. She screamed, "Stop, stop Melvin something is wrong."

Melvin knew that this was her first time. He hugged her tightly, looked down into her face and doubled his efforts. He watched the fear, then the pleasure that washed over her body and showed in her eyes like fire. Watching her aroused him so much that he came right along with her.

"What was that?" Helen breathed heavily.

The thought occurred to Melvin that he was the only one to ever make Helen experience *Le Petite Morte,* 'the little death' as they called it. This made him feel like a God. He felt he held such power. When he laughingly explained what she had just enjoyed, she blushed a bright red. He hugged her "I love you so much."

She looked at him and started to ask a question but stopped. He urged her to say what was on her mind. He told her to never be afraid to talk to him, because he didn't ever want her to feel like she had to go and ask someone else about anything.

She looked him in the eye and giggled.

"What is it woman?"

"Can you make it happen again?"

He burst out laughing. Of course he was more than willing to oblige. He could not get enough of her. Her skin so smooth and free of blemish, and her long, soft hair always smelled of the gardenia scented soap that she used. This is what made him rush home every night. He hired someone else to help his brother with the pool hall in the evening and the gambling at night. Some mornings he could not imagine getting out of the bed and leaving her side; some he just didn't.

Since Helen had bled that first night, Melvin took it for granted that she had been a virgin. She did not see any reason to tell him any different. As far as she was concerned, she had never been with another man because Mr. Macklin was something that had happened to someone else.

Melvin never thought it was possible to love someone any more than he did Helen. Her innocence was so refreshing and different compared to the others he had known. He had an overwhelming desire to protect her and keep her safe from all the ugliness that he had seen in the world. She was his and it was going to be that way until the day they died if he had anything to say about it. Lord have mercy on the man who tried to take his Helen away. Just the thought of her leaving him sent him into a panic. He could not control his temper whenever they were out and he spied lust in another man's eyes as they visually devoured her. He had gotten into more than one fight over men trying to speak to

Helen. He knew she loved him, but for some reason his jealous nature always kept him on guard and made him feel insecure.

Melvin had gone to an old voodoo woman and had her to make up a potion to ensure Helen's love for him. He slipped it into her drink one evening. Of course there was no visible difference because it was not humanly possible for her to love him any more deeply than she already did.

Melvin had known this old Guiche woman since he had been born. She was the midwife that his mother had used and had brought all of his siblings into the world. She had also given him a *gris-gris* bag to put under their bed at night for fertility. He wanted her to get pregnant as soon as possible.

Helen

The wedding was wonderful. Helen felt like a princess in a fairy tale. Everyone who was important in her life was there. Only one thing put a damper on the ceremony. When the preacher said, "If anyone here knows of a reason why this marriage should not take place, let him speak now or forever hold your peace."

A woman charged into the isle of the church and said, "He shouldn't be marrying her because I'm pregnant with his baby."

Melvin turned to Helen and said, "One second, let me take care of this."

Melvin went to the woman and told her, "You need to leave and stop embarrassing me. I done told you before that I am not going to marry you."

"You no good dirty…"

Her words trailed off as Sadie grabbed her by the arm, "You heard what my brother said, and I done seen you all over town with a bunch of other men. I don't believe for one second that the baby is his."

Sandra was trying to get her arm out of Sadie's grip as she was hustled towards the door, "Let me go, you bitch. You don't know nothing about me, this is his baby."

"If by some miracle it is, so what? He still ain't gonna marry you."

Sandra made the mistake of taking a swing at Sadie. The door of the church closed and all you could hear was a loud scream. Sadie ducked her swing; growing up with brothers, she knew how to fight. She knocked the girl out cold with two punches.

Sadie walked back into the church, "Ok Father, go ahead."

The ceremony went smooth with no other disturbances.

Helen noticed a white man standing at the back of the church, for some reason she had a really funny feeling, like she knew him. When the ceremony was over she looked for him at the party but he was not there. She had seen Annie talking to him briefly and asked her about him.

"You know who that was? It was your father. Here you are. Willie gave me something to give you." Annie handed her an envelope.

Helen looked inside the envelope full of one hundred dollar bills, "I wish I could have spoken to him."

"For what? He didn't speak to you your entire life. He wanted to buy you and raise you as a white girl. Honey you are black and you better remember that 'cause you can sure believe he does. You didn't see him running around here telling anybody he was your daddy did you?"

As usual, momma was right.

Gena loved standing up at the front of the church. Helen looked so beautiful, and so did the guy who was sitting on the groom's side in the fifth row. He kept waving at her. If her mother wasn't right there in the front row, she would have waved back. But there was always later.

Gena

Helen would take the long way to the store to avoid passing Sandra's house. Sandra had some nerve interrupting her wedding like that. She lived around the corner, four houses from the little neighborhood store.

This day, Helen was in a hurry and hadn't thought about anything but hurrying back to finish dinner before Melvin came home.

Helen had gotten pregnant on that first night, and her stomach was just starting to show. She was five months along and happy about it. She had already started decorating the nursery.

When Helen walked out of the store, she regretted not going the other way. Sandra and her mother were waiting for her, "You know Melvin still comes around here to see me? He was with me last night. You thought he was at the club, but he wasn't. He only married you because he was scared your mother would do something to him since you were pregnant. You ain't no better than me. I hope you know that," Sandra boasted with her hand on her hip.

Helen had taken enough from this whore and the other jealous women who were sick with envy cause Melvin had married her. She could not go anywhere without someone telling her something about her husband and another woman. At that time Melvin was spending so much time and energy on Helen that she knew that it was not physically possible for him to be servicing all of them.

Helen had grown up watching women fight over men and thought it was the stupidest thing in the world. *If a man wants to be with you, he will and you beating up some woman that he may or may not have been screwing ain't gonna make one bit of difference. If they had any good sense at all they would be kicking his ass.*

"Unless he can be in two places at one time, you are a liar, Sandra. He was home with me all night. Warren told Melvin that you were sitting in the club waiting for him to show up, so he decided to come home to me to avoid you. As far as him marrying me because I was pregnant, when Melvin and I got married we hadn't had sex yet. I was a virgin on my wedding day."

Sandra's mother was taking off her shoes while calling Helen foul names and talking about kicking her ass and fucking her face up so bad that Melvin wouldn't want to be with her anymore.

Gena had tired of sitting at the house on her own. Bob was with his father and it did not look like Annie was coming home anytime soon. She decided to go and see Helen.

As she rounded the corner she saw Helen in front of the store. The crazy bitch from the wedding grabbed Helen from behind. An older woman picked up a bottle from the gutter and broke it on the curb.

Gena assessed what was going on and ran up behind the woman grabbing her by the hair. She jerked so hard that she fell on her back. Gena sat on the woman's chest with her knees on her shoulders, her fist went to town on her face.

"Get up off of her Gena! She's knocked out, come on let's go!"

Helen pulled Gena up.

Sandra was lying on the ground, her knees pulled up to her chest whining in pain.

"Good thing I came when I did or that would be you on the ground crying," Gena joked.

"You're probably right," Helen handed her a peppermint stick.

Gena lectured Helen about standing up for herself.

"You just like to fight, that's why you kept getting kicked out of school. When are you going to start acting like a lady?"

"Fighting is a lot more fun than getting beat up like a lady."

It was true. Gena did enjoy a good fight; she did not care who it was: girl, boy, woman, man. She had even fought with one of Annie's boyfriends. She did not understand why her mother sliced anyone for the slightest little thing, yet she would get with men who liked to beat her up, until she got to the point she did not want to be bothered with them anymore, she would take the abuse, and seemed to like it.

Gena could not stand Annie's current boyfriend. His name was Luther and he was a blood-sucking leech. He walked around the house as if he owned it. He did not pay any bills, or buy food. He sat around eating and drinking at Annie's expense, hitting her upside the head at any time for no good reason.

One day he told Gena to fix him something to eat. She looked at him as if he had two heads. Gena and Bob were sitting at the table working on a drawing for school.

Luther was drunk as usual, and walked over to the table and got in Gena's face, "Didn't I tell you to fix me something to eat girl?"

Gena stood up and told him, "I'm not fixing to do nothing for you, you need to get out of my face."

"You need a lesson on how to respect your elders, little girl," Luther started unbuckling his belt.

"You must be fixing to change your pants, 'cause if you going to try and do what I think you gonna try and do with that belt, you are going to be one sorry soul."

Luther lifted the belt with every intention of whipping Gena. She hit him with a hard right on his jaw and came back with an upper cut. He fell to the floor and she grabbed the belt from his hand and started whipping him like he was a two-year-old.

Annie walked in the door and heard all the screaming. She laughed at what she saw.

"Momma, he tried to beat me 'cause I didn't want to fix him nothing to eat."

Annie stood over Luther, "Is that true?"

"Girl ain't got no respect for her elders. You better be glad your mother walked in when she did, 'cause you gone make me hurt you little girl."

"Uh Uh Mister. You the one should be glad I walked in when I did, cause this little girl may not look like much, but she can do some damage." Annie warned.

He charged at Annie who pulled out her straight razor, "I might take a little beating off of you 'cause I was a mind to, but I ain't never gave you leave to put your hands on my children. I think you done just about worn out your welcome here."

Luther was familiar with her reputation. The kids stood up, ready to come to Annie's defense. Luther turned and went in the bedroom and gathered his few belongings. That was the last they saw of him.

Melvin Jr.

Gizelle called Helen one afternoon and told her the baby was coming that night. Melvin and Helen packed a small bag and went to Annie's house. Gizelle and Celeste were already there. Annie could handle the birth herself, but Helen was just as much their daughter as Annie's.

Shortly after their arrival, Helen's water broke. She had seen plenty of babies born and was very calm. She knew exactly what to expect. She pushed out a pretty baby boy with wavy black hair.

They named him Melvin Paul Broussard, Jr.

Gena was an aunt now. She loved little babies.

Bob was excited and told all his friends that he was an uncle.

Two days later, Helen prepared to get back to her own cozy little nest where the nursery was waiting for Melvin Jr. who was a good baby. He rarely ever cried and had a good appetite.

Gena was off work for the next two days and went home with Helen.

Melvin was a proud papa. He had to learn how to hold his son and give him his sugar tit after Helen breastfed him. He was glad that he had a son, that way, the girls that came next would have the protection of their big brother from men like himself.

Melvin had a daughter by a woman, Eunice who lived in Lafayette. Helen met her and the two year old, named Joyce.

Eunice made it a point to let Helen know that she was not after Melvin. Matter-of-fact, she had not even told him about the baby until after she was married her childhood sweetheart. Their relationship was something that happened when her and her man had been going through a rough patch.

Helen and Eunice came to be friends and Joyce spent time with the Broussard family often. She could not fault Melvin for something that happened before her.

Melvin had four other little girls before his marriage to Helen by bitter women who harbored animosity because they were not Mrs. Broussard. Even though he did not tell her about these children that he did not claim, it was not long before she learned of them. In small towns like Lake Charles and Lafayette, Broussard and New Iberia, there was no such thing as a secret. Bad news, trouble and scandal traveled twice as fast as good news. People loved to see others in pain. What do they say? 'Misery loves company.'

It was a good thing that men did not have to pay child support back then, because if they did, Melvin would not have had a dime. Most of the women eventually married other men; all but Sandra.

Gena

Now that Helen was gone, all Annie's attention focused on Gena.

Gena had spoken to her mother about letting her date now that she was fifteen.

Annie was firm on her, "No."

Gena was still a virgin, but was getting curious. All her friends were having sex, and she felt left out.

There was a boy in the neighborhood that had been walking her home until Annie found out and threatened him. He was so scared he would not so much as say hello to her anymore.

Every day, Gena picked Bob up from school. She gave him a snack and helped him with his studies until Annie came home. The neighbors told Annie that they had seen Gena with a boy and she beat her and accused her of having sex. She even checked her to see if her hymen intact. She knew that if she did not keep a close eye out her daughter would not stay that way.

Annie felt Gena was too much like her when she was young. She knew the signs. She had seen her flirting with boys.

Gena felt Annie was being mean, but she was only trying to protect her.

Gena was tired of being the good girl and sick of Annie always accusing her of doing something when she was not. She wanted to live like Helen, in her own house, without her mother always looking over her shoulder. She had been sneaking around with Bruce, the guy she had met at the wedding, for two years now.

Gena told Bruce, that she was ready. He was older by five years. He always brought her candy and magazines. He was so much more mature than the boys that went to her school. He walked her and Bob home several times a week. Sometimes he came in the house and often had to run out the back door to avoid Annie when she came home early.

Some Sundays, Gena would make up an excuse so she would not have to go to church. Annie was gone all day out to Rebi's. She spent the whole day with Bruce. They talked, laughed and never bored of each other. He never tried to do anything more than kiss her.

Bruce had his own apartment behind his parents' house. He was a bellboy at a downtown hotel. He got off work in the early morning and waited down the block until Annie left for church. Gena came out to the car that he borrowed from his father. He wanted to make this a special day. They went to a restaurant for breakfast, then to a matinee at the picture show.

Back in the car Bruce asked Gena, "Do you still want to go through with this? Because if not, it's all right with me. It's not like I'm rushing you or anything. You do know that don't you?"

"It's ok. I'm ready."

They went to his apartment and drank some rum. Gena realized that he was more nervous than she was.

"Gena I have to tell you something. This is my first time."

She did not believe him. He was tall, handsome and had a job.

All these things made him quite a catch. She had assumed he was experienced.

Bruce explained that he had fallen off a horse and was paralyzed when he was twelve. The doctors said he would never walk again. He spent all his time before this last year, at home, with his parents taking care of him. His life was spent between the bed and a wheelchair. He had not been able to feel anything from the waist down until this year, when one day he woke and was able to move his legs. Melvin's brother, Warren had been his best friend before the accident and never stopped coming to visit him. That is how he came to be at the wedding.

"Maybe you're the one who is not really ready?" she said.

He did not say anything for a time, then took her in his arms and kissed her, nothing urgent, just kind of exploring and that was enough for today. It was getting late and she needed to get home.

Bruce was relieved that it had not happened today. He felt like they had gotten much closer. On the way home, they talked about what a future together would be like.

Gena got home before Annie and ate before going to bed to dream about her life with Bruce. He had not actually said anything about getting married yet, but had hinted at it.

Every day that week he picked them up from school. Thursday, he was extra quiet and she could not get two words out of him. When they got into the house she asked, "Bruce what's wrong with you today? Why are you so quiet?"

Bruce sat down at the table. He fumbled in his pocket for an envelope. When he looked up he had tears in his eyes. She read and now she was teary too. It was a draft notice. He was going into the army. They sat and talked for a long time until he had to leave for work. They decided to spend every day they could together before he had to leave in two weeks.

Gena went to see Helen who was now pregnant with her second child. She told her about Bruce. Helen knew that Gena had been seeing him. She also knew that her mother would not approve and knew what Gena was feeling.

"I'll tell mama that I want you to stay with me for a while because Melvin is always working and that I need help with Melvin Jr."

Annie volunteered to stay with Helen herself, then suggested that Helen come stay with her until the baby was born. Helen agreed to return when it was closer to her delivery time. She just wanted Gena around for company and help when she was feeling tired. Annie agreed.

Helen told Gena all about sex. She could not wait to try it, but was scared she would get pregnant. Gena had gone with Annie on several occasions when she was doctoring and remembered her telling a woman that if she put grease inside of herself, it would stop the little swimmers from making it to the eggs. If she did get pregnant, she knew about the tea that would bring your period down.

Bruce quit his job and Gena stayed with him. If Annie came over they would say that Gena had gone to the store. Helen would call Bruce's house and he could run her right over. It was only a few blocks away.

Warren explained everything there was to know about sex to Bruce and gave him an illustrated book.

Gena knew that Bruce was afraid of going into the service. He had never had a fight in his life, but had to do what he had to do. They were like a married couple after a few days. Gena cooked and cleaned.

Their nights were experiencing, experimenting, expressing and learning to move in one motion with each other. Then they slept in each other's arms through the morning until the afternoon sun woke them.

On Saturday, Gena and Bruce went to a concert with Helen and Melvin to see Curley and Joe play the blues. The next week went by fast—too fast. They had agreed not to mention his going away until the day before he had to leave.

Helen, Melvin and Warren went to the bus depot with them to say goodbye. Melvin had gotten a draft notice also. Sadie had been dating one of the recruitment officers who was able to get his report date delayed since he had a pregnant wife.

Gena held back her tears until the bus pulled away.

During the next three weeks, Gena felt tired. She would come home from school and went straight to bed. She woke up in time to clean and prepare dinner before Annie got home. It seemed like every morning she was throwing up and her period never came. She knew she was pregnant.

She received letters from Bruce every week from basic training in Alabama. She missed him something terrible. She decided not tell him that she was pregnant so as not to distract him.

Gena quit school and got a job cleaning house for a family on the prominent side of town. She got no argument from Annie, who thought school was a waste of time for girls anyway.

Bob Jr.

Bob spent most of his time with his father who he adored. He had two little brothers.

Annie either had company or was asleep and he was tired of watching all different men come and go. He did not like any of them, and the ones who tried to be nice, he ignored because they were not going to be around that long. Plus, he had a daddy. He did not understand why she was not married to his father anymore. The church was the most attended in town.

Bob liked his father's new wife. She treated him no different than the two boys she had by his father. They lived in a big house. Each child had their own room, including Bob. Elizabeth was definitely a preacher's wife. Sometimes he wished that Annie was more like her, but she was not, and he loved her anyway, and she him.

Annie adored Bob and never found cause to beat him because she did not feel like she had to protect him the way she did the girls. In her eyes, he could do no wrong.

Charlie

Annie had been seeing a man named Charlie. She liked him well enough and let him and his piano move in. It proved to be a big mistake.

He was a good musician and in demand. He was a sharp dresser and always wore gator shoes and he had a lucky hat that he had been wearing for years. The truth was, it was the one thing his father had left behind when he walked out on his mother and the six children he had given her.

Charlie would play a particular song for Annie every night after dinner before he left for work every night. It was titled, '*When he meets me at the River.*'

Charlie walked Annie to work every morning. When she got off, he would be waiting by the gate. He bragged to his friends that he had to go and pick up his pan girl. They all knew that he had more than one woman around town.

The Judge suggested Annie closed the club. Since prohibition was over and alcohol was now taxable, the government was focused on any illegal establishments.

Charlie had watched Annie carry on for years when he frequented the club. He could not believe that she was his woman now. He was obsessed with the thought of her stepping out on him as she had so many others. Sometimes he took off work and hid in the bushes to see if she left the house or had visitors. So far, the two times she had left, she had gone to deliver a baby and help someone who was sick. He knew it was crazy but he could not control his insecurities.

Charlie sometimes worked out of town, and came back swearing up and down that he knew she had been with someone. They had terrible fights, followed by passionate, angry sex. They were okay as long as he knew where she was every second.

Annie was starting to tire of the routine and resented always having to prove where she had been and with whom. The last couple of times, he had threatened her with his six-inch knife. So hid it, afraid he would use it while drunk.

Bob did not like Charlie at all and told Annie, "I always see him coming out of other women's homes, and I heard him bragging about how he has you under control."

Bob stayed over when they fought to insure his mother's safety.

Lately when Charlie was away he called Annie every night and got no answer. He knew what she was up to. She had been hinting that he should move out.

One day, preoccupied and angry about not being able to reach Annie, he ran into an old woman, knocking the bags out of her hand. He was angry and told the woman, "Watch where the hell you going, you old bitch."

She looked up at him and shook her finger, "You help me pick up my food, young man."

Charlie laughed at her.

She pointed her finger, "You are going to die with your hat and your shoes on."

He spit on the ground and walked away.

Charlie had been away on a gig for two weeks. When he returned in the middle of the day. He was hanging out with some of his friends in front of a bar killing time until he went to get Annie from work.

Several of his buddies told him about Annie in the clubs with some guy. He was angry. He had warned her that he would kill her if she messed around on him. Charlie never let on that he was upset.

They made love and ate dinner, after he called Annie into the front room, "I want you to stand right here and listen to this song, it's gonna be the last thing you hear because when I finish playing this, I'm gonna take this here knife and kill you." He laid another knife on top of the piano, "I know you took my other one but I got me a new one just for you, because I warned you not to be messing around on me." He thought himself justified. She had been with someone else.

Annie knew that Charlie had gotten word about her carrying on. He did not see his infidelities as being cause for her to do the same. She had gone to every club in town with another guy. She wanted him out - she was tired of him and figured going out with someone else would do the trick. She also knew that he was violent and would try to hurt her. That is why she had the knife she had taken in her apron pocket.

Annie let Charlie get almost to the end of the song, and then she took the open knife and stabbed him under the arm puncturing his lung. He could not believe it. Never had it entered his mind that she would defend herself.

Charlie stood up and reached for Annie. She stepped back, just out of his reach. The blood in his chest was rising and coming out of his mouth. He needed help and realized he would not be getting any from her. He shuffled toward the door and opened it. He could not yell out for anyone. He felt like he was drowning.

Bob and Gena were on their way to Annie's when they saw the

man coming down the walkway. He stumbled to the middle of the street and fell down on his face. A man ran out to help him. He felt for a pulse but there was none.

Charlie's hat never did come off his head and his gator shoes were still on his feet. The old woman had been right.

Annie was released when the police determined that it was self-defense. When she walked out of the station, Bob and Gena were waiting for her. She got out of that one because of the Judge, but things like that were not going to happen anymore, because soon afterwards the Judge died; he had a heart attack. He weighed over three hundred pounds and the strain had finally caught up to his heart, which failed.

Annie's house no longer felt comfortable. She decided to move. She felt Charlie's presence and the blood in the floor would not come out. She put the house up for sale, rented the other out. She leased a house a few blocks over.

A Cheating Heart

Helen had another son. His name was Curley, after Melvin's brother. Helen was the perfect wife, homemaker and mother. She stayed home with the kids, took in laundry, and sewing.

Helen was in the attic one day and found pictures of herself that had been used for some sort of Voodoo ritual. She phoned and described the things in detail to Annie, who told her that it was to ensure her love for him. At first, she found it endearing, but the implied accusation was totally unfounded. She never so much as looked at another man.

The only problem was her husband. She did not know what happened, but he had started to stray. It was his way, almost as if he could not help himself, and she did not know how to handle it. Seemed like he always had somewhere to go, or something to do.

People could not wait to tell Helen where and who her husband was dallying with. She was getting tired of his running around, and when she confronted him, of course, Melvin denied everything. He would start arguments over nothing so that he had an excuse to walk out. She was not stupid, she knew exactly what he was up to.

Gena had seen Melvin around town with another woman. She did not like the way he was treating her sister. She told Helen about it, but what could she do? She tried not to let on how much Melvin's cheating ways hurt her, but Gena knew.

One day… Helen waited until he left and asked one of the neighbors to watch the boys. She knew where the woman he was cheating with lived. She was going to see for herself. She decided that if the rumors were true she would confront Melvin and leave him. Looking through the window, low and behold there sat Melvin with the woman on his lap. She was feeding him, and before every mouthful they kissed.

Helen waited for Melvin to come home. She thought about all the women who had called to tell her that they had slept with her husband. Well, if he wanted to run around, he could do it without her in his life.

Someone told her that he had a new child across town. She already knew about Sandra, who had the nerve to name her son Melvin Jr.

Melvin was overbearingly jealous of Helen. Annie had warned her girls that a man who is stepping out will always accuse you of doing the same thing. He knows that he is doing wrong, so his biggest fear is being done wrong.

Melvin sprinkled flour on the front porch so that if disturbed he would know that she had left the house, or someone had been there.

When Melvin came in, he heard Helen's voice in the dark living room, "I know where you went Melvin, and I think you should just go on back there and stay with her. I don't want any man who has to run around on me."

He turned on the light. "What are you talking about? I been down to the pool hall."

She was so mad that she could have hit him over the head. "Melvin, I saw you through the window; don't lie to me."

"You must have seen someone else and thought it was me. If you didn't put your hand on me, then it wasn't me."

She was flabbergasted. How stupid did he think she was?

"I'm leaving you, Melvin. If you won't go, then I'll go."

Melvin hit her.

That night, when he left for the club, she packed their things and headed for Annie's, children in tow.

Before the night was through, Melvin was at the door apologizing and begging her to come back home. She did.

Melvin stopped seeing that particular woman, but there were others knocking on the door professing their love for her wayward husband, most of them angry because he had stopped seeing them.

Helen got to the point that she did not care what Melvin did anymore. She was content with him keeping food on the table and a roof over their heads. She loved him, but she was not going to concern and upset herself with his running around, that was between him and God.

"Most men are that way. It don't mean that they don't love you and the children. They can't help themselves and you can no more stop him from running around than you can stop him from breathing air. Just thank God for the good times, and the others, pray," Annie said.

One day, Melvin's brother Joe saw the black eye and bruises on Helen and it angered him to the point that he fought with Melvin. Warren had to break them up. They tried to talk to him, but he would not listen.

Helen later decided that she was not going to take it anymore and started fighting back. She hit him with everything she could lay her hands on and screamed, "Get the hell out."

When he tried to apologize, she was not going for it.

It took Melvin three weeks to get back into the house and after she finally forgave him, he thought twice about putting his hands on her. He had received a visit from Annie. Although Annie had her theory about men and their running around, she was not going to have this boy beating her daughter and she went to the pool hall and told him so. She showed him a doll fashioned in his likeness.

Melvin knew what Voodoo dolls could do, and he knew better than to tangle with Annie. He promised that he would stop being unfaithful. He loved Helen very much and was afraid that he had come very close to losing her. He was going to try and straighten up and fly right. They both knew that was not going to last long, but at least he would be much more discreet so as not to be caught.

Gena

Helen noticed the way that Gena doted over the new baby, Jerry. There was something personal about it. She also saw how much she was eating lately. "Gena, what is going on with you? Why you getting so fat? I notice your breasts have suddenly gotten huge. Is there something you want to tell me?"

Gena sat down on the bed with the baby and looked at her big sister, "Can you tell?"

Helen looked at her, "Yes, and pretty soon momma will be able to also. What are you gonna do?"

"I want to have this baby, Helen; I can't do anything to hurt this baby, any more than you could do something to Jerry," she started to cry.

Helen got out of the bed and hugged her sister, "Don't worry. Everything is going to turn out all right. I'll help you. If you have to, you can come and live with me."

Little Jerry moved and when Gena reached to touch his cheek, he gripped her little finger.

"See, even Jerry will help take care of you." They laughed.

For the next two months, Gena wore loose fitting clothes so as not to arouse Annie's suspicion. One day Annie was entertaining friends. Gena brought in a plate of chicken and placed it on the table.

Lucy turned to get up and bumped into Gena's stomach, "Girl, you pregnant?"

Annie looked up, snatched Gena's blouse up and realized Lucy was right.

Gena hurried out of the room. She was so scared that she went out the back door and walked down the street. A neighbor was just getting into her car and she ran over and asked for a ride.

"There really isn't anything she can do now, you're too far along. She'll be mad for a minute but what do you think she's gone do? She can't beat you, you're pregnant," Helen held her sister who was shivering with fear.

"You're right, and when she had you she was way younger than I am now," Gena got ready to walk home.

Gena walked in the door and Annie flew at her. She grabbed her by her hair and snatched up her blouse. She was hurt, mad and cursing up a blue streak, "You little heifer, you done went and got your stupid ass pregnant. You didn't have the good sense to tell anybody in time to do nothing about it," she hit her upside the head.

Gena screamed and tried to get away.

"Don't run from me," Annie grabbed her shirt.

Gena lost her balance and fell against the Victrola, hitting her stomach hard. She fell to the floor in pain.

One of the neighbors heard the screaming. When he looked inside the open window and saw what was happening, the man ran into the house and called an ambulance.

Annie was so busy hitting Gena that she had not noticed the blood on the floor, or the neighbor until he grabbed her arm in mid-air,

"Annie, stop it. You're going to kill her, she is bleeding," he pulled her away.

Annie had been drinking with her friends all afternoon. By the time Gena returned, she had worked herself into a frenzy. She had not meant to hurt her like this. She pulled up Gena's skirt. There was a lot of blood, "Oh My Lord what have I done?"

Annie heard the ambulance sirens. Gena was crying from the pain. Annie was afraid Gena and the baby could die. Annie rode to the hospital and stayed by Gena's side while she had the baby. It was a boy; he lived for seventeen minutes.

The woman at the hospital tried to tell Gena that if someone had beat her and caused this child's death she should say so, "That person should go to jail, where they will be for a long time."

Gena would not say anything. Annie heard this and realized that Gena was not going to turn her in, but she also saw that her daughter would not speak to her either. She had never been so sorry in her life as she was at this moment.

The nurse knew that someone had beaten this girl. She had bruises everywhere and the blow to the stomach had burst the placenta that housed the fetus; the baby was too young to survive outside of the womb. Gena stayed in the hospital for but would not say anything when the woman came to her room every day.

Helen and Melvin picked Gena up from the hospital two days later. She did not want to see Annie. Helen told her that she had talked to her, and that she had not meant to do it. She had been disappointed and angry, that is why she lost her temper. She was really sorry. Gena stayed with them until she saved enough money to get her own place. She had experienced enough of Annie's anger to last a lifetime.

Gena was glad she had not told Bruce about the baby, and now that she had lost it, what would be the point? The doctor said she could have more children, and that was just what she planned to do. When Bruce came home he wanted to marry her and she had written him back, telling him that she could not wait to be his wife.

The next time she saw Bruce was at his funeral; he was killed in action.

Jerry

Helen's son, Jerry was another beautiful baby. She was hanging sheets on the clothesline and looked down at the front of her dress and saw the two huge circles of breast milk that had let down. That was strange, usually Jerry cried to be fed before this happened.

Suddenly, a terrible feeling gripped Helen. She ran into the house to Jerry's crib. She picked him up, but he did not wake as he did when she touched him. She tried shaking him and breathing into his tiny mouth. He was dead. He had died in what they call 'A crib death.'

Helen sat down on the floor and started to cry. Melvin Jr. walked into the room and saw her. He went and got Curley who he always did funny stuff to make Mother laugh. All Curley's antics did not move her. Melvin Jr. went next door to get mother's friend.

Dahlia came into the room. "Helen what's the matter?"

"Jerry won't wake up, here you try," Helen got up off the floor and rushed to put the baby in her friend's arms.

Dahlia took Jerry. She looked up at Helen with tearful eyes. She herself had lost a child to crib death, but she had four others to keep her going, and they were her only solace and source of strength at that difficult time. "You have to look after your other children now. Helen, right now you have to think of them and thank God for the time that you had with Jerry and know that He is taking care of him now."

Helen looked at her as if she were insane, "He's not gone, he's just sleep; don't say Jerry's dead." But she knew he was. She reached down in her soul and looked at her two children who were standing there with tears rolling down their faces. Still, she could not understand it. Why did God let her keep this child for almost a year before taking him? Why do little babies have to die? With all the violence in the world, were there not enough grown folks dying every day? She kept on going through her depression. She had her other children to look after, including the one in her womb.

Anna Lee

Helen and Melvin finally had their first girl. She had been born on April 12, 1941. It was a beautiful day in Lake Charles, Louisiana and she was a beautiful child. She was born with a head of snow white hair. It took Helen three days to get up the nerve to attempt to discuss this oddity with Melvin.

Melvin laughed at her obvious dilemma. What apprehension she must have been feeling?

She did not understand why he was laughing until he told her, "When I was born, I had the exact same white hair. He showed her the pictures of himself when he was an infant. He had gotten them from Sadie, wanting to explain to Helen that Anna Lee's hair was not going to stay that color; it would get darker as she got older. They often laughed about this subject during their twenty-one years of marriage.

"Look at that baby. Now you know that ain't none of that niggers' baby." People used to say things like that as soon as they thought Melvin and Helen were out of earshot; they just laughed at their ignorance. Anna Lee had Melvin's features and Helen did not really care what anybody else thought, she knew whose child it was.

Sadie made a remark, "Momma's baby, papa's maybe."

Helen cursed her out that day, which surprised everyone because Helen did not curse. She knew Sadie was in cahoots with Melvin's carrying on with other women and that he often took them to Sadie's house. That told her side that woman's bread was buttered on.

Sadie stood there with the rest of them, her mouth hanging open, "My God, Melvin, you better be careful. Who'd have thought that sweet Lil' Ole' Helen had some curse words in her, and a temper too. This girl got backbone boy. One day she gone catch you wrong and go upside your head. Mark my words," Sadie laughed.

Anna Lee grew and learned fast because she had to keep up with her brothers. She was named for one of the white women that Annie cleaned house for. Helen had known this woman all her life; she was a nice, kind-hearted woman who adored her namesake. As soon as Anna Lee started to walk, she often picked her up to go on outings and visit with friends. Once she took her to a luncheon in a huge mansion just outside of town. Anna Lee was two years old at the time, but she still, to this day can recall the resplendence of the house and the elegant woman whose name she shared.

She bought Anna Lee clothes and pretty patent leather shoes with horse taps. Anna Lee drove everyone crazy with her constant tapping.

Sadie

Sadie had a reputation around town for being a hell raiser. She always gave parties and on the quiet block where she lived, the neighbors did not like it. Too many undesirables. Several times, the sheriff had been called because of the noise. The neighbors put together a petition to get her to move out.

She had always been a good time Sally, or should I say Sadie. She drank a lot and was very high-natured. She went through men like water and there was always some drama around her.

Sadie met a bartender who was not going to put up with her foolishness. His name was Oliver and everyone called him Suk. He made good money and liked to gamble a little bit, his preference being the horse races.

Suk had a relationship with God; he was not a holy roller or anything like that, but he did have moral fiber. He had plans to get out of Louisiana and open his own bar in Los Angeles, California.

Sadie did not understand Suk, but she liked him. He was not going to chase her; he was not going to beat her, he simply wanted to love her and if that was not enough for her, then he would leave her alone, and told her so.

Sadie understood men who wanted to try to beat her into acting right and had no respect for them, she fought back and often times won, but she understood them. She understood the men who followed her around and spied on her to see what she was doing. She did not like them either and as soon as they caught her she simply told them it was over.

Oliver Rogers was a whole different story. They had been dating for over a year now and he warned Sadie several times, "If you want to be with me you gone have to change your behavior." One day Suk walked into her house, as usual there was a house full of people. Sadie was on top of the table dancing with her skirt pulled up and her blouse unbuttoned. He decided then and there that he was through talkin' and busy walkin'. She saw the look of pure disgust on his face and it panicked her. He shook his head, turned around and walked out the door. She ran after him.

Sadie caught up to Suk and grabbed him by the arm, "Wait a tic, where are you going? I was just having a little fun; don't be salty with me."

Suk turned and looked at her, "You are not the kind of woman that I want to be with. I don't want anything to do with a woman like you. Ain't you got no pride in yourself woman?"

Sadie started to say something, "Don't waste your breath," he shook her off and walked away.

Sadie went back into the house and got good and drunk. The sheriff showed up because one of the neighbors had called to complain about the noise and they walked in on a huge fight. Men and women both were swinging.

Come Monday Sadie received a visit from town dignitaries who wanted her to move. They did not just want her off the block; they wanted her out of the town. They threatened to make life difficult if she did not take their lucrative offer.

The offer was a good one, but she hated to leave this house. It was part of her parent's legacy to her and her brothers. On the other hand, if they wanted to pay her twice the value for the house, she was going to take it. After all, she did not really have a choice. She took the offer and divided it up among her brothers.

Sadie was heartbroken over Suk, and Louisiana was fast losing its appeal. He had told her, "I want you to be a better person, I love you for what you can be; not for what's between your pretty legs like most men." No one had ever told her anything like that before. He was not wrong for wanting to be with someone he could be proud of and he had given her that chance, but like a fool, had not taken him serious. Maybe, just maybe, he would be willing to give her one more chance. She had to find out.

Sadie found out where Suk was from Joe, who had moved to California right after getting out of the military, "Come visit; you know you are welcome to stay with me, but I don't think you're going to need to."

Sadie bought herself a train ticket and headed for California. She stood in the doorway of Suk's club. He could not believe his eyes. He had missed her. He acted as if he was not happy to see her but he was.

They were married two days later.

Johnny

One day Annie was coming up her walkway and was surprised to see a man sitting on the front porch swing.

Lucy, who lived next door, saw Annie coming down the street and ran over to meet her at the gate, "Girl, I came over here and tried to wake that fool up, but he is out cold."

Lucy rattled on nonstop as Annie examined the man sitting with his head slumped over and a jacket on his lap, then she noticed blood dripping onto the porch, "Lucy, shut-up. He ain't drunk, he's hurt. Now help me get him inside."

They got him to the backroom, "Get some rags and warm water so I can clean him up and find out where the bleeding is coming from." Annie removed his shoes and turned her back to him so she could struggle his pant legs.

Lucy walked in and dropped the bowl, spilling water on the floor, "My God, I ain't never seen one that big."

"What is wrong with you?" Annie asked as she finally got his pants off.

Lucy was standing there with her hand over her chest looking as if she was going to have a heart attack.

Annie turned around to see what the problem was. The man's penis reached damn near to his knees and he did not even have a hard on.

"Whoa," Annie stood there for a few moments admiring and paying homage. When he groaned she remembered what she was supposed to be doing, "Girl will you go on and get some more water and get up the water you spilled before you ruin my new floor."

Annie discovered a bullet wound high up on the pelvis. One inch over and he would have lost his blessing - the bullet had stopped at the bone. She dug it out. It had not hit any major veins, so she cleaned and stitched the wound. She made a poultice with crushed garlic, honey, clove, horse balm soaked in liquor and aloe.

Annie made him a ginger and chamomile tea and added a lot of whiskey; she spooned it into his mouth. He never woke up. She checked on him often through the night.

The next day, he opened his eyes briefly while she spooned him chicken broth loaded with garlic and onion. The fever finally broke that evening.

Lucy came over, "I found out what happened to him. He was caught climbing out of Sacha's window. Her husband came home unexpectedly. He didn't get out of there fast enough and got shot."

"Boy, that Sacha always was a hot number, wasn't she?"

"Not anymore, girl her husband Cliff lost it. After he went chasing after this one and couldn't find him, he went back home. I guess Cliff figured he had taken her cheatin' one too many times. Sacha is in the hospital. She had to have stitches where he took a straight razor to her face. It's a shame 'cause she was such a pretty woman,"

Cliff had loved Sacha from the day he had seen her fifteen years ago walking down the street. She was twenty years old, high yellow with brown hair down to her waist and light gray eyes. She was recently divorced.

Cliff was a red-boned, half Indian man with a mild-manner, except when it came to Sacha, who loved to play around. She loved Cliff, but liked a little variety. She found his jealousy amusing. Well that was all over now; he had sliced her beautiful face so badly that it took over a hundred stitches to close the wounds. She was not going to be having too many admirers.

The funny thing was, after Cliff cut her, Sacha started feeling some respect for him and realized how much he loved her.

Cliff gained a confidence about himself. He did not see the horrible scars on her face when he looked at her. In his mind's eye, she was as beautiful as the day he met her.

Finally, Johnny opened his eyes. He had heard them talking about Sacha. Shame, he thought. She had picked him up in the park. During the two weeks he had been in town, he had many women trying to get him into bed. He knew that easy women came with some kind of foolishness and usually a husband. He had no problem turning them down… until Sacha. They were just about to have sex for the third time when he heard the front door open. He grabbed his clothes and was high-tailing' it out the window. Sacha had gone into the front room to try to delay Cliff, but one look at her hair and the sweat between her breasts told him all he needed to know. He retrieved his gun from the bureau drawer in the front room and ran for the bedroom.

Cliff knew he had shot the man because he saw the blood, but when he went outside he could not find him. Johnny was hiding under the porch. He lay there for what seemed a long time. He heard Sacha scream. He assumed her husband was beating her. He did not understand men who beat their wives, or women who liked to get beat. If he had known that he was cutting her he would have gone back in and tried to stop him. He stayed put until he heard a car start up and drive away.

Johnny climbed out from his hiding place. A nosy woman who lived across the street had seen him. She came out to tell him about Annie and gave him directions. She also told him "Get yourself patched up and come on back and visit me." She had seen the whole thing from the time he had gone into the house with Sacha. He cut through some yards and found the house. No one answered Annie's door. Suddenly he felt very weak. The next thing he knew he was waking up listening to Lucy and Annie talk about Sacha.

Johnny tried to rise up and felt a sharp pain. He fell back to sleep, waking when Annie pulled back the covers to bathe him. She had a gentle touch. As she bathed between his legs, his nature started to rise. She worked her way down his legs to his feet and when she looked up, he and his penis were wide-awake. "Hi, my name is Johnny. You Annie?" he asked.

"Yes," she said while trying not to stare at his member. She busied herself bathing his chest so that she could turn her back to it.

"How long have I been here?"

"Three days now, but you are going to be all right. You are lucky that you didn't lose that toy that got you in all this trouble. The bullet just barely missed it."

"I know I owe you. How much?"

"You just concentrate on getting better." Annie went to the kitchen and fixed him some soup.

Johnny was thirty-seven years old. He was here from California visiting family. They talked well into the night, and then his eyelids started drooping. She realized he was still weak. She checked his wound and gave him some tea and a stiff drink. He was asleep within minutes.

Johnny called his family and told them where he was. He did not mention what happened to him.

Annie wasn't able to get the blood out of his pants, so she gave him a pair of Bob's.

The next morning Johnny was up and out of the bed and limped up behind her, "The food smells good and so do you."

She turned the fire off under the food and followed him to the bed. Even with his wound, he was good. She had to get on top after he had brought her to orgasm because she could see that the pain had come back. She rode him until she finally felt his spasms. They fell asleep.

Annie got up and finished cooking their breakfast of sausage, cheese grits, diced potatoes with onion and bell peppers and a pot of tea. She brought it on a tray, and Johnny ate with relish.

"Cooking this good is hard to come by. Where's your man?"

"I don't have one."

"You do now." Johnny said.

They stayed together for more than a year.

Cliff never did see Johnny's face, so when they walked past him on the street, he and Annie looked at each other and laughed.

One day Helen, Melvin and their three children were visiting Annie, whose house backed up to a creek that fingered through the neighborhood.

There was, and Gena was crossing a little, narrow bridge at a low point. Just as she was getting to the other side, she heard something beneath her, looked down and saw a wide mouth filled with dozens of razor sharp teeth. She started running and the alligator took off after her. She never knew gators could move so fast.

Everyone was in Annie's backyard when they heard Gena screaming for all she was worth. She ran right past them and stormed in the back door, "Get in the house. Get in the house," she warned.

Following her instruction, they all plowed into the back door.

They saw the gator. Curley pointed his little finger and said, "Doggie." Helen scooped the kids and put them on the table.

Annie got her pistol and went outside where the menacing creature was waiting in front of the stairs to the back door. She shot in the air but the gator did not move. "Gena, what have you done to this gator to make him sit here and wait for you?"

Melvin joked with Gena, "He come a- courtin' Aunt Gena," Melvin said to the boys.

Melvin Jr. chimed in, "He wants to take you on a date. He told me to tell you come to dinner; he's serving Aunt Gena." Everyone laughed.

Finally after he did not move, Annie shot the gator in the head. That evening they sat outside laughing at Gena as they dined on barbecued gator.

The next week Bob was gifted a horse for his birthday from his father. Johnny had grown up with horses and noticed the saddle was not on properly. He taught the boy everything there was to know about taking care of a horse. He was showing the boy how to clean the hooves when Bob asked him point blank, "What do you want with my momma?"

"To do whatever I can to make her happy; she saved my life."

"You plan on beating her?" Bob asked.

"There ain't no reason on this earth for a man to hit a woman. I hope you remember that when you are a man."

Melvin

Because of the war, sugar, flour, tobacco, gas, shoes and meat were hard to come by. These things were rationed with tickets that were received every month. There was a serious recession and people were going hungry. The Broussard's were doing all right, but they had to be careful with their money.

The Broussard family was a sight to see on their many outings. They did not have a car, so their mode of transportation was a bicycle. Melvin sat on the seat, Helen on the handlebars holding Anna Lee, and Melvin Jr. and Curley were on the little seat over the back tire. It was a hilarious sight, but they got where they were going.

Just when they had gotten past Melvin's infidelities, and Jerry's death and their marriage was going smoothly, Melvin got a draft notice. This time he had to go. It did not matter that he had a wife and three kids.

Helen received letters from him and she wrote constantly. Neither of them wrote very well, but they understood one another's letters. He was gone for a year and a half and they missed him something terrible. It was rare that he would get leave and when he did, it was not enough time for him to go to Louisiana from California where he was stationed.

Melvin told Helen, "I hate being in the military, but what can I do, I have to serve my country in order to keep things safe for my family." He missed his friends and family, not to mention the fact that he did not like getting up at five o'clock in the morning to do drills. He could not stomach the bland food and sorely missed Helen's good cooking. He was not that good at following orders, and the sergeant did not like him.

Melvin and his friends slept on Sadie's floor while on weekend leave. She put the bug in his ear about moving to California, "Why not? Joe is already here, Warren and his wife are coming. There ain't nothing left in Louisiana for the Broussard family."

Melvin was somehow injured. It was suspected that he had shot himself in the foot, whether by accident or intent no one ever knew. He was in the hospital for a few weeks, then was allowed to go home for a visit. He was on crutches, but enjoyed his time with his family and dreaded the day when he would have to go back and finish his tour. While home he spoke of nothing but moving to California and told Helen all about Central Avenue and the hot Jazz musicians he had seen; Bird, Lady Day, Louis Armstrong.

Helen Heads For California

Melvin's last letter came with money, his discharge date and instructions for her to pack up everything, rent out the house and bring the kids to live in California.

Helen took their furniture and stored some in Annie's vacant room and at Gena's until they found a place to live and send for what she needed. She bought tickets on the train and boarded with her little family.

All the Broussard boys were migrating to be with their sister whose description of Los Angeles had them all raring to leave Louisiana.

The kids were excited. Anna Lee was three, Curley just turned four, and Melvin was five. The train was full of soldiers, traveling to their families or back to duty.

Helen was still a looker with a good figure. All who spoke to her hoped that maybe the children's father had died in the war or she had dumped him. Even when she told them that she was happily married, they sat and talked to her about their families and girlfriends. They bought the children goodies and played games with them. The trip was quite entertaining.

At every stop, men got on and vied for Helen's attention and the kids made new friends. The children were disappointed when the train pulled into Los Angeles Grand Central station. It was their first time traveling.

They stepped into the ornate building with all the people bustling about. Helen barely keep the children under control and instructed them to hold hands.

Suk and Sadie came down to pick them up. The kids were happy to see their aunt who they had missed over the last couple of years.

Helen was told that the California streets were paved with gold. She soon found out that the only gold was in the jewelry stores. She was going to need jobs to survive in this expensive city.

They stayed in the same building with Sadie and Suk in South Central Los Angeles. The apartment consisted of one bedroom, a living room and a bathroom. There were three other occupied apartments in the building and a community kitchen.

Helen had a lot of respect for Sadie's man because it took a special person to love Sadie, just as it took a special person to love Melvin.

Suk thought Helen to be a saint. Sadie and Melvin were both cut from the same bit of cloth. Many a night they sat and talked, in an attempt to reinforce one another's spirit when their spouses pushed them to the brink of giving up. The bottom line that they had to remember, was that after all the people their spouses had experimented with, it was them who they chose to marry in the end. They never let themselves forget that God must have a plan, and that through prayer one day these people would change.

Oliver Rogers

Suk's bar on Central Avenue was right, smack dab in the middle of all the happenings. Sadie was anything but a typical housewife. Not to say she did not love her some Suk, but every now and then she got a little restless.

One morning Anna Lee was talking to Uncle Suk as they walked out the back door. They had been living here for a year now and she loved spending time with Uncle Suk whom she adored. From this spot if you looked out you could see onto the patio next to the kitchen. Anna Lee saw a cloudy expression on her uncle's face and looked down to see what was making him angry. Aunt Sadie was sitting on some man's lap, they were kissing and hugging like there was no tomorrow.

Anna Lee not knowing what to do started talking loud.

Sadie heard her and looked up just in time to see Suk's back disappear into their apartment. She ran up the stairs rushing past Anna Lee into the bedroom where she found Suk throwing his clothes into a suitcase.

Anna Lee sat in the living room. She heard the raised voices and from what her young mind could comprehend, Aunt Sadie did not want Uncle Suk to leave. She heard her Aunt Sadie telling him that she loved him and that he could not leave her like this. Obviously, this was not enough to convince him. The next thing she heard was a loud bang that sounded like a car backfiring. When the door opened she saw Suk lying on the floor groaning and holding his foot. Aunt Sadie had shot him.

Suk was determined that he was going to leave Sadie because he was not putting up with this foolishness. Being a bartender none of her little escapades got by him, someone always knew someone who had seen something that Sadie had done. She had the nerve to shoot him when she was caught dead wrong. Well, she had pushed him to the limit this time. This was not what he wanted in his life. He wanted someone he could trust and love.

Sadie stayed with Suk in the hospital and even though he would not speak one word to her, she would not leave his side. She tried to explain herself to him, "I have been so wild for so long, when my parents died I was still in my teens with no one to teach me all those mother/daughter things. I started doing stuff to block out the pain of losing my parents. Sleeping around, drinking and fighting are things I do to get out of myself sometimes. Even though I go to church every Sunday without fail, sometimes it seems like the devil just gets into me."

When Suk finally turned and looked at her she found the nerve to continue, "The only time in my life that I feel like I have half a chance to fight this devil and not let him take over is when I am with you, Oliver Rogers; my strong, sweet husband who deserves maybe more than I'm capable of giving, but I am going to try, if you just give me one more chance. Oliver you are my Savior and without you and God, I will die."

Suk listened, but he would not comment. It took Helen to tell him that now was not the time to give up on Sadie. He was the only man that she had ever expressed love for. If he thought her behavior improper, he was right, but change is definitely coming about because of love and prayer, "You give up on her now, you may as well throw her to the dogs."

When Suk and Sadie home it seemed like they were always kissing and hugging. He never saw, or heard of her messing around again. They were steeped in their post-shooting honeymoon.

They never took an interest in getting a car and rode the bus everywhere. If the bus could not get them there, they had friends who were only too eager to give them a ride, because if you were with the Rogers, a good time was guaranteed.

On Suk's days off they enjoyed taking the bus downtown to the courthouse to sit in on trials. After that they had a restaurant lunch before spending the rest of the day at the racetrack. They never spent more than they could afford, and loved the excitement of their money sitting on a horse's nose. One day Sadie picked a winner and won four thousand dollars. She took the entire amount and put it on a little two bedroom house on San Pedro Avenue. It was the cutest, neatest little place you ever wanted to see. Sadie spent all her time and energy decorating and redecorating.

Anna Lee

Melvin finished his stint in the military and found a good job downtown cleaning offices with Sadie. Since the shooting, they had been invited to leave the building. "Undesirable by Association" is what the owner said. Helen found them another place to live, if that is what you could call it. It was a back porch. It was tight, but Helen was able to make it habitable; actually, it was quite comfortable. Helen had the porch set up with the children's bed on one end, dressers in the center on each side of the kitchen door. She and Melvin slept on the other end behind a sheet.

During the 1940's, times were hard for everyone with the war and all. It was a depression. Many people with large homes had fallen on hard times and rented rooms out to keep up with the mortgage. The kids loved it on the back porch of the huge house. It was right next to the kitchen and since someone was always cooking, it was quite warm.

The house was elegant. The living room was huge and furnished in elaborate gold carved furniture, a baby grand piano, and the heavy fringed, damask draperies.

Every chance the kids got, they snuck into the main house. In the entire year they lived there, Anna Lee never once got a chance to go up the mahogany staircase. The closest she got was peeking up when someone opened a door.

The tenants were a varied bunch, a married couple, an old woman, one single man, and two single women who lived in the upstairs bedrooms.

The two ladies were really beautiful and well dressed. Anna Lee held them in awe. Every chance she got, she watch them. Their fashions and mannerisms were something that she swore she would emulate when she grew up. The problem was, they never paid her any attention.

Every Sunday they took Melvin and Curley to church. They even bought the boys suits so that everyone could ooh and ah about how handsome they looked.

Each Sunday Anna Lee hoped this would be the day that they would take her too, but it never happened. She cried to Helen about it sometimes, but she just said "Don't worry, we'll do something fun together." Even though she enjoyed the time alone with her mother, she still could not help getting her hopes up every Sunday.

Helen had another son that year. He was named Charles Anthony Broussard and called Butch.

The Projects

Helen put in an application for the Projects on Crosus Street in Watts. The new development was government property and rent was adjusted to your salary. They were approved for the courtyard building with a huge, park-like area in the center of four sets of buildings that housed eight apartments. One side was two-story apartments, and the other side, single levels. Their apartment had a huge kitchen and dining room behind a big living room, with three bedrooms upstairs. They grew vegetable and flower gardens in their backyard.

They were a close knit community, like one big happy family. There were the black-boned Gibson's, called that, because they were so dark-skinned, they had five girls. The Kings - Marie and Harry with one boy and one girl. The Woods - Helen and Ray with two boys and two girls. The Lewis's - Doll and James with their eight grandchildren; six boys and two girls. The Holly's - Woodrow and Verteen, who hoped to one day have children. The Howard's, - Larry and Esther with two girls and The Williams, - John and Jenna, with four girls.

They moved in the week of Anna Lee's birthday. Sadie and Suk came over to visit that Saturday. Suk was always good to the kids and visited often. He would play ball and tell them stories for hours. He and Sadie did not have children and he always said, "You are my kids."

On Anna Lee's birthday, he gave her a whole dollar and told her to go down to the corner store and buy as many all-day suckers as she could. When she came back, Suk gave her a handful of them and started passing the rest out to the neighborhood children. The word was out that a man was giving away suckers. Kids came from everywhere. He gave Anna Lee a five-dollar bill. "Get whatever you want and two dollars' worth of all-day suckers."

Anna Lee was a hit because he told everyone in the neighborhood that the suckers were for her birthday. From that day on she had friends for life.

All the parents looked out for one another's children. You could not do something wrong and not have everyone know it by the time you got home. The neighbors had no problem with beating your butt before sending you home to get another whipping. It brings to mind the phrase, "It takes a village to raise a child."

During the summer, the kids would walk around to the five and dime store where Uncle Buddy's daughter, Carolyn worked at the food counter. She would save the popcorn from the bottom of the machine for them. She would have it set aside for them when they came along with a cold drink. Anna Lee looked up to Carolyn, she was so pretty and had a job, and a boyfriend.

Anna Lee did not like Mr. Williams. He was always beating up his wife and kids. Melvin bought a B. B. gun for the boys and taught them how to use it. Anna Lee was mad because she always asked him for lessons and he would say, "Girls don't need to know how to shoot." One day she got hold of the gun. Everyone else was outside playing. She took the gun and got in the window looking for something to shoot. She spied Mr. William's brand new black Cadillac convertible and pointed the gun and shot. This resulted in several little cracks in the window of the car.

There was a knock at the door and Anna Lee answered it. Mr. Williams was standing there. "Ms. Lewis and her son told me they saw you shooting that gun at my car."

"Uh, Uh, I ain't been shooting no gun; a lot of people around here have B.B. guns, they can't say it was me," Anna Lee lied.

"First of all, young lady, I didn't say it was a B.B. gun, and second you are holding the gun in your hand behind your back right now." he took it from her hand, "I'll be back here when your parents come home, young lady."

Anna Lee was dreading every moment. She sat on the couch and willed the clock to stop ticking; she knew she was in big trouble. Mr. Williams was sitting in his car waiting. When she went to the window to see if he had gone inside, he had not. He was showing her mother his cracked window shield.

Anna Lee ran upstairs to her parent's room and found a spot in the back of the closet and covered herself up with the long dresses like Curley did when he was trying to hide from a punishment. She forgot that they always found him. She remembered just as mother pulled the clothes from in front of her. All she saw was the belt and knew by Helen's face that she should not even try to lie. She got the worst whipping ever that day. She lay in her bed and cried herself to sleep. She had been sleep for about an hour when she heard her father yelling, "I don't go to work to have to bring money home and pay for somebody else's goddamn car window because that child thinks she's Wyatt Earp. That window is going to cost me more than a whole day's pay." The door flew in and so did Melvin. He grabbed Anna Lee up by her ankle and held her upside down while he whipped her with a belt.

She did not even get out of the bed the next day.

Saturday, all the kids all met in the center courtyard and played ball, which she loved to do. Everyone knew that she had gotten whipped and what for and she was embarrassed. She stayed in the house the whole weekend. Sunday she played sick so she would not have to go to church.

Finally, on Monday afternoon when Anna Lee went to meet the girls that she walked to school with at the gate, they all patted her on the back. She did not understand at first. Even the Williams' girls were telling her what a great thing she had done by shooting out Mr. William's window, and how they wished they had the nerve to do something so bold.

The school was a fifteen minute walk down 102nd Street. Anna Lee attended the afternoon session and the boys went in the morning. One day the girls were gathering to walk home as they did every day. They had one route that they were supposed to take. Walk down the street on the same side as the school until you came to the stop sign and then cross the street all together.

Anna Lee had a Déjà vu thing happening that day. As they walked out of the gate she saw a man sitting in his car and somehow knew something was wrong. "Let's cross the street right here you guys. The man in that car is going to try to do something bad to us. For real ya'll, he is up to no good."

Nobody questioned her; they had all grown up with families that knew not to ignore their intuition.

The girls crossed the street in the middle of the block, even though they knew they could get in trouble for it.

The man jumped out of his car,. "Hey you, little girls, look what I have for you. Come here would ya." He held up a bag that looked like it was from the candy store.

They all looked at each other and without a word to one another walked faster. They had all been warned about the dangers of taking candy from strangers.

He yelled out again, "Look, Look, Look."

They turned around and the man had his coat spread wide open. He was naked as the day he was born.

They started ran screaming all the way home. The girls told their mothers about it. Two fathers followed the girls' home from school every day for two weeks. They were hoping the man would show up; they had something for him.

Butch must have had a tapeworm or something. Every day at dinnertime he would go to everyone in the courtyards house. Of course, when they are feeding their children if he was there, they are going to feed him too. He went from house to house eating dinner.

Helen would be coming in and people would tell her, "I already fed Butch dinner." Sometimes four people would tell her that he had eaten at their house. She got on him about it, but that did not stop him. He never gained any weight. He was able to eat more than anyone else at home. Helen thought he must have a hollow leg or something because she never heard him say the words, "I'm full."

Uncle Joe And Aunt Bessie

The babies just kept on coming for Helen and Melvin; Francis, JoAnn and Jonathan were born while they lived in the projects. JoAnn and Jonathan were born on the same date as Anna Lee.

Helen's breast turned out to be a gold mine. They raised the money that purchased their first house. Rich white women who had a baby and could not, or would not breastfeed because she did not think it was good for her figure, or for whatever reason was not that invested in parenting would pay a wet nurse for their milk.

Helen had more than enough. She also felt that she was helping the child become healthier. Formula babies were sickly. A limousine came to the house three times a day to pick up the milk that she pumped from her breast into sterilized bottles. The twenty-five dollars a week went directly into a bank account that Melvin knew nothing about.

Helen rode to work with neighbors who had helped her get the job at the shipyard at night.

Melvin worked during the day at the steel factory and was home at night to watch the kids. Melvin and Mr. Holly walked to work because they lived so close to the good job. Melvin had a second job cleaning offices during the wee hours of the morning. The kids were asleep by then and Doll who lived next door, would watch out for the kids until Helen got home.

Helen put half of her paycheck from the shipyards into purchasing savings bonds. Melvin was supposed to be doing the same. They had a trunk where they locked up all their valuables. This is where

Melvin was supposed to be putting everything. They were saving to buy their dream house.

When Melvin got laid off from work on his day job and he and Mr. Holly decided to open a shoeshine stand. Of course, they needed money to get it started and guess where it came from?

The little stand they rented was on 103rd Street and Central Avenue. They sold soda, candy, chips and shined shoes. They made pretty good money, but times were tough all over for everyone. If you did not have two jobs, you had better find a hustle, because nothing was guaranteed.

Uncle Joe, as the kids called him, and his girlfriend, whom the kids called Ms. Bessie rented an upstairs bedroom with them. The kids loved this because he was a lot of fun and never walked in the door from work without treats.

Miss Marie and her husband Lawrence also rented out a room at their house. Times were hard and people had to survive the best way they could.

Bessie was a very light-skinned woman with bright red hair. She wore the nicest clothes. Anna Lee would be walking down the street with her Ms. Bessie, who had a figure that would not wait; men would holler and whistle every time. She did not look cheap; she looked poised, like what every woman should aspire to be. Her walk was one of confidence. She had it, and she knew she had it and knew she did not have to flaunt it, either you did or you didn't.

Her expensive clothes and her hair were always to perfection. Every day she wore coordinated outfits, even her underwear matched. One thing that really set it all off was the fact that she wore stockings and garter belts every day, "Something about those straps attached to the top of a woman's stockings made a woman feel sexy inside out, from the top of your head to the tips of your toes, no matter what you got on girl, if you wearing nice underwear it's gon' show in the way you walk and carry yourself," Bessie always said.

Uncle Joe was so jealous of her that he would follow her to the store and half the time get in fights with men who were admiring her. He would tell her, "You need to stop wearing them damn dresses and high heel shoes."

Bessie was a beautician and made good money in one of the most popular shops in town where Helen and Anna Lee got their hair done. Boy, after she finished your hair, you felt like a movie star. She really knew what she was doing. She spent a good portion of her money dressing Uncle Joe in the best suits, shoes, cologne and hats. "Don't my man look and smell good?" she would ask the kids every day before they went out.

Someone was always coming into the beauty shop selling clothes or something. Joe was not shabby about his appearance; he always took a lot of time getting dressed. Anna Lee loved to sit in the bathroom and watch him primp. It seemed like he would gargle forever. She wondered when he was going to stop to breathe. He knew how much this amused her and loved to hear her giggle.

Uncle Joe had gone out cattin' around with Melvin on Saturday night and somehow he was crazy enough to take a picture with a woman sitting on his lap at a nightclub. He had bought the picture home and given it to Melvin to put away so Bessie would not find it. Melvin put it in a cigar box in the top bureau drawer.

To show you what a sense of humor God has, that Wednesday, Bessie was going to wear her red and-white polka dot dress that was made of chiffon and needed a half-slip. She asked Helen if she could borrow one and Helen told her to look in the top drawer.

Helen did not know anything about the picture. Bessie went in the drawer, and being nosy by nature, she opened the cigar box. For a few days, she did not say anything.

The next week, Joe was in the bathroom when Bessie walked in and threw the picture at him.

"Where did you get this?" Joe yelled.

"Don't matter where I got it, why did you do it?"

Helen and the kids could hear the raised voices coming through the door. Then they heard rumbling and crashing that seemed to go on forever.

Helen ran outside to get help. Melvin was coming up the walk with Mr. Holly. "Hurry up, they gone kill each other," Helen screamed.

Melvin and Mr. Holly banged on the locked bathroom door. All they heard was swearing, punching and slapping. They used a screwdriver to get the door open.

Ms. Bessie's shirt had been torn off and she was fighting like a cat, Uncle Joe was in the corner of the tub trying to fend her off.

Melvin and Mr. Holly rushed in and got Uncle Joe and pulled him out of the room. Ms. Bessie was steadily coming after him. The children were standing at the top of the stairs. After things calmed down a bit, Helen told Anna Lee to go in the bathroom and get Ms. Bessie's shoes. Anna Lee came back with her shirt that had been ripped into two pieces, "There weren't any shoes in the bathroom, Mother."

"That's 'cause I didn't wear any," Ms. Bessie said as she packed her bags. She left Uncle Joe that day. She had walked out with two white-and-brown suitcases without as much as a backward glance at Uncle Joe, even though he was begging her not to leave him. "Please baby, baby please don't go," he pleaded.

The next week, Joe moved out. He had rented an apartment further down Central Avenue. A couple of days later, Uncle Joe came to Helen to apologize for his thoughts, "I'm sorry; I thought you had given Bessie the picture. I should have known better."

Mother was stunned. She had never guessed such a thing could even cross his mind. "Now Joe, what would make you think I would ever do something like that? It ain't even got nothing to do with the fact that I don't get in that kind of mess, but I love you, and I love Bessie, and even though you did not have no business out cattin' around and taking pictures of it, I would never do anything to hurt ya'll."

Bessie and Mother had gotten to be good friends and often came by to visit after she moved in with her sister. Mother and Bessie liked to have fun, just as much as Melvin and Joe. Bessie suggested they go out and paint the town.

They were sitting in a club and had just ordered a round of drinks when the darkest man they had ever seen walked into the door. He was even darker than the black-boned Gibson's. He was, "dressed to the nines," as they would say in those days.

Jefferson was shooting the breeze with coworkers from the oil plant. He stood six feet, five inches tall; his moniker was ape, because of his broad flat nose and blue-black skin. Contradictory to his looks, he had never hurt anyone in his entire life. He was as mild-mannered as a kitten.

He turned around to see why all his friends had stopped talking in mid-sentence; their mouths hanging open. He saw the red head walking out of the bathroom. "Ooh Wee, she looks like some Lord have mercy with some good googly woogly on top," he admired aloud.

Jefferson could not help himself. It was as if a magnet was drawing him to her. He knew that he had no chance with a lady that looked like that, but just wanted to hear her voice, even if it was just to hear her say, "Go away you big ugly baboon." He told the waitress that he wanted to send them all a drink.

Mother had called Marie King and Helen Woods who were only too glad to join them. When the waitress brought the drinks to the table and pointed to Jefferson, three of them smiled and lifted their glasses in a salute. Bessie had her back to him and when she turned, stared at him for more than a second. Then a big smile spread across her face.

Jefferson just knew that God decided to let the sun shine in the middle of the night. He had never seen anything so radiant.

"Ooh Wee, Look at big man," Ms. Helen said.

"Yeah he's a big man all right. If what's in his pants is half as big as he is, honey you better run the other way," Ms. Marie said. They all started laughing and making jokes about his appearance.

"Well, I like the way he looks and I'm going over to thank him for the drinks," Bessie said.

Every jaw at the table dropped as they watched her rise up,

She appeared to be moving in slow motion as Jefferson took in every step, movement and muscle. Her ample hips, tiny waist and full breasts had him captivated. He stood rooted to the spot. His friends started adjusting their clothes and wracked their brains for a line that would stop this woman.

"She either has a weak bladder, or she's coming this way so I can talk to her. She just went to the bathroom," Reg said. He was so full of himself. He was the best looking guy in the club. He was Indian and black and had long straight black hair pulled back in a ponytail that hung down his back. Women found his high cheekbones and dimples irresistible and he just knew that she was going to be his next conquest.

"What this? Naw," he did not realize he was speaking out loud, but he could not believe his eyes.

Bessie approached Jefferson and reached way up to put her hand on his shoulder. "Thank you for the drinks; that was very kind of you. I hope I'm not out of line for coming over here like this, but I wanted to thank you personally."

Not that anyone could tell, but Jefferson was blushing from his head that was holding up his mohair hat to his white size fourteen, Stacy Adams shoes that were under his tailor-made pen-striped suit. He did not know what to say, "Uh, uh, uh," was all that came out of his mouth. Stanley hit him on the back to try to loosen his tongue.

"You're very welcome," Jefferson said. He was looking down at the floor, smiling from ear to ear.

Bessie lifted Jefferson's chin so she could look in his warm gentle eyes, "If you like, you can join us or what would be even better is if you and I can sit somewhere together," she blushed and giggled. "I don't even know if I was the reason that you sent the drinks; maybe I'm being too forward here," she turned as if to walk away.

Jefferson reached out and grabbed her arm. "It was for you," He stood up.

She turned, "Excuse me?" She liked the fact that he towered over her. She envisioned herself in his arms. She imagined it would be a secure fatherly feeling.

"They were because of you." Jefferson said.

"I don't understand," Bessie said.

"The drinks, I sent them over because of you." He took her arm and led her to a booth toward the back of the club. Everyone in the place stared at Bessie and Jefferson. It was that way for the rest of their married lives, because they stayed together until he died fifty years later at the age of eighty-four.

Mother Buys A Car

Helen was so tired of taking the Red Car; it was what they called the streetcar. They had to ride it everywhere unless someone with a car was willing to take them. She bought a car from the man down the street and he agreed to teach her how to drive. She was motoring around in no time. After a few more lessons they went down and got her driver's license.

Melvin was proud of Helen. They piled the family in for drives every weekend. They went visiting, had picnics and went to the beach. The car opened up a whole new way of life for them.

Helen kept asking Melvin to let her teach him how to drive, but for some reason he kept saying no.

One Sunday after church Melvin had given the kids a quarter. In those days a quarter paid for admission, popcorn, candy and a drink. Just about every kid in Watts went to the movies on Sunday. This week they were running Tarzan.

Wednesday night Helen left to pick up Melvin from work and bring him home to eat and change clothes before going to his night job.

While she was gone, Melvin Jr. got out of bed. He had a great idea. He took a long rope and somehow fastened it to the light fixture in the ceiling of the living room. He took the rope and went to the stairs and swung himself off, "Aah aah aah ahh yay," he hollered as he swung on the rope.

Anna Lee and Curley heard him and got out of bed. He swung back to the stairs and landed in front of Anna Lee. "I Tarzan, you Jane," he handed her the rope.

She swung to one side of the room and back again. "That was fun."

Then it was Curley's turn. He was swinging back to the other side of the room, "Don't stop, Curley, keep swinging," Melvin Jr. yelled. He jumped onto the rope with Curley. As they swung back towards the stairs the light fixture came out of the ceiling and crashed to the floor.

"Uh, oh," they all said at the same time.

Helen had cut several slices of bologna from a long roll wrapped in red plastic. She was going to prepare sandwiches for Melvin to take to work. Melvin Jr. went to the refrigerator and opened it. He gave Anna Lee a slice, took one for himself, and gave Curley one. Curley loved food more than anything. As they ate he told them, "Curley you are gonna have to take the fall for this one ok? You just say you did it and next time something happens, one of us will take the blame. Don't make sense for all of us to get a whipping, does it?" Then he held out another slice to and when Curley reached for it, he pulled it back, "Ok?"

Curley said "Ok" as he grasped the bologna. When Mother and Melvin walked in the door, they hit the ceiling.

"Who the hell did this?" Melvin asked. Curley took the blame and the whipping. He never did squeal.

The next week, Anna Lee was upstairs when she heard a crash. Mother had a big china doll that she had since she was a little girl. They all had heard the story of how Gena's father, Horace, had given her the doll at the Louisiana fair.

Mother was at a fair the same day Grandma Annie had brought him home to meet her. While walking around, Helen had noticed a booth filled with china dolls. Annie and Horace were sitting on a bench talking and Helen slipped through the crowd back to the booth. She stood there gazing so intensely that she did not hear them calling her name.

Horace found her and picked her up, "We have been looking for you little girl." he said. "Baby, you see something you want?"

She looked up at him and did not say anything because she did not really know him and her mother always said, "Don't take anything from someone you don't know." She looked to her mother, hoping she would say it was all right; she wanted that doll so badly. When Annie nodded her head, Helen pointed to a small little China doll. He told the man, "Give us that one and the one behind it that looks like the mother." The doll was almost as big as she was.

After that, Helen started talking to Horace and as far as Helen was concerned, Horace was the only father she had ever had. When he died, the dolls were the only things that she had left of him. She had taken good care of them all these years.

Melvin Jr. and Curley had been throwing the doll back and forth as if it were a ball, when Melvin Jr. dropped it. The face broke into five pieces. When Anna Lee came down, Melvin Jr. told her, "Anna Lee, you gonna have to take the blame for this one, ok?" Anna Lee looked at him and nodded.

When Helen and Melvin came home, Anna Lee took the blame, but when Melvin took off his belt, before he could start spanking her, she yelled out, "Daddy, I didn't do it."

The belt hung in midair as she explained. "I just said that 'cause Melvin Jr. told me to," Anna Lee said. She never thought that her father would really give her a spanking and since she did not do it, so she was not going along with the plan.

Melvin knew his little girl; she had always been his favorite and always would be. He knew when she was lying. He spanked her on the butt with his hand. "That's for telling me you did it in the first place."

Melvin Jr. got whipped and when it was over and his parents were not looking, he told Anna Lee, "I'm gonna beat you up for squealing on me." Anna Lee ran to her daddy and told him what Melvin Jr. said.

He got another whipping.

Helen did not look up at Melvin as she kneeled down on the floor with tears rolling down her face, "If you knew how to drive, I could quit leaving them alone in the middle of the night and I would still have my doll that Horace gave me."

Melvin hated to see her crying like this. She was right. It did not make sense for her to have to go out in the middle of the night. He was a man. If she could drive, so could he. "This weekend you can teach me how to drive, ok." he knelt down and took her hand, "Go on and wash that pretty face of yours, I'll get this up."

Melvin gingerly put the pieces in a bag. He knew what that doll represented to her. Having lost his parents at a young age, he knew how important these things could be; he still had the dice that his father had used while teaching him to shoot craps when he was only six years old. The reason he had refused every time she offered to teach him was because his parents had been killed in a car accident.

True to his word, Saturday morning the family piled into the car for Melvin's driving lesson. Melvin just could not seem to get the hang of shifting the gears and using the clutch at the same time. Helen was being very patient with him, but for some reason that frustrated him even more. "That's enough for today." They went home.

The next day was no better. Melvin got so frustrated that he jumped out of the car in the middle of the street and left the whole family sitting there.

"Who does she think she is? Just 'cause she can drive and I can't. She's making me look stupid in front of my kids," he muttered to himself as he walked down the street.

Helen was so angry with Melvin that she was having a conversation of her own, "That stupid fool could have killed us all getting out the car like that and leaving us sitting there in all that traffic," At their front door, she turned to the children, "Kids, go over to Aunt Doll's house until I tell you to come back."

Everyone could hear the argument through the walls. Then they could hear the fighting through the walls. "What in the world is going on over there?" Aunt Doll's husband, James asked. After the children explained what had happened he went next door and without knocking, he let himself in.

James had to stifle a laugh. Helen had Melvin pinned up against the wall and was holding a vase which she had every intention of hitting him over the head with. He noticed bruises on her arm as he came up behind her and took the vase out of her hand, while moving between the two, "Come on Melvin. Take a walk with me so I can talk to you."

When Melvin did not move, James grabbed him by the arm and, led him to the front door. Once outside, James picked up a six-pack of beer that he had left on the porch. He opened and handed Melvin a can of beer, "Follow me boy, we gonna have you driving in no time," he said.

The two men walked over to his Buick and he let the hood up. "The first thing you need to know is how a car operates." He explained every part and purpose before they got into the car.

James drove to a vacant lot on Central Avenue. Within two

hours, Melvin and James had polished off the six-pack, along with two more besides while Melvin drove them around.

Helen was standing at the sink washing dishes when Melvin walked up behind her and wrapped his arms around her waist, "I'm sorry," he took her hands out of the water and picked up a towel to dry them off before leading her to the dining room table.

"What do you want Melvin? I'm busy, I still have to fix dinner."

"Hush, woman and look in the package."

She had not noticed it in the chair. She tore the paper away. Tears formed in her eyes as she examined her doll. She marveled at the workmanship. There was no way that the naked eye could ever discern that it had ever been broken.

Helen opened the china cabinet and placed the doll right in the center and this time, she took the keys from the top drawer and locked it. She placed the keys in an envelope on top of the cabinet so that the children would not be able to get their hands on them. She turned into Melvin's arms and they just held each other for a good, long while.

Melvin saw the kids on the stairs over Helen's shoulder, "Troops, fall in. Helen, bring the car keys; don't worry about cooking dinner tonight."

They climbed into the car. Melvin drove them to Stops Hamburger Drive-In. They ate hot dogs, burgers and fries and washed it down with strawberry shakes as he drove them around.

Though Helen was glad to see Melvin driving, it had been three hours and she was ready to go home, "Melvin it's time to take these kids home, they're all asleep in the backseat and they have to go to school in the morning."

"Ok, sugar, just a little while longer, it's not like they ain't getting their sleep."

Helen fell asleep herself and when she woke looked at her watch.

She could not believe it had been two hours since she had last asked him to take them home, "Take me home right now, you driving fool." They laughed.

Vacation At The Beach

The Broussard family was going to take their first vacation, they were going to spend a week at the beach. Things had slowed down on Melvin's job and he was laid off. Helen had vacation time coming from her jobs. The children were off for summer vacation. Now that they had the car, there was nothing to stop them.

Helen borrowed camping gear from one of her clients. They had a huge tent, a propane cook stove, fishing poles, sleeping bags, coolers, pots and pans and a first-aid kit.

The kids decided to practice setting up the tent when Helen told them it was in the car. They decided to sleep in it that night and when asked Helen said, "I don't see why not."

The neighborhood kids were soon begging their parents to let them sleep outside too. They fashioned tents out of blankets held together with clothes pins over the clothes lines and held them down at the bottom with bricks.

Everyone had a good time that night. George, who lived behind them, was a butcher at the meat market on Imperial Avenue. He brought meat home and sold it to the residents of the projects. They wrote down their orders on Thursdays. Friday was payday for every household in the projects. George and his Jewish boss filled the trunk of his car with the orders, loading in extra cuts of meat just in case.

George delivered, and as he collected the money, he was to pocket the funds until he had the equivalent of his weekly salary. The rest he put in an envelope and on Monday morning the boss would split the profits, giving him a third of everything he had sold.

The women fired up their grills and stoves and prepared the slabs of ribs, hotdogs, hotlinks, chicken and steaks. Ms. Helen left her job at the neighborhood store with two big bags of corn, potatoes, and bread.

The men made a liquor store run. The parents were outside socializing, drinking, dancing and playing cards long after the kids had fallen asleep. Friday night was always fun in the projects. Most of the residents had two whole days off before Monday morning when they had to return to their jobs.

First light Saturday morning, Melvin got a phone call. He had was called back to work. He had to be willing to work nights, weekends and over the holidays. He could not afford to turn down the work. Those who declined were never called back, or at the very least, their names went to the bottom of the list. The company was having hard times and they remembered the employees who were loyal.

The kids started to whine. Helen said, "One monkey don't stop no show, what are y'all crying for, we still going."

They loaded up the car and headed for Long Beach. They found a spot and set up camp a few yards away from a man who had built a hut out of bamboo and canvas against the face of the tall mountain cliff.

Before long, the kids had befriended Mr. Smith. Once a year. He left his wife, kids and company to get away for a few weeks. He took time out from his hiatus to teach the kids to fish. They returned with a rope strung through the mouths and gills of the fish.

Helen insisted Mr. Smith join them for dinner, which turned out to be quite a feast. Nothing tastes like a fish you have caught, scaled and gutted yourself.

Mr. Smith went scuba diving daily and bought back lobsters and crabs. He taught the children to dig clams out of the sand, and pry muscles from the rocks. They laughed as they watched him eat the slimy, snotty looking raw substance right out of the shell. Helen fried theirs in cornmeal in a cast-iron skillet on the butane stove. The children collected shells and Mr. Smith showed them how to make necklaces, bracelets and wind chimes by boring holes and stringing them together with fishing line. They made hats to shield their faces from the sun by weaving strips of palm trees together. Every day was an adventure. Mr. Smith's time with the kids gave Helen a chance to catch up on her sleep. The days flew by much too fast.

Melvin surprised them the day before they were scheduled to leave by coming down to spend the night with them. The kids pulled him over to Mr. Smith's hut, all the while praising all the great things he had taught them. Melvin was polite. He thanked the man, but when he got back to the tent, he was angry, "What is that man doing playing with my kids?"

"Melvin, you being stupid, he's just a nice old man," Helen said.

"I wanted to be the one to teach them all that stuff."

"But you couldn't because you weren't here, were you Melvin? Besides what do you know about making jewelry and straw hats? There is no one else out here camping and I thought it would be safer with someone else close by. Now, can we just enjoy our last night on the beach, please?"

Melvin spent the next day swimming and fishing with the kids. He was having such a good time that he announced over dinner that they could stay a couple more nights. Helen protested about getting back to work, "In the morning, we will drive to a phone and you and I will call in sick, simple as that. What are we working so hard for if not to be able to take out a little time to be a family? Don't argue with me, woman." As if she really would. She and the children laughed.

Melvin asked Mr. Smith to keep an eye on the sleeping children so he and Helen took a nice, romantic, moon lit walk down the beach. That was the night Joann was conceived.

Two days later, at first light, the kids complained as they were forced to pack up to go home. Helen and Melvin were due at work in less than three hours. The kids ran off to say goodbye and help Mr. Smith tear down his hut. He too was heading back to the real world.

Melvin climbed the stairs and opened the trunk of the car to discover it was full of bamboo and canvas. Melvin Jr. and Curley had decided they were going to keep Mr. Smith's hut materials to build their own house at the projects. They started crying when Melvin made them replace it with their borrowed camping supplies. They hid the bamboo and canvas in a small cave they had discovered.

When the family arrived home, Melvin Jr. and Curley went to their little cigar boxes where they kept the money that they had saved from pulling weeds and washing cars. They both had close to ten dollars. They told some of the neighborhood boys about their week on the beach and that they had decided to go back there to live. They wanted to go too.

The remainder of the afternoon, the boys put a plan together. The next morning, when their parents had left for work, they met at the gate with pillowcases full of what they thought they would need to survive. They looked like a band of miniature vagabonds with their pillowcases tied on sticks and fishing poles.

One of the boys swore that he remembered how to take the red car to the beach because he had been many times with his family. They made it to the beach and marched down the steps. Melvin Jr. and Curley supervised while the others worked at reconstructing Mr. Smith's hut.

They played in the water all morning and fished for their dinner all afternoon. They prepared the fish on sticks over a small fire. Soon after dark they were worn out and sleeping. Everything was going great until they woke to thunder and lightning. Soon, rain was pouring in through the collapsed canvas. Within minutes, the hut was in broken pieces blowing down the beach into the raging surf.

The boys ran to the cave but it was soon filled with water and they were forced back out on the beach. The stairs that led up to the highway had been destroyed by lightning.

There was so much water coming down the hill that they did not know which way to go. The tide was getting closer to them and they knew that before long the water would be too high. They huddled together, terrified.

That evening, the projects were in an uproar. Worried parents did not have a clue as to where the eight little boys could be. On her return from work, Helen found the neighbors congregated outside talking. After listening to them, she rushed home to see if Melvin Jr. and Curley were there.

Helen questioned Anna Lee who told her, "They went to the beach to live." Helen took Anna Lee outside. The parents loaded into four cars and headed for the beach. They were worried, because when the weather was rainy, the water at the beach sometimes rose up to meet the mountain cliff. They drove as fast as they could, but it was slow going because this was a serious storm.

The boys were so happy to see flashlights at the top of the cliff. They whooped and hollered. Soon, they saw two sets of headlights coming down the beach. The boys ran toward the cars before they realized it was their parents. For a moment, they all thought about running the other way into the surf. They would have preferred to take their chances with the ocean rather than face their parents, but it was too late.

Melvin Jr. Gives A Party

Melvin Jr.'s moniker was Crickett because he was so short. He was in the fifth grade and was eleven years old. Somehow, he was the president of a club called the Black Swans that had members who were as old as seventeen.

Helen and Melvin were going to a dance that coming Saturday night, and Melvin Jr. decided it would be a perfect opportunity to have a party. He told everyone that when they saw the porch light come on that was the signal the coast was clear.

The house was packed full of people. Melvin Jr. made a big pot of Kool-Aid and someone poured liquor in it. There were so many people that they were spilling out of the house. The music was blasting and everyone was having a good time. Anna Lee was standing there looking up at all these people. She told Melvin Jr., "Ooh you gon' git' a whipping." He asked her to make some snacks, but she was not having any parts of it.

Melvin and Helen picked up Verna and Warren and decided they were not dressy enough after seeing their attire. When they turned into their parking lot, they saw all the kids on the lawn and wondered what was going on. No one had mentioned a party to them.

Doll had been burning up the phone lines calling the parents of the kids she saw going into the house. She told them to "Come and get yo' kids; they over here at the Broussard's acting like little hoodlums." She was really glad to see Helen and Melvin coming up the walk. "This is gonna put the icing on the cake," she told Daddy James as she went out to meet them. The other parents were standing outside, getting ready to go in and get their children who knew they did not have any business being in there.

Doll and James met Helen and Melvin on the walk. "You didn't tell nobody you was having a party. You guys are either really brave or really crazy having all 'dem kids in your house, and believe you me, some of them don't look like kids," Doll said.

"Doll, what are you talking about a party? We ain't having no party," Helen said.

"You could have fooled me," Doll waved her hand as if to say, "What's this?"

Melvin took off running to the house and told James to catch the back door. "Make sure they ain't stole nothing." He got to the door and looked around at these kids who were obviously drunk and ransacking his house. Suddenly the lights came on and all you could hear was, "Ya'll get the hell out of my house." Melvin roared.

Kids were running out the front and back doors like ants, only to run right smack dab into their parents—some standing there with belts and extension cords.

You never heard so many kids pleading their cases. "Please don't whip me. I just came to see what was going on. I came to get my brother out of there." None of the excuses did them any good. For the next month, the projects were quiet. All the kids were on punishment.

Melvin Jr. got the beating of his life, and was grounded forever; but he remained the youngest President in the history of the Black Swans gang until he stepped down when they moved out of the projects.

Hillford Avenue

It was 1950 and Helen finally had saved enough money for a down payment on a house. She found a brand new house in the city of Compton on Hillford Street. She had filled out all the papers and the bank had approved the loan. The only thing left to do was take in the down payment. She went to the chest where the savings bonds were. She could not believe that she was actually about to do this. For years, she had looked forward to and dreamt about this day. For eight years, she and Melvin had faithfully put half of their checks into this box in the form of savings bonds and now they were going to buy a house of their own; be property owners, she thought, as she unlocked the chest.

WHERE THE HELL WERE THE SAVINGS BONDS??

She went to Melvin's job. "Melvin, where are the savings bonds? The man at the bank is waiting for me."

"Ain't they in the chest?" he stalled while trying to come up with an explanation.

"No, Melvin, they are not in the chest and if you don't know where they are then I am going to call the police so that they can find them."

"Helen, just hold on until I get home and we'll talk about this then. Don't go getting all worked up and calling no police. Everything is going to be all right; I promise."

Helen smelled a rat. She had an account that he knew nothing about and had been socking money away for years. She signed the papers and took Melvin's name off everything. If he wanted his name on the new house, he would have to pay. What she wanted to know was where were her savings bonds that represented her blood, sweat, and tears over the last twelve years.

When Melvin came home, the tension over dinner was so thick you could slice it with a knife. Helen had not even picked up her knife and fork. The kids were already finishing up and dressed for bed, so that was not going to buy him any time.

Helen told them "Go and watch television 'til time for bed."

They knew something was going on and knew to move when told.

The Broussard's were the first in the projects to have a television. One of Helen's employers gave her their old one. When they first got it, there were not many channels available; only fights and sports. Now they had a variety of shows that the kids watched every night before bed.

Before Helen could start fussing, Melvin handed her some money. It was not enough to cover the down payment, but it was close. "When I was laid off from work, every now and then I would take one of the bonds and cash them for pocket money. I had planned to put them back."

Helen was furious. "How did you cash my savings bonds with my name on them, I'd like to know?"

"Well I kind of got Sadie to do it."

"So you and Sadie stole my money and you never bought any savings bonds with your paycheck, am I right?"

"It wasn't like that Helen."

"Then just what was it like Melvin; give me one good reason why I shouldn't put that sister of yours in jail? Or why I can't get the house that I have worked for and dreamed about all these years? You want to explain that to me Melvin Paul Broussard? You can't can you?"

"Helen, I will get the rest of the money; don't worry," he pleaded.

Melvin did not realize that Helen was not worried one bit; he, on the other hand, should be. She told him in no uncertain terms, "If you don't come up with every cent of my money; when it comes time to move, you won't be joining us."

The bank manager had a soft spot for Helen. She had told him all about the savings bonds. "I tell you what I'm going to do; I am going to push your loan through with whatever you can afford to give me right now and when your husband comes in with the rest of the money for the loan, we will put the funds into your private account and he'll never know a thing."

By the next week, Melvin miraculously came up with the balance and they moved in as planned. Helen loved having her own home. Every spare moment was spent painting, planting, sewing and decorating. Her clients were happy for her and gave her house warming gifts. A big truck pulled up in front of the house on Hillford Avenue. All the nosy neighbors came out and oohed and aahed for a good while. A huge custom-built Cherrywood dinette set arrived. It was a true work of art and Helen cherished it for years.

Alice Morehouse, Helen's employer of six years, redecorated as often as some folks changed their underwear and had sent the China cabinet and dining room table and chairs as a housewarming gift.

Helen called to thank her, "We are just so proud of you, I'm going to have to drive down and see your new home; you, my dear, are a credit to your race."

Helen ignored the patronizing remark, she knew Alice didn't know any better and meant no harm, "You come by anytime you want, Ms. Alice, we would welcome a visit from you. Call and let me know when you are coming so I can cook something nice for you."

The next day, Alice surprised them with a visit. Her tune suddenly changed. It disturbed her to see that Helen's brand spanking new house was bigger and nicer than the one she lived in.

When Helen finished work the next week, Alice gave her a check and said, "We will no longer be in need of your services."

Helen did not care. People were always looking for a good cleaning woman. When she got into her car, Mr. Morehouse came running down the drive, waving for her to wait. "Don't mind my wife; I am very proud of you and your accomplishments - she's just jealous. I want to thank you for the many years you have served us." He placed an envelope in her hand. She thanked him and headed home. When she parked in her garage, she picked up the envelope. She smiled as she counted out two hundred dollars.

Tonsils

Within a month, Helen's house was a home. The four bedrooms, large living room, kitchen, dining room and bathroom were just what they needed. She had painted each of the children's rooms in cheery colors. She made curtains, comforters and pillows, they even had matching pajamas.

"Melvin you gon' get rings on my table. I declare, anyone would think you can't see those coasters sitting right under your nose." Helen chastised.

"Well if I can't sit my glass on the table, where can I put it? Sometimes I think you love this Furniture more than you do me."

She retorted, "Huh, only sometime?"

It was not long before Helen found another job. The Steinman's, a Jewish doctor and his wife, had a three-story house in the Wilshire district. She had called saying that she could not come in until her husband was home from work after three o'clock in the afternoon. Two of the kids were sick with sore throats; it seemed that when one came down sick, it had a domino effect.

The doctor asked Helen, "Are your children getting a lot of sore throats and colds?"

"Lately yes; it's as if I can't get them over it."

"You should consider having their tonsils removed. If you like, I can examine them and do the procedure myself. It can be done in one day."

The next week, Helen put all the children in the car and headed for General Hospital. They took them in one at a time, about half an hour apart. While the last child was in surgery, Helen drove back home and with the help of some neighbors took all the furniture out of the living room and lined all their beds along both walls. "This way, I can sleep in here right alongside my chittlin's; I know they are going to be calling for me all night."

Helen went to the grocery store and picked up every flavor of Jell-O they had, along with several gallons of ice cream. She bought some board games and cards to keep them occupied while convalescing. When Helen brought the children home, they were still loopy from the anesthesia. She and a neighbor carried them inside and put them to bed. Helen took the opportunity to nap herself. When she woke, they were still asleep, but she knew that would not last long. She went in the kitchen to prepare bowls of Jell-O for each of them. She lined the Jell-O up on the counter and taking one bowl at a time, she placed two scoops of each flavor of Jell-O and two scoops of ice cream. She placed the bowls in the children's red Ryder wagon and pulled the bowls into the living room, while blowing one of their kazoos.

The pain in their throats was a small price to pay for all the ice cream and Jell-O you could eat.

"Mom, it looks like a hospital in here," Melvin Jr. said.

"Yeah," said JoAnn. "We can play hospital and I'll be the nurse."

"Nope, what y'all gon' do is get yourselves into these pajamas.

I'll be the nurse, and whoever gives me the least trouble will be my assistant tomorrow," Helen said.

They lay in the bed for a week and had a good time watching television and playing games. Even after they were feeling better, they faked sick for another few days to get out of school. Helen knew what they were up to, but was really enjoying herself. She planned to take full advantage of this rare opportunity to spend time with her children.

Gena Comes To California

By the time all the children were of school age, Anna Lee was old enough to help out. Helen started working for the movie studios as a maid. They assigned her to actresses who were in town temporarily for filming. She cooked and cleaned at the leased homes. They all fell in love with her thorough work and good food. Many tried to get her to go back home with them. "I appreciate your offer, but I got babies and family here," she explained. Whenever they were in town they requested her. She always received a generous tip or an expensive gift.

Christmas was a special time for the Broussard family, Helen made sure of that. Each child had plenty of gifts that Helen had sewn, knit or crocheted. The children were given money to shop for one another's gifts.

They always rode up to the mountains to the tree farm the day after Thanksgiving. They rode home singing carols, with the tree tied to the top of the car. They strung popcorn and cranberries, and the kids made all kinds of ornaments. They had a contest for the best angel, the winner getting the place of honor on the top of the tree. The rest adorned the end tables.

Helen and Melvin had been living in the house on Hillford Avenue for two years when Gena came from Louisiana and moved in with them, along with her seven children: Poopie, a very mature eight- year old; Donnie, six; Jr. Boy, five; Jeanann, four; Virginia, three; Pat, two; and Clarence, who was not yet one. Gena was not well physically and could not work due to an accident that injured her back.

Caring for the children fell on Poopie and Anna Lee's shoulders. For months, they prepared breakfast and sack lunches after getting the kid's ready for school. After school they came home to make dinner and get the kids ready for bed. Gena took care of the little ones while they were gone and that took all of her energy.

Melvin and Gena always fought. Melvin felt that if he and his wife could work two jobs each, Gena should get off her butt and find one. "Gena is not well, Melvin," Helen said.

He was not buying it. There was always tension between them and Helen was forced to mediate.

Sometimes Gena would do things like leave the cloth diapers in Melvin's way, knowing that this was one of his pet peeves. She liked getting him riled up. She did not like him because he was not as good as he could have been to her sister.

Annie's House

Annie loved her little one bedroom house in Watts that her brother, Buddy had found for her. There was a little store across the street owned by a Chinaman.

Buddy lived right down the street from her. He had a gigantic two-story house, twelve children and a wife. They had a huge back yard, full of chickens and ducks. They also had a huge turtle that the kids rode on.

Buddy had walked into Annie's club one night ten years ago and found his long lost sister. He had advanced on his job through the years and was now a ticket master. His friend Hank, who was head porter, always talked about a speakeasy he frequented.

"There's a joint that is always jumping, I'm going to take you there tonight if you ain't too tired." They would be staying with his relatives. The train had pulled in at noon. They had three days off and planned to take full advantage of them.

Hank borrowed his sister's car after they changed clothes. "Let's go paint the town red." They were sharp as a tack in their suits and hats.

Buddy walked into the club and knew he was going to have a good time; the place was rocking with music drifting from upstairs. The atmosphere was charged with electricity, and the aroma coming from the kitchen reminded them that they had not eaten.

"Man I'm going to sit down at this table and have a big plate of that down home Louisiana cookin' I smell up in here; ooh wee it takes me home," Buddy beckoned the waitress to their table.

Hank watched the waitress butt as it retreated to the kitchen with their food orders, "I'm going to get with one of them sweet, sexy ladies that work out of the house next door."

"My wife is all the woman I need. The only thing I'm going to get with is them dice," Buddy said trying to get a closer look at one of the women who came out of the kitchen. There was something very familiar about the short, little woman who was running around overseeing everything with such efficiency that he had to admire her.

Someone called out "Annie." Buddies heart skipped a beat. Could God be this good? He looked in her face as she walked past their table. There was no mistaking his mother's features. He followed her to the kitchen.

Annie moved quickly around the room as she prepared plates. When she noticed the man standing in the doorway, without looking up she said, "The waitress will take your order; go on back to your table and I'll send her over."

"Lil' Annie," Buddy stepped into the light.

She stopped cold; there was only one person who had ever called her that. Could it be? She turned toward the voice of her youth and looked closely. She could not believe her eyes - other than some gray hair and a little weight, he had not changed in twenty years.

"Buddy is that you?" she screamed.

He nodded and spread his arms wide.

She let out a holler and flew into his arms, jumping up and wrapping her legs around his waist as she had done when she was a little girl. They held each other tightly for a long time, tears streaming down their faces.

"I hadn't heard nuthin' about you. I didn't know where to find you when Momma and Daddy died. I thought I ain't had no kin left in this world, but my kids and their children, but looky here," Annie cried and held onto him as if she was scared he would vanish as mysteriously as he had come.

"I came back to look for you and everyone said that you left town when Ma and Pa died. They said you didn't want nuthin' to do with the land. No one knew where you were." Buddy squeezed her as tightly as she did him. His family.

"I had to leave; that old overseer told me that I would have to work the land to pay off their debt and he came every night trying to make me do things. He told me I had to see to his needs or I would end up swingin' from a tree. I couldn't take it no more, I packed a bag and left."

Everyone was jammed into the doorway trying to find out what all the commotion was about.

"This here is my big brother, Buddy. I ain't see'd him nigh onto twenty years. I thought he was dead, but here he is."

Everyone made him feel welcome.

Annie fixed him and his friend a big bowl of Gumbo and as they finished off three helpings, he told her all about his job, wife, kids and the big house in California. They went upstairs to the club where they drank and danced the night away. Hank gambled for a while and then went next door to spend some time with the girls.

Buddy helped her clean when the club closed. They sat on Annie's bed and talked. He leaned up against the headboard and she nuzzled against him as she had done when they were children sleeping on a cornhusk mattress. This was the first time she had felt safe since Horace had left her. They fell asleep, both having lightened their burdens by sharing the good and the bad.

Around noon, Bob Jr. let himself in. He looked suspiciously at the man who was sitting in the kitchen drinking coffee, "When you finish your coffee, you can let yourself out. My momma likes to wake up alone if you know what I mean."

Buddy jumped out of his chair laughing and grabbed Bob in a bear hug, "So you're Bob, huh? Big boy ain't you? I'm your Uncle Buddy boy." Bob did not know what this crazy man was talking about.

He wrestled himself free and ran into the bedroom, "Momma, who is that fool in the kitchen?"

"Bob, that's my brother Buddy; your uncle I been telling you about all these years. He came in last night." She smiled and went back to sleep.

Bob walked back in the kitchen and this time returned the hug from his uncle. Buddy fixed them some breakfast and they talked for hours. He liked his uncle. Buddy went next door and borrowed the car keys from Hank. Bob was taking him to meet his nieces and their broods.

When they got to Helen's, she knew who Buddy was because Annie had called her before day in the morning all excited about him finding her after all these years. Gena arrived shortly after to meet her newfound, long lost uncle, who sat in a chair bouncing Melvin Jr. and Curley on his knees while Jerry slept in the crib next to him. He stayed until dark.

Buddy went back to Annie's. His friend was talking to Annie while she cooked. He was stuffing his face with fried catfish and potato chunks. Hank went to spend some time with his sister and Buddy stayed with Annie.

Buddy was proud of his little sister and told her so. He visited often over the next few years. She closed the club and he helped her move into her new house. After the judge died she really had nothing to keep her busy.

Every time Buddy left, he made California sound so good that she found herself contemplating moving. The last time Buddy visited, he was not happy with what he found. Annie's physical condition was not good. She could not have weighed more than ninety pounds and her complexion was sallow.

He spoke with Lucy who lived next door, "Buddy you got to help her. She drinks all the time now; she's not happy. She hardly ever eats. Since the girls moved to California and she closed the club, it's like she ain't got nothing to live for. You know she's sick and she won't see a doctor."

If Annie had not been so stubborn, he would have packed her up and brought her home with him that very day.

Bob was visiting his sisters in California. He had gone into the Air Force and could fly whenever he wanted. He had recently come back from overseas and had not gotten to Louisiana yet.

Bob and Uncle Buddy discussed Annie, "She said that she would move here as soon as she sold the house."

Bob looked at him as if he had lost his ever-loving mind, "What are you talking about? She don't own that house; she's renting it."

"Damn it; she done bamboozled me."

The next day, Bob put in for military leave. The day after that he was en route to Lafayette. He had to fight back tears when he saw his mother. Annie was as thin as a rail; alcohol and lack of food had taken its toll. Bob immediately started making arrangements.

Bob called Helen and since she was not home, he spoke with

Melvin. "Of course she can stay here. Your mother needs help - that's all there is to it. We'll do our part."

Bob spent a week ignoring Annie's complaints and threats while he packed, sold and gave her furniture away. He sent her clothes to Helen. She fussed through the whole train ride.

Once Annie arrived, Helen insisted she see Dr. Steinman, who told her, "If you keep drinking, you are going to die; I guarantee it." With the help of her children and grandchildren, she stopped drinking and eventually got healthier.

One day, Anna Lee was talking to the other kids, "I'm gonna call my grandmother 'Granny' from now on."

Annie turned around and gave her such a look that Anna Lee felt about two inches tall, "I ain't yo' damn Granny! You can call me Annie or you can call me Grandma, but you do not call me Granny."

Anna Lee ran to her room in tears.

Helen had heard the whole thing. She sat next to Anna Lee on the bed and pulled the crying child into her arms, "Honey, don't take it so hard; your Grandmother's parents were slaves and the word 'Granny' is something that the white folks used to call the older black women. Some words remind people from down South of a time in their lives that wasn't very nice."

Annie swore that she was going to get better so that she could get a place of her own. She stopped drinking and followed the doctor's instructions and between his medicine and her own, it was not long before she was looking like her old self. She liked the fact that she had grandchildren, but dealing with thirteen of them every day, all day, was a whole lot more than she could sign up for.

When Gena moved into her own house, she asked Annie to live with her. Annie found herself working harder than she had on any job. She would get up in the morning and get the children ready for school, do the washing, cleaning, cooking and ironing, plus take care of the toddlers who were not yet old enough for school.

Gena had a new man, Cubie. The two of them would stay up all night watching television since he came in from work in the middle of the night. When it came time to get the children off to school, Gena stayed in the bed. She had eight children and one more on the way.

It was definitely time for Annie to move. Buddy's house was not an option. He had twelve kids whose kids were having babies all over the place. She could not take it anymore. She liked kids and loved her grandchildren, but she had raised her own already and was not going for another round. She needed a place of her own, now, before she went crazy.

Gena

Gena had been a California resident for the required minimum of one year. She was eligible for housing and financial assistance. Helen had thought about signing up herself when she saw how much money she got, but she enjoyed working. "If you ain't doing anything, then you might as well lie down and die," was one of Helen's favorite sayings.

When Gena had packed all their things and was leaving, she turned to Melvin, "There will be chicken-shit growing on these walls before I set foot into this house again Melvin Paul Broussard."

"You promise?" Melvin said.

Gena moved across the street from Green Meadows Park by San Pedro. She had two more children by Cubie, Larry and Terry. He was a bit older than Gena but she loved him.

Gena practiced the Voodoo she had learned from Annie. She had also known another woman who liked the dark side and had taken her lessons well.

Gena had a jealous streak that ran long and deep. She loved Cubie, but even though he loved her, she knew that like most men, he liked to step out every now and then.

One morning they were about to make love and Gena told Cubie, "I want to measure how long your dick is when it's hard."

He thought she was playing another one of her sexual games, so he went along. She took the string and tied a knot in it at the length of his member when it was at its longest and placed it in the nightstand.

Cubie got dressed and went out as he usually did on Friday night. Gena retrieved the string from the drawer. She lit a candle and prayed over the string. Then she tied seven more knots, and tied it around her waist.

Cubie went to a bar that he had frequented for years. "Hey, Shelly, been waiting long, baby?"

"No Sugar, I just got here. I had to wait for Lester to leave on his fishing trip. I was scared for a minute that he wasn't going." They had a few drinks before going back to her house. Shelly was hot as a firecracker. By the time they made it through her front door good, she was out of her clothes. Cubie had been waiting on this night all week long. Not that he did not enjoy Gena, he just needed a little variety every now and then. Cubie had been seeing Shelly every Friday night for two months now. Her husband went fishing every weekend, or so she thought. Actually, he had a woman that he was spending weekends with up in the mountains. Come Sunday, he would go by the lake on his way home and buy fish from some guys he had an arrangement with.

"Baby, are you ready for me?" Shelly asked as she crawled under the covers with Cubie.

"Oh yeah, Sugar." He raised himself over her and prepared to penetrate, but there was nothing to work with. His dick was as limp as a wet noodle. Okay, I can fix this, he thought as he attempted to will his penis to rise.

Shelly tried dancing for him and fixing him strong drinks, but nothing helped. Finally, he gave up and went home.

When Cubie came home, Gena took the string off and placed it back in the drawer. To his amazement, as soon as he climbed in the bed with Gena, his penis rose like a hot air balloon. They made love. He was relieved. Thinking she was asleep, he prayed. "God thank you for restoring my manhood. I praise you for that."

Gena smiled as she listened.

Sadly, after three weeks of the same performance, Shelly found herself someone else to spend her time with.

Cubie told himself that maybe it was Shelly and picked up a woman named Brenda that he knew had eyes for him. When he left her house, her laughter was ringing in his humiliated ears.

Cubie stopped going out on Friday night's altogether. What was the use? He started taking Gena out on Fridays. They would go out to eat and listen to jazz, or go dancing.

Gena liked the way that things had changed and she told him so one day. He smiled and held her closer. Lately, it seemed like Cubie was always talking about what she should do if something were to happen to him. It was as if he planned on going away or something. He spent all his free time with his boys, and though he never paid much attention to the other kids, he did not ignore them, but he did show a preference.

Annie told Helen she wanted a job. Helen had been working for a family called the Sterns for three years cleaning their home twice a week. They had recently opened a motel in the Wilshire district and she recommended Annie for the job at the motel and their home.

Helen cleaned other people's homes by appointment and always had a full schedule, she took Annie to help. When they arrived at the Sterns house, they discussed Annie's employment. Mrs. Sterns had taken ill and was unable to get out of bed. She needed someone full-time. She hoped Annie would consider living in. Of course, Helen could not take the job because of her children.

It would be the perfect job for Annie. She could move out of Gena's and make money doing just what she had always done for the Judge back in Louisiana. Mrs. Sterns agreed to try her out for a few days and see how it worked out.

Mrs. Sterns was feeling worse than usual one day and asked Annie to prepare a roast for dinner. Usually, Mrs. Sterns prepared the meals. Helen would always put the meals she prepared in the oven so that they would be ready by the time Mr. Sterns came home. The couple was so impressed with Annie's cooking, that they proposed she live-in. "Hallelujah," Annie said.

Every other week, Annie had the weekend off. Transportation was a problem though. If Helen was busy, she had no way to get back to Compton and would have to stay at work, which meant Mrs. Sterns would expect her to work. They made other arrangements for someone to pick her up and she would stay with Helen, Gena or Buddy. She was used to having a place of her own and when Buddy found a little house around the corner from him, Annie jumped on it with two feet.

Bob got Annie some furniture. She did not need much and with the money she had saved, she turned her house into a home. Her first weekend off, she and Buddy planted a vegetable, herb and flower garden. She liked fresh everything and swore that no store could produce anything that was even close to what she could grow, "I don't have a green thumb. I got me a green hand," she boasted.

Chester lived across the street from Annie. She did not like him because he was mean to the neighborhood children who ran by with sticks that they clicked on his picket fence and he would have a fit, as if the darn thing would fall down from a little touch. He would come outside cursing them.

Chester always spoke and waved to Annie in an attempt to strike up conversation when she was in her garden.

Every time Annie came home, it was obvious to her that some-one had been in her garden. She was all right with someone helping themselves, because she had more than she could ever eat, but what she did object to was that they seemed to tear it up. No one had to do this much damage to get what they might want; crushed flowers, stepped on tomatoes, herbs uprooted. This was just plain old vandalism.

Annie's neighbors felt it was their duty to tell her that Chester was the one going in her yard. She crossed the street one-day, "Chester, I don't mind you helping yourself to my garden, but from now on try to be more careful or better yet, just ask me or my brother Buddy to get whatever you want."

He started ranting and raving, "I ain't been in your yard. I don't need that stuff you growing. If I want something, I know how to get up and go to the store," he got up and went inside, slamming the door.

Two weeks later she found her garden in the same state and again the neighbors told her it was Chester.

"Why you got to keep tearing up my garden?" she screamed walking across the street. "I told you we would give you whatever ever you wanted. I'm warning you Chester, if you go in my yard one more time you are going to be sorry."

"I done told you once you crazy old bitch, I ain't been in your yard," Chester yelled back.

"Oh, so I'm a bitch now, huh?"

Annie went into her house. When she left to go to work, Bud-dy's oldest son, Train, got the keys from her. Having grown up in this neighborhood, Train knew the people who lived right behind Annie. He let them know that in the evening, he would be going through their backyard to get to Annie's house. They had no objections. That night when Train got off work he climbed the short chain link fence and let himself in the back door. He lay in Annie's bed with his Polaroid camera and waited. A streetlight shined down on the garden. He should be able to get what he needed without using a flash. He was dozing when he heard the gate closing. He snapped off pictures of Chester as he foraged through the garden, filling a paper bag. Then he watched him crush flowers, squish tomatoes and pull-up greens, just making a mess.

The next week Train picked Annie up from work. On the way home, he picked up the incriminating pictures from the developer. Buddy and Train wanted to beat Chester up.

"I will handle this myself, thank you very much."

Annie took one of the pictures and placed it inside a book along with an old-fashioned key tied with a string. She placed the book on the windowsill facing the garden when she left the house. The next week she came back the garden had been totally destroyed. Not one flower, vegetable or fruit was left intact. She took the book and placed it on its side, standing up inside the door facing Chester's house. This was on a Friday night.

Every Sunday that Annie was off, she fixed a big dinner and everyone came over. Helen, Gena and Buddy with their children went outside when they saw lights flashing. They all watched as Chester was brought out of the house and loaded into an ambulance.

Annie went over, the concerned neighbor that she was, "Is Chester going to be all right?"

The paramedics told her, "We are going to do our best for him, Ma'am."

Annie asked, "Can I speak to him before he leaves?"

"Of course," The medic said.

She put her lips right next to his ear, "I told you to stay out of my garden, now look at yourself. Guess I'm not such a stupid old bitch now, am I?"

His eyes bulged and he tried to get off the stretcher to come after her, but the paramedics thought he was having a fit so they gave him a shot.

Helen stopped her when she got back across the street. "Momma, what did you do to that man?"

Annie just gave her a smug look, "Who wants some of my pecan and sweet potato pie?" Then she turned and laughed her way into the house. She was still laughing when she brought the warm pies out and put them on the table.

Chester never did come back home. He ended up in an old folk's home where he spent the rest of his days having his diaper changed and being fed through a straw.

Gena

Things had being going well for Gena and Cubie. She stopped using the string because he never went out never wanted sex. She had known that something was wrong for a long time. He obviously was not feeling well, and was going to the doctor's a lot. He finally told Gena about the cancer. He was hospitalized for two months while they ran tests and tried all kinds of treatments on him, but nothing helped.

The doctors sent him home and told him to try and enjoy himself and relax as much as possible. They gave him bags filled with medications and she had to fight with him to get him to take or eat anything and when he did it was very little and came back up. He drank constantly, even though they told him not to mix liquor with the pills. When Cubie was at home, he stayed in the bed. He was unable to play with his boys.

"I do care about Cubie. I feel so helpless, I don't know what to do for him. I think he needs to be somewhere where they can take care of him and make sure he gets some kind of nourishment. His food always comes up and he can't even go to the bathroom on his own anymore. Frankly Helen, the smell makes me sick. I'm trying to do it on my own but the doctors say that he needs nurses."

Gena wanted Helen to tell her that it was all right to put him in a convalescent home, but she did not say anything. She listened letting her put voice to her concerns. Cubie was almost twenty years Gena's senior. He had a rare form of cancer that they could not do anything about.

Gena spent his last few months going back and forth to the convalescent home where he was being fed through tubes. Most of the time, he was sleeping or incoherent and did not know she was there. It upset the boys that he did not know them. The doctors said that the only thing they could do to make him comfortable was to keep him asleep. He was given painkillers through his IV every three hours.

Butch

Curley and Melvin had to do the yard every week. If the yard wasn't cut and cleaned properly, the boys got the whippings of their lives. One day Butch, whose job it was to pick up all the trash in the yard, had missed a bunch of papers by the back fence.

Melvin was already angry because he and Helen had argued about some people calling and telling her that he was with another woman. The pieces of paper were not even what he was so angry about and he inadvertently took it out on Butch.

He got the extension cord from the iron and hit Butch so hard that he turned a backwards flip, and still Melvin continued hitting him.

When Helen came home, she looked at her bruised and bloody child. When she found out the reason Melvin beat him she went out in the back yard and picked up the papers. Butch had sworn to her that he had picked up everything in the back yard.

The address on the papers was for the people who lived behind them. The owner had thrown the papers over the fence, trying to hide some bills from his wife.

Helen came inside and showed them to Melvin, "I don't care what those kids do. Don't you ever put your hands on my children that way or so help me God I will have your black ass thrown under the jail."

Helen went around the corner and told the neighbor what he had caused by throwing that paper in the yard. When he tried to deny it, Helen walked past him before he could stop her, to the woman that sat on the couch and asked her had she thrown the papers in the yard. The woman looked at the papers and started screaming and throwing things at her husband. The papers were disconnect notices for the bills that the man should have paid the month before, but his gambling had taken all the money; he was going to pay them with his next check and had hoped that his wife wouldn't find out, there had been several times that the lights and water had gone off because of his habit.

Melvin was always tight as a drum when it came to money. When he got his check, he usually told Helen that he hadn't gotten paid. Only when absolutely necessary did he get up off of any for the household.

Melvin had a hiding place that no one knew about; so he thought. He took the panel off the back of the china cabinet and placed the money back there and screwed it back on. He had been hiding money there for years, but little did he know; Melvin Jr. and Curley had been taking money out for years.

One day Helen needed money because she had some traffic tickets to pay or she was going to jail. She had asked Melvin for the money and he had sworn he didn't have any. She was on the phone trying to scrape together one hundred dollars.

Butch and Melvin Jr. got up from the couch, "Momma we know where some money is."

"Where?" Butch went and got the screwdriver and opened the back of the china cabinet. She took all the money out and counted it. "There is over one thousand seven hundred dollars here."

Helen paid off her parking tickets and went and bought herself some new tires, then she took the kids shopping for clothes. *Now he really doesn't have any money*, she thought.

Helen went and got some smaller denominations, instead of twenties and fifties. The bills at the very bottom were fives and tens and she put half of the original money back over the top so that if Melvin looked in the back of the cabinet he wouldn't be able to tell anything was missing. The way the money had been folded and thrown in the cabinet, she was sure he hadn't kept a tally. Whenever she needed money, she just went and got the screwdriver.

Helen found out the boys had been going in there for years, so the damage had already been done if he ever decided to check. "Shoot, half of that money is probably all my savings bonds and we'll just look at this as compounded interest, even though he did pay back the principal." Helen laughed.

Bumpy

Jonathan was inquisitive about the machinations of everything. He was always taking a clock or radio apart and putting them back together. No toy could avoid being dismantled and rebuilt. It was a passion for him.

His nickname was Bumpy because when he was little, he would bump his head against the wall whenever he could not get his way.

Bumpy had three good friends who lived in the neighborhood; Ronald, Michael and Joe. The four of them were always hiding out in his bedroom. Anna Lee thought they were in the room being good studious boys, reading or building something. Years later when he was an adult, Bumpy told her that they were in the room experimenting with marijuana. Had she known, she would have whipped all their butts.

Helen had taken them all to the movies in Hollywood at the Groman's Chinese Theater. She had been given ten tickets by a lady whose husband worked for the studios. The tickets were for the premier of Peter Pan. Helen was lucky enough to find a parking space right across the street from the theater. They walked past the people who were standing in line to get tickets right up to the ticket taker. The kids felt really important. All those folk's mouths dropped open watching their little troupe escorted inside and shown to the best seats.

After the movie, Anna Lee was looking pale. Mother reached over and felt her forehead. She was warm. By the time they arrived home, was asleep. When the others had gotten out of the car, she reached over to shake her; she was soaking from sweat. Helen went to pick her up and got scared, she was burning up.

Helen rushed over and asked Mrs. Versie who lived next door to keep an eye on the kids for her. She rushed Anna Lee to General Hospital and the doctors said that she had Polio, which later they recanted. She remained in the hospital for an entire month.

The afternoon Anna Lee came home, that there was a nice breeze blowing. Bumpy liked that Peter Pan could fly; he decided that if Peter could do it, so could he. He and his friends climbed up on the roof with an umbrella. Ronald went first.

The umbrella caught a wind and he drifted leisurely to the ground. Bumpy did not factor in that Ronald only weighed about thirty pounds soaking wet. Bumpy could not wait to go next. As soon as Ronald came back up the ladder, Bumpy grabbed the umbrella and took a running start from the other side. The umbrella caught a wind, then collapsed. He went crashing to the ground; there was a crunch. Suddenly, he was looking at the bone sticking through the skin of his arm.

Bumpy lay there moaning and Ronald went inside to tell Helen. Once again this month, she was back at General Hospital. Bumpy was happy about having a cast; it was a big deal to the other kids and they all wanted to sign it.

One day Bumpy had another great idea -, he found some Drano drain cleaner in the kitchen and thought it must be something like the salt that is used to make ice cream, but wasn't sure. He went to his younger sister Francis and asked her to taste it. She did. After two seconds, she was screaming her head off.

Anna Lee ran into the kitchen to see what the problem was. Francis was foaming at the mouth. Anna Lee held her over the sink and rinsed her mouth out. Then she grabbed her up and took her next door to Mrs. Versie who was a nurse. She rinsed her mouth a few times and gave her some milk to drink, just in case she had swallowed some and then they headed back to General Hospital. Francis' tongue was swollen, red and irritated but she would live.

Bumpy, always the inventor, had another experiment underway. He and his friends were going to make a bomb. They collected the powder out of the fireworks they picked up in the street after the Fourth of July. They found a box of bullets and emptied the shells. Sitting at the table with a box of kitchen matches, they carefully removed the fire making tips and put them all in a coffee can. They went behind the grocery store and threw firecrackers into the can. When it exploded, it was like a grenade. Their hands and torsos were showered with the shrapnel from the can.

His love of mechanics is why he grew up to be a master machinist.

When Bumpy was a teenager, Helen asked, "How come the tomato plants that are growing next to your window don't bear anything? I been waiting for months and checking it every week and it hasn't grown one yet."

He did not know what she was talking about, so he and Ronald walked around to the side of the house. They looked at each other in amazement. "Naw, it couldn't be, we not that lucky," Ronald said.

As soon as Helen left for work, they took some of the leaves and put them in the oven to dry out. It smelled like marijuana, "Man, you know we been throwing the seeds out of the window when we cleaned our herb for years. No one ever goes on this side of the house," Bumpy said.

"You mean no one except your mother looking for tomatoes," Ronald laughed as he rolled the joint. They discovered that they had a very potent product. Every week, they would pull up a plant, dry it out, bag it up and sell it.

Someone dropped a dime on them. Bumpy went to jail for cultivation. Bumpy's girlfriend bailed him out of jail. When he went to court, one of his teachers helped him out by speaking on his behalf and he did not get any time. He went to school, learned a trade, and got a good job.

Gena

This time around, Gena was not going to end up with a man who died on her. She always got with older men because her father, Horace had been torn from her life at such an early age.

Gena spent her afternoons in the park with the kids. She watched the neighborhood boys; if you could call them that, play basketball. There was one in particular, Clifford who always made it a point to talk with her.

Clifford had one of those bodies that was built for performance. He had an engaging smile and a confidence that she could not ignore. There was no denying that he was a handsome young man, but that was just what he was, a young man.

Clifford persistently asked her out and she kept telling him, "Boy you are way too young for me."

"Age ain't nothin' but a number Miss Lady. Once you realize that, I am going to make you a happy woman."

Finally, Clifford caught Gena at a weak moment. It had been a year since Cubie had died and she had not had, "a good, satisfying screw," as she liked to put it, in a long time.

Gena ran into him at a neighborhood bar one Friday night. They danced the night away. She forgot all about his age and started having a good time.

When the place closed, he insisted on giving her a ride home because she was tipsy. She had driven her car but it was just down the street -she could go and pick it up the next day.

Clifford and Gena sat in front of her house talking until daylight. She could not believe that they had been telling each other their life stories for over four hours now. He had not tried to do any more than kiss her. She thoroughly enjoyed the touch of his lips on hers.

Gena saw the kids looking out the window and had to go in and get some food in her stomach to soak up all the alcohol she had drank that night. Clifford asked if he could take her out that night.

"That's not a good idea because on Sunday, my sister and I are taking the kids to Knox Berry Farm. Two nights in a row is too much partying for me."

"Well, it's not like I don't know your kids. If it's all right with you, I would like to go along."

Gena did not see any harm in it. "I'll see you Sunday morning at nine o'clock," She kissed him one more time before going inside,

They had a great time and the kids seemed to like him. Gena and Clifford started seeing each other every day after he got off work. Soon, the age difference did not bother her and he was the best that she had experienced in bed. He moved in with her and before she knew it, she was pregnant with Clifford Jr.

"Helen, you better go find yourself a younger man. They know some new tricks in the bed that you couldn't begin to imagine," Gena said.

"That's why your old ass can't get out of the bed lately, all those new tricks? You know you too old to be trying to bend and twist your body like some double-jointed circus act. Come on now, tell the truth.

Ain't that how you sprained your back last week?" Helen asked.

Gena pulled the sheets up over her face, "Yeah," They both roared with laughter.

Clifford kept Gena on her toes. More than a few times, she had spied girls, much younger than herself flirting with him. This made her feel insecure. She did not want to lose him and lately he had taken to staying out all night.

Gena prepared a string for him; the same kind of string that she had made for Cubie. He suffered a serious bout of depression over the resulting problem. Of course, there was no problem with Gena.

Clifford was good to all her children and in return they all loved him.

For years Clifford tried and could not perform with other women, yet when he was with Gena, his erection was just fine. Gena knew that Clifford loved her. He hardly ever went out without her anymore.

One day they had just finished making love, Gena was tipsy and made the mistake of showing him the string and telling him what it was.

Clifford got the wildest look in his eyes, jumped on top of her straddling her chest and started beating her. He did not stop until he was out of breath, "If I ever think that you are trying anything on me again, I will come back here and so help me God, I will kill you dead."

He packed his bags and moved to New Mexico. He sent her money for his son every month and visited now and again, but they never got back together.

The next time Gena used the string on a man, she was not crazy enough to tell him about it.

Helen

Melvin and Helen had a '57 Chevy that she bought to replace the old black Chevy, which died after four years. Mother worked in the Valley, Melvin worked downtown. It was hard on them only having one car and it was on its last leg.

Mother saved her money until she had enough for a down payment on a brand new car. Melvin went to the dealership with her to fill out the paperwork. The papers in order, the salesman handed the keys to Melvin.

When they got outside she said, "Give me my keys."

"You go on home in the other car, I'm going to try this one out for you," Melvin said.

She went on home and when he had not shown up an hour later, she grew angry. She stomped around the house fussing up a storm.

Anna Lee asked, "What's wrong, Mother?"

"He done drove off in my new car that I just bought and ain't come home yet."

Finally when Melvin returned, she asked for her keys and he

would not give them to her. Every day she went through his pockets looking for the keys, but he had hid them.

"Melvin, I saved for six months to put a down payment on that car and I haven't driven it once since I bought it. Give me my damn keys," she screamed at him.

"It's my car, it's got my name on it and ain't nobody but me going to drive it, or ride in it."

She thought he was joking at first, but whenever they went somewhere he would take the family out in the old car and when it died and she told him that they needed to share the new car; he would not cooperate.

Some days when Melvin did not come home on time, Helen had to pay one of the neighbors to take her to work, come back and pick her up. She had to cancel jobs because she had no transportation. Well, she was going to put an end to this. She was not driving the car, so she was not going to take her hard earned money and pay the bill. For that matter, she was not going to pay any of the bills until she got herself another car.

One of the neighbors was selling a car when he had taken delivery on a new one. She had a mechanic check it out and gave the man some good faith money so that he would not sell it to anyone else. He told her she could take the car and pay the balance in monthly installments. He found her quite attractive and relished the thought of seeing her beautiful face every month. He told her she could make the payments as low as she wanted, he was in no hurry for the money. He also suggested that maybe she would like to go out with him for dinner and drinks. She declined his invitation, she got the shivers just looking at his wrinkled old butt.

Helen asked Melvin for the balance of the money, but he said he did not have it. She knew he had to be lying, because she paid most of the household bills. One day she was looking for something in the attic and came across a big box full of Melvin's old shoes. She picked one up that had fallen out of the box and some tiny pieces of paper fell out. She picked one up. Money; it was money - bills folded up really tiny and stuffed into the toes of the shoes. She started peeling them open and found several hundred and fifty dollar bills.

They had been going through a rough patch and she had borrowed money from her friends and employers to get them by, "This son-of-a-bitch knew we needed money. I am wearing myself out working two and three jobs to cover a balloon payment on the house and that bastards been stashing money up here and in that China cabinet all these years and refuses to lift a finger to help. Well, I'm gonna fix his little red wagon."

Helen went through every box and trunk that was in that attic and did not stop until she had the remainder of the money she needed to pay for her car free and clear.

While in the attic, she found a lot of hoodoo stuff – pictures of her covered in blood and dolls fashioned in her likeness with pins in them. Mother showed the stuff to Annie, who was visiting.

"This stuff ain't going to work like this. Just take it outside and burn it, he had better remember that I know how to do it the right way so that it will work. If he don't want his dick to fall off, he better stop fooling around," Annie said.

The next day, Helen picked up her car, drove it home and parked it in the garage. When Melvin came home and asked her about it, she told him it was hers.

"Well, where did you get the money?"

"It fell out the sky. Oh and the one you been driving around in, if you don't make the monthly note, they are going to repossess it." She gave him four pieces of paper the one on top said just that. The other three were shut off notices for the lights, gas and water.

"What are you doing, woman? Why haven't you paid the bills? All this stuff is going to be turned off."

Helen looked at him and picked up her purse and sweater, "Pay them your damn self," and walked out the door.

The utilities were still on the next week. Melvin had paid them on Monday morning.

The bumper and one of the side panels needed to be replaced on Helen's car so she asked Melvin to follow her to the junkyard so she could find the parts she needed.

Mr. James, who owned the junkyard had been an acquaintance of Helen's for a long time. He always told her that if she ever needed a man, he was the one. He forgot about Mrs. James.

It was late in the afternoon and Mr. James and his employees were winding down with a six-pack of beer when they arrived. They figured out the parts she would need and one of the guys went to look for them.

Mr. James gave Helen and Melvin a beer while they waited. They were all sitting around talking when Helen pulled Melvin to the side and suggested he go to the store and buy a six-pack of beer, since he had just drank their last one. Melvin did not agree.

"James Jr. is going to the store to buy more beer. You want anything, Melvin?" James asked.

"No thanks," Melvin replied.

She pulled him to the side and told him, "You shouldn't be freeloading. You need to put some money in, since we are going to be here for a while."

"They offered and I drank. That don't mean I owe nobody nothing."

Helen gave James Jr. a five-dollar bill.

Melvin got angry and took off, leaving her behind, "Who she think she is, telling me what I should spend," he fussed on the way home.

By the time Melvin got to the house, he was furious. He ate dinner and changed for his evening job. He could not find his white shirts and stormed into the living room, "Anna Lee, where are all my white shirts? Why is there a dirty pile in there that hasn't been washed and ironed?"

"Daddy, you always tell us not to wash and iron your shirts. You want them to go to the cleaners, remember?"

"Girl you getting smart with me?"

"No, Daddy. I can show you where some clean ones are in the closet."

"Don't you be sassing me girl," he said as he walked to the closet and took the electric cord off the iron.

"Daddy, I wasn't getting smart. I promise I wasn't." She jumped up and ran to the closet. He was standing at the door, when she walked out with shirts in hand.

Melvin beat her until she was nothing but a mass of bleeding welts. Melvin Jr. and Curley were hollering for him to stop, but it was as if he could not hear them.

Helen walked into the house and saw what was happening. "Melvin, what are you doing? Stop it, you're going to kill her!" She grabbed his shoulder. He turned around and hit her. She picked up the phone to call the police and he yanked the cord out of the wall. She ran out of the door to one of the neighbors and called.

Melvin grabbed Anna Lee and put her in the back seat of his car and took her to Sadie's house. When Sadie saw Annie Lee, she turned around and lit into him, "You crazy asshole, why the hell did you do this? Look at her. She is all cut up and bleeding. Answer me, you stupid fool. What could have possessed you to do this to your child?"

Melvin stood rooted to the floor, tears falling from his eyes. He could not say anything that would justify what he had done. Anna Lee had always been his favorite; he had never really whipped her before.

"I was mad at Helen. Anna Lee hadn't done anything. I took it out on her. I know I was wrong, but Helen done called the police on me and if they see her like this, I'm going to jail for sure. Sadie, please help me," he pleaded.

"Go on to work, I'll do what I can."

Sadie put Anna Lee in a tub of Epsom Salt and let her soak to help take down the swelling. She got her out of the tub and dressed the open wounds and put her in the bed and lay down next to her. Anna Lee tapped Sadie on the shoulder and her tiny little voice asked, "Sadie why does daddy get so mad?"

"Don't you worry about that honey, it will never happen again."

Helen called Sadie and told her what had happened.

Sadie lied, "I don't know what done got into that boy. Wait till I see him. I'm gonna kick his ass about beating that baby like that. If I hear anything from him I'll call you."

The next morning, Melvin came to get Anna Lee.

"If you ever beat one of those kids like that again I will personally beat the shit out of you and call the police myself. Do you understand me Melvin Paul Broussard?"

Melvin took Anna Lee straight to school.

Anna Lee's teacher saw blood on the sleeve of her sweater and called the nurse. They took her down to the office and after examining her more closely, were required by law to call the police. They called Helen who picked her up. She cried as she redressed her wounds and put her to bed.

The police went to Melvin's job and arrested him. Helen got a restraining order and had talked to the husband of one of the women whose house she cleaned. He helped her to get papers started for a separation.

Helen had taken enough of Melvin - twenty-one years of his anger, running around and stingy ways was enough. She was through.

She was lying on the couch when Sadie and Warren walked in. She was pissed off at Sadie because she had lied about Anna Lee being at her house. Sadie sat down on the couch next to her as if she wanted to talk. Then she picked up an ashtray and swung it.

Warren caught her by the arm, took the ashtray and pulled her outside, "That bitch done put my brother in jail."

When Melvin got out of jail he stayed with Sadie until he found a room to rent. He took some of his clothes and moved out, thinking that they would work things out.

As far as Helen was concerned, that was not going to happen.

When he realized they were not going to reconcile, he found himself a home on the west side.

One day Melvin came to collect his things and when he went into the attic and found the boxes of shoes gone, he went running to Helen, "I gave that stuff to the goodwill." When he looked in the China cabinet, he noticed that there was not nearly as much money as he thought there should have been. He yelled at her.

"I don't know what you are talking about Melvin. You always told me that you didn't have any money, so how could I have taken some from you? Oh yeah, I did find all that Voodoo mess. You didn't do it right. If you mess with me again, you better remember that my mother knows how, and she can make your dick fall off."

Helen was crying a lot and the kids noticed her depression, but after about a month it passed and she saw a lawyer to start proceedings for a divorce. She learned that when the divorce was final, she would have to sell the house and give him half of the money. She had paid the bulk of the bills during their marriage, so she decided that rather than sell the house, she would borrow as much money on it as she could and then stop paying the mortgage. The house would go back to the bank. If he wanted it, he could pay for it himself. She had taken and given all she was going to. Melvin Paul Broussard was her past. Now it was her time.

Mr. Willie

Helen and her friend Janice were at a restaurant and club when she met Willie Bruce. Janice was going out with his brother and talked her into going along. She knew he was bringing his brother, but did not tell her friend. When they sat down at the table, Helen could have killed Janice. All her friends knew that she did not like being fixed up. She had been divorced for five years and was not looking for a relationship.

In spite of her anger, Helen found herself having a good time. By the end of the evening she had made a date with Willie for the next night.

Willie came to the house and was not greeted warmly. Melvin Jr. and Curley asked him a bunch of questions. They felt it was their duty to protect their mother, especially since they had just managed to get rid of Fred, the last guy who had attempted to date her.

Clyde had brought it to Melvin Jr. and Curley's attention that Fred always wanted to pick up JoAnn, who was seven years old at the time. He never played with any of the other kids, just JoAnn. If you watched closely, you could see that sometimes while he was swinging her, his hand would graze inappropriate places. They watched him closely the next time he came. They sat Mother down and told her what they thought.

"I won't see him anymore," She knew that children's intuition was not to be ignored. She was in no hurry to find a man, and knew that she would never find one that the kids would like, but like any red-blooded woman, she had her needs.

Helen had been seeing a man for six months before finally deciding to sleep with him. They were at a motel, when he took his pants off she knew she could not do it, "You ain't a man, you a horse," she exclaimed.

"This ain't the first time that Johnson has scared off a good woman," he said.

"Look, I don't want to waste your time; you are a nice man, but I know that I will never be able to handle anything that big." That was the last she saw of him.

Helen met Willie at the restaurant to keep down confusion. The third time she went out with him, she did not come home until the next morning, where she found the kids sitting in the living room waiting for her, "If you are going to stay out all night you should call," Anna Lee said.

The next time Mother went out with him, he picked her up and she told Anna Lee to meet her at the club at seven o'clock so they could go clean the Temple. The previous evening, she had catered a party there and the clean-up was part of the contract.

Anna Lee arrived and Helen was not there. It was eight o'clock when she arrived. You would have thought that Anna Lee was the mother and she the child.

Helen, Mr. Willie, his brother and his wife walked into the house one day; the children did not have school the next day so they watched television.

Helen took her company to the dining room table. None of the kids tried to keep it a secret that they did not like Mr. Willie. They felt he was taking up the little spare time that she had for them.

First Helen saw Willie once a week, then it seemed like he was there every day. The kids had even seen his car parked down the street at the gas station. He would leave his night job and instead of going home, parked down the street to bring her donuts and coffee before she went to work. On his nights off he went along to help her clean buildings.

Helen found herself pregnant at the age of fifty. No one was more surprised than she. When she told the kids, they were angry, and told her she should get rid of it. The last three pregnancies had almost killed her due to toxemia. They did not want her to risk her life trying to have another child.

Before the child was born, Willie insisted that Helen marry him. Willie strutted around like a peacock, telling everyone that he still had it. This would be his first child. Helen had to stay in the bed for the last trimester. Little Willie was born premature, but flourished and soon became a healthy child.

Helen and Willies marriage lasted twenty-one years - the exact same as her first marriage.

Sadie

Suk was sick. Sadie knew that she was going to lose him. She had always been into the church, but now redoubled her efforts. She needed a miracle to change Suk's diagnosis. He had undergone two cancer surgeries. The first time, it was prostrate. The second time it was in his stomach. He got better, but two years later it came back.

Sadie prayed while he wasted away before her eyes. Anna Lee and Melvin Jr. came over to take care of Suk while Helen and Sadie went out to take care of some business.

"It's not good for you to stay locked up in this house day after day. Sometimes you have to get out for your own good. I'll come by a couple of days a week and watch Suk for you," Helen told Sadie. After a long debate, she finally agreed.

After the last surgery, Suk was bedridden. After they opened him up it seemed that the cancer accelerated. They could not close the huge wound where they had removed the cancerous tumor. The doctors said the hole needed to heal from the inside, but it would be a slow process.

Sadie looked forward to the days when she could get out. She and Helen had their rough patches over the years, but at the end of the day, they were there for each other.

Going out did not take away from the fact that Sadie was losing the only man that she had ever loved or the only man that loved her for more than her body and money. It was a genuine, wholesome, "I know everyone of your faults, and love you anyway," kind of love.

"Why does this have to happen now? Have I not lost enough in my life? I lost my parents in a car crash at a time when a girl needs them the most. I was a teenager for Christ sake. I had to grow up in a hurry to take care of my brothers. I have taken more than my share of hard knocks, but I have to remember that God has a plan and stay strong," Sadie prayed on her knees.

Helen instructed Anna Lee - fourteen and Melvin Jr. – sixteen, on care and medication for Suk, "The bandage should be changed every three hours or you run the risk of an infection. He needs to eat, even if he says he's not hungry, and make sure he takes his pain medication every four hours."

It got tough when it came time to change the bandage. Melvin Jr. took the old bandage off and jumped up and ran into the bathroom and threw up. With the sight and the smell of the wound came the reality that his uncle, who he loved and respected, was dying. He did not know how to handle this.

Anna Lee finished changing the dressing and was grateful that Suk was sleeping when Melvin Jr. ran out.

When she went into the bathroom, she saw Melvin Jr. sitting in a corner holding himself and crying. When Anna Lee reached down and touched him, he turned away, embarrassed to have his little sister see him like this.

Anna Lee was not going for it. She pulled him to her. He looked up at her and said, "Why Uncle Suk?" Then he let go all the tears that were stored up in him.

Anna Lee had never seen him cry. He was always too busy being tough. At this moment, he looked like a little child and she never felt closer to him. She could not help but cry along with him.

When they finally came out of the bathroom, Suk pretended to be asleep. He had woken when Melvin was pulling the tape off the wound. He knew he was dying and what bothered him most was his loved ones' pain. Suk had a good life with Sadie and her brother's children and even though Sadie had not been able to have any children, he had enjoyed each one of his nieces and nephews as if they were his own. Sadie had been a good wife; she made sure his food was on the table and the house was always as neat as a pin. She believed in God and was one of the cornerstone members of the church they attended. He remembered the surprise on everyone's face when the Pope, the actual Pope from the Vatican in Italy, had walked into the church and asked for Miss Sadie Rogers.

It seemed that she had been writing him for years and on a visit to Los Angeles, he made it a point to visit her. After church he had come to their little home for dinner and it really amazed everyone that he was a down-to-earth person, just like everyone else. Sadie had slipped into the kitchen to check on dinner. The Pope walked in and caught her having a little nip. He took the bottle from her hand, picked up a glass and poured himself a drink. She looked amazed at the fact that the Pope was having a drink. He told her, "Taken in moderation, drinking is not a sin." They had a good laugh.

Sadie still sinned occasionally, but she had a good heart and a lot of love that she was not afraid to give openly. She was definitely high-natured, which meant she enjoyed sex, but she said, "I ain't ashamed of the fact that I enjoy myself in bed and anyone who looks down on me because of it, ain't never had an orgasm and is jealous."

Suk laughed out loud and called Anna Lee and Melvin Jr. into the room. They were walking around on eggshells as if he was already dead, "Hey what's with the long faces? I ain't dead yet. Melvin Jr., go get those dominoes so that I can give y'all another whipping." Both of them laughed.

"Now there, that's much better, I don't want to hear about ya'll being all down-in-the-mouth about me no more. Where I come from in Louisiana, people celebrate the time they have together. They don't mourn it. Ya'll understand what I'm saying?"

"Yes sir, whatever you say," they got comfortable on the bed to play dominoes. They knew he would win, he always did.

Overdose

Crickett was what they had always called Melvin Jr. He was seventeen and worked as a janitor at a hospital. It seemed like he could never make his paycheck last from one week to the next. He paid some of the bills around the house to help Mother, and by the time he went on a date, he was broke.

He went to lunch with Edward who was from New York and worked in the hospital pharmacy.

"If I could get my hands on some pills, can you sell them?" Edward asked.

Crickett saw where this was going, "Red Devils?"

The next week Edward took a bottle of Red Devils and replaced the missing pills with some that looked similar, but were actually placebos so that the inventory would not come up short.

Crickett knew lots of people who took pills to get high. He was going to make a lot of money.

Marvin Johnson who lived down the street came by the house. His eyes popped when he saw the jar of pills. He had an affinity for drugs and Red Devils were one of his favorites. He did not have any money, but knew where he could sell a lot of them.

Crickett did not doubt him; he had met Marvin's friends. "Here's fifty pills … you pay me for thirty-five and the other fifteen are your cut." He knew that Marvin would not sell the extra fifteen, but take them himself.

Marvin washed down two of the pills with a beer. Fifteen minutes later, he took two more.

Crickett warned him to be careful and went into the front house to eat dinner and make some phone calls. He later sat down to watch television and fell asleep on the couch. He did not wake up until the next morning when it was time to go to work. He was not surprised to see Marvin asleep in a chair; he often spent the night. He threw a blanket around him and headed to work early so that he could make some deliveries on the way.

Crickett met Edward at lunch and gave him two hundred dollars.

When Crickett got home from work, Marvin was in the same position.

Curley asked Crickett, "What's up with Marvin; I came home at lunch time and I tried to wake him but he wouldn't budge, now six hours later he still won't wake up."

Crickett walked over to him, "Hey Marvin," he shook him. Still no response. Melvin was starting to worry, "Hey Curley get some water, I got to try and wake him up. I gave him some reds yesterday and he must have taken too many."

"Man, people die from them things. I watched a dude fly off a building just last week and today they said that he was high on reds," he took a mirror and held it under Marvin's nose, "Well, he's still breathing. Maybe he just has to sleep it off."

The next day, Marvin was still sleeping it off when Anna Lee went to tell Crickett that he had a phone call. He was getting a lot of phone calls and traffic in and out of the backhouse was heavier than usual. It seemed like every two minutes, someone was walking down the driveway to see Crickett. None of them were staying more than five minutes.

Anna Lee did not know Crickett had left a few minutes earlier. When she went in, she saw Marvin sleeping. Marvin's mother had been calling all over the neighborhood because he had not been home. Anna Lee tried to rouse Marvin with no luck.

She went into the house where Helen was cooking dinner, "Mother, Marvin is in the back sleeping and I can't wake him," Anna Lee said. Mother picked up the phone and called Mrs. Johnson. She was there in two minutes. When they went into the back room and she could not wake him, Helen went next door to get Mrs. Versie, the nurse.

Mrs. Versie took his pulse. "Helen, go in the house and call an ambulance."

Before the ambulance came, Crickett walked in and was surprised to find them there.

"What's going on?" he asked.

Mrs. Johnson flew at him, "How long has he been here like this? Didn't you know that I have been looking for him?"

"No, I didn't. I don't know how long he been here. I haven't been home for the last couple of days."

Anna Lee and Helen looked at him suspiciously, because they knew that he had been there last night. Sirens could be heard coming down the driveway.

"Why don't you wake him up and ask him what he's been up to? I thought he was just tired so when I came in this evening, I left him alone and let him sleep."

Paramedics were coming through the door.

After they left, Helen turned to Crickett, "What is wrong with him Melvin Paul Broussard, Jr.? If you know you had better tell me right now!"

"I don't know Momma."

Helen and Anna Lee went to the hospital so that Mrs. Johnson would not be alone. The diagnosis was that Marvin had overdosed on Red Devils; he had taken at least eight and was in a coma. Had they not gotten to him when they did, he would have died.

When Helen returned she went straight to the back house. Crickett was not there, but Curley was. When she told Curley what had happened and that Mrs. Johnson was planning to call the police, he told her everything.

"Where are the pills now?"

"He hid them in the house after the people took Marvin away."

"You are going to show me where they are right now. You fools were gonna let that boy sit back there and die. You got all these junkies running in and out of my house. You're just as guilty as he is 'cause you knew it was happening. I got half a mind to call the police on your dumb asses right now."

Curley pulled down the stairs to the attic. The bag was hidden behind some old furniture. She snatched the bag from him. There was the bottle of pills and half a shopping bag full of Marijuana. She flushed it all.

When Crickett came home, Helen waited for him to go into the attic. When he came down she had a belt and started wailing on him before he could get off the stairs, "If that boy dies you are going to jail for a long time, so you had better get down on your knees and pray to God that he doesn't."

Marvin came out of the coma two days later. He never did tell where he got the pills. Meanwhile, Crickett had to give all the money he made from the pills to the dealers who had given him the marijuana on consignment.

Helen's Social Club And The Matadors

Helen belonged to a social club that organized dances, barbe-cue's, and picnics that everyone in town looked forward to attending. They raised money and at the end of the year, gave a big free dance. They did a lot for the community. If someone fell on hard times, they held bake sales. If someone needed help paying their rent, they orga-nized a rent party. If someone was sick and could not pay their doctor bills, they sold fish dinners. They cared for the sick and their children and delivered meals to the elderly.

Clyde was the president of a car club called 'The Matadors.' He had a green Chevy. Crickett, was vice-president, he had a bright pink car that his girlfriend, Yvonne picked out. The club started out with six members. Every time they gave a function membership grew. They met in the garage apartment to plan events where they charged a fee at the door and sold drinks and hot dogs.

They had members who were going in, or coming out of the military. Others had jobs or were in college. Soon, over sixty members rode around with The Matadors plaque in the back window of their cars.

They rented mansions and clubs for parties and halls for dances. Summers, they had picnics at Griffith Park and overnight beach parties at Cabrillo beach.

They advertised on the radio and when people saw flyers for a Matadors function, they canceled any previous plans because nobody was going to miss out on the fun.

Helen's social club cooked and sold food at The Matador functions. The Matadors made their money from the door, alcohol and sodas. Both clubs donated a portion of the profits to a local orphanage, or for research on a disease that was affecting the community, Sickle Cell Anemia.

The Los Angeles Police Department gave The Matadors respect because they hired off duty officers as security. Anyone who made trouble was put out immediately.

Churches that wanted to expand or needed money came to The Matadors for assistance and used their name for fundraisers. New businesses gave them discounts on merchandise in return for their endorsement.

Crickett and Curley were turning the garage into an apartment. Their friends, Emmit and Joe, helped with the remodel. A wall with a sliding glass door replaced the garage door. Carpet was laid. A couch, some beds and the transformation was complete.

Anna Lee was seventeen and had been dating Joe. Helen and Anna Lee pulled into the driveway after cleaning buildings all night to find Joe pacing back and forth in the front yard, "Where have you been? We supposed to get married," Joe said.

"We are?" Anna Lee said with obvious confusion. Over the eight months that they had been dating, the conversation had come up, but she did not remember setting a date.

Helen assumed Anna Lee was pregnant and drove them to the courthouse where they married. They stayed for two months before Joe decided they were going to live in San Diego in his mother's apartment building.

A few months later, Helen, the kids, and a few friends, which included Clyde, drove down early Christmas morning in four cars to surprise Anna Lee.

They did not have a phone, but Anna Lee had been calling home once a week, but Helen needed to lay eyes on her child to be sure everything was as it should be. Everything seemed to be all right.

One April day, Helen got an anonymous phone call from someone, "You need to get down to San Diego and check on your daughter," and then they hung up.

Ms. Marie was visiting and did not like the look on her friend's face, "What's going on, Helen?"

"Somebody said I had better get down to San Diego to see about Anna Lee."

"Well then, that's just what we gone do," Ms. Marie said.

When they arrived, they could tell Anna Lee had not been eating. She was so skinny that her dress looked like it was on a clothes hanger. That was all they needed to see. They packed her things while Anna Lee told them what had been going on, "Joe takes off for days at a time. I know he's with other women. Ain't no food in the house, I used to go to his aunt's store and shop, but the last time she told me that the bill is too high because Joe has not paid it in months. I was too embarrassed to go back. When I asked Joe about it, he hit me. He won't let me get a job or leave the house. He even told his mother not to let me use the phone anymore because he was not going to pay for the calls."

Bags loaded in the car, they went upstairs to say goodbye to Joe's mother. When they were leaving Joe appeared at the bottom of the stairs, "Hey, Ms. Helen, how you doing?"

"I'm doing fine, and she's going home."

"Nobody's taking my wife anywhere."

Anna Lee looked at him and said, "I'm leaving you, Joe. I'm not going to stay here and be treated like this."

"Only way you are leaving here is over my dead body."

Ms. Marie reached into her ample cleavage and pulled out her switchblade. When the blade popped out, so did Joe's eyes, "Is that the way you want it?" Ms. Marie asked as she walked down the stairs. Before she reached the bottom, he was gone.

Helen prepared all Anna Lee's favorite foods in an attempt to fatten her up.

Crickett was furious about how his little sister had been treated. "If I see that nigga' again, I'm gone kill him."

Crickett and Curley told Anna Lee, "It's time for you get out and have some fun. Go get dressed, we are taking you to a dance."

Helen had seen Joe and two of his friends from the kitchen window when they pulled up, "You might as well come on in," she fixed them something to eat.

"Ms. Helen, I was a stupid fool and I want to try again. We can stay here if she wants to, but I love her and I want her back," Joe pleaded.

"You have to talk to her about that, but if she were to get back with you and I hear of you mistreating her again you gone be sorry mister," Helen warned.

"I understand, Ma'am."

They waited quite a while for Anna Lee to come back. It was evident that Helen was falling asleep.

"We'll come back later," Joe said. He dropped his friends off at home and came back and waited down the street.

It was four in the morning when they got home from the dance. Joe waited a few minutes before going to the door, "Can I talk to you?" he pleaded when Anna Lee opened the door.

"We ain't got nothing to talk about," Anna Lee said.

Helen told her, "There's a right and a wrong way to do everything. Go on in the kitchen and talk to him."

"I am not going back with you. I don't want to be married to you anymore and that's all there is to it," Anna Lee said once in the kitchen.

Joe stepped toward her and when she retreated a pot fell off the counter to the floor.

When they heard the crash, Crickett, Curley, Clyde, Jesse and Boot were in the doorway in a flash.

"What the hell is going on in here?" Crickett said.

"Nothing; I'm just talking to my wife."

Anna Lee walked to the door and said, "We're through talking," and walked out of the room.

Joe went to the door as if to follow her.

"It's time for you to leave, you can use the back door," Curley said.

Joe left and that was the end of that.

Twenty years later, Helen was walking out of the door of her thrift shop and saw a man walking around her car, obviously looking to steal her hubcaps, "Can I help you?"

"Oh, I was walking by here this morning and I dropped something, I was just trying to find it," he lied.

When he looked up, she recognized him. It was Joe and he had definitely fallen on hard times.

"Joe, is that you?" she asked.

He squinted his eyes and stepped closer, "Hey, Ms. Helen, I didn't recognize you. How you been?"

"Better than you looks like. Come on in here boy."

She gave him a hot meal, some money, and clothes. She could tell by the needle marks on his arm that his problem was much bigger than just hard times.

"My mother died and the apartment building went back to the bank after I missed a few payments; I thought it was paid for." Joe explained while he ate.

Actually, he had drugged away the money after selling the property. He could not keep steady work because he was unreliable.

When Helen saw Anna Lee she told her, "You should be thanking your lucky stars that you didn't stay with him."

Clyde

Clyde had grown up in the projects and was good friends with Crickett, whose skinny little sister, Anna Lee, had grown into a real beauty, and it had not escaped his attention. She had really blossomed since returning from San Diego.

That Christmas he had drove down with Helen, his intuition had told him that something was not right. When they walked outside he asked Anna Lee, "Is everything alright here? For some reason I feel like something is wrong."

Joe came outside. Clyde could tell she wanted to tell him something, but could not speak in front of her husband. He never did like Joe Collier. When they got into the car to leave, he pressed some money and a piece of paper into her hand and told her, "Take care of yourself. Please call or write me if you need anything."

When Clyde heard that they brought her back and how Joe had treated her, he found himself angry. That night after the dance he was hoping that Joe would do something to give him the opportunity to kick his ass. He had been the first one in the doorway and was disappointed when Joe tucked his tail between his legs and slunk out the back door.

Clyde had been in the Air Force for a year now, stationed in Arizona. The others who had joined at the same time were ashamed of themselves for washing out after Helen's social club had given them that big, going away dance. Six of them had gone in and found they could not deal with the discipline and had dropped out of basic training one by one. One of them even shot himself in the foot to get out. Clyde was the only one who had hung in there.

When he returned to base, Anna Lee was on his mind. He wrote her a letter. Nothing special, just a 'Hi, how are you,' type of thing. He spoke of how much he was looking forward to being discharged and his future plans. He was pleasantly surprised when she wrote back. Soon they were corresponding regularly.

Anna Lee had been in a beauty contest and sent him some pictures - sexy ones in bathing suits. They were not an item yet, but when his Air Force buddies saw the pictures, he did not tell them that.

The pictures somehow disappeared from the wall next to his bunk. It was a week before Clyde found out who had them. A guy who worked in the mess hall had stolen the pictures and was telling people Anna Lee was his girl.

Clyde went to the mammoth looking man and for some reason, he was too angry to be scared, "You got some pictures that don't belong to you and I want them back," Clyde said.

The guy looked down at Clyde, who was much shorter than he was and could not weigh more than one hundred and fifty pounds soaking wet. "And just how do you plan to get them from me, little man?" He stood there crossing his arms over his six feet five-inch frame that held two hundred and fifty pounds of pure hardened muscle.

"By whatever means necessary," Clyde said and put up his fists.

The guy could not help but laugh. You would have thought he

had taken the actual girl, and not just some photographs, the way this man was prepared to risk life and limb.

He lifted his fists and after a few seconds dropped them, "All right. I'll give them to you. I like you. You're either crazy or got a lot of heart. I'll get them back to you as soon as my duty is up here." He chucked Clyde playfully on the chin.

Guys were patting Clyde on the back, "Alright man." They had actually taken bets on whether or not he would walk away from the confrontation alive.

That night as he lay in his bunk looking at the pictures, he recalled how his heart had been ready to jump out of his chest when the mammoth had lifted his fists. At that moment, he knew that he was about to die, but he wanted those pictures back and in the end he got them.

Clyde hopped a military flight and spent his leave with Anna Lee. He never thought that he could get a woman as beautiful as her.

He was sent overseas to Guam where he was injured when he fell from a cliff. The rocks and coral scraped the skin off his leg and while being carried back to the camp the mosquitoes and insects got to the open wound. His fever was so high that the veins in his legs were affected. When he went back home, it was to the Veteran's Hospital where he spent a lot of time before he could walk again. The doctors diagnosed him with thrombophlebitis. The veins in his legs were so thin that he would have to take a blood thinner for the rest of his life.

When he got out of the hospital, Anna Lee gave him the good news. During one of Clyde's many visits home, Anna Lee had conceived. Clyde could not have been happier. When her time came to have the baby he was right by her side; well, somewhat by her side. During the delivery, he looked through the window and when he saw the blood and the baby coming out, he fainted. The family still laughs about him hitting the floor to this day. They had a girl who they named after his sister, Claudette. Her middle name was Kim.

Clyde went to school at Trade Technical College to be a Tailor. He worked in the evenings cleaning buildings. He had several bad times when his blood would not circulate properly and was hospitalized for months at a time.

Clyde and Anna Lee married when Kim was one year old. Anna Lee was cleaning offices and a house for a woman who worked at Mattel Toys. The woman gave her lots of prototypes from work. Kim had every Barbie doll there was.

Clyde doted over his little girl and almost every day when he had money, he would bring some little trinket for her when he picked her up from Helen's where she stayed during the day while they worked.

The Imperial Garden Projects in Watts was home for five years. Clyde had been fighting with the government for years to get his disability. Even though he was spending months at a time in the hospital, they did not want to give him total disability. He was a proud man and wanted to support his family, but it seemed that when things started getting good for him and he landed a good job, he would fall sick, thus losing his employment.

God may not always come when you call, but he is always on time. After five years of correspondence with the government, they finally gave him total disability, along with back pay for the last five years.

This money enabled him to move his family out of Watts to Compton. Clyde spent a lot of time in the hospital every year, but when he came home, he always got right back out there to support his family.

Crickett Goes To Jail

Crickett worked in the morgue at Cedar Sinai Hospital. His job was to bring the bodies down and put them on a slab, then log them in.

He came running into the house one day, "Mother I'm quitting that job," he was jumping around.

"Boy, calm down. What is wrong with you? You gon' wear a hole in my carpet with all that pacing," Helen was trying not to laugh, but he looked so comical.

"I brought a body down and while I was sitting at the desk filling out the paperwork, the body started sitting up. Momma, I like to tore that place apart trying to get out of there."

When Crickett went to work the next day, his supervisor was still laughing. "We'll find you something else to do; you are a good worker and we don't want to lose you."

Crickett married Yvonne, and they had a daughter named La Shaun. Yvonne was light-skinned and very beautiful. He, like his father, was jealous and the full-figured, curvy grace that she carried herself with gleaned a lot of attention which made him insecure.

Crickett and a friend planned to break into a men's clothing store through the skylight. Unbeknownst to them, the skylight was connected to a silent alarm. They had piled up suits under the skylight on a table so that they could lift them out.

When the police showed up, his friend who was on the roof was arrested. It took them a while to find Crickett; they had to use a police dog. He was hiding under the pile of suits.

Anna Lee, Yvonne and her sister Sharon were on their way home from work, when they heard Crickett's name over the radio. The D.J. was describing the bungled burglary. They were all cracking up about how stupid the burglars were. Then the D.J. said their names.

Anna Lee could not believe her ears. Yvonne was inconsolable. What was she going to do now, she had a baby and a husband who was going to jail?

When Crickett got to jail the woman who did the fingerprinting looked at the policeman who bought him in, "Is this some kind of stupid joke? I don't have time for this, don't you see all these people to be booked in and you playing games." She looked in the file and took out a sheet she had finished less than an hour ago.

The policeman looked at the file and could not believe it. This other person who had been brought in an hour ago had the exact same name and description. He had to see this for himself. He and the woman walked back to the cells and were amazed at what they saw, "You have a brother with the same name?" they asked the prisoner.

"No brothers and no sisters," he said.

They got the first Melvin Paul Broussard Jr. out of his cell and led him into the booking room where the second Melvin Paul Broussard Jr. stood.

"Why would you lie about having a twin brother?" the woman asked the first one.

"I don't have no brothers or sisters. So I don't know what you are talking about lady," he said just as his brother walked into view.

They circled one another; it was uncanny. They could have been looking in a mirror. They booked in the second Melvin and put them both in the same cell. "Seems like you two got some talking to do," the jailer said.

Well, after comparing backgrounds, they realized that they were brothers. This was Sandra's son. They had moved to California during the same year.

Crickett told him, "When I get out I want to take you to meet our father."

He declined the invitation, saying, "The bastard never wanted to know me, so why should I want to know him?"

Annie

Annie loved starting mischief. One Sunday when the family was over for dinner, she kept repeating her little saying, "Confusion is my heart's desire, peace I do despise."

Everyone was uncomfortable when she did this because they knew she had a card up her sleeve, and until she played it no one knew who was to be the victim.

They were sitting around the table after dinner. Melvin Jr. with Yvonne, watching her breastfeed La Shaun. Curley was bouncing Curley Jr. on his knee, next to his pregnant wife Mary.

It seemed to Annie that they were way too happy, "Melvin Jr. and Curley, I told you I don't mind you bringing your little floozies over here when I'm at work, but if you are going to lay up in my bed with them, you make sure you change the damn sheets."

"What and who is she talking about, Melvin?" Yvonne yelled waking the baby.

Mary stood up over Curley, "You mean to tell me you been bringing girls over here and sleeping with them while I'm walking around here all blown up like a balloon carrying your child?"

Annie sat back and smiled. "Confusion is my heart's desire, peace I do despise," she said and watched the fireworks. They stood outside and argued for a good while before leaving.

Annie was tickled pink. She died in 1969.

GiGi

While Crickett was in jail, instead of rehabilitation, he had gotten an education. He kept in touch with his friends from jail, and hung out with them at the clubs. "Birds of a feather flock together."

GiGi made a lot of money every day and after six months with her current pimp, Sammy, she was still living in a motel on Sunset. He had not gotten her an apartment of her own because he was putting all of the money from her and two other women in his arm and up his nose.

GiGi and her two-year-old son, Johnny, were from Germany and had just gotten off a plane at the Los Angeles airport when she was approached by Sammy, who was a handsome man. He gave her his phone number.

She was running from an abusive boyfriend who had sworn that if she ever left him, he would find her and kill not only her, but her son. A few weeks later, she called Sammy.

She was working at a massage parlor in Hollywood. They went on a few dates, the first a trip to Disneyland with Johnny. Of course, he did not tell her that he was a pimp, but she knew; her mother had been a prostitute.

Sammy hired a young black girl named Stacy, who he introduced as his cousin, to take care of Johnny while she worked. One day she was coming in early after breaking luck with a very generous trick. When she walked into the motel, Johnny was standing in the hallway alone crying. She used her key to open the door. Sammy was in bed screwing his so-called cousin.

GiGi flew at Sammy. She really did not care about him sexing Stacy, but the fact that any pervert could have walked up and taken her son; that bothered her.

Sammy beat her, "Bitch you are out of line."

GiGi picked herself and her child up, and went down the street to the club where people in the life hung out. He followed.

Crickett was at the bar having a drink with friends when out of the blue, GiGi approached him. She had a fresh black eye, a fist full of money, a baby on her hip and an irate pimp on her heels.

She had seen him in the club before and knew he was not in the game. Yet. She decided that life might be a little easier for her if she chose a square and turned him out. She walked up to Crickett, tapped him on the shoulder, and when he turned around she took his hand, placed the bills in it and said, "I choose you."

"Cop and blow," was the primary rule of the game. No pimp was guaranteed to keep a woman. She could wake up any day and leave. All they could do is get everything they could as long as she stayed. If a woman decided to go to another pimp, she announced her decision and chose her new man by paying him. The one that she left was expected to accept this. Unfortunately, her pimp, who was not new to the game, did not honor this rule. He tried to pull her away and when Crickett stepped in front of her, he tried to hit him.

Crickett had been taught by Sadie and Annie to use a straight razor. From that day, Sammy was known as Scarface.

That's the night Crickett turned out to the game.

He told GiGi about his wife and daughter and explained that he rented an apartment from his mother. He confessed that he knew nothing about the game.

She told him she knew all there was to know and that a pimp is only as strong as his bottom woman.

Helen had a house on Avalon at the time. Crickett and Yvonne lived in the back apartment building, which had two apartments. He took her to Helen's and introduced her so that she would know her son would be safe.

Yvonne babysat kids during the day and Johnny would be one of them. The little curly-haired child was adorable. He was the same age as Lil' Willie. Mother did not know what was going on, but she agreed to keep him in the evenings.

That night Melvin took GiGi back to Sunset and got a room in a hotel. That night Sammy's other two women chose him.

Two days later, GiGi saw the young girl who was supposed to be Scarface's cousin, battered and bruised, wearing what used to be her clothes. She was standing on the corner, working. She stopped and talked to her. The girl was a runaway that he had picked up at the bus station. He had forced the young girl out on the street when GiGi left.

His other women followed GiGi's lead after finding out that he was sleeping with the young girl who had not given him a dime.

Crickett took their money and rented an apartment for his three women.

Unlucky for Sammy, Stacy's first customer was an undercover cop. The scared fourteen-year-old told them all about him beating her and forcing her onto the street for prostitution. He was arrested and went to jail for corrupting a minor, statutory rape and pimping and pandering.

There was no stopping Crickett after that. Eventually, he told Yvonne what he was doing. Even though he had no intention of her working, bought her a new car, and gave her all the money she could spend, she told him that if he did not quit, she would leave him.

This was eight months after GiGi had started schooling him. He was now eight women deep, and hooked on the money that poured in every day.

Yvonne's ultimatum was the end of their marriage and a year later they were divorced. She eventually remarried.

Wicked Crickett was famous across the country. At the height of his career, he had thirty-two women at one time and a beautiful house in the Hollywood Hills. He could be seen checking his traps on Sunset Boulevard in a customized burgundy van with an airbrushed Gladiator on the side, or his white Rolls Royce. He was a king when, "Pimpin' and ho'in was the best thang go'in.

The Restaurant

Helen cleaned offices at night and during the day she cleaned houses for several women in the San Fernando Valley and Beverly Hills. She drove a truck, and arranged her schedule with their garbage pick-up days. One of her favorite sayings was, "One man's trash is another man's treasure."

You would be amazed at the stuff rich people throw out. Refrigerators, furniture, fur coats, jewelry; some pieces were worth a lot of money. All the women she worked for let their friends know to drop off anything Helen might be able to use. She had clients who when they fell sick, hired her to stay and take care of their children and cook. They loved her cooking. A lot of them said that her cooking cured whatever was ailing them. Soon, she was catering parties. She prepared and served the whole meal. Word of mouth kept her in demand.

In 1969, Melvin Jr. decided to invest some of his earnings into something legal and leased a block of storefronts on Vermont, right before Slauson. When they were through renovating, they had a shoeshine parlor, pool hall, a restaurant called Mom's Soul food, a record store, and a second-hand store.

Mom's Soul Food became very popular. Helen served breakfast, lunch and dinner. The menu varied from day to day, depending on what she felt like cooking when she woke at five o'clock each morning. The grandchildren and Lil' Willie helped run the restaurant. By the time they were eight, most of them knew every aspect of preparation, other than standing over the pots. They could clean and strip the vein out of the chitin's, cut up sausage and okra, clean shrimp and chicken, mix the eggs, and prepare the meatloaf and burger patties. They took orders, waited on and cleaned the tables.

Helen could always tell when someone was down on their luck. They would order a roll or a piece of pie. The longing look at some-one else's full plate of meatloaf, macaroni and cheese, greens and corn bread, or fried chicken, mashed potatoes, string beans and garlic toast, told her the whole story.

Helen would bring the person a full plate and set it in front of them. They would say, "Mother, I don't have enough money for this," or "This isn't what I ordered."

Helen would say, "Oh shoot, well I done fixed it now; you might as well eat it or I'll just have to throw it away."

They knew that she was being kind and appreciated it. When things got better for them, they would always come back and leave big tips, sometimes more than their bill.

Helen never made anyone feel that they owed her anything. They knew that if they tried to give her the money she would never take it. Some people ate there every day and paid their tab when they got their weekly checks. People came from as far away as the San Fernando Valley for Mom's Soul Food.

Sundays, everyone in the family ate at the restaurant.

Crickett

In 1985 Crickett opened a beauty supply store and a club in the Valley. He was not able to get a liquor or club license, so he rented it out for private parties.

One night, Crickett got a call from a girl he had been trying to add to his stable. He had told her to meet him at an after-hours club in Los Angeles. Two days later, no one had heard from him. The family was worried. It was not that he did not take off occasionally, but he always checked in. He missed an important medical appointment and his stepdaughter's school concert. Everyone was trying to track him down.

Miko, his woman, filed a missing person's report. The next afternoon, the police called. Crickett was in Centinela Hospital, in Inglewood. He had undergone two surgeries and was in intensive care listed under critical condition. They had identified him by his fingerprints. When he finally woke, he gave the nurses numbers to call. He had been there for two days and they were not optimistic.

Before leaving for the hospital Miko called Helen and Crickett's best friend, Dooby. Word spread like fire. The hospital waiting room was packed with family and friends within two hours.

The police questioned Crickett, "I don't know what happened." When they departed he told the nurse, "I need to speak to Butch, Curley, and Dooby." They were next to his bed within moments. "I was leaving the club off of Normandy where I had met with Rochelle. You know that Suzie choosy broad? She called, asking me to meet her at the after-hours. She didn't have no choosing fee so I told her to call me when she could come correct. She left the club before me. I left about a half hour later to check my traps. A car blocked me at the intersection. Rochelle was sitting in the car with some guy. When I got out of the car, I saw the shotgun too late. The next thing I knew I was here."

Family was allowed in one at a time for two minutes. The monitors suddenly went crazy; they rushed Kim out of the room and took him back to surgery. The doctors opened up his chest in an attempt to massage his heart. It was a futile effort, Melvin Paul Broussard Jr. suffered a heart attack and died.

The police got nowhere questioning everyone in the waiting room. "I don't know anything," was all they heard. The police would only get in the way, they had their own investigation going.

Rochelle had been with several pimps for short times over the last year. Each one told their own stories about the girl. They found that they had one thing in common; each had been robbed shortly after she left them.

The night that Melvin Jr. disappeared, a white guy had been trying to get in the club but was told to go away. He stood outside hollering for Rochelle. He had asked several people to tell her to come outside.

Rochelle was released from police custody. The only fingerprints found in the Rolls Royce belonged to her boyfriend, who was in solitary confinement for his own protection.

The funeral was huge. Pimps and players came in from all over the world. Melvin Jr. had been a pimp for over thirty years. Helen looked around at all these people attending her first-born son's funeral, "If you could only make them listen or plan their lives out for them. A mother should not be burying her own son."

Family and friends were outraged when the Judge called the murder a crime of passion. Rochelle's boyfriend was sentenced to two short years in a country club prison.

Davonne

Kim had been working at Blue Cross of Southern California in the San Fernando Valley. Her title was, 'Membership Examiner.' She had been staying at Crickett's and right before he died had moved into an apartment not far from them.

Kim and her Jewish attorney proved that the supervisor, who had an intense dislike for Kim, was falsifying quality control reports in an attempt to get her fired. She was four months pregnant when the woman physically attacked her in front of several employees on the work floor.

The doctors said Kim could no longer work and would have to be on bedrest.

Helen lived with Melvin Jr. over the last ten years because he did not want her cleaning and cooking for other people. He told her that he made enough money that if she insisted on working it would be for him.

When Crickett died, Helen moved back to Los Angeles, Miko retired and moved away.

Helen's house had five bedrooms and two bathrooms. JoAnn and her daughters—Tracy and Kenya, Curley's second wife's children

- Patrick and Sheila, Butch, and her niece Virginia— all lived with her.

Even though they were divorced, Mr. Willie came by and Helen fed him before sending him off to his apartment. He wanted her back, but she liked things as they were. He was not doing well, he had prostate cancer.

Helen convinced Kim to move in with her, "Since you are on workers compensation and after the baby is born, maternity leave, you may as well save the eight hundred dollars a month that you are paying for rent. This way you can be around family and we can help you."

This being her first child and all, Kim was afraid and agreed it would be better with family around.

"Kim, you can't be reaching over your head like that, it will make the cord wrap around the baby's neck," Helen warned as they packed her things.

"Mother, is that another one of them ol' wives tales that you always talking about? Like don't sit on the ground or your period will be hard and you'll have back problems, or coffee will make you black," she joked.

"It sure is and you better pay it some mind, Miss smarty pants."

Kim was enroute to one of her frequent trips to the bathroom when suddenly her water broke, "Mother! Mother!" she screamed holding her gown up around her thighs.

Helen had already driven Kim to the hospital all the way in The Valley on two false alarms this month, "I cannot for the life of me understand why you refused to change doctors."

"Mother, I like my doctor," Kim said.

"Humph, you know we don't really need to go to a hospital. I delivered more than a few babies in my time."

"For one thing, you cannot give me an epidural, and I am not trying to have this baby without some pain killers."

They took the hour-long drive to the Valley. Every time Kim felt a contraction she would start laughing her head off. Helen knew that she had always laughed when she was scared or angry.

At three o'clock in the morning, Kim was on monitors. She was on the phone talking to her father. He never understood how she could laugh at times like these, "Get off the phone and concentrate on what you're doing."

The nurses and doctors who were not busy stood outside the door; her laughter was amusing and contagious.

Nurses and doctors ran into the room in answer to the alarm on the fetal monitor. Something was wrong; the baby's heart beat weakened with each contraction. Kim was prepared for a Caesarean section. She was crying and laughing at the same time. She did not want to lose her child.

The anesthesiologist administered medicine, her hysteria would not help matters any. Though unconscious, she was still laughing when rolled into surgery. Helen sat in the chapel praying for her granddaughter and great-grandson.

Five hours later, Helen sat by the bed holding her great- grandchild. Kim opened her eyes and tried to sit up, but the pain stopped her. She looked at her Grandmother and the little bundle and smiled. "Does he have any hair?"

"Have a look see," Helen brought the baby boy over to the bed and removed the swaddling. She saw that Kim was overcome by the perfection of her beautiful son.

Helen knew just what she was feeling; she had experienced the same wonderment with the birth of each of her children.

"So sleeping beauty is back with us I see. Are you ready to feed your son?" the nurse asked as she sailed into the room. She positioned the bed and placed the baby in a feeding position. He knew just what to do. "Ten minutes on each side, then great-grandma can burp him for you. You are not going to want to sit up just yet with those stitches," the nurse said on her way out.

"What are you going to name him?" Helen asked. "Davonne Clymel Harold." Kim said.

"Are you going to tell us who the father is now?"

"I am his Mother, and I am his Father." Kim's tone let her know that was the end of that conversation.

When Clyde and Anna Lee arrived that afternoon, Kim was asleep. She woke up to her mother clipping off her five-inch fingernails. Kim tried to pull her hand away.

"Don't you move; how do you think you are going to change the baby? Hell, I don't know how you manage to wipe your own ass," Anna Lee admonished.

So much for her bi-weekly visits to the nail salon, good-bye seven color airbrush designs. She knew her mother was right. No need to protest, it would not have done any good anyway.

Kim called the nurse to bring Davonne. For a moment, she thought her parents were going to come to blows. She watched them debate over who was going to hold him first. Finally, they compromised and held him together. It was a nice, long visit. Visiting hours had been over for two hours when the nurse discovered they were still there and put them out.

A week later, the night before Kim and Davonne were to go home, the hospital provided a candlelight lobster dinner. It was meant for the parents of the newborn. Kim invited Helen.

Helen stayed the night in the other bed. Kim explained to the nurse that the long ride for her grandmother was really inconvenient since she had to come back in the morning to pick them up.

"I'm sorry, that would be against hospital policy," the night nurse said.

Fifty dollars bought them an exception to the rule.

Davonne's crib was set up in JoAnn's room in the front of the house. Kim slept on a big comfortable reclining chair in the living room. Her stitches were still fresh and it was much easier for her to stand up from the chair than had she lain down in the bed.

Davonne rarely slept in his crib. Kim always fell asleep with him on her chest. Every night Helen patiently watched television while waiting for Kim to fall asleep. When she heard Kim's low snoring she took her great-grandson to her room at the back of the house.

Helen enjoyed the time, just as she did with all her children and grandchildren. "Da Da" which is what they called the baby, was her sixth great-grandchild. Clymel stood for Clyde, his grandfather and Melvin his uncle.

Helen knew that just like his namesakes, Davonne was destined to do something good in this world; she prayed it would be something legal.

Two weeks after Melvin Jr.'s burial, three pregnancies were announced in the family: Carol; one of Melvin Jr.'s women, Tanika; Willie's woman, and Kim.

As they grew older, the three healthy boys exhibited character traits that ironically mirrored the uncle they had never met.

Kim ended up back in the hustling life after a while. She got in some trouble and had to leave town. She sent for Helen and Davonne who was three years old, to stay with her in Las Vegas. When she left Las Vegas at the invitation of the police, Helen took Davonne home with her. They spoke over the phone often and she sent money and toys, but it was seven years before Davonne saw his mother again.

Helen Goes To Texas

Kim sent Helen plane tickets to visit her in Texas where she lived with her man who had rescued her from the fast life. They bore a son, Colin Jr. who came into the world on May 25, 1993. Helen was the first to hold him after his father. He was a beautiful healthy child.

Mr. Willie succumbed to cancer in 1994.

Helen arrived a few days after Kim's third child, Colina, was born. Her plan was to arrive before the due date, which was May 25, the same day as Colin Jr. They were Irish twins, born within the same year. Daddy's lucky day was Labor Day, but this child had decided to come three weeks early on May 5. She had been there for the birth of all her other grandchildren and great-grandchildren.

Helen stayed for a month and as with every other, she took care of the baby and insisted mommy rest. Were it up to Kim, she would never have gone back home.

On May 25th they had a big party in a park, celebrating Colin Jr's 1st birthday and Colina's birth. Over a hundred people came. Helen and Kim prepared all the food: hamburgers, hotdogs, potato salad and baked beans and purchased two full sheet cakes.

Helen held and tended to Colina that whole day. She did not believe in passing newborn babies around to strangers. They could look, but only the few who were good friends to Kim held her. Everyone else, she would just retrieve the bottle of water she kept in her pocket and tell them it was feeding time or that the baby had just fallen asleep.

A couple of months before Colina was born, Kim had gone to Lafayette and the stories that Helen and Anna Lee had told literally came to life.

While in Texas Helen would sit and retell stories of her life. Kim sat at the computer and took notes. That is how this book came about.

Helen's children got together to clean out the house. The Board of Health had threatened to condemn the property. The neighbors, who really liked Helen, had called them, anonymously of course.

The boxes and piles of debris in the garage and in the house were a breeding haven for rats and roaches. Although Helen tried, it was impossible to organize all the things that she just could not bear to part with. She insisted that one day she was going to open another second hand store.

Helen was visiting Kim in Texas and her absence was just the opportunity they needed. They ran an advertisement in the Los Angeles Times and organized a yard sale that lasted three weeks.

It was like walking down memory lane. The boxes in the garage held clothes that they had worn over forty years ago. Furniture had them reminiscing about their childhood. Anything that did not sell, went to the dump.

They scoured every inch of the house until it sparkled as much as it could for such an old place. They used some of the money from the sale for necessary repairs, paint, carpet and flooring. The rest went into Helen's bank account.

They felt Helen did not need this big house anymore. Her health would not allow her to carry such a load. They did not want to lose her to stress related illness, and hoped that after the initial shock, she would come to see that this was for the best.

Helen had lost her right breast to cancer. Her diabetes and blood pressure levels were out of control, and she had arthritis. The doctor told them that if she continued at her current pace, she would die. He suggested that she move into an assisted- care facility.

When she returned from Texas and Helen walked in her door, they just knew that they were going to have to turn around and take her to the hospital. She was fit to be tied, "Where is my stuff? Who told ya'll to come in here messing with my stuff?" she screamed.

Helen did not speak to them for weeks. She knew they were doing this to help her, but she had not asked for their help and always said, "If you are not doing something to keep yourself busy then check your pulse, because you're probably dead." What they saw as junk, she considered her life. "One man's trash is another man's treasure." They thought she was sorting through piles of trash, but she was actually sorting through memories.

How could they do this? She was a grown woman, and they had no right.

Helen was having money problems because she had taken a loan out on the house for ten thousand dollars for home improvements and family emergencies. Without Melvin Jr.'s financial assistance, the bills became overwhelming. She had too much pride to go to her children and tell them her predicament. A man came to the door and offered to take over the payments on the loans and help her before she lost the house back to the bank. She took the offer. She did not know that he was a con man who had had been tipped off by a loan officer in the bank. Within a few months, she lost her home. Even the lawyers that the kids hired could not prove any wrongdoing on the man's part. The court's hands were tied. Everything had been done nice and legal.

Helen could have moved in with any one of her relatives, but was too stubborn, "I have been taking care of myself all my life, I need my own space."

The kids found a retirement community and leased an apartment for her. She had a living room, a bedroom, a kitchen with a little balcony. They would all pitch in to pay the monthly bill. There were scheduled activities and weekly trips to her favorite place in the world, Las Vegas for five dollars. They hoped she would make friends and the family would put together a schedule so someone would be looking in on her daily. There were nurses who would check her sugar levels and blood pressure daily.

The only problem was who was going to tell her about it. No one wanted to volunteer. They were scared of what her reaction would be.

The next week, Anna Lee and JoAnn picked Helen up to show her the place. She was totally against it, but she knew she had no choice. She settled in and soon had to admit this was a lot easier than taking care of a big house. She spent her extra time and money visiting her family.

A few years later, Helen suffered a series of small strokes. No one noticed until she started to say things that did not make sense. She mistook her grandchildren for her own children, and her speech was slurred. She became so sick that it was necessary to place her in a facility where she could be monitored and medicated.

During a surgery for a malignant spinal tumor, she suffered a stroke and lapsed into a coma.

Mother was aware of the many visitors she received. She floated around on the ceiling, watching and listening to her children talk and read. Occasionally she would fight through the fog and utter a word.

Kim brought her family for a visit and would sit at her bedside reading the book she had been putting together.

The other family members asked, "What is that?"

"Mother's memories," Kim explained.

Since everyone was interested in reading it, Anna Lee made a few copies. Before she left, everyone told her their stories and urged her to finish the book. When she returned to Texas, the family would call her with amusing tidbits she could add. Some of them sent cassette tapes with their memories.

Helen prayed for God to come on down and take her. Early one morning he did.

The Funeral

Helen walked around the room. She was amazed at how many people attended her funeral. She walked from person to person, reminiscing over special moments they had shared. So many funny things happened during her life, like when Kim was seven years old and Lil' Willie was four. She cleaned a large building in the Wilshire district at two o'clock in the morning. She took Kim and Lil' Willie inside and settled them on a couch in the lobby to sleep while she cleaned the upper floors before buffing the marble floor in the lobby. Helen stepped off the elevator and was nearly mowed down, "Yee haw," Kim and Lil' Willie were having a good time.

"Look mother, we helping you." They were both standing on the buffer. Of course, they could not control the machine. Mother ran and got her liquid wax, since the kids were having so much fun she would kill two birds with one stone. She poured the wax onto the floor and showed them how to lean from one side to the other to direct it.

She sat down, put her feet up and watched them ride. It generally took her about an hour and a half to do the floor herself. After thirty minutes, she pulled the plug and the floor was shining like the top of the Chrysler building.

Another time, Mother had arrived home at Slauson and Avalon at five o'clock in the morning. She was beat and went directly to bed and at seven o'clock a friend who lived clear on the other side of town at Crenshaw and Slauson called her, "Did you know that Kim and Lil' Willie rode their bikes clear over here?"

Helen could not believe that they had done that, her granddaughter was thirteen and her son was ten and they had no business riding so far away, anything could have happened to them. When they walked inside, she was waiting for them behind the front door with a belt. They both got a good spanking that day.

She continued to the next row, where Kenya and Little Jay sat. These two had shaken her up more than once. Her car was acting up and she had taken it to a mechanic. Kenya was nine, and Bumpy's son, Little Jay was eight. They were inside the car, she stood next to the mechanic who was under the hood trying to see where the knocking noise was coming from.

Kenya and Lil' Jay loved to dare one another and he dared Kenya to drive the car. Kenya climbed into the front seat and moved the gearshift to 'R.' The car took off with the mechanic stuck under the hood, which closed down on his back.

The car stopped in the middle of an outdoor restaurant. Luckily, no one was hurt and only a few empty tables had been knocked over.

It took Mother ten minutes to get them out of the car. They had climbed into the back window in an attempt to avoid punishment. She whipped their butts with the belt from her purse.

The mechanic stood there shaking his head, "Ma'am, I can fix your car tomorrow, but please, don't bring those kids."

Helen saw the tears rolling down the cheeks of her children and grandchildren and great grandchildren. She felt bad about the pain they were feeling, but knew they realized that she was going home, back to God and heaven where she belonged.

Helen saw the white light and knew that it was time for her to go. They were waiting for her to join them, Annie, Melvin, Mr. Willie and Crickett waved for her, behind them was a long line of and a long line of friends and family were waiting to welcome her home.

Helen knew that she would be back to look in on her family from time to time. Who else was going to keep them out of trouble—and she had to make sure that Kim finished her book.

Epilogue

Melvin Jr. married once to Yvonne, they had a daughter named La Shaun. They divorced. He had a lucrative pimping career for over thirty years; he lived by the sword and he died by the sword.

Curley's wife Mary bore him three children: Curley Jr, Christopher and Michelle. He went to jail for ten years and was divorced during incarceration. When he came home he started his own construction company and remarried. His second wife Diane had two children - Patrick and Sheila whom he adopted.

Anna Lee married Clyde when he discharged from the military. They had one daughter, Claudette Kim. Anna Lee was head of Quality Control in Electronic assembly for over thirty-five years and Clyde was a tailor.

Butch married twice. His first wife Jackie bore a daughter, Dana. His second wife Diane had a baby girl named Jacqueline. Butch went to jail for bank fraud and the government offered him a job in bank security. They offered him a million dollars a year. He turned them down, "That would be against the game." He painted murals for exclusive homes in Palm Springs.

Frances is the head of Escrow for one of the biggest banks in the country and married to Hakim, they are Muslim. He was an Animal Control agent for years. They had five kids: Aiesha, Hakim, Munir, Abdull, Asia, and Hakim Jr.

Jonathan is a master machinist. He married a nurse, Phyllis. They had two children, Jonathan Jr. and La Keisha.

JoAnn married Jim and they had two girls, Tracy and Kenya. Jim went to jail and when he got out they divorced. JoAnn remarried and was an electronics engineer for the last forty years.

Willie followed in Melvin Jr.'s footsteps and started pimping and dealing drugs. He went to the penitentiary for burglary and was sentenced to twelve years. He had three boys before taking this vacation and later married and had twins. He is a truck driver now.

Different But Better

When you are different
Seen through other's eyes
Their cruelty is away to disguise their fear
Rather than understand something unfamiliar
Tear it down and destroy it, don't encourage it to thrive
But this adversity can get the opposite results
Making the tortured smarter, stronger,
Much more determined to survive.
More open and accepting to help others
Indian heritage says, "All on this earth are brothers."

Unshackled

No longer a runaway slave trying to dig her own Bayou grave,
Through knowledge she has tools to make her brave
Standing up against the world, strong and unafraid,
Armed with an occupation, something of value to trade.
When your first experience in love is dirty and degrading
Relationships become something you spend your life evading
But when romance comes knocking at your door, feelings rise to the
surface like never before
You discover a ship in a safe port
Something to cherish and hold close to your heart.

Marry Me

Mama it is with much pride that I tell you I want to take a bride
This is something for years you prayed for
Now our family name will endure
The search for someone has taken years
There have been plenty in my bed
But none who could assuage my fears
And get so totally into my head
Children looking for an education
Not knowing how to deal with prejudice and aggravation
Running from school, victims to arson
Families going to church wanting to pray
Reverend turned into strange fruit hanging from a tree
Blood at the Root,
Blood on the leaves.

In Love With A Dream

When you are in love with a boy
And discover that for him you are a toy
Someone to be played with
Just another colored in his Daddy's employ
When you discover that you're not going to be his wife
Even though the baby you carry should be in his life
You learned the hard way but you got the lesson
In this child you have a blessin'
Dark as the night and just as short
Learning to live with a broken heart
Any man would have to do their part
Peace I do despise.
I, like everyone else will
Live and stand one day in God's court
Until then, heart please be still
My life is now going to change
Against the world my husband and I will hang
Right from the start, I knew I was his
Real love is a river that runs as deep as our kiss
In all my life I never knew such bliss.

Mother

She walked with Christ, worked hard all her life
When it came to dedication
She was about being a mother and wife
If it was in her power
She'd never hesitate or pause
If there was a person she could help
She took it on as her own personal cause
Through two hard to get along with husbands
She went beyond the call of duty
No matter what, she continued to love them?
That was a major part of her beauty, knowing that one day
Her body would cease to breathe
She was comfortable with her spirituality
When the time came, she was ready to leave

Here I Go Again

Lord help me, he was gorgeous, with an intriguing mystery

And a smile that was contagious, we are going to make history

I look in his eyes, and to my surprise, something dead starts to stir

Past pains are now a blur, I can drop my armor and disguise

The first time we met he did the funniest thing

He placed on my finger a diamond ring

Then he left and I feared I'd never see him again

All my heart and soul wanted was to be with this man

Kim Robinson

The Roux in the Gumbo

Family Tree

Elizabeth Troudeau-Le Criox: Wife to Marcelle, Mother to Jennifer

Marcelle Le Criox: Husband to Elizabeth, Father to Jennifer, Sponsor to Lizette, Father to Jeanine, Father to Marcus.

Lizette: Lover to Marcelle, Mother to Jeanine, Mother to Marcus

Jennifer Le Croix-Boneaux: Daughter to Elizabeth and Marcelle Le Croix, wife to Jacques Boneaux, Lover to Indian Sachwaw, mother to Tallulah Jacques Boneaux: Husband to Jennifer, Owner of slave Riva, Father of Riva's daughter of Effie, Brother to John.

Sachwaw: Lover to Jennifer, Father to Tallulah, Son to Weena

Tallulah: Daughter of Jennifer & Sachwaw, Granddaughter to Elizabeth & Weena, Wife to Shaw, Adopted mother to Gizelle

Gizelle: Parents were slaves, she did not know them.

Adopted daughter to Tallulah, wife to Grayson, Mother to Jimmy & Jerry, adopted mother to Annie Thomas

Grayson: Son to Rebi and Lucien Masters, Brother to Celeste & Mason, Brother in Law to George, Husband to Gizelle, Father to Jimmy & Jerry

Rebi: Mother to Grayson, Celeste, Mason, Wife to Lucien, Daughter to a slave brought over from Haiti, who practiced voodoo and passed it on to Rebi, wife to Gerard, mother to Gerard Junior

Celeste: Daughter to Rebi, sister to Grayson & Mason, wife to George, Mother to George Jr. and Chastity, Kathy & Katy.

Mason: Son to Rebi, Brother to Celeste & Grayson, Father to Tanner & Jake

Buddy: Sister to Annie, Wife to Martha, Father to Train, Pauline, Soloman, Phillips, Richard, Lewis, Verna, Julie, Ora, Michael

Annie: Sister to Buddy, Lover to Willie Simpson III, Adopted daughter to Gizelle, Mother to Helen, Genevieve and Bob, Wife to Horace, Wife to Bob

Horace Smith: Husband to Annie, Father to Genevieve, adopted father to Helen

Larry Watson: adopted brother to Horace, husband to Wilma, father of Larry Junior.

Wilma Watson: Wife to Larry, Mother to Larry Junior.

Oren Archer: stalker of Wilma

Helen: Daughter to Annie, Daughter to Willie Simpson III, Wife to Melvin Paul Broussard, Mother to Melvin Jr., Curley, Warren, Anna Lee, Butch, JoAnn, Francis, Jonathan, and Willie Bruce Junior, Wife to Willie Bruce.

Melvin Paul Broussard: Brother to Joe, Sadie, Curly and Warren, Husband to Helen, father to Joyce, Melvin Jr., Curley, Warren, Anna Lee, Butch, JoAnn, Francis, Jonathan, Melvin Jackson.

Mr. Willie: Husband to Helen, Father to Willie Bruce.

Genevieve Smith: Daughter to Annie & Horace Smith, sister to Helen & Bob, Mother to George Jr., Donnie, James Jr., (Junior Boy), Jean Ann, Virginia, Clarence, Patricia, Clarence Jr, Hubert, Terry, Clifford

Joyce: Daughter to Melvin & Eunice, Wife to Paul, Mother to Ronald, Clauderick, Natasha & Evonna

Helen's children: Melvin Paul Broussard Jr: Son of Helen & Melvin, husband to Yvonne, Father to La Shaun Curley Broussard: Son of Helen & Melvin, Husband to Mary & Diane, father to Curely, Christopher and Michelle, stepfather to Patrick & Sheila

Warren: Son to Helen & Melvin, died at age one

Anna Lee: Daughter to Helen & Melvin, wife to Clyde, mother to Kim

Butch: son to Helen & Melvin, husband to Diane, Father to Dana,

JoAnn: daughter to Helen & Melvin, wife to Jim Mother to Tracy & Kenya

Francis: Daughter to Helen and Melvin, wife to Hakim, mother to Aiesha Asia, Abdull, Hakim, Munir

Jonathan: son to Helen and Melvin, Husband to Phyllis, father to Jonathan Jr., and La Keisha

Willie Bruce Junior: Son to Helen and Willie Bruce, father to Darnell and Willie Bruce III

Genevieve's children:

George Jr.: Son to Genevieve & George

Donnie: Son to Genevieve & Bennie, father to two children

James Jr. (Jr. Boy): Son to Genevieve and James, no children

Jean Ann (Joann): Daughter to Genevieve and James, Mother to Deon & Terrell

Virginia: Daughter to Genevieve and Clarence, Mother to Lamar & Toney

Patricia: Daughter to Genevieve & Clarence, Mother to Tanya, Brian, & Inesha Clarence Jr.: Son to Genevieve & Clarence, Larry: Son to Genevieve and Hubert, husband to Jo Ann Terry: Son to Genevieve & Hubert, father to Chanise Clifford: son to Genevieve & Cecil

Family Photos

Anna & Clyde Harold

Anna Lee Broussard

Anna Lee In A Beauty
Contest

Anna Lee Harold & Kim
As A Child

Annie Thomas Before She
Died

Butch, Curley, Melvin
Jr., Melvin Sr., & Uncle
Buddy

Francis Broussard

Uncle Buddy & His Wife
Martha

Martha, Uncle Buddy,
Aunt Sadie, & Melvin

Helen, Francis, Crickett, Curley, Anne, Butch, & Jo Ann

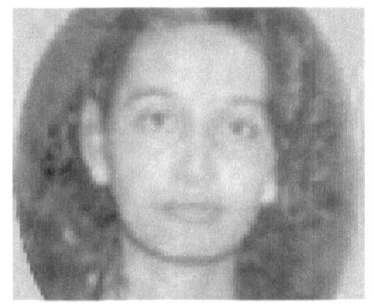

Helen When She Was Younger

Anna Lee Broussard & Friend

Jo Ann Broussard

Gena In Her 30's

Helen & Melvin Paul
Broussard Sr.

Helen's Obituary

Obituary

Sunrise: December 8, 1920 - Sunset: November 9, 1997

HELEN TERESA SIMPSON was born December 8th, 1920 to the late Annie Thomas and Willie Simpson in Lake Charles, Louisiana.

While in Louisiana she met and married the late Melvyn P. Broussard and moved to Los Angeles, California in the early 1940's. To that union seven children were born. The eldest, Melvyn P. Broussard Jr. preceded her in death in 1985. Curley, Anna, Charles, Frances, JoAnna and Jonathon. In 1959 she met and married the late Willie Bruce and to this union Willie Bruce Jr. was born.

Twenty grandchildren, Claudette, LaShaun, Poncho, Chris, Michelle, Dana, Tracy, Kenya, Alexis, Ayesha, Asia, Hakim, Munir, Abdul, Jay, LaKisha, Willie III, Adrian, Ricky and Anthony; and seventeen great-grandchildren.

"Mother" or "Mom" as she was so affectionately known, was loved by many. She will never be forgotten for her willingness to help others in spite of her needs and obligations.

"Mom" leaves to cherish her precious memories a beloved sister, Gennie V. Smith and a host of nieces, nephews, great-nieces, great-nephews, relatives and friends.

THE DEFINITION OF BLESSED

Yes his eye is on the sparrow, and Mother is by his side. Their love combined will comfort us, and dry all the tears we've cried. Her beauty is unimaginable, it surpasses what's merely seen. It was the love, the strength, the kindness, the sincerity, and everything in between. From her soft soulful eyes, to her quiet sweet smile-she was a mother to all... everyone was her child. Her soft golden skin would shine like starlight - she's in heaven with Jesus, now everything is alright. I can still feel her kiss, still see her smile. And although she's gone away, I know I'll see her in a while. Her love remains with mine, it will never fade away... but grown deeper still until I reunite with her one day. Yes, she's a woman of infinite beauty, with qualities that very few possess, to have known her, loved her, and received her love... to me - is the definition of Blessed.

LaKisha R. Broussard

To my grandmother... one I love so much. You were there for each and everyone of us. All of us were blessed by God to have you in our lives.

Love, Kisha
Nov. '97

Order of Service

Processional

Song .... "His Eye Is On The Sparrow" .... Kisha Thornton

Scripture

Prayer

Solo .... Rev. Rodney Friend

Remarks .... 2 Minutes Max.

Obituary .... Stephanie Sanchez

Eulogy .... Rev. Rodney Friend

Parting View

Recessional

Interment
Park Lawn Memorial Park
6555 E. Gage Ave.
Commerce, California 90040

FAREWELL MAMA

As I look back on yesterday the memories of you are still clear. And I want you to know I will always hold you near. I will never, ever let the memories of you fade away. Because in my heart you will always stay. I know I didn't get to say I love you, or see you smile again, but please know that you left me with enough love that will never end. We have all come this far by faith and determination alone. And the memories of you in our hearts and minds will always remain strong. Mama, I know we will meet at the crossroads and see each other again. So don't worry about me because this is not the end. God has bestowed upon us a strength that can not be destroyed by sorrow. Because we have faith in His word and a better tomorrow. Although Mama you must make this journey alone. May peace be with you forever more. I will always love you and hold you close to my heart. And believe me nothing will ever tear us apart. I love you mama.

Your Son,
Willie Bruce, Jr.

INGLEWOOD CEMETERY MORTUARY

Directors In Charge

423